Raven Fire

Fire-Walker part Four

This is for you.

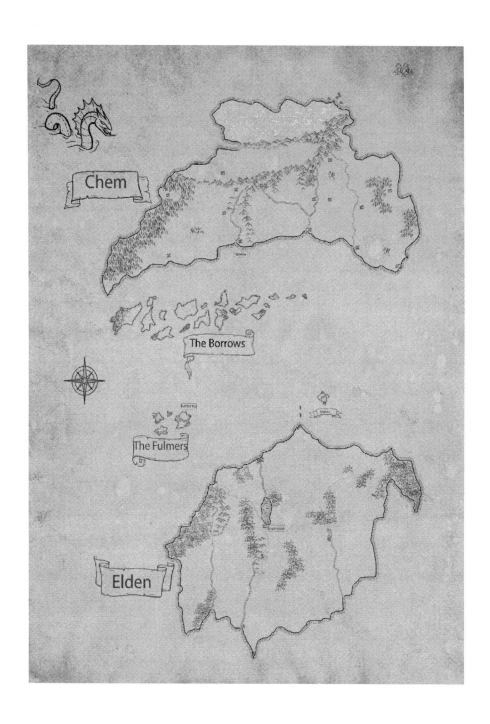

Chem

The Borrows

The Fulmers

Elden

Chapter One

Arridia; Kingdom of Elden

The sun touched her skin where the soft beams slipped between the moving canopy of leaves. Arridia closed her eyes, breathing in the earthy scent of the forest. Freckle plodded steadily beneath her, his hooves making a rhythmic clip on the dry trail. The breeze was gentle, only the lightest of chills brushing back her long black hair. When she opened her eyes again, the tower peered at her through the distant trees and her lips parted just a little.

Home.

Her heartbeat quickened, and Freckle tossed his head.

'Come on, Riddi!' Azrael darted across the path in front of her, Freckle barely paying the crazy fire-spirit any attention. 'Hurry up!' He flared brighter, losing his human shape and appearing more like an inverted teardrop with a long tail.

Arridia smiled, but she settled back in her saddle and didn't hasten. She'd always preferred the peaceful harmony of nature to the disquiet and chaos of a hold or a city, and it was rare she ever had any time on her own. Azrael hummed incessantly, and with a sigh Arridia gave in to the tiny fire-drake, urging Freckle into a gallop.

They burst into the clearing, passing through the ring of braziers that illuminated it at night, giving early warning of anything approaching the hold. She raised a hand to the warriors watching from the outlying walls, and they opened the gates without challenge. Azrael streamed ahead as they wove through the houses of the outer circle, Freckle barely slowing. For a moment she thought she'd have to pull the horse up, but the inner gates also drew back as someone shouted down, 'Welcome home, my lady!'

Apprehension tightened her chest, and she drew in a sharp breath. Freckle slowed to a trot as they rounded the solid walls of the keep. The Raven Tower loomed above them and she leaned back, straining her neck to gaze up at the highest windows, the sun reflecting off the leaded glass. Azrael shot away, spinning up toward the loft where the ravens roosted.

With no prompting, Freckle headed into the long stable building through the open door. Arridia slipped from the saddle and looked around. She took a moment to draw it all in. The scent of the hay and the horses. Soft breathing and the stamp of a hoof. The calm, warm, deep feel of the man who'd quietly watched over her for much of her life. He was cleaning out a stall, his sleeves rolled back over his muscled arms, his almost colourless mousey-brown hair falling over his eyes.

'Riddi.' He propped his broom against the stall and took two strides towards her, before hesitating.

Arridia didn't. Her feet took her straight to him, and she threw her arms around his ribs, squeezing tightly.

'Nip. I'm so sorry about your dad.'

Nip stiffened a little but didn't let go. 'Thank you, Riddi. I got your letter. It... it meant a lot to me.'

He was the first to step away, although his hands rested gently against her arms as he regarded her, eyebrows drawn in over his dark-grey eyes. It had been almost two years since she'd last been at Northold, a short visit between being assigned first to the Fulmers to finish her *walker* training, then later to Caergard in Chem. She'd been a girl then, but it was a young woman who stood before Nip now.

Arridia swallowed, heat spread from her pounding heart to the skin of her face and neck. She longed to use her *knowing*, to be sure of what Nip was feeling, but she didn't dare. Instead, she stepped back and surveyed the immaculate stables. 'How are the horses?'

Nip straightened up, clearing his throat. 'Destiny is very well; your father still takes her out most days.' He walked deeper into the extensive building, stopping at a stall to unbolt the half-door. The black mare within stepped forward to snuffle at Nip, blowing out air as he rubbed her neck. Destiny was Freckle's mother and the horse Arridia had first learned to ride on. She couldn't help the smile that came to her lips. She'd been much too young, and Destiny much too big, but with her affinity for animals, Arridia had known Destiny would never let her fall. Her father and mother hadn't shared her confidence, and they had confined her to the hold for a week.

'Griffon?' She joined Nip, standing on the other side of the mare to stroke her nose.

Nip laughed, and it warmed Arridia's heart, easing the nervousness that had locked her muscles. 'As cantankerous as ever. The old boy still thinks he's king of the stables, gelding or no.'

Arridia chuckled and her eyes met Nip's.

'Arridia!'

Both she and Nip started, stepping apart guiltily as Arridia pivoted to face her mother.

'Mumma.' She hurried into her mother's bruise inducing hug.

'Oh, look at you!' Kesta stepped back, gazing up into her eyes. It shocked Arridia to realise she was taller than her formidable mother. 'You get more beautiful every time I see you.'

'Mum.' Arridia's cheeks tightened, and she glanced over her shoulder toward Nip.

'Joss is here,' Kesta told her.

Arridia groaned. Not that she didn't want to see her brother, but Joss didn't go anywhere without his entourage of young warriors and Ravens. Her seventeen-year-old brother had a bigger court than the king of Elden.

Kesta glanced around. 'Where's Azrael?' Her eyes narrowed, and she placed her hands on her hips. 'Where's Eila?'

9

Arridia sighed, stopping herself from rolling her eyes. 'Azrael has gone straight to Father; Eila has gone to her mother in Farport.'

'Why has your cousin gone to Farport?' Kesta demanded. 'She's supposed to be guarding you.'

'She's pregnant.'

Kesta's mouth fell open.

Eila had married her fellow Raven, Neffy, over a year ago, so it was hardly shocking news. Arridia knew it wasn't that her mother was angry about though, and she braced herself.

'Why didn't your cousins or your aunt assign you another partner?' Kesta threw her hands up, her eyes blazing. 'Wait until your father hears about this.'

Arridia ducked her head to hide her expression. Her father would be upset, but he wouldn't explode like her mother. 'They thought Dierra would suit me best, and she's here with Joss. I came straight here, Mother.'

Kesta stilled to regard her, obviously not quite convinced. 'You should have brought an escort. Azrael knows better than that, as do you.'

Arridia sighed. 'Mum, I really need to be alone sometimes.'

Kesta sagged a little, holding her gaze. She reached out and squeezed Arridia's arm. 'You're so like your father. But you know I can't help but worry.'

Arridia nodded, swallowing and looking away from the intensity of her mother's love.

'Go on.' Kesta shook her head, a smile creeping across her lips. 'Go see your father. I'll get your old room ready.'

Kesta strode out of the stables, and Nip stopped pretending to be busy and came to take Freckle's halter.

'Um.' He cleared his throat and looked at the horse rather than at her when he spoke. 'Now I no longer need to care for my father, I could travel with you as your escort and guard.'

The stables suddenly felt very warm and Arridia tugged at the neck of her iron-studded tunic. The idea of having Nip as her bodyguard was both exciting and terrifying. 'Oh, um, that's kind, but I should probably have a woman with me to, you know, share my room and stuff.'

'Oh, well yes, of course.' Freckle tossed his head and Nip had to step back.

'I'd best see my father and check what Azra's up to.'

He looked up and met her eyes, Arridia caught her breath.

'I might see you in the great hall later then, my lady.'

'I hope so.' She smiled awkwardly, then hurried out into the ward to hide her blushes.

She blinked at the bright light, a wide smile growing on her face as her eyes fell on the wooden door of the Raven Tower. It stood slightly ajar, the darkness within inviting, rather than intimidating. She was running across the grass before she realised her feet had moved and she thrust the door open. Placing a hand against the stone wall for balance, she took the spiral staircase two at a time. When she reached the top, she paused a heartbeat to catch her breath. She lifted the latch and stepped into her favourite place under the sky.

'Riddi.' Her father stood from his soft chair by the fireplace. As tall as she was, Jorrun still towered over her.

'Father.' In three steps she was in his arms and she drew in a deep breath, taking in the scent of the cinnamon and jasmine soap he still used, as he kissed the top of her head.

Azrael hummed and buzzed as he flew around them in excited circles.

Jorrun stepped back to search his daughter's face. 'Azrael told me you travelled here by yourself.'

Arridia scowled. 'Azrael is a tattletale.' The fire-spirit gave a squeal and poked out a fiery tongue. 'I crossed the sea with Raven Scouts, we only rode through Elden alone. Mother's already torn off my ear.'

'We just want you safe.'

Arridia threw herself into the chair opposite her father's worn-out favourite one. 'Ow.' Something bruised the back of her thigh and she reached beneath herself to pull out the book she'd sat on. 'We've heard nothing of Geladan in fourteen years.'

'Doesn't mean we won't.' Her father sat slowly, Azrael coming down to hover at his shoulder. Jorrun's neat beard was more grey than black now, but his hair was still almost as dark as her own. 'Azra told me about Eila. We could have sent Dierra to you.'

Arridia shrugged, holding his gaze. 'I took the excuse to come home.'

His eyebrows drew together. 'You need an excuse to come home?'

She shifted in the chair, hugging the book in her lap. 'Not exactly, but there's always another assignment, then the next one. I guess I just grabbed my chance before they gave me another mission.'

'You could always say no.'

Their eyes met, and they both laughed. It had taken years of persuasion from Tantony, Rosa, and the Icante for both Kesta and Jorrun to slow down and stop running to everyone's rescue.

Jorrun held up a hand. 'Okay, point taken. I'm really glad you're here, Riddi, will you stay a while?'

'A month, if I can. I thought I could return to Chem via the Fulmers when Joss goes out there.'

Her father smiled. 'He'll love that. He's missed you. Although being assigned to Elden and the court of Taurmaline has suited him a little too well.'

Arridia snorted. 'I can imagine.'

'Do you want to join him now?'

Arridia screwed up her nose and shook her head. 'Not yet. I want to enjoy the quiet a while longer. What are you working on?' She looked toward the cluttered table.

'Earth-spirits.' Jorrun nodded at the book in her arms. 'We still know so little about them and we have seen none in years, but for allegations some escaped from Yalla's staff in the Fulmers. I heard an interesting story recently, though.'

Azrael's dark-blue eyes widened, and he drew closer to the Thane. Arridia grinned when she realised she'd leaned forward herself. 'Go on.'

'A farmer in Southport swears a fairy ruined his crops. Says it looked like a man, but thinner and hairless, with glowing eyes. Apparently, its skin was the colour of earth.'

'Did anyone else see it?' Arridia asked.

Her father shook his head. 'Bractius thinks it was just an excuse for not paying his taxes.'

'What do you think?'

One side of Jorrun's mouth curled up in a smile. 'I think something blighted the man's crops and left a trace of magic.'

Azrael grew larger, contorting his face dramatically and making Arridia laugh.

'Riddi!' A familiar voice bellowed up the stairs. She held her breath. 'Get your head out of those books and come fight me!'

'Go on.' Jorrun shook his head.

With a grin, Arridia handed him the book and kissed his cheek, before hurrying down the stairs. She broke into a run as she neared the end, using her momentum to launch herself off the steps at the figure who stood at the bottom. He caught her, squeezing her hard as he spun her about and set her on her feet. Her brother's guardian fire-spirit, Doroquael squealed at her in delight.

'Spirits, you're getting heavy, Rids.'

She scowled at her brother, punching him in the arm. He was a good three inches taller than her now, his muscled frame making him much broader. He'd had his black hair shorn close to his scalp at the sides, although it was longer on the top of his head.

'I like it,' she said, reaching up to touch his hair, but he ducked out of her reach.

Despite being in the safety of the hold, he was dressed in his light armour.

'Trouble?' Arridia frowned.

Joss grinned, revealing his even white teeth. 'Nope, the ladies love an armoured and polished warrior.'

Arridia clicked her tongue and rolled her eyes.

Doroquael made himself bigger, flaring bright to gain their attention as he drifted closer to the stairway.

Joss laughed at his elemental friend. 'Go on and see Azra.'

Doroquael shot up the stairs at once.

'Come on, Rids, you're missing all the fun.' He put his arm around her shoulders and steered her out into the ward.

Noise spilled out of the keep before they reached it, sounding very much like a busy geranna house in a Chemmish city. Arridia realised she'd tensed and forced her muscles to relax.

The great hall was a flurry of activity. The familiar sight of it made her heart ache. Joss's Ravens had gathered below the high table to the left of the hall. To the right, three children sat shaping letters with chalk on a slate. A woman sat between them; her grey hair plaited in a coil about her head. She was rounder than Arridia remembered, her face creased with more lines, but the kind brown eyes were just the same.

'Rosa.'

The woman stood up, squinting before her eyes widened. 'Oh, my goodness. Arridia!'

Arridia's own eyes prickled as Rosa wiped at hers, struggling a little to climb over the bench. Realising the gaze of most of those in the hall were on her, Arridia kept a dignified fast walk to reach the woman who had been, in all but name, aunt and nanny. Rosa was soft and smelled of lavender, her head coming just above Arridia's shoulders.

'Look at you.' Rosa wiped at her eyes again. 'You've grown so much.'

Although her parents had been to Chem frequently, neither Rosa nor Tantony had made the journey in quite some time. They'd written often, but Arridia realised with a stab of guilt that she owed this kind and exceedingly brave woman more than letters.

'And you, Rosa, are you well?' Arridia studied her face.

'I'm well enough.' Rosa smiled.

'And Uncle Tantony?'

'I shall fetch him from his study, he'll be so happy to see you.' Rosa grabbed up handfuls of her skirt ready to hurry from the room. Arridia's hand moved to press against her chest when she saw the dagger tucked into the much older woman's boot.

'Come on.' Joss took her hand and almost dragged her across the room to his friends. Several of them she recognised, including her cousin Dierra. Like most of those of Dunham descent, Dierra had dark hair. Unlike Arridia, her skin had the paleness of Chem, and her eyes were brown. She was between Joss and herself in age and like them had trained in the Fulmers, Chem, the Borrows, and Elden.

One of the young men broke away from the others, reaching out to clasp her wrist and kiss her cheek with a grin. 'Riddi.'

She smiled back at him, keeping hold of his hand as she regarded his unusual amber eyes. He'd tied his long auburn hair in a tail. 'Alikan.'

The Chemmish Raven was a brother to them, having been raised alongside them at Northold. Although about eight years older, he'd become Joss's closest friend and had naturally moved into the position of her brother's bodyguard.

Alikan snatched a glass up off the table and poured some wine for her.

'Welcome home, Arridia.'

Chapter Two

Scarlett; Kingdom of Elden

A large man barrelled into her and Scarlett cursed, pulling her hood down lower and stepping into a muddy puddle to get out of the oaf's way. She was tempted to reach for her narrow blade, but she didn't want to draw attention to herself. As much as she feigned toughness, the docks always sent her heart racing. They were busy, loud, full of rough and mean-looking men.

A familiar voice spilled out of a tavern and she breathed a little easier. Her rapid, but small steps faltered as she drew close to the door. It was a common enough tune, but the notes of the lute accompanying the rich vocals were mesmerising, weaving intricately with extraordinary speed.

The doors flew open, and Scarlett staggered back with a gasp. A bearded man leered down at her; Scarlett ducked beneath his arm and scurried into the tavern. It was dark, only a little daylight seeping in through the small, dirty windows. Her fingers rose to her nose and she tried not to breathe in the awful stench of body odour, stale ale, and old vomit. The room was crowded, every table full, provocatively dressed women squeezing between the standing patrons to deliver more alcohol to the tables.

Nearly every eye was on the singer perched on a barrel at the end of the bar. His head was bent over his lute, his curly mop of brown hair hiding his face. She frowned at the undyed linen shirt he wore, and the plain labourer's trousers. He didn't look like a prince; he looked like a nobody. Scarlett shook her head slightly. That wasn't quite right. Her brother almost glowed when he sang, just like Temerran the Bard.

The door behind her opened, and someone shoved past her, breaking into her momentary daydream. With a scowl, she made her way over to her brother, trying her best not to touch anyone.

'Luce,' she hissed.

Her brother's fingers barely faltered as they caressed the strings of his instrument, but he glanced up, his brown eyes almost black in the tavern's darkness. When his song ended, he slipped off the barrel, his lute held in his arms as carefully as a baby.

'Scar, you shouldn't be here.'

Their parents hated him calling her 'Scar'. Only her brother and Joss still did so, if only in private. She rather liked it herself. It made her sound fierce.

'Father's looking for you, I couldn't cover for you forever.'

Lucien closed his eyes and groaned.

Several of the tavern's patrons had already started grumbling and shouting out for another song.

'It's kind of good news.' Scarlett grinned. 'Riddi's home.'

Lucien straightened up, a smile forming on his own face. He waved a hand towards the tavern's owner and pushed toward the exit, using his body to protect his precious instrument. Scarlett tugged her hood down lower again and tried to keep up with him, breathing in deeply as they reached the open street.

'What did you tell father?' Lucien asked.

'Nothing.' Scarlett winced. 'Aiden the Page warned me, he'd just run a message from the pigeon loft. I was... well, I was taking your place with the master of arms.'

It wasn't the first time, and it wouldn't be the last. Scarlett loved anything martial. Tactics, fighting, history, she absorbed it all like a starving thing. Her father indulged her to an extent, he'd even allowed her to train with Heara and Cassien, but no matter how hard she tried, he never took her seriously. Lucien hated it all. His love was music, books, and poetry. Despite their differences, Scarlett was closer to her brother than she was to her own twin sister. Eleanor was their mother's shadow, and she obsessed over all things feminine. As much as Scarlett looked down on Eleanor's pastimes, she did love her delicate sister, and Eleanor always covered for her, just as she herself did for Lucien.

'Did you beat him?' Lucien asked hopefully.

Scarlett screwed up her nose and shook her head. 'Not yet. But with Riddi home, Father might let us spend time at Northold, so I'll snag Merkis Tantony for a few more lessons.'

Lucien gave a bark of a laugh. The king of Elden wasn't all that keen on Jorrun and Kesta's influence on his children, but they knew full well what his intentions were for Lucien and Arridia. Jorrun had warned them all Bractius had designs on adding magical bloodlines to his royal one, and told them in no uncertain terms that they should decline any kind of arranged marriage. Arridia and Lucien loved each other dearly, but they'd grown up together like cousins. With an overprotective Mother, Scarlett had been late to rebel and join the circle of Northold friends; it hadn't helped with her being the youngest, but Arridia had always treated her with patience and kindness when they met.

As they approached the castle gates, Scarlett's feet faltered. The guards had stepped forward from their posts, standing tall to peer above the heads of those entering the grounds. As soon as they spotted Lucien, one of them hurried to meet them, making a hasty bow.

'Your highness, your father is looking for you.'

Lucien swore. 'All right, thanks. Hide this for me.' He handed his lute to Scarlett, then taking a leather thong from his pocket, pulled his unruly mop of hair back into a tail. As he reached the castle gates, he broke into a run.

With an embarrassed glance at the guard, Scarlett followed at a dawdle. Instead of choosing the main entrance, she took the back way through the kitchens. She opened the door to her room and started when she saw someone sitting on her bed.

Eleanor put down her embroidery hoop. 'About time. Did you find Lucien?'

Scarlett relaxed, holding up the lute as evidence. 'Thanks, Eleanor. Have we been summoned to Father?'

Eleanor shook her head. Physically, she was identical to Scarlett in almost every way. They had the same sandy-blonde hair that fell below their shoulders, the same pale-hazel eyes. The only actual difference was that Scarlett was left-handed, while Eleanor favoured her right hand. It was easy enough for them to pretend to be each other, although it was a rare thing for Scarlett to have to cover for her quiet, obedient sister.

'Not yet. I don't think he wants us spending more time in Northold, if that's what you're hoping.'

Scarlett pressed her lips together in a pout and sat heavily on the bed beside her twin. 'It's the best place to learn anything. I don't see why I can't be a Raven. Even Luce got to be fostered for a while in Chem with Merkis Teliff. None of the other allied countries treat their women like nothing more than an ornament.'

'Well, lucky for you, Mother thinks Northold is the best place right now for us to secure a good husband with power and influence.'

'Really?' Scarlett pivoted to regard her. Then the reality of her twin's words burst her excitement. 'Oh no. What's she plotting?'

Eleanor shook her head and rolled her eyes. 'Joss's friends include those who will go on to run the provinces in Chem. But...'

'What?' Scarlett sat up straighter.

'Oh, nothing.' Eleanor gave a small smile, not meeting her sister's eyes.

'No, tell me.' Scarlett leant forward to tickle Eleanor, who squealed and tried to fend her off.

'Girls!'

They both shot to their feet, straightening their clothes. Scarlett's face heated when she recalled she hadn't changed out of her trousers and hooded tunic. Their mother glared at them, folding her arms slowly across her chest.

'Your father has ordered a formal gathering next week.' Queen Ayline's gaze moved away from Scarlett toward her sister, and Scarlett let out the breath she'd been holding. 'You're sixteen now. When I was your age, I had my sights set on a throne, and I won it.'

Scarlett's lip curled up in a sneer, but she quickly hid it. Elden was the only kingdom, the only throne – unless you counted the self-proclaimed Queendom of Snowhold – and it would be inherited by their brother, a young man who didn't even want it. Scarlett herself didn't care about the throne, but she cared about her land, her people. She longed to have the power to protect, to make decisions. She dreamed of being wise, inspirational; a warrior queen. But it was just that, a dream. She was of Elden, where they had no magic, and royal women wielded nothing but the potential for a political alliance.

The queen's delicate nose wrinkled. 'Invitations have been sent out and we will receive a delegation from the Fulmers and Borrows shortly. I expect you to behave in accordance with your status. Speak to those with influence and cultivate a rapport. Avoid those who do not deserve your regard.'

Scarlett was well aware of who her mother meant. The queen despised both the Icante of the Fulmers and the Bard of the Borrows, but she was painfully polite to both because of their power. Sometimes Scarlett wondered how her mother kept so up to date with who was rising in importance and who was out of favour. Her knowledge of Chem's provinces and who was most influential in each Coven was uncanny, considering the woman had never set foot there. She couldn't help but imagine her mother as a spider, sitting in the centre of her web.

'May I have a new dress?' Eleanor asked wide-eyed.

'Of course.' Ayline smiled, although what lit her eyes didn't seem to be humour. She held out her hand and Eleanor leapt up to take it.

Ayline looked Scarlett up and down. 'Sort yourself out, Scarlett, you're a princess, not a palace guard.'

The queen pivoted and marched from the room, Eleanor giving her sister an apologetic smile over her shoulder as the door closed behind them. Scarlett gripped her sword hilt. As exciting as the prospect of a busy court full of interesting people was, it would be a difficult few days.

Lucien was going to need her.

She unbuckled her weapon and let her practical clothes fall in a pile then rifled through her dresses to pick out a plain blue one. As always, she'd dismissed her lady-in-waiting, and she swore several times over the laces as she tried to tie them behind her own back. She hurried to her brother's room, knocked once, then called out, 'Luce, it's me,' before opening it a crack. Lucien jumped up from his seat beside the window. He was dressed now in a green tailored jacket, a long dagger on his belt.

'Where's my lute?'

Scarlett blew air out loudly. *'Thanks for risking your hide for me, Scar.'*

Lucien winced. 'Sorry, sis. Thanks, I really do appreciate it.'

'It's in my room.' She sat on his bed. 'Well?'

Lucien groaned and threw himself face down beside her, making her bounce. 'Gods, this is a nightmare, Scar.' His voice was muffled as he spoke into his blanket. He sat up slowly, meeting her gaze. 'Father wants me to "charm" Arridia when she comes to Taurmaline and try to "win her over." He claims she is the key to Elden retaining power against the growing magical strength of our neighbours.'

'He talks as though they're our enemies.' Scarlett frowned.

Lucien leaned forward. 'He says we have to look ahead, be prepared for any eventuality. He doesn't want Elden to be beholden to the other nations, that we need to protect ourselves.'

'Well, that makes sense,' Scarlett mused. Lucien opened his mouth to protest, but she shushed him. 'It doesn't mean you should be made to marry Riddi if you don't want to, but I can see why Father is worried and his need to plan ahead. What of Riddi's cousins? Or any of the other Ravens? Are there any of them you like?'

Lucien looked away. 'Well, Arridia is pretty much my closest friend, and she is beautiful, but… but I just don't feel…' He glanced at her and ground his teeth. 'Gods, I can't believe I'm talking about this stuff with my sister.'

'Why not?'

'For a start, you're just a child.'

'I am not!' She glared at him. At times their five-year age gap had come between them, but despite his teasing, Lucien had always given her more respect than anybody else. She wondered suddenly if her brother was lonely. All of them had grown up having to hide how they felt, disguise who they really were to please their parents, and live up to their demanding expectations. Was there anyone she was truly herself with? She didn't think so.

Lucien tilted his head to regard her. 'Would you tell me who you're attracted to?'

'Of course!'

'Really?' He narrowed his dark eyes at her.

Scarlett squirmed a little, feeling heat rise to her cheeks.

'See!' Lucien poked her in the arm, his laughter quickly faded. He sighed. 'I've met plenty of women I'm attracted to, but none that, well none that I seriously thought I might fall in love with.'

'What are you going to do?' She asked in concern.

Lucien picked at his thumbnail, his eyes growing distant. 'I shall tell Riddi the truth and see where I go from there.'

Chapter Three

Cassien; Free Provinces of Chem

'Fifteen slaughtered.'

He closed his eyes, jiggling his baby son in his lap. Enika was red-faced but had stopped crying. Cassien thought he might start himself, as much from frustration as grief. 'When is it going to end?'

'Maybe not in my lifetime.' Rothfel sat heavily in the chair opposite him, rubbing a hand over his face and tugging at his greying brown beard. 'Hopefully in your son's, though.'

The candle flickered, sending shadows darting across the study. The palace was quiet, but for the city bell striking twice.

'Do we know who?'

'Raven scouts think it's just the usual bandits, self-entitled men who use us as an excuse to rob, kill, and enslave.'

'Did they take prisoners?'

Enika gurgled.

Rothfel nodded. 'The Ravens caught up with them. They took three bandits captive to question, the rest fought to the death.'

'Did the prisoners survive?'

Rothfel stared at the candle. 'They did. Some of them weren't in good shape though.'

Cassien clenched his jaw and his temperature rose. Enika squirmed and grizzled again, and Cassien tried his best to relax and cool his anger.

'All right.' Cassien sighed. 'Thanks for the report. Why don't you get yourself off to bed?'

The alchemist and former thief placed his hands on the table. 'I reckon I might. The kid okay?'

Cassien looked down at his son. 'I think he may have another tooth coming through.'

Rothfel grunted. 'Good luck with that.'

Cassien gave the man a brief smile as he stood to leave, closing the door softly behind him. Cassien leaned back in his chair, cuddling Enika closer. It was fourteen years since they'd taken Eastern Chem and united the land under the Raven Laws. Every year the struggle to maintain peace, to ensure freedom for women, got a little easier; but there were always uprisings, new factions trying to revert things to how they had been. They'd been through two years of terrible earthquakes, followed by a poor harvest, but his wife's careful planning and foresight had meant Caergard had thrived and remained one of the most stable provinces in Chem.

The door opened a crack and an anxious young face peered in.

'Father?'

'What are you doing up?'

Raith let go of the door handle and crept in, his eyes wide in the candlelight. The eight-year-old boy had his mother's dark hair, but Cassien's silver irises. 'I heard Enika crying and you leaving your room. Dad, I...' Raith bit his lower lip.

'What is it?' Apprehension tightened Cassien's chest muscles.

Raith's eyes brightened, but he couldn't get his words out, shifting his feet. Cassien opened his mouth to reassure his son, but the boy beat him to it. He raised a hand and an erratic flame sparked and guttered in his palm.

Cassien leapt up, his son's name coming out in a shocked whisper. He put Enika down carefully on the chair and hurried to kneel before Raith, taking his hands and kissing his forehead. 'You have power!'

Raith nodded rapidly.

'That's wonderful. Does your mother know?'

Raith shook his head. 'I didn't want to wake her.'

'She'll want to be woken up for this.' Cassien smiled and brushed his son's hair back behind his ear. 'Let me just get Enika.'

Cassien blew out the candle and followed his eldest son out into the hallway. A single guard kept watch, and he gave Cassien a polite nod of acknowledgement. They made their way up the two flights of stairs to where their rooms were, two more guards stepping aside to let them pass.

'Everything all right, Raven?' One of them asked.

Cassien nodded. 'All good.' Not entirely true, but there was no need to reveal news of raids in the outer province just yet.

Kussim stirred as soon as Cassien opened the door to their bedchamber. The powerful Chemmish sorceress sat up slowly, calling a small flame to her palm to illuminate the room.

'Cass?'

He waved a hand at her, balancing Enika in the crook of his other arm. 'A late-night report, but it can wait for now. Raith has news.'

'Raith?' Kussim sat up, her long black hair a messy tumble across her shoulders. The flames in her hand vanished, but several candles around the room instantly ignited.

Raith glanced at his father and swallowed, then straightened himself up and held up a hand. Cassien heard his wife draw in a sharp breath, and he wondered if she could sense the magical power in their son. Raith's face reddened a little, and Cassien realised he was holding his own breath as he tried to will his son strength.

With a loud exclamation, Raith staggered back, and flames spluttered momentarily from his fingertips.

Kussim thrust aside the blankets to throw herself to the carpet before Raith. 'Oh, well done.' She wiped at his face and Cassien realised with a jolt to his heart that Raith's nose was bleeding.

'Is he okay?' He asked in concern, striding across the room to place Enika in his cradle.

'It's normal.' Kussim smiled, although her blue eyes were serious. 'Do you have a headache now, Raith?'

The boy nodded.

Kussim kissed his forehead. 'Get yourself to bed, I'll bring you a tonic in a moment.'

Raith obeyed at once, but he grinned up at his father as he passed him, causing Cassien's heart to swell with pride.

As Kussim moved to her large herb chest to mix a painkilling tonic, Cassien told her of Rothfel's report. She frowned, but she didn't appear as upset as he had been. Seeing his expression, she said, 'It's one more gang of bandits who won't trouble us again.'

'But the cost was high to our people.' Cassien shook his head. 'We need to take out these lawless murderers before they slaughter innocent civilians, not after.'

'You can't save everyone, Cass,' she said gently, placing a hand on his chest as she crossed the room to tip her mixture of herbs and powders into a glass of water.

Cassien didn't reply. It was a conversation they'd had many times over the years. No matter how much Kussim tried to reassure him, every death by purposeful violence in their province felt like a failure to him, every loss of life was another tear in his soul. He checked on Enika, then sat on the edge of the bed while Kussim tended Raith. The murmur of their voices in the other room was as soothing as the shush of gentle waves.

Someone knocked firmly but quietly on the door. With a frown, Cassien got up to open it. Surely it couldn't be a second report in the middle of the night?

The captain of the palace guard himself stood there, and from the dishevelled state of his hair and his incomplete uniform, it was clear the man had been woken from sleep.

'Forgive me, Raven.' The captain's eyes were wide. 'We, er… we have visitors.'

'Visitors? At this hour?'

'What is it?' Kussim asked as she joined him, wrapping a cloak about her shoulders.

'It's a small party,' the captain explained. 'Two men, two women, and a boy. I would have accommodated them and woken you in the morning, it's just that…'

Cassien gritted his teeth, wishing the man would spit it out.

'Well, the woman claims to be the Queen of Snowhold.'

'Catya.' The name burst from Cassien's lips and he quickly clamped his jaw firmly shut. He could feel his wife's gaze on him. It had been fourteen years since he'd seen his ex-lover, fourteen years since she'd fled without a word. The volatile young woman had taken control of the northernmost province of Snowhold, claiming the title of Queen. As far as he knew, Catya had never set foot back in the Free Provinces since winning her crown. Rothfel had been involved with the conquest of the only Chemmish province not under the rule of the Raven Laws, and was one of the few Ravens invited to the Queen's palace. The Ravens had sent several delegations in recent years; Cassien himself had refused to go.

'What should I do?' the captain asked.

'Where have you put her?' Kussim stepped in.

'The official receiving room. I've had warm food and wine arranged.'

'Thank you, captain,' Kussim replied. 'Have rooms prepared for them in the west wing and meet us outside the receiving room.'

The man gave a slight bow and hurried away.

'Gods, what does she want after all these years?' Cassien rubbed at his jaw. 'And why sneak about in the middle of the night?'

Kussim gave a snort. 'Because she's Catya. Come on, let's get dressed and find out what she's up to. I'll get Orla to watch Enika.'

Cassien's apprehension grew as they approached the receiving room. He and Catya had not parted on good terms. He glanced at Kussim and she briefly took his hand, before letting go as the captain of the guard opened the door for them.

Cassien made a quick observation of the five people in the room. They were all dressed in a mixture of black leather and white fur, even the boy armed with a sword. The two men had dark-brown hair and beards, one in his twenties, the other closer to forty.

One of the women was striking. She was tall with flame red hair and green eyes; but it was the other woman who held Cassien's gaze. It relieved him when the old wound in his heart didn't open, leaving him instead with a dull ache of apprehension.

'Cass, Kussim, how are you?' Catya strode toward them, the red-haired woman eyeing them with distrust, her hand near her sword hilt.

It was Kussim who replied, a smile on her face if not in her eyes. 'We are well, Catya. Oh, forgive me, should we address you as *your majesty*?'

Catya gave a snort and flapped a hand. 'Don't be daft.' She planted a kiss on Kussim's cheek. Cassien shrank back, his muscles tensing as she kissed him as well. Her light-brown hair was tied in a single neat plait and she flicked the end of it back over her shoulder. 'I'll get to the point. I'm in Chem because I'm taking my son to meet his father.'

Time seemed to stop, Cassien's heart missed a beat. He shifted to regard the boy and his eyes widened a little. The boy was too young to be his, around the same age as Raith. His irises were unmistakable; Cassien had only met one other person with eyes the colour of bright amber.

'I believe Alikan is in Northold with Joss Raven?' Catya turned her back on them to pick up a glass of wine. 'I didn't want to pass through Chem without saying hello. I wondered if you might be so kind as to escort me across the Free Provinces to Navere, and onward to the Fulmers before I continue to Elden?' She pivoted to catch Cassien's eyes.

He froze, his mouth falling open.

'It would be quicker for you to go straight south and sail from Parsiphay,' Kussim said. Cassien could hear the strain of tense muscles in her voice.

'I know.' Catya shrugged. 'But I'd like to visit Navere, it's been so long, and it will be good for Merin to see more of Chem and the places where we made history.'

'Merin? Oh.' Cassien shook his head. Of course, she meant her son.

'We can provide you with Raven Scouts if you'd like an escort,' Kussim said. 'Rothfel is here, he might even go with you.'

Catya rolled her eyes, exchanging a glance with the red-haired woman. 'Oh, come on, I haven't seen you in years and we have so much to catch up on. Will you take me, Cass?'

His fingers clenched and unclenched. 'All right.'

Catya's face lit with a grin, and she swigged back her wine.

Cassien didn't dare look at his wife's face.

Chapter Four

Joss, Kingdom of Elden.

Joss swallowed back his ale and smoothed down the front of his dark-blue jacket. His training kicked in as he surveyed the room before stepping further in. King Bractius sat at the high table, laughing loudly with the Jarl of Southport. Bractius was drinking from a large, ornate tankard carved from the bone of an enormous animal and traced in gold. Joss startled, his eyes narrowing. Had the king forgotten it had been a long-ago gift from the murderous delegation from Geladan? Bractius's astute brown eyes travelled around the hall even as he joked with his subordinate. He'd allowed his sandy beard to grow long, plaited and held by silver beads.

Queen Ayline was standing apart, Eleanor at her side. The young princess was wearing an elegant gown that hugged her slender figure, and Joss raised an eyebrow.

Alikan nudged his arm hard, and Joss only just avoided splashing ale over his expensive clothes.

'Hey!'

'Keep your eyes in your head.' Alikan scowled.

Joss grinned. The king's hall was an array of very tempting young woman, but Elden wasn't the Fulmers, as his parents were fond of reminding him. There was a sudden buzz in the conversation, and many turned toward the main doors. A man strode in with a retinue of Borrowmen warriors on his heels. Bard of the Borrows and captain of the *Undine*, Temerran's striking red hair seemed untouched by grey despite the years he'd accumulated. His green eyes sparkled with mischief as he bowed to both men and women on his way to present himself to the king. Temerran's first mate, Nolv, was a more sombre figure, in practical loose clothing of salt-splashed grey.

'Your majesties.' Temerran gave a low and flamboyant bow. The man never forgot to include the queen, and despite her dislike of the Borrowman, Ayline flushed and smiled.

'Temerran.' The king gave the Bard the courtesy of standing but didn't move to greet him. 'How good of you to come.'

'It honoured me to be invited,' Temerran replied.

Movement caught Joss's eye, and he turned to see his parents slipping in quietly through a side door. As ever, his father wore perfectly tailored black, but his mother had chosen bright red, and unlike the women of Elden she allowed her long dark hair to fall loosely around her shoulders. Despite their discreet entrance, they stood out like hawks in a flock of doves.

Doroquael gave a sudden squeal and flew out of the torch in which he'd been hiding. Joss's hand twitched, readying to draw power, before he realised the fire-spirit was excited, not alarmed. Alikan took a step forward, putting himself between Joss and the room.

'It's okay, Ali.' Joss's heart beat just a little faster as he squeezed through the crowd, hurrying toward the main doors through which Doroquael had vanished.

One of the king's stewards loudly announced, 'The Icante of the Fulmers.'

The Icante stepped in, wearing a pale cream dress with a sky-blue cloak wrapped around her shoulders. Unlike her daughter, the ruler of the Fulmer Islands had her steel-grey hair coiled artfully about her head. The warrior Gilfy flanked her, along with the *Fire-Walker*, Eidwyn. Dia Icante's new apprentice, Vivess, and the formidable scout, Heara, followed behind. Despite being in her sixties, Heara moved with energy, her bare arms still tight with muscle. As far as he could see, Heara was the only one who'd dared bring weapons into the king's hall; her two long knives tucked into her belt.

Joss appraised his grandmother's new apprentice before moving forward again to meet them. Vivess had lighter hair than most of those in the Fulmers, a dark chestnut, almost red where it caught the light. She was about Joss's age and had one grey eye, one green.

'Grandma.'

'Joss.' Dia's serious expression melted into a joyful smile and she halted to hug him. 'Are you well?'

'I am.' Joss waved a hand at Doroquael. 'Calm down!'

The fire-spirit ceased his noisy buzzing and made himself small, coming back to Joss's shoulder.

'Did Grandfather not come?'

Dia's smile faded, and anxiety squeezed Joss's heart. 'Your grandfather was a little unwell. Joss, I'll catch up with you as soon as I can, but it would be rude of me not to go straight to the king.'

'Oh, of course.' Joss's face warmed, and he glanced around, realising many eyes were directed his way. 'I'll find you in a moment.'

Dia Icante smiled, then turned to continue to the high table. Heara gave Joss a huge grin and a thump on the arm as she passed. Alikan ducked in time to miss the scout's hand as she tried to clip him around the head.

Despite his laughter, Joss felt uneasy. His grandmother had seemed worried.

'Joss?' Alikan prompted. 'We're kind of in the way.'

Joss spun on his heels to see another group entering the hall. The steward announced them as Thanes and their wives from Promise and Haven on the small Eldenian island of Mantu.

'Let's get the good wine,' Joss suggested. They moved closer to the high table, Joss giving his most charming smile to a trio of young women. He narrowed his eyes as he poured wine from a decanter into two glasses and glanced at Alikan. 'Have you seen Riddi yet?'

'No.' Alikan stiffened. 'But she's probably putting off leaving the quiet of her room.'

'Doro?' Joss looked up at the fire-spirit, who made himself a pair of fiery shoulders to shrug.

'Sshall I find Azra, Joss?'

Joss winced. His sister was more powerful than he, and perfectly able to take care of herself. There was no reason for him to worry. 'Not yet, I'm sure she'll turn up.'

'Joss, Ali!'

Joss turned at the excited voice and peered down into smiling hazel eyes.

'Scar.' Joss reached out and tucked a stray strand of her fair hair back in place and she blushed as red as her name.

'You own a dress then,' Alikan teased.

Scarlett's hand self-consciously brushed at the satin material.

'You look great,' Joss reassured her. She looked more than great, in fact, but she was the king's daughter and a very long way out of bounds; though his mother would probably skin him alive before Bractius did.

Scarlett's eyes barely left his face, and he swallowed, reaching past her to pick up his wine.

'Would you like a glass, your majesty?' Alikan asked.

Joss groaned; he should have thought of that.

'Oh, yes please, Ali.' Scarlet fidgeted. 'I see Heara is here.'

'Want me to see if she'll give you some more lessons?'

'I would love that.' Scarlet bounced on her heels.

'You know, I could teach you—'

Alikan cleared his throat loudly and passed Scarlett her wine.

Joss was saved by Temerran who began to sing, everyone's attention immediately turning to the bard.

'Oh, but where's my brother?' Scarlett stood on her toes to peer around the room. 'He never misses a chance to hear Temerran.'

Joss looked up at the high dais. The king was speaking with Dia, who was seated at his side, Vivess hovering attentively behind her. He glanced over the in-favour Jarls and his eyes met those of the queen. Ayline was staring right at him, the slightest hint of a smile on her face that sent a shudder down his spine. He looked away before she did.

'Oh, there he is.' Scarlett pointed and Joss followed the direction of her finger, noting with a smile that her nail was chipped.

Prince Lucien and Arridia walked into the room together, Azrael trailing behind them. They made a striking couple, heads bent close in quiet conversation. The prince and the *Fire-Walker*. Joss looked at Alikan, who shrugged, though his amber eyes showed concern. Dierra followed a short and discreet distance behind them, slipping in and out of the crowd like a shadow.

'Shall we say hello?' Scarlett suggested cheerfully. She grabbed up a handful of her skirt to hurry across the room before they could protest.

Joss gestured to Doroquael, and with a happy chirp the fire-spirit sped across the room to his friend.

His mother beat them to it. Kesta stood glaring at poor Lucien through narrowed eyes while the prince squirmed. Arridia seemed totally unphased, speaking with her usual calm serenity.

'Your highness.' Joss gave a hasty bow, trying to catch his sister's eyes, while Alikan's bow was slow and smooth.

'Joss, Alikan.' The prince nodded at them with a warm smile. 'Will you be staying at the castle again for a while?'

Joss glanced at his mother, knowing how much she disliked the castle of Taurmaline. 'A few days if I can. It will be great to have some time with you, Luce, if your duties permit?'

'I'll make time.'

'You haven't been to Northold in a while,' Kesta said. 'You know you don't have to wait for an invitation.'

'I know.' Lucien didn't meet the eyes of Joss's formidable mother, despite the fact he loved her like an aunt. Kesta had always encouraged the prince to be himself, but even in Northold the king and queen of Elden had informants ready to report back on the young heir. 'It's just hard to get away.'

'Tell me about it.' Joss sighed. 'I used to think that when I became a man, I'd be free of lessons and chores. If anything, I have more.'

'Stop learning, and you'll soon stop living,' Kesta admonished.

Joss caught Arridia's eyes, and they both grinned. Their mother had been threatening them with that line for years. Joss saw his mother's glare and his smile quickly vanished.

'Scarlet.' Kesta turned to the princess. 'We haven't seen you at Northold for a while either. Are you well?'

'I am, Silene,' Scarlett replied politely, using Kesta's Fulmer title. 'I would visit every day if I could, but Mother thinks you are a destructive influence and I don't act like a lady enough as it is.'

Joss's mouth fell open. His mother threw back her head and laughed.

'You've made my evening.' Kesta grinned. 'The world wouldn't be right if your mother and I got along, Scarlett.'

Scarlett blinked rapidly, obviously unsure how to best reply.

'Honesty is good,' Kesta said a little more seriously. 'Always speak your mind to me. But even I had to learn diplomacy.' She gave the startled girl a wink. 'Anyway, I'll leave you children to it.'

'Hey!' Alikan protested. 'I'm twenty-five, remember?'

Kesta jabbed him in the ribs with two fingers as she passed, slipping away into the crowd.

Alikan turned straight to Arridia. 'Everything okay?'

Arridia made a quick scan of those around them, then held Lucien's gaze a moment before she replied. 'King Bractius has ordered Luce to *court* me.'

'What?' Joss spluttered, his eyes widening and his shoulders pulling back so that his chest expanded.

'Shh!' Arridia scowled at him. 'This isn't the place. Don't worry, Luce and I have a plan.'

'I bet it doesn't involve telling your mother,' Alikan muttered.

'Look.' Lucien drew himself up and regarded them all. 'Let's just enjoy tonight's party. We'll meet tomorrow.'

'Not too early.' Joss raised his wineglass and looked meaningfully at the content.

'Not too early.' The prince's sombre expression lifted a little. 'Well, I have to mingle.'

'Majesty.' Arridia gave a slight bow, as though formally dismissed. Joss didn't miss the soft and heartfelt smile the prince gave her.

Scarlett groaned, shifting from one foot to the other, her glance going from her brother to Joss.

'Your majesty,' Joss jumped in quickly. 'May I fetch you anything?'

Scarlett let her brother go. 'I'd love to get nearer to Temerran, I can barely hear him above all the chatter.'

Joss held out his arm, and the princess took it. Alikan rolled his eyes, while Arridia narrowed hers.

'What?' Joss mouthed at her silently.

Arridia gave a slow shake of her head, but her smile made him grin. Dierra stepped in quickly as they left, and Joss glanced at his own bodyguard. Alikan appeared completely relaxed, but the Raven sorcerer's eyes flitted everywhere. Joss examined every face they passed, his eyes lifting to the torches high on the walls and the candles in the iron candelabra's that hung from the high ceiling. He felt, rather than saw, which flame his faithful fire-spirit now hid within.

'Joss?'

Scarlett's voice brought him back to the young woman beside him. 'Sorry, Scar, I can't help my scout's training sometimes.'

She sucked in a breath and bit at her lower lip. He wondered if she realised she was gripping his arm a little tighter. 'What are you looking for?'

'Anything out of place, really.' He turned to look into her hazel eyes. 'I'd love to teach you scouting.'

'I'd love to learn.'

He looked away quickly, scanning the room, this time to see who was watching *them*. There were more than he'd expected, and he almost pulled his arm away from the princess. Almost.

Instead, he straightened his spine and took her directly to the table below where the Bard of the Borrows performed. A few glares from Alikan and people made way so Joss could pull out a chair for Scarlett.

'Go fetch us some more wine, Ali.' Joss waggled his eyebrows at his friend.

Alikan opened his mouth to protest, then breathed out loudly, his chest deflating as he shook his head and moved away to grab a decanter. Temerran was singing a ballad from the Borrows, his voice soaring and somehow reverberating within Joss's ribs. He recognised the harmonic tingle of magic.

'It's beautiful.' Scarlett sighed, her lashes fluttered, and her pale-pink lips remained parted.

Joss pinched his leg and snatched up a jug of water, which he gulped down. A glance toward the king quickly put any foolish ideas out of his head. Bractius was presently engaged in what appeared to be a heated discussion with Joss's own father, Jorrun.

Temerran's song ended, and he jumped down from the stage with the energy of a much younger man, handing his lute to one of the Elden musicians.

'Joss. Your Highness.' Temerran gave Scarlett a low and intricate bow, taking her hand to kiss it. Then he turned to Joss, clasped his wrist, and pulled him into a brief bear hug. 'How is Elden suiting you, Joss?'

Joss glanced at Scarlett before grinning at the bard. 'It suits me very well. I've been touring the country to get to know all the Jarls and Thanes, and updating them on the provinces of Chem.'

Temerran screwed up his face. 'I'd rather be fighting slimy sea monsters.'

Scarlett giggled. 'Oh, me too!'

'Yes, but they're not half as pretty as the women of Elden,' Joss said with a swagger.

He felt Scarlett stiffen. Temerran's eyes went so quickly from the princess back to Joss it was hardly noticeable. Joss's cheeks burned. Spirits, she'd think he was the biggest oaf going.

'Oh, I don't know.' Temerran leaned forward conspiratorially. 'There was this giant squid once...'

Joss's guffaw was a little forced, but Scarlett seemed to relax.

'Hey, Tem.' Alikan squeezed between Scarlett and Joss, a carafe of wine cradled in his arms. 'How are you?'

'I'm good.' Temerran smiled, his green eyes alive in the candlelight. 'Do you still have that scruffy cat of yours?'

'I do.' Alikan's own amber eyes softened. 'Although he stayed in Navere.'

'How old is Trouble now?' Scarlett asked.

'About fifteen,' Alikan replied.

'Did you know Ali used to believe the cat spoke to him?' Joss teased.

'Hey.' Alikan's eyebrows drew down low. 'There're worse stories I could tell about you, remember?'

'Like what?' Scarlett demanded, looking from one of them to the other. 'I want to know.'

Joss noticed a change in the sound of the great hall. Both Temerran and Alikan pivoted to look toward the centre of the room. A middle-aged man with short-cut blonde hair and a slightly curling beard was pushing his way to the high dais. Joss recognised him as the king's newest advisor, Merkis Shryn. He had a scroll clasped in his hand.

'Talking of trouble.' Temerran began making his way to the king. Without realising he'd done so, Joss grabbed Scarlett's hand and followed.

Jorrun stood as the Merkis approached and the king tensed, although he kept a smile fixed to his face. Shryn handed the scroll to King Bractius, leaning close to speak rapidly into the king's ear. Bractius stilled, handing the scroll to Jorrun, his smile still frozen in place.

'What is it?' It was Scarlett who asked as she reached her father.

'Nothing for you to worry about, my dear,' the king replied.

Jorrun studied the scroll, then he looked from Joss to Temerran. 'There have been reports of another magical attack in Elden. This time not a farm, but an entire village. Teriton.'

'That's just fifteen miles south of here,' Scarlett exclaimed.

'Magical attack?' Temerran demanded.

Bractius waved a hand to hush them. Queen Ayline was working her way closer, trying to be subtle.

Jorrun lowered his voice, and Joss strained to hear his father. 'They claim some kind of curse, a huge man-like demon made of earth.'

Joss sucked in air. He darted forward and dropped to one knee. 'Your majesty, allow me to investigate on your behalf.'

King Bractius raised his chin a little, his eyes narrowed. Jorrun stiffened, his gaze fixed on his son, although he said nothing.

'Father.'

Joss turned, startled to see Prince Lucien only a few inches behind him.

'Father, I will be grateful for Joss's aid, but I will lead the investigation into these wild claims for you.'

King Bractius looked his son up and down, no hint of pride on his face. 'Very well. Organise your expedition. Leave the day after tomorrow.'

Lucien gave a short, slow bow. As he straightened up, his eyes met Arridia's across the room.

Chapter Five

Kesta; Kingdom of Elden.

Kesta wiped the tears angrily from her face, looking from Dia to Jorrun. 'There must be something we can do?'

The exchange of glances between her mother and husband made her curl her fingers into fists and dig her nails into her palms.

Dia sat slowly on the bed. 'You know your father's health has been declining—'

'But I didn't realise he was this bad.' Kesta threw her arms up in the air. 'Why didn't you tell us before? Why have you even left him?'

The pain in her mother's face sent a lightning blast of guilt through her chest.

'I wanted to tell you in person,' Dia replied gently. 'But we should make our way back to Fulmer Hold tomorrow.'

Kesta nodded distractedly. It had been a good six months since she'd last been home to the Fulmer Islands. Even then her father had been less energetic, much quieter than usual; retiring to his room early rather than being last to leave the feast. She'd dismissed it as his age, although she'd never considered him old.

'We can try, can't we?' She grabbed Jorrun's hands, squeezing his fingers hard as she gazed into his pale-blue eyes.

'Of course.' He forced a smile, but she could see the doubt in his eyes. Despite years of trying, only Jorrun and his sister, Dinari, had mastered the skill of healing with magic, and as yet they didn't understand why. The magic itself was also limited, able to mend wounds and reverse the damage of poison, but not cure disease or sickness.

Dia sighed quietly. 'I'll leave you to get some sleep.'

Kesta nodded distractedly, then kicked herself, hurrying after her mother to give her a hug. 'Are *you* all right?' She stepped back to look into her mother's mismatched eyes.

Dia gave a thin-lipped smile and squeezed Kesta's arm. 'I'll be fine.' With a glance at Jorrun, the Icante of the Fulmers slipped out of the room.

Kesta immediately started packing. Jorrun wisely remained out of her way, a worried frown settling on his face.

Kesta swore and straightened up. 'What do we do about the children?'

'They'll want to see their grandfather, but they have other duties. And they're hardly children. You were helping kill Dryn Dunham at Arridia's age.'

Kesta flapped a hand at him dismissively. 'Doesn't mean I had an ounce of sense. To be fair...' The tension eased a little from her muscles and she smiled. 'Riddi is a lot more sensible than I ever was. She must have got that from you. Trust Joss to suddenly claim a quest! He won't like backing out of it.'

'No, he won't.' Jorrun crossed to the window to gaze out at the darkness. 'And I'd hoped Arridia would go with him. I don't like this appearance of an unknown magic.'

Kesta sucked in a breath and held it, biting at her lower lip. 'You think it's Geladan?'

'I don't know what to think, yet.' He winced. 'I was hoping to keep an eye on Joss and Lucien myself.'

Kesta wrapped her arms about her body. 'Perhaps you should.'

He turned and in two long strides was holding her gently. 'As hopeless as we might believe it, I have to at least try to heal Arrus. I'll never forgive myself if I don't. And it's time we let go of Joss a little. We've trusted Arridia out on her own for four years.'

'It's not a matter of trust.' Kesta looked up at him.

He nodded. 'Arridia should go with him, though. She's stronger than us.'

Kesta's chest muscles constricted. Their daughter might be strong in magic, but it still killed Kesta not to be watching over her children herself.

'All right.' She sighed. 'But they won't like not coming with us to Fulmer. I guess it will make them hurry on this mission and get safely back to us quickly, though.'

'Do you want to try to sleep?' He studied her face.

'I... I might just go for a brief walk.'

He nodded and kissed her. 'Try not to find any more trouble.'

She grinned at him before stepping out of the room.

Most of the torches in the hallway had been extinguished, the sparse few that remained danced in the drafts that wandered the castle. Kesta ran her fingertips along the wall as she trod the carpets soundlessly. It was over twenty years since she'd first come here, seeking aid for her people. More than twenty years since she'd first seen Jorrun, seated in his black chair beside the throne, with eyes like ice. Warmth flowed through her heart and she smiled despite the pain. They'd been through so much together. As had her parents. Her feet stumbled, and she choked back a sob. Her father wasn't gone yet, she was borrowing pain before time.

Kesta drew in slow, deep breaths, straightened up, and headed for a door leading to one of the lower battlements. As soon as she stepped out, she was struck by the chill, but she proceeded slowly, drawing in the fresh petrichor scent of the night. A few stars shone bright and steady; the small clouds slow to move. Kesta leaned out through a gap in the crenulations, gazing over the rooftops of the city below. She noticed her shadow move and twisted to look up and find the source of the light. A tall tower stood at the corner of the castle, the uppermost window lit, most of it hidden from her view as it looked out over the lake. She smiled to herself, reminded of the Raven Tower at Northold. Who else would be awake in the early hours of the morning? A guest, perhaps? From the brightness and the way the light moved, she guessed they had a large fire burning in their hearth.

Goosebumps prickled her skin, and uneasiness shuddered through her. With a frown, she drew up her *knowing,* reaching out her magic to feel for any threatening emotions. She touched on Jorrun's anxiety, then drew back as she hit the edge of her mother's grief. She pressed her face into her hands; her legs shaking a little as she stepped back from the edge.

She lowered her hands slowly.

There had been something else there. It felt like magic.

There were several within the castle with power. Her fellow *walkers*, the sorcerers of the Ravens, and Temerran the Bard. This had felt different, though, it almost had a taste – like herbs, like earth.

The night grew suddenly darker, and looking up, Kesta realised the light had gone out from the window. Not a slow fading, but a sudden extinguishing.

She hurried back to her room, almost breaking into a run. As soon as she opened the door to their bedchamber, she called flames to her hands to illuminate it.

'Jorrun, do you know who uses that room way up in the tower over the lake?'

Jorrun groaned and sat up. 'No, I don't. It's rarely used. Too many stairs for most people.'

'I think someone is using magic up there.'

He narrowed his eyes. 'Okay. Bractius has lots of guests tonight who use magic. I can't really go waking up the king to find out who he put in the tower.'

She growled at him in annoyance. 'I think we should investigate. I need you to… I need you to have a sniff. Something reminded me of the dream herbs you use.'

He sat up a little straighter. There were a few Ravens who could dreamwalk like him, but none were present in Taurmaline. He rubbed at his eyes and beard, then threw off his blanket. 'Come on, then.'

While Kesta dug about in her bag for something, Jorrun quickly got dressed. He led her unfalteringly through the maze of corridors and stairs, nodding to two curious guards who didn't dare ask the Dark Man what he was up to, wandering in the early hours of the morning.

Jorrun took the tower stairs two at a time with his long legs. By the time they drew near the top, Kesta was a little out of breath, although she tried her best to hide it. Jorrun held up a hand to halt her, leaning close to the wood of the door to listen. He closed his eyes for a moment, while Kesta shifted from one foot to the other.

'I can smell something,' he said, softer than a whisper. 'Someone has definitely burned herbs. It's…' He closed his eyes again. 'Pine, cedar, possibly hemlock. They might just like the scent.'

Kesta pulled a face at him and hissed. 'Can't you detect the traces of magic?'

She sensed him call his power, and she herself drew up her *knowing*. She could feel no one in the room.

'I think they've gone,' she whispered.

'We should come back in the morning—'

Kesta pushed him aside and tried the door handle. It was locked. Unperturbed, she drew out her lock picks with a grin.

He rolled his eyes but didn't stop her.

She nudged the door carefully open a crack, then a little more, shifting so she could put an eye to the gap. Only a tiny amount of light flowed in through the open shutters.

The room was empty.

She thrust the door open, and Jorrun made a sound of protest. Kesta went straight to the fireplace, grabbing up a poker and moving it about in the grainy ashes. There wasn't even a hint of a spark, it was completely dead. She held a hand over it, then touched the grey remains. 'It's as though no one has been in here for hours.'

Jorrun examined the bed and the two chairs either side of the fireplace, then went to the chest at the foot of the bed and opened it. 'Nothing.'

'But you smell it?' She implored, wondering if maybe her tired mind had played tricks on her.

He nodded. 'I do. And I feel the buzz of old magic.'

Kesta clenched her fists. 'But what magic?'

Jorrun drew in a deep breath, crossing slowly to the window to look out. 'I don't know. Herbs are used to help with many things, but...'

'But?' She scurried to his side and took his arm, looking up into his beautiful eyes.

'Herbs are the influence of an old magic. Earth magic. The magic of Elden.'

***

Kesta blinked at the light, then pulled the blanket up over her face. She wished she could somehow make today unreal; avoid the awful truth. The bed gave way as Jorrun sat on the edge. He took a strand of her hair and ran it gently through his fingers. She sat up suddenly, hugging him as tightly as her muscles would allow.

He kissed the top of her head. 'Come on, we're so late for breakfast it's more like lunch.'

She drew back as though stung. 'I need to check on Mother.'

'Heara's with her,' Jorrun reminded her.

Kesta pursed her lips in a humourless smile, then shot out of bed in alarm. 'Oh, but shouldn't we be on our way?'

Jorrun held up both his hands. 'I sent a raven to Tantony. Rosa will pack our things to go on to the Fulmers. We'll take my ship and follow Dia as quickly as we can.'

Kesta nodded, already scrambling into her trousers and tunic.

'I arranged a private room. Riddi and Joss should be waiting for us.'

Kesta clutched at her stomach. She didn't want to have to endure this herself, never mind tell the children. There was some water on the washstand, and she splashed it on her face, quickly dragging a brush through her hair.

'So, the magic,' she said as she pushed open the door and proceeded him into the hall.

'If we had time, I could do more research into the herbs we scented.' His long stride easily matched her hurried steps. At an intersection, he pointed right.

Kesta nodded, holding to the banister as she scampered down two flights of stairs. 'I hope it's nothing.'

'Me too.'

Jorrun opened a door, and Kesta froze. Arridia was sitting in a soft chair next to the window, her cousin Dierra perched on its arm. Joss sat at a table, still picking at the large array of food. The fire-drakes were hovering near the whitewashed ceiling, singing nonsense rhymes. Alikan spun about, drawing magic, but he quickly shut it off when he saw who had entered.

Kesta was proud and relieved at the young man's caution. The Chemman was as much family as her own children; but her family weren't the only ones in the room. Prince Lucien sat beside Joss, laughing at the antics of the fire-spirits. On the other side of Joss, one of the twins was leaning back in her chair, nibbling at an oatcake. For a moment Kesta wasn't sure which princess it was until she realised she was using her left hand. Scarlett then.

Her heart and stomach sank at the thought of having so private, and difficult, a conversation with an audience.

Arridia stood at once, her blue and violet eyes wide. 'Mumma?' Arridia looked from Kesta to her father. All jollity in the room ceased at once. Azrael started keening and Arridia waved a hand at him gently to be quiet.

Lucien stood, giving a slight bow despite himself being a prince. 'Would you like a moment alone?'

It was Jorrun who answered. 'Thank you, your Highness, for you're consideration, but I think you should hear this too.' He turned to Kesta, but she still couldn't bring herself to talk. She detested that she was being a coward. Jorrun continued. 'Arrus Silene is unwell. He's... he is very unwell. Kesta and I will head back to the Fulmers today. I shall try to heal Arrus, but I have to be honest... it's unlikely it will work.'

Joss shot to his feet and turned to his sister.

It was Lucien who spoke again. 'I am very sorry for your news. Is there anything I can do?'

Kesta smiled at the young man, a surge of love gripping her chest as tears blurred her vision. 'You are very kind, Luce. Just look after yourselves on your quest and get back safely.'

'Wait.' Joss looked from Kesta to his father. 'I... we.' He ground his teeth. 'What about Grandfather?'

'If you need to go, I understand,' Lucien said quickly. 'I can take warriors south.'

'No.' Joss turned again to his sister as he replied to the prince. 'You're investigating magic, Luce, you can't go without someone with power. I'll go. Riddi, you can—'

'Your grandfather will be fine for a while.' Kesta stepped forward. She hoped it was true. 'Go on your quest, keep each other safe, then join us at Fulmer Hold as soon as you can.'

Arridia stood slowly, avoiding everyone's eyes, and clenching her jaw as she hurried stiffly across the room to hug her. Kesta forced her own tumultuous emotions aside to try to offer comfort. She quickly wiped at her eyes and let go of her daughter. Joss had stepped closer, Alikan at his shoulder. Both the fire-spirits were wailing.

Kesta took in a deep breath and drew herself up, clapping her hands together loudly to silence the raucous spirits. She regarded Lucien and Scarlett. She'd known them since they were born, and although she wasn't particularly fond of their parents, she had a lot of affection for both of them. With a glance at Jorrun, she warned them all of their suspicions someone was practising an unknown magic within the castle. Lucien looked deeply concerned, while Scarlett seemed excited, animated.

'Oh, but we must find out who!' She almost danced in her seat.

'We will, carefully.' Lucien met Kesta's gaze despite his shyness. 'When we get back.'

The door opened behind her, and Kesta turned to see her mother. Heara was just behind her, but it was another of the Icante's close friends whose arm she leaned on. Temerran bowed politely toward Lucien and Scarlett.

'Grandmother.' Joss pushed back his chair and hurried around the table to hug her. Kesta was shocked at how small her mother appeared in the arms of her grandson.

Temerran shook Jorrun's hand, then addressed the Elden Prince. 'With your permission, your highness, I would like to accompany you on your quest.'

Lucien's eyes lit up, and the prince seemed to grow taller. 'Thank you.' Lucien gave a small bow of his own. 'Your company would be greatly appreciated.'

Jorrun took hold of Kesta's hand and their fingers intertwined. Kesta's heart felt lighter. As much as she trusted Arridia, it would be a relief to know the resourceful bard would be with them. She looked up and met Jorrun's eyes; he nodded.

Chapter Six

Arridia; Kingdom of Elden

Arridia realised she was clenching her teeth and tried to force her jaw to relax. Every instinct urged her to escape the enclosed room and get out to open sky. Despite her efforts to shut down her *knowing*, the emotions of the others assailed her like nettles.

'I'm sorry, Riddi.'

She turned to find her grandmother gazing at her, the wrinkles around her eyes more pronounced in her concern.

'Oh, no.' Arridia shook her head. 'Don't apologise, Grandma, you can't help how you feel and… and please don't think you have to suppress it for my sake.'

Dia smiled. Despite everything, the Icante still held herself with poise and grace. 'I need to get ready to leave, anyway. I wanted to see you though, before I left.'

'We'll be with you as soon as we can.' Arridia's attention was caught by Joss, who was gesticulating wildly as he discussed his upcoming quest with their parents. Jorrun had a shadow of a smile on his face, while Kesta frowned at him. Lucien also looked wary, sitting quietly in the corner.

Heara met Dia's eyes and nodded. She sauntered toward Joss and Alikan. 'Well, we have to go. Good luck hunting your monster, and I'll see you in the Fulmers soon.' She reached out a hand and Joss went to clasp her wrist. Without warning, the scout hooked a foot behind his ankle, twisted his arm, and threw him onto his back.

'Ow!' Joss landed with a thud.

Heara and Alikan both laughed, while Scarlett drew in a loud gasp.

Heara grinned. 'Enthusiasm's nice. Caution is better. I'll see you for lessons in a week or so.'

Scarlett followed the scout with her eyes, mouth open. 'Will you teach me that, Joss?' she asked, as he scrambled to his feet, cheeks red.

'Of course—'

Kesta cleared her throat. 'I'll teach you, when there's time. Or Riddi will.'

Dia touched Arridia's arm, and she turned to hug her grandmother. Heara opened the door for the Icante, both fire-drakes streaking after them to give their goodbyes.

Arridia was breathing hard. She needed to run. Looking up, she met her mother's eyes. Kesta gave her a wave of her hand, and Arridia didn't need telling twice. She hurried from the room, head down, gulping in air. She wiped her clammy hands down her trousers, feeling the fluttering of her heart ease.

'Arridia?'

She closed her eyes briefly and groaned, glancing over her shoulder to see Dierra scampering after her. Arridia slowed down a little, trying to push away her resentment. It wasn't her cousin's fault her parents and the senior Ravens were so overprotective of her and Joss.

'You want some space.' Dierra winced as she caught up. 'I get it. Unfortunately, I can't hide in lanterns like Azra.'

Arridia laughed, her muscles easing a little more. 'I'm sorry, Dierra, it's nothing personal.'

Dierra shrugged. 'I know. I was told that being around people can be tough for you. If you like I could hang back a bit, pretend I'm just, I don't know, a chair or something.'

Despite the ache in her heart, Arridia laughed again. 'No, it's okay, walk with me.'

'Just your luck you got assigned a chatter box, eh?' Dierra nudged her arm.

'Hey, I'm used to it, I've lived with Azrael all my life.'

'Oi!' A disgruntled buzz came from one of the wall sconces.

'Do you want to practice some magic, or some swordplay?' Dierra suggested.

'Actually, I was just hoping to walk down by the lake or something.'

Dierra's shoulders sagged a little. 'Okay.'

'We could work at some water magic when we get there,' Arridia conceded.

Dierra immediately brightened. It wasn't long before she was compelled to break the silence again. 'So, you spent a lot of time with Lucien last night.'

'The prince is a good friend.' Arridia glanced at her cousin with a scowl, then she recalled that speculation about the two of them had been exactly what she and Lucien had planned to get the king off his back for a while. 'I haven't seen him in a long time. You've been assigned to Elden for a while now, haven't you?'

'A year.' Dierra pushed open a door, checked who was about, then held it wide for Arridia. 'I stayed at court for a few months, assigned to the king as a Raven apprentice, then did some training with your parents at Northold. They were considering reassigning me back to Chem to allow someone else a chance to train with them but thank the gods my sister got pregnant and they assigned me to you.'

Arridia's eyes widened a little. It was odd to hear a member of her family talk so casually of gods. Her father rarely mentioned them, her mother did, but not in a good way. She wondered which gods Dierra even meant, the belligerent and vengeful false ones of Chem, or the more benign and absent Eldenian god and goddess?

They descended to the ground floor, and out through the main doors of the castle, Dierra giving a nod to the guards as she continued to chatter. 'I kind of like it here. You'll think I'm mad, but I enjoy dressing up in skirts and jewellery. Think I'd hate it in the long term though, being seen as little more than a decoration, or a prize to be won. I admire Queen Ayline though. She's done a lot to gain respect and recognition as queen in such a patriarchal land.'

Arridia raised her eyebrows but said nothing. She supposed Ayline had used every tool she could to gain position in her own court and with her husband, but many of her methods hadn't exactly been... honest.

'Where's your favourite assignment?' Dierra asked her as they crossed the ward towards the gates.

Arridia saw the number of people passing in the street beyond the portcullis, and her heart sank.

'Riddi?'

Arridia shook herself. Where was her favourite place? It wasn't so much a country, as a state of being. Peace. Clean air. The sound of birdsong and the rush of the wind in the trees or the shush of the ocean. But places? She drew in a deep breath, recalling the smell of books, or of horses and hay.

She smiled. 'Northold.'

'Well, it is your home, I suppose.' Dierra stepped out into the street without hesitation. She gave a shudder. 'My childhood home wasn't so nice. But when things were more settled, and I moved back there with Mother as head of the Coven, that was good. I enjoy being in a large seaport though, although Navere is much better than Farport. If I had to go to Chem, I was hoping to finish my training there under Rece and Calayna.'

'I'm sorry.'

'Oh no, don't be.' Dierra took her arm and Arridia had to fight the compulsion to pull it free. Touch made it harder for her to block other people's emotions, but Dierra's flighty, happy thoughts were actually oddly soothing. There was a peculiar mix of surface dancing and deeper concentration. 'I'm honoured to be your partner and finish my training with your parents and the Icante.

'I was worried at first about coming to Northold with Joss and Ali, though I didn't tell them. The original conquerors of Chem!' She waved her free hand dramatically in the air and Arridia glanced about to check if anyone was watching them. 'And both your parents were so formidable. Fierce Kesta, and the powerful Dark Man. I bet you were scared to be naughty as a child!'

Arridia smiled to herself. 'Actually, quite the opposite. Mother always encouraged us to indulge in our curiosity, to explore and challenge. But she taught us responsibility and consequence as well. She's actually... well, she's no fool and won't take any nonsense, but she's incredibly kind. As for her temper, it made me feel safe, because I knew she would protect me, no matter what. And my father, he's wise and strong, I've rarely seen him angry. He always had far more patience with us than Mother, but he never... well, he always talked to me like an adult, never a child. Sometimes I appreciated it, other times I wished he would play with me.' She shook her head. She'd said far too much, even though Dierra was family.

'Do you remember the attack from Geladan?' Dierra asked quietly.

'Kind of.' Arridia chewed at her lower lip. 'Mostly I remember how I felt. Terrified. Excited. Vulnerable. Loved.' She shook her head. 'Azra will tell you later if you really want to know, he'll jump at the chance to tell a story.' She surveyed the street before them, then guided Dierra into a quieter side road. A slender figure was hurrying just ahead of them, and there was something familiar in the way she moved. As the young woman turned off, Arridia glimpsed the side of her face.

'That's Scarlett, isn't it?' Dierra indicated with her head.

'We left the castle before Scarlett.' Arridia frowned. She picked up her pace to catch up with the hooded figure. 'But I can't imagine it would be Eleanor. I know Luce sometimes disguises himself and sneaks into the city, but I don't believe Eleanor would.'

'I guess Scarlett could have taken a different route from the castle and got ahead of us.'

'Maybe...'

'Look, she's carrying a basket over her left arm. Scarlett's the left-handed one, isn't she?'

'Yes.' The young woman turned toward the docks, with barely a glance behind.

'Should we see what she's doing?' Dierra asked eagerly.

'I'm not sure we should really intrude on the princess's privacy.'

'What if she gets into any trouble?'

Arridia sighed. The girl was probably looking for a moment of peace and normality, just as she was. 'All right then.'

Dierra grinned.

They shadowed Scarlett until they reached the crowded waterfront, where they lost her. The wharves were lined with taverns, fishmongers, second-hand shops, and an occasional ale and wine merchant.

'I can't imagine a princess going into any of these.' Dierra gazed up at the signs. 'Perhaps it wasn't her after all.'

Arridia looked up and down the street, her attention was caught by one ship tied at dock. Sunlight glinted off its polished wood. Its tall masts and sleek lines made the other ships appear like uncarved logs. While the other vessels rocked and bobbed, even at anchor, the *Undine* gave the impression of gliding.

Dierra followed her gaze. 'Oh, by the gods that's the *Undine*, isn't it? Didn't you sail on her? I spent six months in a god's forsaken Borrow village for that part of my training.'

Arridia didn't reply. She'd been a little uncomfortable, a little intimidated, onboard the *Undine* among all the Borrowmen; even with Azra and Eila at her shoulder and Temerran in charge. She'd only sailed for a month, and although she'd enjoyed being on the sea, being trapped in a small area with other people had been unpleasant. Despite that, seeing the ship was like encountering an old friend. The *Undine* wasn't alive, but it somehow projected something like emotion, as though the wood had absorbed the lives of those aboard it. The Borrowmen might come across as coarse, rough, and dangerous, but the overwhelming feeling from the ship was love and courage.

'Riddi?'

'Would you like to take a peek?'

'Oh, would I?' Dierra's brown eyes widened. 'Lead the way.'

Scarlett forgotten, the young women wove their way along the wharf, taking the wooden walkway running alongside the ship of the Borrow Bard. Arridia recognised the figure who leaned against the railing, watching the people passing by with a slight scowl.

'Nolv!' Arridia raised a hand politely to gain the first mate's attention. He straightened up, squinting to see who it was.

'Mistress Arridia.' He smiled, revealing gaps where teeth had once been. 'Come to visit the lady?'

She nodded.

'Come on up.'

Despite the fact she was a strong sorceress, Dierra stayed close to Arridia's side as she walked up the gangplank. Most of the Borrowmen warriors were making the most of the harbour facilities, but two sat watch on the deck, perched on barrels and playing dice. One of them had his hair plaited and coloured ash smeared about his eyes like a mask, as though he were going on a raid.

'This is my cousin, Dierra Raven,' Arridia introduced. 'Nolv, first mate of the *Undine*.'

Nolv gave a slight bow, which Dierra returned. 'You know your way around.'

'Thank you,' Arridia replied.

Nolv went back to leaning on the rail and watching the docks while Arridia led Dierra around the deck. The young Chemmish woman leaned over the prow, and Arridia held her breath at how precariously her cousin balanced.

'This figurehead is amazing!'

Arridia smiled. She herself had taken a turn to wax the wood to protect it from the weather and the sea. The *Undine's* figurehead was of a woman, her long hair streaming back behind her to caress the prow. Instead of legs, eight tentacles curled about the ship. Dierra reached out to touch one. 'They even carved in the suckers!'

Arridia laughed, glancing over her shoulder to see that Nolv was smiling. 'Want to look below decks?'

'Oh, yes,' Dierra said, her excitement evident.

Arridia took her down to the narrow corridors of the crew deck and the galley, both of them calling power to light their way. Arridia breathed in deeply, the smell of the wood not dissimilar to that of an old library.

'Goodness, it's so cramped below, isn't it?'

'It is just here.' Arridia brushed the wall with her fingers. 'These are the quarters of Nolv and the other crew who've earned a private cabin over the years. But come forward.' Arridia pushed open a door and a much wider space opened up before them, hanging cots and hammocks, with chests stowed neatly below them, spread across the room. Two steep stairways led up to hatches, and a large, covered hatch went to the deck below. Arridia pointed. 'That's the stores down there.'

'Did you have to sleep in here when you served on the *Undine*?' Dierra asked in horror.

'No, they gave me one of the cabins.'

The *Undine* creaked gently, and Arridia stood listening for a moment to the lapping of the waves against the hull outside. The ship barely moved.

She sighed. 'Let's get back up to the sunlight.'

Dierra shrieked when Azrael appeared suddenly above the hatch they were climbing out of.

'Ssorry!' Azrael made himself small, but he looked more pleased with himself than apologetic. 'Riddi, your parents are getting ready to leave and want to see you.'

'Already?' Arridia climbed faster, turning to give her hand to her cousin and help her onto the deck. 'Where are they?'

Azrael pulsed brighter. 'Heading to the Icante's longship.'

Arridia hurried to the gangplank, throwing a smile toward the first mate as she strode down it. 'Thanks, Nolv.'

'Anytime, miss.' Nolv gave a nod.

'Gosh.' Dierra panted as she kept up with her cousin. 'The people on the Borrow Islands were never that polite. In fact, they seemed to frown at some manners.'

'It's a harsh land,' Arridia replied. 'Even before the blood curse.'

Azrael streamed ahead of them, chuckling as people almost threw themselves out of his way in a panic. Arridia rolled her eyes, but she was in a hurry, so she didn't stop the fire-spirit from having his fun. They reached the longship before her family; the warriors were loading the supplies they'd traded for. Half as long as the *Undine*, and much narrower, the Fulmer ship was designed for shorter distances between the islands and for fending off raiders. It had only two decks, above and below. The lower deck was used for storage, sleeping, and for rowing when the wind wasn't with them. A simple screen was used to segregate off an area for privacy for the Icante and her female companions.

Arridia recognised some of the warriors and raised a hand in greeting.

'Here they come.'

Arridia twisted around to follow Dierra's gaze. Jorrun was easy to spot, taller than everyone around him, red-haired Temerran at his side. Her mother walked behind them with Dia and Eidwyn; Gilfy and Vivess taking up the rear. Heara strode ahead, bellowing when someone didn't move quickly enough. All of them carried their own belongings, including the Icante.

Arridia instinctively clamped down tighter on her *knowing*.

Her father spotted her at once. He didn't smile, but there was warmth in his sky-blue eyes. He gave her a hug and kissed the top of her head. 'I'm sorry, Riddi, you've not long arrived here to see us and already we're leaving.'

She shrugged. 'It's okay. Grandfather is more important, and we'll be there as soon as we can.'

'Just investigate.' Kesta looked sternly from Arridia to Dierra, then pointed a finger at Azrael who squeaked. 'No risks, unless you're absolutely sure you can handle it.'

Arridia glanced at her father, who couldn't help but smile. He hid it quickly as his wife turned to look at him. Arridia knew very well the pair of them had taken tremendous risks in their lives to do what they thought was right. She swallowed. She'd been independent and lived away from her family for years, but this parting really stung.

'Come on.' It was Heara who prompted them, taking the Icante's bag and throwing it to a warrior. Dia turned to Temerran to say goodbye, the bard holding her as gently as though she were a snowdrop.

'I'll bring the children as quickly as I can,' he promised.

For once Arridia forgot to be offended at being referred to as a child, as with a jolt it hit her why Temerran had offered to remain here with the *Undine*.

'Take care.' Dia placed an icy hand briefly against Arridia's cheek as she followed Heara and Gilfy onto the longship.

Kesta drew in a breath and regarded her. 'Don't let your brother do anything too stupid.'

Arridia couldn't help but grin.

Kesta grabbed her wrist and kissed her, hiding her face as she stepped toward the ship. 'We'll see you soon.'

Jorrun held Arridia's eyes a while longer, then followed his wife aboard.

Unable to bear prolonging the goodbye, Arridia nodded to Temerran and headed back along the dockside with long strides. Dierra scampered to keep up with her. With a sharp intake of breath, Arridia turned around to look. Temerran stood on the wharf, completely still, watching as the longship sailed out onto the lake.

Pain was what she had felt from the Bard.

And heartbreak.

Chapter Seven

Scarlett; Kingdom of Elden

'It's not fair!'

Scarlett quickened her pace to keep up with her father's long strides as he made his way from the audience room to his private study. The king didn't answer, and she glared at his back.

'It would be an excellent opportunity for me to learn, and for people to see that I'm as capable of acting as my brother.'

'That's as may be.' She heard some frustration in her father's voice. 'But you're a girl. You can't go gallivanting about the country on quests.'

'The Ravens do!' Scarlett tried to keep pace at his side, to catch his eyes.

'You're not a Raven, you're a princess, and you're of Elden, not some Islander.'

'And shouldn't a princess learn to rule?'

'No.' Bractius pushed open the door to his study, but he held it wide for her to follow. 'A princess must learn to serve.'

'Serve!' Scarlett's eyes widened in affront.

'Yes.' Her father sat down heavily in his chair. 'To serve Elden and your future husband.'

Scarlett folded her arms across her chest, then realising her mother did exactly the same thing, quickly unfolded them again. 'But what if something happens to Lucien? Surely, you'd want me or Eleanor to rule after you, not whoever we marry who isn't of your descent?'

Her father's eyes narrowed. 'Nothing will happen to Lucien. If it does, I can have another son.'

Scarlett doubted her mother would be happy with that idea, but she was wise enough to remain silent. She tried a change of tactics. 'Would it not be advantageous for others to see how strong your children are? That even your daughters know warfare and leadership? Are you not proud of me, Father?'

'Of course, I am.' Bractius smiled and reached out to pat her arm, though he barely looked at her. 'But if you act too wild, how will we find you a good husband?'

Scarlett's nostrils flared. 'I wouldn't want a husband who couldn't respect who I am.'

The king regarded her, and he didn't appear pleased. 'I haven't decided on your husband yet, but whoever I choose, you will obey him.'

Scarlett stared at him. This wasn't her father; this was the king. There was no softness, no love in his gaze, only calculation and... and annoyance.

She couldn't help thinking she'd be better off in Chem. Then his words struck her, and her heart gave a flip. 'Do you have someone in mind for me and Eleanor?'

'I have a few options.' He picked up some papers on his desk and pretended to read them.

'Are we allowed to know?'

'I'll tell you when it's decided. Don't worry, I'll ensure you're safe and retain the status you deserve.' He offered her an indulgent smile that didn't quite reach his eyes.

Scarlett supposed that was as close as she'd get to affection from him. She wished she was Kesta and Jorrun's daughter. It was worthless being a princess without freedom or power. Her cheeks flushed a little as her thoughts turned to Joss. She forced the words out. 'Thank you, Father.'

'Go on, now, I have work to do.'

He didn't even glance up as she left the room. She looked down at her clothing. She'd worn a full skirt, though it was split for riding, and she'd buckled her thin blade to her side in the vain hope she'd be allowed to go with her brother.

With a heavy sigh, she made her way down to the courtyard where the grooms were preparing the horses for the prince's quest. Several warriors were there waiting, including Merkis Adrin, whom Scarlett supposed her father had put in charge. She cringed inwardly on Lucien's behalf, Adrin wouldn't make things easy for her gentle brother. She noticed someone perched quietly out of the way, slicing off bits of apple with his knife and popping them in his mouth. Alikan met Scarlett's eyes and smiled, giving a slight gesture with his head to invite her over. Adrin straightened up on seeing her, visibly startling when he turned to see where she was heading; the arrogant warrior hadn't even realised Alikan was there.

'Hey, Ali.' She hopped up onto the crate beside him.

'No bags?' His brows drew together in concern.

She shrugged. 'Nope. Apparently, princesses shouldn't go on quests.'

'I'd have thought quests should be exactly where princesses should be going.'

'Well, sadly you're not the king,' she grumbled. 'How am I supposed to learn anything useful?'

'Oh, I don't know.' Alikan grinned at her. 'Sewing's quite useful!'

She tutted and shoved him in the arm.

'Seriously, though.' Alikan held out his apple core to his patiently waiting horse. 'What will you do?'

She looked out across the courtyard. Supplies were being loaded onto the heavy-set baggage horses. 'There's still Kesta's mysterious magic to investigate.'

Alikan placed a hand on her arm, and she blushed at the familiarity, at the same time as loving the unabashed acceptance. 'Be careful, your Highness. Do you have anyone you trust who can work with you?'

Her immediate answer was no, but she thought about it. 'I'll ask if Eleanor will help.'

She could see by the expression on the sorcerer's face that the idea of both princesses looking into the magic did quite the opposite of reassuring him.

There was an increase to the chatter in the courtyard and Scarlett looked up to see her brother had arrived with Joss, Arridia, and Dierra. Doroquael flew low over everyone's heads, pulling a face at Adrin, who scowled and ducked. A moment later, Temerran emerged from the castle with two of his Borrowmen warriors.

Alikan jumped off his crate and went to meet them without a backward glance at Scarlett. 'Your Highness, good morning.' He greeted the prince.

With a sigh, Scarlett wriggled off her perch and dawdled across to her brother.

'Is everything ready?' Lucien raised his voice a little more than usual, sounding full of command and confidence. Scarlett wondered if it was down to Temerran's presence.

'Highness,' came a chorus of mumbled replies.

Pages presented Temerran and the Borrowmen with horses and they quickly secured their few possessions. Arridia was quiet, stroking her horse's nose before getting into the saddle. Beside her, Dierra chattered away.

'We won't be gone long, Scar,' Lucien reassured his sister.

'I should be allowed to come.' She pouted.

Lucien lowered his voice to a whisper. 'One day I'll be king, and things will change.'

'It will be too late by then.' Scarlett almost stamped a foot. 'I'll be married to some awful old man who won't let me do anything.'

Lucien winced. 'I'll do my best not to let that happen.'

'You're not even allowed to decide who *you* want to marry.'

Lucien took a step back from her, raising his chin a little to regard her from beneath his wayward curls. 'We'll see,' he replied quietly. 'Stay safe, Scarlett.'

He turned his back on her, getting onto his dappled horse and urging it forward to join Arridia. There was no sign of Azrael, but Scarlett knew the fire-spirit had likely gone to scout ahead.

'See you soon, Scar.' Joss vaulted up into his saddle with a wink that made her skin grow warm. She watched as the party clattered out of the courtyard and vanished through the gate.

Someone cleared their throat. 'Can I help, your highness?'

She realised she'd been standing in the middle of the courtyard for some time. She barely glanced at the groom. 'No, thanks.'

She grabbed up a handful of her skirt and hurried back inside the keep and toward her rooms. No one could stop her taking up the quest within the castle and proving her worth. She knocked on her sister's door, not waiting for a reply before pushing her way in. Eleanor sat at her table with her lady-in-waiting, and Scarlett's too. Both the young girls stood up to bow, Eleanor put her pen down in its stand to regard Scarlett.

'Can we talk alone?' Scarlett asked at once.

Eleanor frowned, but she turned to the two ladies-in-waiting and gave a polite nod. With curtsies, the girls hurried from the room.

'You really should try to do more with Riane,' Eleanor scolded. 'The poor thing keeps coming to me to ask what to do, with you disappearing all the time.'

Scarlett waved a hand impatiently. 'I never wanted a lady-in-waiting. Do what you wish with her. Listen, Elle, do you want to help me on a quest?'

'You know we can't go leaving the castle—'

'No, it's in the castle! Come on, it'll be fun.'

Eleanor shrank back in her chair. 'I don't want to get in any trouble.'

'You won't,' Scarlett reassured her. 'All we have to do is look around a room for clues, then keep our eyes and ears open.'

'That's it?' Eleanor narrowed her eyes.

'Well.' Scarlett cringed. 'I might have to go to Northold, but—'

'You'll never get permission to go to Northold, especially as Arridia's not there now.'

Scarlett rolled her eyes. 'Let me worry about that. Are you in?'

'What exactly are we looking for?'

'Magic.'

Eleanor froze. 'Magic? Won't that just be one of the Ravens?'

Scarlett shook her head and quickly explained, while Eleanor turned paler.

'I don't think we should mess with that. Let's tell Mother.'

Scarlett gave an exasperated groan. 'Come on, Eleanor, let me have one adventure. What harm can it do, looking in a room?'

Eleanor threw her hands up. 'Oh, all right.'

Eleanor instructed the girls to work on their tapestries, then she walked beside Scarlett down the long corridors.

'So, whose room is it?' Eleanor asked.

'Well, I made some enquiries with one of the older maids,' Scarlett told her enthusiastically. 'Originally it was used by our ancestor, King Medric, until he tired of all those steps and moved into what are now the royal suites. The maid said it was rumoured that some kings would keep mistresses hidden away up there.'

'Do you think Father has a mistress?' Eleanor demanded. 'Maybe a *walker*?'

'No, of course not,' Scarlett retorted. She'd heard the rumours her father had loved a *walker*, some red-haired woman who was murdered and reputedly haunted the castle still. The air caught in her lungs. Could what Kesta had smelt result from a haunting? She dismissed it at once, although the idea didn't quite leave her.

'Well, go on.' Eleanor nudged her in the ribs.

'Well, the maid says the room hasn't been used in years, but that sometimes servants go in there just to keep it tidy.'

'Hide out the way of chores, more like, lazy things.' Eleanor scowled. 'Well, there's your answer. It was probably some servant attempting a daft love spell or something. Anyway, if Kesta and Jorrun found nothing, why would you?'

Scarlett's heart sank, but she refused to give up. 'Because they went late at night, and they didn't stay long. Oh, come on, Elle, it could be fun.'

Eleanor shook her head, but she followed her sister up the long staircase.

Scarlett touched the door handle. She held her breath, her heart beating just a little faster. She tensed and pushed the door open. Eleanor made a startled sound and Scarlett froze.

'What?'

'Oh.' Eleanor's eyelashes fluttered. 'I just thought it might be locked.'

The room wasn't as dramatic as Scarlett had expected. It was bright with its one large window open wide to the sky and the lake. A bed took up most of the space, the only other furniture was two chairs by the fireplace, a clothes chest, and a small table under the window.

'Can you smell anything?' Scarlett asked as she stepped cautiously into the room.

'Dust,' Eleanor replied, screwing up her nose.

Scarlett surveyed the room. It *was* dusty. A fine film lay over everything, but there were exceptions.

'Look at this.' Scarlett crossed to the table. There were three circular marks that had probably been made by bowls just larger than her hand, one of them had been pushed across the table leaving scuff marks. Then she noticed something red on the windowsill, a crescent-shaped stain had been left. She leant closer to sniff at it, then touched it with a fingertip.

'Ew, Scarlett, don't touch anything.'

She touched her tongue to her fingertip, ignoring her sister.

Eleanor squealed in disgust.

'It's wine.' Scarlett gave a nod of her head. 'Someone has definitely been using this room. What's in that chest there?'

Eleanor drew her hands up to her chin and screwed her face up. 'It's filthy.'

Scarlett rolled her eyes and pushed past her sister. Scarlett took hold of the leather handle and lifted the lid. She let out a breath and sagged. It was empty.

'There's nothing here, Scarlett.' Eleanor huffed. 'Let's get back to our rooms.'

Scarlett ignored her, taking a poker and sifting through the ashes as Kesta had done. She got onto her hands and knees to look closer. Eleanor tutted.

'You'll get your dress dirty.'

Scarlett pulled a face, then sat back on her heels. Her heart sank. There was nothing there.

But something niggled in the back of her mind, and she turned. She reached out, lifting the valance around the bed and looking beneath. Amidst the dust was a small object. She grabbed it and held it to the light.

'What is it?' Eleanor demanded.

'Some kind of crystal,' Scarlett replied. It was as long as her index finger, six sided, pointed at one end and rugged at the other, as though it had been torn from something. It was darker at the base than at the point and looked as though swirling smoke had somehow been caught within.

'Put it down,' Eleanor said, wide-eyed. 'It might be dangerous.'

Instead, Scarlett slipped it into her pocket. 'I'll ask Joss and Riddi when they get back. Scarlett, I need to go to the Raven Tower to do some research.'

'Don't be stupid. You'll never be allowed to visit Northold, what reason could you possibly give?'

Scarlett's heart sank. She couldn't think of any with Arridia being away.

'Let's just tell Mother.'

'No, Elle, promise me you won't, not yet.' She grabbed her sister's arms and gripped them tightly.

'Ow! Okay.'

Scarlett let her go. 'Thanks. Would you, um... would you cover for me if I—'

'No, Scarlett, I'm not getting into trouble. Just wait until Arridia gets back or write to Lady Rosa if you must.'

Scarlett gave a loud sigh and ground her teeth a little. 'Oh, all right. But keep quiet about this, Elle.'

'I still think we should tell. Not that it's anything other than some stupid, love-sick maid anyway.'

Scarlett gave a snort. Her eyes travelled to the window, and she moved closer, gazing down at the lake and the boats that crossed it. An idea came to her, and she smiled, quickly hiding it as she turned back to her sister. If she could find a boat to take her, she could head out to Northold at night, and be back before anyone really missed her.

Chapter Eight

Cassien; Free Provinces of Chem

Kussim had been polite in public at Cassien's agreement to go with Catya, but she had plenty to say when they were back in their rooms. Not that she didn't trust him, she just hated the idea Catya might assume she could still manipulate him. Their parting had been a little uneasy, and Cassien's stomach had taken a long time to settle; he realised it was guilt. He might not love Catya anymore, but she had been a huge part of his life. Her absence had been like a missing tooth, a constant reminder of something being incomplete.

Manipulate him was exactly what Catya had done.

He'd chosen one Raven sorcerer, Sonnet, and two scouts to travel with them, as well as six warriors and a handful of servants to manage their shelters and supplies. It was unlike the scouting missions he and Catya had taken together many years ago, just them with nothing more than blankets and their weapons.

They'd crossed through Caergard without incident, and through the south-eastern corner of Arkoom Province. The long miles of Navere stretched before them, its city standing on the far western side where Domarra's river ran down from Mayliz and through Margith to join the sea. It had been over a year since Cassien had last visited Free Chem's new capital, and part of him was excited at the prospect of seeing it again. Navere. The city he had helped liberate in what felt like a lifetime ago with Kesta, Jorrun, Jagna, and the master who had saved him. Osun.

Catya and Dysarta stumbled out of their tent, their laughter sharp in the subdued camp. Their hands were entwined and Catya leaned against Dysarta. The red-headed warrior's cheeks flushed when she realised everyone was staring at them, but the women joined amber-eyed Merin as he quietly ate his breakfast.

Sonnet cleared her throat. 'Those two, um… are they—?'

'Yes.' Cassien interrupted quickly.

'Sooo,' Sonnet lowered her voice. 'Catya seduced a Raven so her kingdom could have an heir?'

Cassien shushed her. 'I doubt Catya even thought about it. Enough though, we have to remember she's queen of her land.'

Young Sonnet swept a strand of corn-blonde hair away from her face and nodded.

Cassien stood, brushing off the knees of his trousers. 'Half an hour, then we should get going.'

Catya looked up, her face serious as she nodded.

It didn't take them long to pack up the camp and be ready to leave. Cassien resisted the urge to do the scouting himself and let the two Ravens move out ahead. Catya urged her horse forward to ride beside him, and every muscle in his body tensed.

'You haven't forgiven me, have you? After all this time. Do you really think you'd have been better off with me than with Kussim?'

'Of course not.' He scowled.

'Well then,' she said brightly, as if that sorted everything, as if it rubbed out years of pain. 'I forgave you ages ago.'

'What?' He turned to stare at her. 'Forgave me for what?'

She sniffed. 'Those cruel things you said. Anyway.' She shrugged her shoulders.

Cassien clenched his teeth. 'Why are you really back, Catya? You declined invitations from Jorrun and Kesta, you rarely allowed Raven envoys into Snowhold. What are you up to?'

She rolled her eyes. 'Well, that's nice. I'm here to introduce Merin to his father.'

'Does Alikan even know? Gods, Cat, he must have been just a child himself—'

'Oh, don't start. It was years ago. People can change, you know.'

Cassien shifted in his saddle. He'd certainly changed, although he wondered if he were still being a bit naïve. He shook himself. 'Okay, Catya. So, Dysarta. She seems really nice. She's a Northman, yes?'

'She is.' Catya smiled, and Cassien found himself smiling too. 'She's of The People.'

'Would you tell me?' he asked. 'What happened to you in the north, how did you become a queen in a land where women are slaves? I've heard some of the story, of course, but, well, not from you.'

'Okay.' Catya narrowed her eyes a little, surveying the terrain ahead of them. 'When I left Uldren I headed north, into Snowhold. I think I was looking for a final challenge, an unknown land. Perhaps even a glorious place to end. I found myself instead embroiled in the story of The People, the tribesmen of the north. I fell in love with Dysarta. You won't be surprised to hear I let her down. Anyway, I helped The People take back their land, Snowhold, and I took on the title of Queen as chosen by the true inhabitants of the Glacier Plains.'

Catya told him in more detail as they crossed Navere, and he was surprised at her honesty; she left nothing out, not even her mistakes and her foolhardy pride. Cassien stared at her as she spoke of the strange monsters of the northern mountains, the Rakinya. He'd always half thought them only a tale to scare off would be attackers – even though Alikan and Rothfel insisted they were real – but he could see in Catya's face the Rakinya were no children's story.

He glanced over his shoulder and saw young Merin rode beside Dysarta. And from the calm look on the boy's face, none of this information was new to him. Perhaps Catya had changed.

'I'm sorry about Ruak,' he offered.

She shrugged, although her chin dropped, and she turned away a little. 'Twelve was a good age for a bird.'

As they climbed down into the river valley days later, Cassien's spirits lifted. Caergard was where his family was, but Navere was always home – and not because he had been born there. It made his heart swell to see the city thriving. The women's market had long ago expanded and men now worked and shopped there. The harbour was a chaos of activity and noise, the ships from Elden and the Borrows among those berthed. What once had been the slave pens and skin markets where Cassien had been forced to fight to keep his life, was now the colourful and highly lucrative foreign trade market. Gulls competed with the shouts of men and women. Laughter far more prevalent than anger.

Catya looked around at it all wide-eyed, her mouth open a little but curved up into a smile. 'It's so different!'

They were admitted into the palace grounds and rode through the well-tended gardens towards the stables. A familiar figure stood waiting on the palace steps, and Catya drew up her horse. She turned to Cassien, her eyes widening, then she vaulted off her horse and raced across the grass.

A laugh bubbled up from Cassien's chest. She might be a queen in her mid-thirties, but she was still Catya.

'Captain Rece!' Catya threw her arms around the waiting man. His hair was mostly silver now, still cut short, although it was many years since he'd been a guard and worn a helmet.

'No one calls me Captain anymore.' Rece smiled down at her.

'Hello, Captain.' Cassien grinned.

'Cass.' Rece untangled himself from Catya and held out his hand to clasp Cassien's wrist, before turning back to Catya. 'Well, your majesty, welcome home to Navere. Will you introduce your friends?'

Catya spun on her heels and waved at Merin to join her. 'This is my son, Merin, and Dysarta, my wife.'

Dysarta's face lit up, and she reached out to clasp Rece's wrist, placing her other hand on Merin's shoulder. Catya introduced her two warriors as stewards came forward to take their horses.

'Come on in.' Rece looked them all up and down again, the smile not leaving his face. 'How are your family, Cass?'

'They're well,' he replied, his chest swelling. 'Raith's power has just come through.'

'That's fantastic.' Rece reached out to clasp his wrist again.

Rece led them past the main audience room and took them instead to the vast library. The round window that Kesta had smashed many years ago had been replaced with coloured glass. The scene it depicted was of the Ravens defeating the demon-like creature Navere's high priest had become to attack them.

'Can't say I approved.'

Cassien turned to see the owner of the voice. It was an old priest in plain-looking brown robes, although the material was luxurious. Most of his hair had gone, but the eyes that peered over the book were shrewd.

'Kerzin, your holiness.' Cassien gave a bow in greeting. 'They finally trusted you in the library then?'

'They still keep an eye on me.' The high priest of Navere's temple glared at Rece, but it quickly turned into a smile. He put the book down and stood. 'Your majesty, it's been a long time.'

'It has, Kerzin,' Catya replied seriously. 'I hope you're keeping your gods under control these days?'

He winced. 'Indeed.'

The door opened behind them and Calayna hurried in with Sonnet's mother, Beth. Cassien and Sonnet were greeted warmly, Catya with reservation. A young man followed with glasses of wine on a tray. Navere palace's long-time head of the household servants, Zardin, had died six years ago; they had awarded him a funeral fit for a Raven.

Calayna raised her chin a little, her brown eyes regarding Catya as she came straight to the point. 'How are things in Snowhold? Have you come to make a treaty with Free Chem?'

Catya grinned, glancing at Dysarta. 'It isn't why I'm here. But we can talk. I want lasting peace, of course I do, but we have our own way of doing things in the north and I intend to keep my crown.'

'Sounds like a reasonable starting place.' Rece stepped in. 'But let's get you settled and sit down for dinner before we begin negotiations.'

'Sounds good.' Catya raised her glass.

Cassien found a quiet moment to catch-up with Calayna in Osun's old study and exchange news from their provinces. Jereth, Jorrun's nephew, who had been assigned to Navere permanently, joined them. Cassien thought it likely he would eventually take over from Calayna and Rece. The dark-haired young man was animated as he spoke, taking down ledgers from the shelves to show Cassien, and pointing out places on the vast map that took up most of the wall. Cassien's eyes kept going to the portrait opposite, where Osun's eyes looked down at him, a rare smile just touching the man's lips. It had been painted by Raven Jollen from memory and wasn't a bad likeness.

'So that's about it.' Jereth finished his report. 'Other than the odd murder between rivals and the usual thefts, it's been pretty quiet.'

Cassien met Calayna's eyes, and they both smiled.

'I don't like quiet,' they both said at the same time.

They laughed at Jereth's expression.

'I don't imagine things will stay that way with Catya here.' Calayna raised her eyebrows.

Cassien sat back in his chair. 'Maybe. But I think she has changed. The old Catya is still there, but whether it's Dysarta's influence, or Merin, she seems to have a purpose finally... and a conscience.'

Calayna snorted. 'We'll see.'

***

Cassien sighed, rubbed at his face, then with a groan got out of bed. Despite the size of Navere palace, it was too quiet. He missed the sound of his wife's quiet breathing. He snorted, he even missed Raith waking him up at some ungodly hour and Enika's teething. He dressed quickly, and buckling on his sword out of habit, made his way down to the library. He wasn't surprised to find it occupied, but he was surprised at the occupant.

'Merin, everything all right?'

The boy nodded. An old black cat was curled up in his lap, purring slowly, a bead of dribble forming at its lips.

'Hey, isn't that...' Cassien crouched to stroke the cat. 'Yes, this is Trouble, your father's cat. Alikan hated leaving him here, but didn't think it fair to keep taking him over the sea when he had to travel about so much.'

'Do you know my father?' Merin gazed at him without blinking.

'Well, yes.' Cassien stood and slumped in a chair close to the boy. 'I trained him in a few things. He's a good man.'

'Mother said she didn't know him, but that he was nice, is a powerful sorcerer, and has orange eyes like mine. She talks about you a lot, though.'

'Really?' Cassien shifted uncomfortably.

'Yes. She says you're the best swordsman who ever lived, and that your heart was too soft for a warrior.'

Cassien clenched his teeth, feeling the colour rise to his cheeks. 'Being a warrior doesn't mean it's okay to kill.'

Merin straightened up, making the cat groan in annoyance. 'Mother says that too!'

Cassien tilted his head slightly. 'She does?'

Merin nodded. 'But she also says sometimes you have to be ruthless, to be a queen.'

Cassien grunted. 'I suppose there is some truth in that.'

Merin stroked the cat again. 'Dysarta doesn't like when Mother is ruthless, but Edon Ra tells her sometimes she has to be.'

'Edon Ra?'

'He's mother's Rakinya advisor.'

'Rakinya?' Cassien frowned. 'The monsters from the far north?'

'They're not monsters,' Merin said angrily. 'Edon Ra said you'd all say he was, that's why he's had to hide when we came, but he isn't.'

'Hide?' Cassien froze. 'Hide where?'

Merin's hand flew to his mouth, his amber eyes wide above his fingers. He shook his head.

Cassien held up his hands, leaning forward. He spoke softly. 'It's okay, Merin, remember your mother said I don't like to hurt things. If Edon Ra is your friend, then I'll make sure no one hurts him, and no one will call him a monster.'

Merin lowered his hand slowly. 'You couldn't catch Edon, no one can find him if he doesn't want to be seen.'

'I can believe it. I'm a good scout, but I didn't know he'd come with us.'

'He's the best.' Merin grinned.

Cassien kept his breathing steady, although his heart had sped up. So, Catya had brought one of the northern beast-men with her; but what was she up to?

'I can understand why your mother wanted him to come, to protect you.'

'Oh, no,' Merin shook his head. 'Edon came to protect you, and the other people Mother loves.'

'Protect us?' Every muscle in his body tensed.

Merin nodded slowly. 'Edon Ra is a Rakinya seer. He says something bad is coming, something terrible.'

'Bad?' Cassien swallowed. 'But if something bad is coming, why on earth would your mother take you to it?'

Merin's eyelashes fluttered, and his eyes filled with tears. 'Because Edon Ra says you are the only one who can stop me dying. Only you.'

Chapter Nine

Joss, Kingdom of Elden

'That's it, just there.' Adrin pointed to a small huddle of houses amid cultivated fields. Joss sat up straighter in his saddle, scanning the landscape. There were three houses spread out away from the others. One with a mill wheel that lay oddly on its side, one close to the eaves of a forest, and the third a stone and slate building from which smoke rose. He glanced up at Doroquael and the fire-spirit shot off to take a closer peek.

'We should send the men ahead, your majesty,' Adrin said.

'No need, it's already in hand,' Lucien replied with a smile at Arridia, who rode at his side.

Adrin grumbled to himself, but they ignored him. The Merkis had somehow stayed in Bractius's favour, but never enough to earn a promotion to a higher rank, or to become one of the king's advisors. He was a tool, no more, although the vain man couldn't see it.

Joss urged his horse forward to draw level with his sister and the prince. 'Anything?'

Arridia closed her eyes. Her expression remained serene, and he felt the drawing of her magic.

'There is anxiety, anger even, and some relief now Dierra is there.'

'What?' Adrin twisted in his saddle to gaze back over the others.

Joss chuckled; the idiot hadn't noticed the Raven scout had gone. Adrin's face flushed when the Borrow warriors caught on and laughed aloud. So far, Temerran had hung back, not attempting to take over from the prince – unlike Adrin.

'Let's find out what happened then.' Lucien kicked his horse into a canter and Joss followed, his eyes scanning the crowd of people who waited with Dierra. It seemed the whole of the village had gathered, including the children. Dierra's arms were folded across her chest, her expression serious. The man and woman beside her were better dressed than the others, the woman hastily smoothing back her hair and dipping in a premature curtsy at the prince's approach.

'Your highness.' The man bowed, wringing his hands together. 'We are honoured you would come yourself.'

For a moment Joss wondered if they'd ridden all this way over some neighbours' dispute. He dismounted, placing his hand on his sword hilt and shadowing Lucien. Arridia hung back, needing to keep some distance between herself and the emotions of these people, while keeping her *knowing* open to assess them for Lucien.

'Tell me exactly what has happened,' Lucien asked kindly.

One of the Borrowmen moved off to investigate the area, an instinctive action, but Temerran held out a hand to stop him.

'It was three nights ago.' The villager looked around at his neighbours for confirmation. 'Must have been just past midnight. Some of us heard something moving about outside.'

'Thought a cow had got loose,' a woman said.

'Couple of us looked,' the man continued. 'But we saw nothing. Anyways, we came out next morning, as the sun rose, and found all our ploughed fields covered in rocks and stones, as though they'd rolled there or come up from the ground.'

There was a muttering from the villagers, and Joss shifted his weight. Among the words used were 'magic' and 'cursed.'

'It will take days to get the land cleared. We'd just sowed our crops as well. Anyway, we sent a message straight to Taurmaline for help. Then the next night...' The man shook his head. 'There was an awful sound. None of us dared leave the house. When we came out in the morning, something had lifted the mill wheel right off and lain it on the grass. We haven't dared try to put it back.'

'And last night?' Lucien prompted.

'Last night something broke into our house!' The woman in the finer dress burst into sobs. With a wince and a helpless glance at Arridia, Dierra put her arm around the woman.

'Smashed the front door right in!' The man's eyes were huge. 'I grabbed my axe and crept to the top of the stairs and there were eyes looking up at me, glowing eyes. I've seen nothing like it, it was no beast as I knows of. I'm reluctant to admit it, but I ran back to my room and pushed a chest in front of the door. The creature was shuffling about downstairs, breaking things, and we decided to get out of there. We tied a sheet to the bedpost and climbed out the window, made a run to our neighbours.'

One man raised a hand and nodded his head, as though to corroborate the man's story. Joss tried not to smile.

'A group of us went together in the morning,' the man continued. 'The house was wrecked, though we couldn't see that anything was taken. What do you think it was, your highness? A demon like what was summoned in Chem?'

Lucien drew himself up. 'I don't think it was a demon from Chem, but we'll certainly look into it.' He turned to Adrin. 'Set up camp, a little away from the village but where we can watch easily. Tem, are your men trackers?'

The Borrow Bard gave a polite bow. 'They are, your highness.'

'Good. Coordinate with the Ravens and gather as much information for me as you can.' Lucien regarded the villagers. 'Get any essential chores you need to do done, then stay in your houses where it's safe. We may need to ask you more questions. We'll stay here tonight and see this creature ourselves.'

'Highness, is that wise?' Adrin broke in.

'Yes.' Lucien held his gaze. 'I think it is.'

The village leader stepped forward, then remembered himself and gave a fumbling bow. 'Your highness, I'd offer my house but—'

Lucien held up his hands. 'You're kind, but there's no need. I'm a warrior, a tent will do me just fine.'

Joss raised an eyebrow. He'd never seen the prince so decisive before, and he protested that he wasn't a warrior more often than not. Was this because Temerran was here, or was the prince just more confident away from his father's critical eye?

'Arridia.' Lucien touched her arm briefly. 'Perhaps we could start with the house.'

'I'd be honoured.' Arridia smiled at him.

Joss's eyes narrowed. He was beginning to suspect his sister and the prince's ruse might be no such thing. He jumped when Alikan's hand landed firmly on his shoulder.

'Shall we check the mill?'

'Yeah, sure,' Joss agreed. 'And I'd better see what Doro and Azra are up to.'

Some villagers were still hanging about, watching, despite the prince's directive. Adrin shouted at his men to set up camp. Joss headed towards the mill, surveying the worn but narrow track.

He sighed. 'We'll be lucky if there are any clear tracks left at all.'

'There'll be something,' Alikan replied optimistically. 'If not, it sounds likely we'll get a visit tonight, anyway.'

Joss called up his power and sent a small ball of fire upward, signalling for Doroquael to come to him. The fire-spirit rose from one of the rock-strewn fields and streaked toward him at once.

'Definitely magic!' Doroquael buzzed excitedly. 'It feelss elemental, but it's not a fire-spirit.'

Joss's heart dropped to his stomach, and he felt the blood drain from his face. He glanced at Alikan to make sure his friend hadn't seen his fear. The Geladanians used elemental magic.

'Hmm.' Alikan's stride didn't falter. 'Could be a lot of things. Kesta and a few of us can draw rock up from the earth, but I can't see this being the work of Ravens.'

'Well, let's not jump to any conclusions until we have more information,' Joss said with false brightness. 'Doro, can you make a quick check of the mill. Just make sure there's nothing lurking there.'

'I hope there is.' Doroquael made himself larger and pulled a face.

Joss laughed despite himself. 'Go on. And be careful!'

'Let's search down by the water,' Alikan suggested.

Joss kept an eye as Doroquael made a circuit of the watermill, before disappearing into a window. As they reached the millstream, Alikan crouched, some of his long auburn hair falling over his face as he leant over the ground, running his fingers over the rabbit-trimmed grass.

'It's odd.' Alikan rocked back on his heels. 'There is an impression of something heavy having trod here on the softer earth, but its flat.'

'Flat?' Joss leant closer.

'Yeah. No shape, no distribution of weight. Just flat. I guess it could be a badly made boot, or a man who has no arches, or walks oddly.'

'Like what?'

Alikan rolled his eyes. He stood and tried to demonstrate, stomping, lifting high at the knees and trying to place his feet down evenly all at once, with no bounce or push.

Joss burst out laughing.

'Idiot.' Alikan scowled at him and slapped his arm. 'This is serious.' But the sparkle in Alikan's amber eyes showed his humour.

Doroquael came flying over to them and turned a loop. 'All is well at the mill. There are tracks, though.'

Joss and Alikan looked at each other, then hurried after the eager fire-spirit. They found more of the same tracks Alikan had spotted at the river, and Alikan shook his head over them. They examined the wheel; it appeared as though someone had ripped it off.

Joss blew air out loudly. 'Whatever it is, it's strong.'

'No scorching.' Alikan ran a hand along the wood. 'And I would say wind or a force spell wasn't used either.'

Doroquael flicked out a fiery tongue. 'I can taste magic, though.'

'Where's Azra and Riddi?' Joss stood up on his toes to look around the village. Temerran and his men had gone out to the fields. Despite being ordered to set up camp, Adrin was also trampling about. Joss clicked his tongue in disgust.

'They're still in the house,' Doroquael hissed.

'Let's see what they've found.'

Dierra was examining the ground around the headman's house and Arridia and Lucien stepped out of the building as they approached; Azrael flying out through a hole in the window rather than using the door.

'What did you get?' Joss asked at once.

His sister wrinkled her nose. 'Nothing that useful. As the headman said, it seems nothing of value was stolen. The things that were broken appear random — at least we can see no pattern. Whatever it is, it seems to be just destroying and frightening people for the sake of it. From its obvious strength and power, I believe it could have killed if it wanted to, but it hasn't.'

Alikan grunted, raising his eyebrows. 'Interesting observation. Perhaps its motivation has nothing to do with the villagers themselves.'

'You think it may have been making some kind of point?' Lucien tilted his head a little, peering out from his long curls. 'Maybe to draw us here?'

'Well, that's an unsettling thought.' Alikan shifted his weight.

They all looked at Lucien.

'I'm not leaving.' He glared at them. 'Anyway, it would more likely be a trap for you.'

Azrael gave a squeal.

Joss tutted. 'I don't think it's a trap. It's too unspecific. Anyone could have been sent here to investigate. I say we wait and see this creature for ourselves tonight.'

'Agreed,' Lucien said at once.

Neither Arridia nor Alikan protested, but Joss could see they weren't happy.

They all turned as Temerran called out to them, slightly out of breath. 'There are a few tracks, but we couldn't see where they went, the ground is too hard. Tracks are odd too.'

'Yeah,' Joss called back. 'Alikan can demonstrate the walk if you like?'

Alikan elbowed him hard in the ribs, making him grunt.

'What's the plan?' Temerran turned to Lucien.

The prince drew himself up. 'Sun's fading. We wait and watch.'

Temerran gave a slight bow. 'Very good, highness.'

They returned to where the Eldenian warriors had picketed the horses and set up the tents. The two Borrowmen warriors took over preparing them a meal and Joss was impressed they remembered his sister was a *walker* and didn't eat meat. Temerran drew out his lute, and he handed it to Lucien, whose face lit up.

'Shouldn't we be keeping quiet?' Adrin grumbled.

Even his men stared at him.

'The creature doesn't show until midnight,' Arridia said quietly.

'I'll take first watch,' Alikan told Dierra. She nodded her agreement.

Lucien checked the lute's tuning and picked out a few notes. From the flush of the young man's cheeks, Joss guessed he was nervous at playing in front of the bard – or perhaps Adrin was more the problem. Joss cleared his throat.

'So, Adrin, I heard you saved Mantu from the Chemmish necromancers years ago, but I've never heard it from the man himself.'

Arridia looked up in surprise. Joss winked at her quickly, and she settled back. They both knew very well it was their mother and the fire-spirit, Siveraell, who had done most of the saving of Mantu.

'Ah, well.' Adrin drew himself up. 'Well, I was sent there to shore up the garrison at Haven...'

Joss was sure to nod and make the right noises as Adrin waved his arms about, his voice carrying in the evening air. Everyone else soon had their attention on the young prince and the song he softly sang. Temerran closed his eyes, a smile on his face. Arridia's gaze barely left the prince. Azrael and Doroquael hovered close to hear, and Dierra had to shoo them off to do their scouting.

'That was excellent,' Temerran said as Lucien finished. 'You've improved at weaving your own melodies in and out of the main tune. How have you been getting on with the fiddle?'

Lucien winced. 'Not as well as I'd like.'

'He still isn't allowed much time for his music,' Arridia said, her violet and blue eyes meeting the green ones of the bard.

Temerran looked down at his hands. 'I thought that might be the case.'

Joss realised his attention had wavered and quickly laughed at something Adrin said.

'You play something.' Lucien offered the lute back to Temerran.

'Oh, yes.' Dierra sat up. 'Can you play the Kraken's waltz?'

Temerran grinned, handing the lute back to Lucien as he fetched his fiddle. They played together for an hour. Even Adrin closed his mouth to pay attention. There was no denying the prince had an amazing talent, but instead of feeling pleased for his friend, Joss's heart sank. Lucien was destined to be a king. In Elden he couldn't also be a bard, not if he wanted to keep the respect of his Jarls and Thanes, and he would never be free to sail the seas on the *Undine*.

Alikan swapped places with Dierra and they settled down to wait, some of the Eldenian warriors taking a chance to doze. Temerran and the prince continued to talk quietly, Arridia moving discreetly away a little to give them some privacy. She sat up suddenly, meeting Joss's eyes.

'What is it?' he whispered harshly.

She swallowed. 'The horses are unsettled. They smell or sense something.'

Joss turned to regard the equines. Their ears were up, their nostrils expanding to take in air. He got to his feet, hand on his sword hilt.

'Joss?' Alikan scrambled up.

'We think it's on its way.'

Lucien stood. He was shaking, but no one commented. 'Adrin, your men should guard the camp, but you had better come with me. Arridia, get closer to the village, signal when you see it.'

She moved away at once, Azrael keening a little as he hid within their campfire. Joss couldn't fault the prince's choice, Riddi was an excellent scout, but she could also feel things long before anyone spotted them. Joss turned to Doroquael. 'Stay with Azra until the creature spots us.'

Joss kept his eyes on his sister as they stalked towards the village, knowing that Alikan and Dierra had their backs. The Borrowmen fanned out a little to their left, Temerran staying close to Lucien. A dog barked in the village, followed by a sharp yelp, then silence. Arridia raised her hand and Joss touched Lucien's shoulder, gesturing for him to follow him to his sister.

'The dog is scared,' Arridia whispered. 'Its owner quieted it, but it is desperate to warn them of danger.'

Joss winced as Adrin landed behind them with a scuff and a grunt.

'Anything from the creature itself yet?' Lucien asked.

Arridia shook her head, rubbing at her temples. 'The emotions of the villagers are too loud. The dog has got them all on heightened alert.'

'Good dog.' Alikan grinned.

Joss gave a shake of his head; Ali did love his animals. 'Yeah, but it's not what we needed.'

Arridia raised a hand to shush them, and Joss pulled a face.

Lucien placed his hand on Arridia's shoulder, and her muscles almost instantly relaxed. Joss narrowed his eyes, his mouth falling open a little. What was *really* going on between the prince and his sister?

Then Arridia stiffened and Joss's fingers curled tighter around his sword hilt.

'There's something.' Arridia shuddered. 'It feels... it's similar to a fire-spirit or a sea-spirit. It sets my teeth on edge, like vibrated metal.'

Joss glanced over his shoulder at Alikan.

'Father was looking at earth-spirits,' Arridia said. 'There was something reported a few weeks back that piqued his interest, but this can't be one.'

'Why?'

Arridia pointed, her eyes huge. 'Because it's much too big!'

Joss followed the direction of her gaze and cursed. The creature was bigger than a man, and, as the headman had described, its eyes glowed with blinding brightness, not red, but green. 'You almost got the walk right, Ali.'

'Reminds me of foxfire,' Temerran murmured.

'It has power,' Alikan warned. 'A lot of it.'

Dierra called hers, but Arridia hissed at her. 'Wait!'

Joss held his breath.

'I can...' Arridia screwed her eyes tight shut. Lucien placed his hand on her shoulder again. 'It's furious.'

'We should kill it,' Adrin snarled, his face pale.

'Wait,' Lucien said calmly.

'It's in pain.' Arridia twisted to look them all quickly in the eye, before turning back toward the creature. It wandered into the centre of the village, throwing its arms up in the air. 'It's scared. It... it's trapped. Joss, it is a spirit. It's caught in some kind of spirit trap. Someone is controlling it, but it just wants to be free. We have to help it.'

Joss nodded.

'How do we help it?' Temerran asked.

'If it's a spirit trap,' she replied. 'All we do is smash it.'

They all turned to regard the huge, man-shaped creature.

'I think we need to talk to it first.' Temerran sat back on his heels. 'And since we have a bard—'

'I should do it.' Lucien stood, and Arridia grabbed his arm to pull him down.

'Highness.' Temerran gave his head a slight shake.

'It's my quest.' Lucien raised his chin.

'I advise against it, Highness,' Adrin said. 'Let the bard approach it.'

Lucien narrowed his eyes. 'I'm going.'

'Then so am I.' Arridia stood, giving Temerran a meaningful glance. 'The blood curse.'

The bard nodded.

Joss winced. He knew she was referring to how Temerran and Dia had worked together years ago to save the Borrow islands, but he wasn't convinced mixing song with *knowing* would work here. 'Rids, I think—'

'Me, Arridia, and Azrael,' Lucien said firmly. 'The rest of you be ready.'

Arridia called a flame to her hand, and after a few seconds Azrael came flying out of it.

'Rids.' A huge, expanding rock was growing in Joss's stomach. 'It could be Geladan.'

She pivoted; fists clenched. 'It could be, but that spirit needs help.' She touched Lucien's arm, then stood, taking small steps towards the village. Joss knew better than anyone how strong his sister was, but his heart burned as he forced himself not to move.

Then Temerran sang, softly, subtly. Tension left Joss's muscles.

The creature turned, roaring at Arridia and Lucien's approach; green fire flared from its open mouth, so bright Joss had to raise his

93

arm to shield his eyes. Azrael grew in response until a sharp command from Arridia made the little drake fall back.

Lucien drew himself up. 'I am Lucien, Prince of Elden. You are in trouble and we have come to help.'

The creature's bellowing subsided; its luminescent eyes regarded the prince. Joss felt a tingling in his chest, like pleasant pins and needles as his sister's projected *knowing* added to the magic in the song of the Bard. The creature appeared to relax, its arms falling to its sides.

Lucien's shoulders rose and fell rapidly, but despite his fear, his voice was clear and unfaltering. 'The only way we know to break a spirit trap is to smash it or kill its creator. Is the one who trapped you nearby? What can you tell us?'

The creature roared again; Adrin staggered back. Joss drew several inches of his sword, his left hand clenching and unclenching as he yearned to call his power. Doroquael darted about in frantic zigzags.

The earth-coloured monster flailed its arms, coming closer.

Arridia turned to wave her hands at them. 'It can't speak.'

Joss drew in a sharp breath as Lucien took a small step towards it. 'Okay. We are going to try to free you. Arridia is going to use magic to smash the trap you're in. If you consent, raise your arms.'

The creature didn't move, then slowly, it lifted its hands above its head.

Lucien turned to Arridia. She was breathing hard; chin raised a little. Joss bit at the inside of his lip as she called her power.

'Shield,' Alikan said in his ear.

Joss did so, expecting his sister to send out a blast of power, but she was more subtle than that, cleverer. Planting her feet carefully, she braced herself, reaching out in the same way their mother reached for stone beneath the earth; the way she'd reached within the flesh of the

Geladanian sorcerer who'd threatened them many years ago to rip him apart.

Cracks appeared in the clay skin of the creature and it screamed. Arridia staggered, the prince catching her. Joss darted forward, but Alikan grabbed his arm. Azrael flared, making himself huge. Doroquael and Dierra both called up their power; the creature swung an enormous fist towards Arridia.

Lucien drew himself up, took in a breath. 'No!'

Joss froze, all of them did, even the clay monster.

'He has power!' Joss forced the words out of his constricted lungs. 'Luce has power.'

Temerran sang on, eyes closed, voice calm.

'Okay.' Lucien held up his hands. 'Try again, Rids, when you're ready.'

Arridia unbent slowly, Azrael flittered anxiously to Doroquael and back to her side. Joss shook off Alikan and stepped closer.

Arridia tensed, breathing heavily.

She drew more power and ripped the creature apart.

Hard, baked clay flew out in all directions and there was a sigh, as though a ghostly presence despaired. As the dust settled, Joss lowered his arm, then sprinted to his sister's side. He lifted her and brushed her hair away from her face. She was bleeding from her nostrils and the corner of one eye, but she was alive,

'Your majesty!' Temerran hurried over.

'I'm all right.' Lucien got unsteadily to his knees.

'Look, look!' Azrael pointed frantically.

They followed the direction of the spirit's fiery arm. In the debris of the man-shaped spirit trap, a small being stood. It was the size of a squirrel, its skin a dark brown and wrinkled like the bark of a tree. Its eyes glowed green, and foxfire rippled across it.

It gave a slow bow.

'Are you all right?' Arridia struggled to sit up. 'Are you hurt?'

The little spirit shook its head.

'Who did this to you?' Joss demanded. 'Was it the Geladanians?'

The little spirit shook its head again, but before they could ask any more questions, it seemed to explode, turning into hundreds of tiny beetles that scuttled away, each with a green glow.

'Wait,' Lucien shouted. 'Who was it?'

But the creature was gone.

Joss met his sister's mis-matched eyes, as wide as his own. If not the Geladanians, then who?

Chapter Ten

Arridia; Kingdom of Elden

While Lucien dealt with the villagers, Arridia slipped away to check on the horses, using her *knowing* to send them calm; Freckle's presence soothed her in return. She found her comb and began working it through Freckle's mane.

'Riddi!' Azrael came to bob beside her. 'Are you all right?'

'I'm okay, Azra.' She forced a smile at the little spirit. 'It's just a bit busy and noisy over there at the moment.'

'Do you need to rest?' He fluttered about anxiously. 'You used lots of power.'

'I did, but I'm fine, Azra, honestly.'

Temerran approached them slowly, as though she were a wild animal that might startle. He held a fragment of clay in his hand.

'What is it?' Arridia lowered her comb.

'A piece of the spirit trap. There are runes on it.'

Azrael moved closer so they could better see by his light.

'I don't recognise them.' She looked up to meet the bard's green eyes.

'Part of my training was the study of languages.' He curled his fingers around the shard. 'This is ancient Eldenian.'

'Eldenian?'

He placed a finger to his lips.

As though to remind them of his presence, Adrin's voice was raised in a cheer. Arridia and Temerran turned to gaze back toward the village.

The relieved villagers had brought out what food and drink they could spare to celebrate.

Arridia sighed.

'We should make a search when we have more light,' Temerran urged. 'There could be more pieces intact.'

Dierra stepped suddenly out of the darkness, making two of the horses shy. 'Looks clear,' she announced. She scowled down at the village. 'Just as well.'

'Do me a favour.' Arridia touched the younger woman's arm with the tips of her fingers. 'You're good at talking. See what old wives' tales you can gather. Discover if anyone there still uses old Elden runes for anything.'

Dierra's eyebrows rose, but she nodded. 'What about you?'

'I'll stay with her,' Temerran offered.

'Okay.' Dierra's mouth quirked up, and she almost skipped her way down to the impromptu feast.

'I'm sorry.' Temerran screwed up his nose. 'I hope I didn't offend by offering to stay with you?'

Arridia sighed. 'It's okay. Joss and I are used to it.' She reached up and rubbed at her forehead.

Temerran glanced at the village. 'Do you need to move further away?'

She shook her head, but he made a noise in the back of his throat.

'Arridia, we've known each other since you were born, you don't need to pretend with me.'

She sagged a little. 'I know. It's harder when I'm tired, but I'll manage.'

'Do you have another comb, or a brush?' He indicated her horse. Arridia handed him the comb and dug around in her bags for a brush. He hummed as he worked, then quietly sang. Azrael joined in with a gentle buzz. A pleasant tingling sensation started in her chest and her muscles slowly unknotted. She knew the bard was using his magic, but she let herself relax and fall into it rather than protesting. The intense pressure of her headache eased; the relief was bliss.

The sound of laughter drew nearer, and she twisted to see over her shoulder. Lucien was approaching, he looked pale and more tired than she was. Not far behind him Joss and Alikan followed, side by side. Doroquael sped up to join Azrael.

'I found nothing useful,' Lucien apologised to Temerran.

'Hmm. I'm not sure there is anything to find in the village,' the bard replied.

'Hey, Luce!' Joss called out, a little too loudly. Arridia rolled her eyes. Her brother had clearly been drinking. 'You used magic!'

It was Alikan who shushed him.

'He used the power of command,' Temerran said somewhat sternly.

Lucien glanced at Arridia, pushing his long curls back from his face.

'Discretion, nitwit.' Alikan elbowed Joss in the ribs.

Joss winced, showing his teeth. 'Sorry, Luce.'

'I've had a little bardic training,' Lucien mumbled. 'But people mustn't know.'

Joss's face grew suddenly serious. 'Spirits, Luce, I know you really wanted to be a bard, but you've got to be a king.'

'And why would a king not need the skills of a bard?' Temerran regarded them all, then gestured that they should sit together away from the two men who still guarded the camp. He called out to the warriors. 'Go join the feast, we'll watch the camp.'

The two men didn't need telling twice.

'I mean no disrespect,' Joss said as they sat. 'But Bractius won't tolerate his heir being an entertainer.'

Temerran tilted his head. 'Is that what you think I am, Joss?'

'Well, no, of course not. But you're the Bard of the Borrows and Luce is, well Luce… is Prince of Elden.'

Alikan gave a slight shake of his head, rubbing his face with his hand.

'You don't have to be Bard of the Borrows to make use of the skills of a true bard,' Temerran explained patiently as they sat in a circle. 'You never met him, but the ambassador from Geladan, Ren, had bardic training. He could use his voice to command and manipulate. But it isn't just about the magic. Bards are versed in languages, history, diplomacy, and politics. There are reasons Bractius doesn't want Lucien to learn from me that go beyond his disdain for the profession of musician. Some of those reasons are somewhat petty. Anyway, Lucien wanted to learn, and I have taught him when I could. The fact he can invoke magic should please the king, yet I doubt it will.'

Lucien waved a hand. 'This is all taking us from a more important point. We have an unknown magic, one strong enough to summon and trap a rare earth-spirit. The spirit said it wasn't Geladan, so who?'

Joss clicked his fingers. 'Mother said someone was using magic in the castle.'

'There could be a connection,' Temerran agreed. 'I think for now we should get some sleep, then check over the area and make sure we haven't missed anything.'

Alikan snorted. 'That's if the villagers and Adrin's warriors haven't trampled over everything by then. I'd best keep watch.'

'We'll do it!' Azrael offered.

'Thanks, Azra.' Arridia pursed her lips together in an attempt at a smile. Her eyes were stinging. Lucien stood and held out his hand to help her up.

Joss yawned loudly. 'I guess we'd better send a report to the Fulmers as soon as we can.'

'Already sorted,' Doroquael buzzed, glowing brightly and swelling in size.

'Hmm.' Joss narrowed his eyes. 'I'm not sure that's a good thing, you spirits spreading gossip throughout the fire-realm.'

Doroquael spun back to show his affront.

Arridia went to the tent that had been put up for herself and Dierra. With her assigned Raven and Azrael busy, she had a rare opportunity to be alone. Alikan realised and hesitated.

'It's okay.' She made a shooing gesture with her hand.

She could see the muscles of Alikan's jaw move, but he relented. 'Night, Rids.'

She let out the air she'd been holding in her lungs, her muscles easing, her heart swelling in relief at the love and understanding from her adopted older brother.

She ducked to crawl into her tent.

***

Arridia woke slowly and rubbed at her dry eyes. Her head still felt heavy and foggy. She turned over and seeing she was alone sat bolt upright. She could hear voices outside the tent, they sounded calm, and Arridia allowed herself to relax. She pulled on her boots and a green jacket, untied the tent flap, and peered out, blinking at the light. It was perhaps two hours since dawn. Dierra was sitting with Temerran and Lucien, they had several pieces of clay lain out before them. Arridia scrambled out of the tent.

'Morning,' Azrael chirped.

She looked up to see the fire-spirit drifting high above her. He swooped down, passing her to join the others.

'What did you find?' She stifled a yawn as she wandered over to peer over Dierra's shoulder.

It was Temerran who responded. 'Sadly, not enough to make anything out. There are a few partial runes, but only the one complete symbol.'

'What does it say?' Arridia crouched down.

'Obey.' Both Lucien and Dierra replied at once.

Something prickled on the back of Arridia's neck.

'Well, strictly speaking, the rune denotes mastery over someone.' Temerran picked up the piece of clay. 'But we already know the nature of a spirit trap.'

'We have learnt something though.' Dierra grinned. 'An old wives' tale.'

Azrael turned a little loop.

'Have you ever heard of a golem?' Lucien asked Arridia.

She shook her head. 'I don't think so.'

'It's an ancient magic,' Dierra enthused. 'A sorcerer would bake a man out of clay and with runes and a spell it would animate and follow commands. According to the old tales, you had to be incredibly careful of your commands as the golem was very literal. So, if you said, go chop wood, it would keep chopping wood until every tree in the land was felled. If you asked it to make porridge, it would just make more and more until you drowned in it.'

'And if you told it to kill,' Lucien breathed. 'It wouldn't stop.'

Arridia took in a deep breath and blew it out slowly. 'So, there may be truth to the old tales, but golems were actually spirits in an elaborate trap?'

Temerran gave a slight shrug. 'That's the way it seems.'

'And it's Eldenian magic,' Arridia murmured more to herself than the others. 'Although, it sounds similar to Chemmish blood magic to me. We need my father. He knows more about the old magics than anyone else.'

'We should get you to the Fulmers as soon as we can,' Temerran agreed. 'But I don't like leaving Elden unprotected.'

There was a loud yawn behind them, and Joss staggered out of his tent. 'Have I missed breakfast?'

Dierra picked up a bread roll from beside her and threw it at him. It struck him in the chest, but he grabbed it before it hit the ground.

'Where's Ali?' he asked.

'He's taking a last look around with Temerran's men,' Lucien told him. 'Come on, let's get this camp packed up and get back to Taurmaline.'

Arridia and Dierra took down their tent, while Adrin muttered and cursed around the camp, clutching his head. When she had everything ready, Arridia surveyed the rest of the camp and noticed Lucien was missing. She spotted him some way away, talking with the village headman. The prince handed the man something.

'Compensation,' Temerran told Arridia quietly, following her gaze. 'We ate and drank our way through most of what they had last night, or at least some of us did.'

'Right.' Alikan came striding over to the horses and slapped his thigh loudly. 'Are we ready?'

'We're ready,' Doroquael and Azrael chorused.

As soon as Lucien joined them, they made their way back across the miles to Lake Taur. They kept their pace steady for the sake of the horses, despite their eagerness to report to the king and send messages to Fulmer Hold. When they reached the castle, they were ushered straight to the king's study rather than the throne room. They crowded in, Lucien scowling when he realised Adrin had followed.

'So, what did you find?' King Bractius remained standing behind his desk.

'More than we expected, Father.' Lucien described everything that had happened, missing out his use of bardic magic.

'Old Elden magic.' Bractius sat down, regarding them all. 'I think we need to be discreet about that for now until we find out who's behind it.' He turned to Joss. 'You're sure it isn't Geladan?'

Joss shrugged. 'The spirit said not.'

'Hmm.' The king looked down at the scrolls on his desk. Even with her *knowing* shut down as tight as she could, Arridia experienced the sharpness of his fear. 'Well, then. We shall see what my absent sorcerer has to say and keep our eyes open for anything which might be connected. In the meantime, we'll announce you defeated a golem; a creature from the past who was woken from slumber. Temerran, I'm sure you can come up with something believable?'

Temerran's red eyebrows raised, but he nodded once.

'Good. We shall have a feast tonight to celebrate the success of your quest. Try to look suitably heroic, Lucien.'

Lucien's nostrils flared a little, but he said nothing.

They took their dismissal and filed out into the hallway.

'Hey.' Dierra scowled. 'That Adrin stayed with the king.'

'He'll be spilling his guts about me to my father.' Lucien almost snarled. Then he sighed. 'We best make ourselves presentable for tonight. I'll go find Scar and see if she found out anything else about the lake tower.'

'See you in a bit, Luce.' Joss clapped him on the back.

Arridia and Dierra made their way to their shared guest room. While Arridia took the chance to rest and lay on the bed, Dierra went straight to the wardrobe and started pulling out the few dresses she had with her.

'Oh, these are all useless.' She pouted and scowled. 'Have you got anything, Rids?'

A knock at the door saved Arridia. Dierra opened it and Lucien pushed his way in.

Arridia sat up. 'Luce, what's wrong?'

'Scarlett's missing.' Lucien gave a helpless shrug. 'Eleanor hasn't seen her all day, and neither has her lady-in-waiting. I… I had to ask Mother. She's going mad.'

'Is it like her to go missing?' Arridia asked.

Lucien shook his head. 'For an hour or two, maybe, but not all day. 'Something's happened to her.'

Chapter Eleven

Scarlett; Kingdom of Elden

Scarlett finally secured the knot, then fell back hard as the boat swung about. Her eyes filled with water, but she pushed herself up, rubbing at the top of her arm which had hit the seat. She scrambled to the rudder, squinting through the gloom. Her brother had made sailing his small boat appear easy, but despite everything he'd taught her, she'd struggled to keep it going in the direction she needed and had ended up too far out on the lake. She wiped at her eyes and leaned out past the sail, but all she could see was darkness. It was too cloudy even for the stars to be out.

She drew in a sharp breath, sitting up straighter. Was that light?

She turned the boat toward it, her arm shaking with the strain. It felt like a painfully long time before the light grew any closer, but when it did, she cried out with relief. Northold. There was only the slightest of glows behind the trees from the hold itself, but she recognised the braziers which stood at intervals outside the high walls. Her relief was soon crushed as her brother's small sailboat insisted on fighting her all the way, and when she finally bumped up against the wharf, she could barely clamber out and tie up.

'Who's there?' a man's voice demanded.

She drew herself up, her knees ached. 'Princess Scarlett.'

Someone laughed, but the first man replied, 'Are you? Come closer and take off your hood.'

Scarlett gritted her teeth and fists in affront until her tired mind acknowledged these warriors were just doing their jobs; and she was disguised in the attire of a man. She pushed back the hood and folded her arms.

Two men stepped out of the darkness, one gawping with his mouth open, while the other straightened up and bent in a hasty bow. 'Highness, how may we assist you?'

'I need to see Lady Rosa,' she replied.

'But it's four in the morning,' Gawper spluttered.

Scarlett placed her hands on her hips, trying to appear stern, although inside she experienced the slippery, sick feeling of guilt.

'This way, majesty,' the older warrior invited. He strode ahead, but gradually slowed his pace to better match hers. She expected him to question her, but he didn't say a word as he took her through the gate and past the houses of the outer circle.

The man turned and waved at his colleague, who followed behind. 'Wake the Merkis, I'll take the lady to the hall.'

Gawper scowled, but did as he was told, breaking into a jog to pass between the inner gates.

The older warrior cleared his throat. 'Please excuse me, Highness, I mean no impertinence, but you're not hurt, are you? Is anyone likely to be pursuing you?'

'Oh, no.' She shook her head, slightly out of breath. 'I'm just... I'm on a special mission that urgently requires the Lady Rosa.'

The man didn't appear the slightest bit surprised. 'Yes, if you have an emergency, our lady is the one you want.'

Scarlett raised her eyebrows. She liked Lady Rosa very much; she was a kind, soft, and wise old lady, but not someone she'd have considered in an emergency. The warrior clearly saw her doubt.

'Rosa stood on the walls herself and fended off undead creatures from Chem when grown men very near wet themselves. She fought off an assassin from Geladan with nothing but a bedwarmer, and stood up to their sorcerer with nought but a shoe. Don't underestimate her, your majesty.'

Scarlett nodded, her eyes wide.

The two warriors on guard outside the keep held the doors open for them and they entered the great hall. A few torches burned on the walls, the fire was red and low in the fireplace, the vast, long room filled with shadows.

Scarlett drew in a sharp breath as someone near the fireplace stood.

'Your Highness?'

'Nip!' She hurried across to the stableman, glad to see someone she knew.

'Are you all right?' He looked her up and down. 'Here.' He grabbed up a cup and poured a dark liquid into it from a small pot that was warming in the hearth.

Scarlett took a sip, closing her eyes as the mellow flavour rolled over her tongue. Chamomile and honey.

There was a clatter on the stairs as Tantony descended, struggling into his jacket. Behind him came Rosa, bearing a candle in a small holder, and the warrior who Scarlett would forever think of as 'Gawper.'

'Your Highness.' Tantony gave a hurried bow, scanning the room to check who was witnessing the interaction. 'How may we assist you?'

'Oh, my dear, you look tired.' Rosa fussed. 'Nip, be a darling and get her highness something to eat from the kitchens.'

Nip hurried off at once. At a stern glare from Tantony, the warrior who'd led Scarlett here cleared his throat and straightened up. 'Will there be anything else, Merkis?'

Tantony waved a hand at him and Gawper. 'No, thank you. Feel free to continue your patrol.'

The warrior gave a slight bow, then hastened his colleague out of the great hall.

'Is there trouble at Taurmaline?' Rosa asked, her brown eyes narrowed a little.

'Oh, no.' Scarlett shook her head. 'But then, yes, there might be.' She told them of the room in the lake tower and Kesta's concerns. 'So, with the others away on the quest, and no more clues to be found, I came here.'

'In the middle of the night?' Tantony's eyebrows seemed to bristle. 'I take it your father knows?'

Scarlett bit her lip and shook her head.

Tantony threw his arms up in the air. 'Gods preserve us!'

Rosa tilted her head at him, and he calmed immediately, taking a step back. The former lady-in-waiting held Scarlett's gaze and sighed. 'If the king asks, we will say we thought you were here with permission. Are you willing to take that responsibility?'

Scarlett drew herself up. 'Of course.'

Rosa gave a sharp nod. 'Good. What is it you need?'

'Rosa, I'm not sure this is wise,' Tantony mumbled.

Rosa raised one finger, still looking at Scarlett.

'Oh.' The princess winced. 'Would it be possible for me to use the library in the Raven Tower? I need to research a list of herbs Kesta smelled and their uses.'

Nip returned from the kitchens, an array of fruit and cold cuts on a tray. He waited politely out of the way.

'All right.' Rosa straightened up. 'I'll help you. But as soon as we find what you need, Nip will take you back to Taurmaline.'

Scarlett smiled. 'Agreed.'

Tantony rolled his eyes, holding up his hands in resignation.

Rosa turned to Nip. 'Would you kindly bring that to the Raven Tower for us?'

'Of course.' Nip immediately headed towards the doors.

'Why were you up so late?' Rosa asked him quietly.

Nip glanced at Scarlett. 'I was having trouble sleeping. I thought I might as well wait in the great hall to see if there was any news of Joss and Arridia.'

'There was nothing when I left,' Scarlett told them.

Rosa briefly touched Nip's arm before pushing open one of the heavy doors so they could step out into the ward.

The temperature seemed to have dropped in the short time Scarlett had been inside and she shivered. The Raven Tower was a dark and foreboding shape before them, but Rosa stepped confidently across the grass. Tantony caught them up, a lantern and some tapers in his hands. He opened the door at the base of the tower and moved carefully up the uneven steps, lighting the candles as he passed.

'The first library is where herb lore is,' Rosa called up to her husband.

Scarlett entered the library behind Rosa. Although she and Lucien had been to Northold many times, this was her first look within the fabled tower. As tired as she was, her pulse quickened just a little. Tantony lit four lanterns that stood on sturdy metal stands away from the bookshelves. To Scarlett, it was as though someone had struck a flint inside a cave full of jewels. She spun about, mouth open, as she gazed at the hundreds of spines.

'All this knowledge!'

Tantony gave a huff. 'You're as bad as the Thane. Rose, shall I get some tea?'

'Please.' She smiled at him.

Tantony didn't waste any time in leaving them to it.

'Okay.' Rosa put her hands on her hips. 'Let's find any reference we can to the herbs we're looking for, and list any uses they might have in common.'

They soon fell into a comfortable routine of Rosa digging out books while Nip and Scarlett made notes and marked pages with string. When both of them had a substantial list, Rosa joined them at the table, and they compared what they'd found.

'Okay then, pine.' Scarlett ran her finger down her scrap of parchment. 'So, the resin is used to help with pain and inflammation. Pine needle tea is used for coughs. Pine oil is used for pain and respiratory problems. Anything else, Nip?'

'Those seem to be the main things, but I have a long list of other stuff, like skin conditions.' Nip replied.

'Cedar?' Rosa asked eagerly.

Scarlett turned back to her list. 'Well, there's a link already. It's used for respiratory ailments, also fevers.'

'I have here that it helps with toothache.' Nip tapped one of the books. 'So, there could be a pain link too.'

'Well, that doesn't sound too sinister,' Rosa said brightly. 'What of hemlock, though? I know it's a poison.'

'It's also an important medicine if used carefully.' Nip shifted in his chair. 'My father used it to calm the shaking in his hands. Like the other two, it also helps with coughs.'

Scarlett slumped. 'So, someone had a bad cough.'

Rosa tapped at her lip. 'But Kesta said she sensed magic. I wonder if we're looking in the wrong place.'

'What do you mean?' Scarlett asked, feeling her excitement return a little.

Rosa stood. 'Let's move up to the other library. Jorrun doesn't like people using that one so much, but I hope he won't mind under the circumstances. It's where the rarer and more dangerous books are kept. We should see if we can find anywhere those three ingredients are listed together. It, um... this could take us a while. I don't know those books so well.'

Scarlett stood quickly. 'Let's try it.'

They followed Rosa up the stairs, Nip extinguishing all the lanterns in the lower library. The sun was now up and glowed through the narrow window, the dust dancing in the soft beam as they hurried in. Rosa lit two lanterns from the one she carried, while Scarlett went straight to the shelves. Her heart sank. 'Where do we even start?'

The other two joined her in scanning the spines.

'Hey, Scarlett.' Nip winced and quickly spun about to bow, a hand over his heart. 'Forgive my informality, your Highness.'

Scarlett waved an impatient hand at him. 'Have you found something?'

He reached up and pulled down a book. 'Didn't you say you found a crystal? This is about using them for spells.'

'Ooh, yes.' Scarlett dug in her pocket and drew out the long finger of smoky quartz. She placed it carefully on the table.

Nip handed her the book. 'I'll keep looking.'

Scarlett opened the cover and began scanning the pages, trying to spot any reference to the three ingredients without having to read the whole thing. Rosa and Nip continued searching, both pulling anything they thought might be of use part way out of the shelf rather than remove it and lose its place.

'Ah!' Scarlett sat upright. 'Here's mention of a dark, smoky crystal.' She quickly read as the others moved closer. 'Oh, but it doesn't really tell us much. It's used for clarity of mind, and to connect to spirits.'

'Try this one.' Rosa handed her a wide volume with a blue binding. 'It's about talismans but has crystals and herbs in it.'

Scarlett frowned, but she took it. Nip stopped hunting the shelves and selected a book, sitting in the chair near the window to read.

Scarlett pored through the pages before her. A word jumped out at Scarlett and she sucked in a breath and held it. 'I have something!' She leant forward, running a finger beneath the words. 'Yes, here, hemlock. It says... it says hemlock is used to anoint talismans for destructive work.'

'What kind of destructive work?' Rosa asked.

Scarlett shrugged.

'I have something here on cedar,' Nip said slowly. 'This book is about old Eldenian superstitions. It says you burn cedar in your fire on certain days to bring money and luck in love, but it's also used to invoke revenge.'

'Revenge,' Scarlett repeated slowly. 'Does that book mention pine, or hemlock?'

'A moment.' Nip leafed through the pages. 'Yes, here's pine. It says pine is used for summoning earth-spirits.'

'Earth-spirits?' Scarlett almost knocked her chair over as she hurried to look over his shoulder. 'There are rumours in court of an earth-spirit being seen.'

'And Riddi, Joss, and your brother have just gone looking for some kind of monster.' Nip looked up, meeting her eyes.

Scarlett swallowed.

'Jorrun was looking into the earth-spirit rumours.' Rosa held up a finger. 'He took most of his research with him to Taurmaline, but there might be something on his desk. One moment.' Rosa picked up her skirts and rushed for the stairs.

'Anything else?' Scarlett shifted closer. There was a horsey smell about Nip, but it was warm rather than unpleasant. As he turned the pages, she couldn't help but notice how strong his hands looked. She felt her face flush and took a step back. Nip was much older than her, and only a stable hand.

'Hemlock,' Nip said suddenly, making Scarlett jump. 'It says "burning hemlock enrages the mind for dark magic".'

Scarlett screwed up her nose. '"*Enrages the mind*?" What under the sky does that mean?'

Rosa came scurrying down the stairs and burst into the room, a book clutched to her chest. 'I have it!' She panted. 'A book on old Elden magic.' She placed it on the table, opening it to the page she'd marked with a feather and slapping it dramatically with her hand. 'Summoning and controlling an earth-spirit to do your bidding. It's witchcraft.'

'Witchcraft?' Scarlett and Nip both stared at her.

Rosa gave an emphatic nod. 'It mentions burning cedar.'

'Hang on a minute, though.' Nip stood and began pacing. 'This could all just be someone with a cough, remember. We need to tread very carefully.'

'Is that what you really think?' Scarlett watched him, her eyes wide.

He sagged a little and shook his head. 'No, it isn't what I think, but we still need to be careful.' He sat back in the chair, looking from Scarlett to Rosa. 'Think about it. If someone is using what, to all intents and purposes, is a banned Elden magic, they aren't going to want us meddling in their business.'

Rosa wrapped her arms around herself. 'And from what we've found so far, it points to something bad.'

'Vengeance.' Scarlett sucked in her bottom lip and bit it.

'Tea.' Rosa said suddenly. 'I'll fetch some fresh tea and something to eat.'

They continued researching after they ate until Scarlett's eyes stung and she couldn't stop yawning. Rosa insisted she take a brief nap up on the bed on the top floor. It felt like only moments later that she was woken by Rosa's worried voice.

She groaned. 'What is it?'

Rosa placed both hands to her face. 'A raven has come from Taurmaline. The palace is asking for urgent news of you.'

Scarlett sat up. 'Oh no. Oh, Rosa, I'm in so much trouble.' She twisted about to peer out the window. The sun was getting low.

'Come on.' Rosa held out a hand. 'Nip will get you back.'

Nip was already waiting. He'd put on a jacket and buckled a sword about his hips.

'I'll keep looking through the libraries,' Rosa reassured them as they hurried down the stairs. 'I'll come myself to Taurmaline if I find anything important.'

When they reached the small wharf, Scarlett saw Nip had already tied a rowboat to her brother's small sailing ship. Rosa stood on the shore to wave them off as Nip untied and gave them a shove away with his foot. It was so much easier with the two of them. Nip let her take the rudder while he made adjustments to the sails.

It was dark when they arrived at the castle harbour.

'Your Highness!' Three guards came hurrying to meet them. 'The entire castle is hunting for you, are you well?'

She rolled her eyes and gave a dramatic sigh. 'I'm perfectly well, I've just been out sailing. Tell my father to call off the guard, I shall be there shortly.'

'Yes, Highness.' The man bowed, looked Nip up and down, then pivoted to hurry away. The other two guards insisted on shadowing them all the way back to the castle.

The noise of the feast within spilled out as they reached the castle keep and Scarlett halted, mouth open, her hand on her hip.

'Well,' she exclaimed. 'They can't have been that worried.'

She marched into the castle, Nip hurrying to keep up. Servants bustled about while the guards kept a wary eye. Scarlett avoided the main doors of the great hall and headed for a side entrance. Squeezing in, she pulled back her hood and made a quick survey of the room. She spotted Joss at once, laughing loudly with a group of young noblewomen while Alikan stood quietly behind him. She saw her mother next and cringed. The queen was chatting to two Jarls and their wives, the smile on her face like a painting on glass shards. Then she saw her brother. He was at the centre of the room and it shocked Scarlett to see him dancing. As he turned, she realised his partner was Arridia. Their heads were very close together.

Scarlett turned to Nip. The stableman stood frozen, his eyes fixed on the prince and Arridia. Scarlett touched his arm to get his attention. 'Listen, I'm going to get cleaned up and get changed, join this party and try to get a discreet moment to catch the others up on what's happening before I have to report to my father.' She turned back to the room, finally spotting the king at the far end. Eleanor was with him, along with Mendil, the son of the Jarl of Taurmouth. 'I'll get a servant to sort you a room—' Scarlett turned back to Nip, but the young man had gone.

Chapter Twelve

Joss, Kingdom of Elden

'That must have been terrifying!'

The young woman blinked up at Joss, tossing her hair as she shared a glance with her friend. Joss tried to recollect which Thane's daughter she was, but his attention kept going to where Scarlett stood dejectedly beside her mother.

'Yeah.' He forced himself to turn back to her, trying out his most charming grin. 'Largest monster I've fought.'

Alikan cleared his throat. 'Thought it was your sister who beat it.'

Joss stepped on his friend's foot. 'Anyway, I need to confer with the prince.' He raised his wineglass and excused himself.

The celebration of their victory was still in full swing despite it drawing close to midnight. There had been no sign of Arridia for some time, but Joss wasn't surprised.

'Anything?' he asked Alikan as they stood side by side at a table, pretending to pick at the food.

Since her return, Joss hadn't been able to get anywhere near Scarlett, but the look on her face, and the way she appeared under guard, suggested she was in trouble.

'I can't get close to her either.' Alikan made a quick scan of those left in the room. 'Whatever happened, Bractius really ain't happy.'

Joss scratched at his head. 'Lucien?'

'Adrin's still following him, but I arranged a diversion.'

Joss followed his gaze. One of the Raven Scouts assigned with them to Northold stepped up to the narcissistic Merkis and handed him a flagon of ale. Kistelle was of Fulmer descent and a very intelligent tracker.

'Come on, quickly.' Alikan nudged him and chose a steady, unhurried pace to cross to where Lucien was watching the musicians. Temerran had taken a break and was chatting with the prince and the Thane of Haven. With absolute subtlety, the bard moved the Thane away.

'Joss, Ali.' Lucien stood, but Alikan made the slightest movement with his hand to bid the prince remain seated. Joss grabbed a chair to sit next to Lucien, while Alikan stood behind them, monitoring the room.

'So, what's happened with Scar?' Joss demanded. 'Why have you both been put under guard?'

Lucien ducked his head, as though to hide his words. 'Scar thinks she found evidence of Eldenian magic being used in the castle. She went to Northold to get help from Rosa. She believes the spell cast here was to summon earth-spirits.'

'What?'

Alikan shushed him, and Joss glanced around to see if anyone had caught his outburst.

'Father was furious about her not telling him, and for investigating alone. He blames your parents.' Lucien looked up at Joss. 'He's restricted her to the castle grounds, well, pretty much to her rooms, actually. Father says the two events aren't linked, that it's just her childish imagination.' Lucien shook his head, and Joss saw a hardness in his eyes he'd never seen before. 'He doesn't trust me either, his own son, and has ordered me to stay out of it. He expected me to be a warrior from the moment I drew breath, but he insists on seeing me always as a child.'

Joss winced. 'I don't envy you. What can we do?'

'Careful,' Alikan hissed.

Joss looked up to see Bractius himself making his way toward them, a huge friendly grin on his face. Joss had to stop himself clenching his teeth and fists.

'Joss.' The king raised his hands in greeting. 'Thank you again for assisting my son in sorting our, er, minor problem.'

'It was nothing.' Joss gave a shrug. 'Luce did fine without my help.'

Bractius's smile didn't slip, but his eyes seemed to darken. 'You'll stay with us in the castle a while?'

Joss froze, it was almost as though he could feel the ground slowly slipping out from under him. 'My grandfather is very ill. We need to leave for the Fulmers tomorrow.'

'No,' Bractius said, holding Joss's gaze. 'The treaty we hold with Chem and the Fulmers requires that a strong magic user be based here to protect Elden. With everything that's going on, either you and your sister must stay, or your father must return.'

Lucien leapt to his feet. 'His grandfather is dying!'

Bractius rounded on his son and Lucien shrank back. Joss drew power, but Alikan grabbed his shoulder and squeezed hard.

'I'm sure we can sort something out, your majesty,' Alikan said, his jaw muscles so tight it strained his voice.

'I'm sure we can.' Bractius smiled at them all. 'Write to your father, Joss, sooner rather than later.'

The king raised his decorative horn to them, the horn from Geladan, then sauntered away towards one of his Jarls.

Joss realised he'd stopped breathing and sucked in air.

Lucien swore. 'I'm so sorry, Joss.'

Alikan reached between the two of them to pick up a glass of wine. 'We're going to have to consider this situation,' he whispered. 'We'll use Doro and Azra to communicate. I suggest we bring Tem in on it.'

At his name, the bard turned slightly, with the barest of glances in their direction.

Lucien made an amused sound in the back of his throat. 'I'd say Tem's already in.'

Joss stood, feeling a sudden empathy for his sister's hatred of social gatherings. 'If you'll excuse me, Highness, I'm gonna head to my room.'

'Of course.' Lucien got up politely.

Alikan hesitated to leave. 'Highness, I'd like to assign you a Raven for protection, but I'm not sure how your father would react.'

Lucien snorted. 'Not well, I'd imagine.'

'Well!' Temerran announced loudly, making Joss jump. 'I'd best sing one last song before I call it a night.' The bard passed them to rejoin the musicians, leaning in swiftly to say to them, 'Try to make it the king's idea.'

Joss rolled his eyes. 'Yeah, of course.' Something sent a shiver down his spine and looking up he saw the queen was watching him.

'Come on then,' Alikan prompted. 'You need all the beauty sleep you can get, Joss.'

Joss scowled at him but left the great hall with a bow toward Lucien.

The sounds of the feast faded behind them as they made their way up the stairs leading to their guest quarters.

'Maybe I should stay with you,' Alikan suggested.

Joss tutted. 'Don't be an ass. I'm fine, I have Doro.'

Alikan narrowed his amber eyes at him but went into his room and closed the door.

As soon as Joss entered his room, he called up power and balanced a tall flame on his palm. He didn't move for several minutes, letting his eyes rove over everything to see if anything was out of place. His shoulders sagged, and he lit a branch of candles before withdrawing his magic.

'Doro.'

The fire-spirit appeared at once out of a candle flame, hissing and spitting angrily. 'I wish Dia had never saved that stupid king!'

A nervous laugh escaped from Joss. 'I imagine Grandma has thought the same from time to time, but he is Father's friend...' Joss faltered, his own words tasting bad in his mouth. 'Anyways, could you nip off and tell Azra everything? Don't wake Riddi, no point her worrying until morning.'

Doroquael buzzed. 'I shouldn't leave you, Joss.'

He waved a hand at him. 'It's only for a moment. Ali is just next door. He probably has an ear pressed to the wall knowing him.'

'All right, but I'll be quick.' Doroquael vanished at once into the candle flame.

Joss ran his hand through his hair and sat on the bed. He used to love Taurmaline, the feasts, the busy city life, the excitement of court; even the challenge of untouchable young women. This, though, this wasn't fun at all.

With a sigh, he took off his boots and shirt, crossing to the candles to blow them out.

A soft knock sounded at the door.

Joss straightened up. Perhaps Arridia had been awake and had come straight here. Leaving the candles lit, he padded across to the door and drawing back the bolt, opened it a crack. He stepped back when he saw who it was.

'Scarlett!'

She had changed out of her fancy silk dress and was wearing trousers and a cotton shirt. Her eyes were red and puffy, her cheeks still wet.

'Can I come in?' She asked.

'Oh, I don't—'

She pushed past him, stepping into the middle of the room and gazing around. With a wince, Joss realised it was a mess. He shut the door and darted across to the bed to grab his shirt.

'No, don't put it on.' Scarlett's eyes were wide, like a frightened deer.

'What?' Joss held the shirt against his chest, though he felt suddenly very warm. 'Scar, I really don't think you should be here.'

'My father is going to make me marry the Jarl of Taurmouth's son! He's nearly forty, Joss! An old man!' Scarlett's shoulders shook as she sniffed, and tears slipped from her eyes. 'He says that Lady of Taurmouth is the best position he can get me and keep me in Elden. I'd rather die!'

'What...' Joss shook himself, took a step toward her, then realised he still wasn't wearing his shirt. He hastily tugged it on over his head. 'Does Lucien know? How can he make you?'

'This is Elden, he's the king!' She almost yelled, her face reddening.

'Okay.' He raised his hands, cringing. 'Well, there must be something we can do. I'll tell my mother and father, they'll sort this out.'

Scarlett growled at him in annoyance and frustration. 'They can't do anything about this, no one can. Only you can do something.'

'Me?' He stared at her, mouth open. 'Well, of course. What do you need?'

Instead of speaking, she hurled herself across the room at him, flinging her arms about his neck, her wet cheek pressing against his collarbone. 'I don't want that horrible old man to be the first man I lay with. Sleep with me tonight, Joss.'

Joss almost choked. 'What? No.' Even as he protested, his body reacted automatically and highly inappropriately. He tried to untangle himself from Scarlett. She smelled wonderful. He swayed a little, breathing in deeply. Her body was warm against his.

'Please, Joss, I love you. I want it to be you.'

'I... I like you a lot, Scarlett, I really do, but—'

She stood on her toes, pulling him down so she could kiss him. Her lips were clumsy, her fingers clutching at his neck and hip.

Joss groaned.

He knew he should step away, but instead he placed a hand to her face, slowing her kiss, taking control of it, and gently parting her lips with his tongue.

***

Joss woke slowly, his head heavy and muzzy. He rubbed at his eyes and sat up with a start. The other half of the bed was empty. A quick scan of the room told him Scarlett had gone. A huge smile spread across his face, but quickly vanished when he recalled the seriousness of the situation. He had to rescue Scarlett, somehow.

He winced and put his arm in front of his eyes as Doroquael appeared before him, flaring brightly. 'Kesta is going to kill you, Joss! Sshe's going to be sso mad!'

'Shh!' Joss flapped a hand at him. 'Mother doesn't need to know. Not everything. Anyway, I have a plan.'

Doroquael made a doubtful buzzing sound; Joss scowled. He called up his magic to heat some water and quickly washed. He picked up his crumpled trousers and a clean shirt, dressing hurriedly and stepping out into the hall to knock at Alikan's door. It opened at once, Alikan looked him up and down with an eyebrow raised.

'I was just contemplating kicking in your door to check you were still alive.'

Joss tutted at his friend. 'Can I come in?'

Alikan moved aside and Doroquael flowed into the room behind Joss, the fire-spirit muttering to itself.

'What's up?' Alikan asked as he closed the door.

'Joss has been an idiot!' Doroquael blazed.

'I have not!' Joss placed his hands on his hips and pivoted to face Alikan. 'Scarlett's in trouble and I think it's because she helped our parents look into the magic used up in the tower. The king's planning to marry her off to some old man, the Jarl's son in Taurmouth. I want to help her.'

Alikan narrowed his eyes. 'That doesn't sound too idiotic, so far.'

'He mated with her!' Doroquael pointed at Joss with a fiery arm.

Joss choked, his face rapidly warming.

Alikan stared at him, his voice deep as he replied slowly. 'Tell me you didn't. Tell me he's joking, Joss.'

'I said I have a plan.' Joss glowered at Doroquael.

Alikan threw his arms up in the air. His amber eyes were furious. 'You absolute idiot, Joss.' He swore. 'How many times have I said, not in Elden? And then you sleep with the king's daughter! Do you want your head chopped off?'

'Why won't you trust me?' Joss clenched and unclenched his fists. 'It's fine, I can sort it. I'm going to ask Bractius if *I* can marry Scarlett.' Alikan opened his mouth to protest, but Joss plunged on. 'He's always wanted magical blood in the royal line, he'll let me marry Scar, I'm sure. I know Father's only a Thane, but he's offered him the title of Jarl before. Scar can live safely in Northold.' He gave a firm nod, his confidence slipping a little at Alikan's incredulous look.

'Your mum is going to kill you.'

'Yep!' Doroquael flared.

'And what does Scarlett think of your plan?' Alikan demanded.

Joss sagged. 'I haven't asked her yet.'

Alikan swore again. 'Doro, see if you can get to Scarlett. If she's able to give anyone watching her the slip, ask her to name a meeting place. The sooner the better.'

Doroquael vanished at once through the open window.

Alikan shook his head, still glaring at Joss. 'We need to get hold of Arridia and Lucien, let them know what's going on.'

Joss's heart sank, and a wave of anxiety made him a little light-headed. He sat down. Arridia would be disappointed in him, but she'd understand, he knew it, after all she was herself pretending to let Lucien court her to save their friend being hassled by the king. He sat up straighter, a smile forming on his lips. Perhaps when he married Scarlett, the king would be satisfied and get Lucien to pursue someone other than his sister.

'Whatever you're hatching in your head now, forget it,' Alikan growled. 'Come on, we have to send a message to your parents and tell them Bractius is holding you and Riddi to ransom, and that we suspect a link between the castle and the earth-spirit in the south.'

'We don't need to tell them about Scarlett yet, though,' Joss blurted.

Alikan looked at him. 'No. You can inform them in person.'

Joss swallowed.

Alikan penned a hasty note, then they made their way to the bird loft to get it sent to the Fulmers. Alikan made certain the scribe in charge of the birds never read the rolled message, watching as the pigeon disappeared over the lake. Despite his apprehension, Joss's stomach gurgled, and he insisted they visit the guard's hall to grab some food. They took a small loaf, some cheese, and dried fruit, and headed back to Joss's room. As soon as they stepped in, Joss realised something was out of place, although it took him a moment.

'My bedsheet's gone,' he exclaimed.

'I imagine the servants have been to take the laundry.' Alikan crossed to the window and looked down. Joss's room, like his, overlooked the city rather than the lake.

'Yeah.' Joss replied slowly, breaking off a piece of bread and popping it in his mouth. Why did he have a creeping feeling something was very wrong?

He felt the odd vibration of Doroqueal's magic before the little spirit appeared. 'I've sseen Scarlett! She says there is a servant's stairs leading up to the royal women's quarters. Stay on the stairs and she'll slip out to meet you as soon as she can, but she won't be able to get away for long.'

'When?' Joss asked eagerly.

Doroquael turned a somersault. 'Now.'

Joss rushed for the door, but Alikan grabbed his arm. 'Joss, you're a good kid, and I know you like to be the hero, but don't go saying anything foolish before you've really thought it through.'

Joss pulled himself free and snatched at the door handle to yank it open. 'I'm not a kid, Ali.'

Alikan didn't reply as Joss marched down the hallway. As Raven Scouts, they'd learned the layout of the castle for emergencies, all but the royal apartments themselves. It took Joss only a moment to find the nearest servant's door and use his lock picks to access the warren of narrow stairs and corridors.

Scarlett was already waiting for them, her dark shape recognisable to Joss even though only a sliver of light leaked through a crack in the door behind her. Joss smiled to himself. His princess was no shrinking violet, scared of shadows and cobwebs. She was pacing, wearing a simple but expensive dress.

'Scar!'

'Joss!' She hurried down several steps to meet them. Doroquael made himself brighter. 'What's happened? Do you have news of the castle's witch?'

'I… what?' He blinked at her. This wasn't quite what he'd expected. 'No, nothing new. Listen.' He stepped forward, gently holding her upper arms. She shrank back, staring at him in bewilderment, a blush touching her cheeks. 'Scarlett, I have an idea to save you.'

'Save me?'

'I'll ask your father if I can marry you.'

Her mouth fell open, and her blush deepened. 'But… I didn't realise you liked me that much. And I'm not sure I'd want to marry you. Perhaps in time—'

'But we don't have time.' Joss shook his head. 'When you marry Mendel of Taurmouth, it will be too late. I can save you from being sold off to that old man. I thought… well, I thought last night that you… That I meant something to you, too.'

'Last night?' Scarlett's face creased in a deep frown.

Alikan swore. 'Spirits, Joss, can't you see she doesn't have a clue what you're talking about?'

'But…'

Alikan pushed past him to face Scarlett. 'Did you spend last night with Joss? In his room?'

'No.' Scarlett actually looked affronted; nausea churned in Joss's stomach. 'Of course, I didn't.'

'What?' Joss tried to smile despite the fact the world seemed to unravel around him. 'It's okay, Alikan knows, he'll help us.'

'It wasn't Scarlett.' Alikan's eyes blazed. 'You utter imbecile, Joss. You spent the night with Eleanor.'

'What?' Both Scarlett and Joss demanded at once.

'I don't know what her game is, but Princess Eleanor has played you for a fool.' Alikan glared at Joss.

Joss didn't have time to think, Scarlett launched herself at him, Alikan struggling to hold the furious princess back.

'How could you!' Her fingers were claws, reaching for his face.

Joss could barely breathe, but he didn't retreat. 'I thought it was you!'

'Me?' Scarlet almost screeched. 'How could you think she was me? We're completely different!'

She nearly broke free from Alikan, but he grabbed her wrists. 'Scarlett. Scarlett! We need to find out what your sister is up to. Why would she do this?'

Scarlett stopped struggling and peered up at Alikan through her wild hair. 'I don't know. But I'm going to find out.'

Alikan let go, and Scarlett pivoted, climbing up the stairs with all the dignity she could muster. She narrowed her eyes at Joss, before vanishing through the door.

Joss grabbed for the wall, bile rising from his stomach.

'Sit down.' Alikan ordered him. 'Put your head between your knees. Doro, go check on Scarlett, be as discreet as you can.'

Joss didn't argue. This couldn't be real. Heat flowed through him, even as a chill prickled his skin. 'What am I going to do, Ali?'

Alikan placed a hand on his shoulder. 'We're going to your sister.'

Chapter Thirteen

Kesta; Fulmer Island

Kesta wrapped her arms around herself as they drew closer to shore, the wind driving the surf so it spattered across her skin. She tasted the salt on her lips, bracing her leg muscles against the rise and fall of the longship. The high cliff rose before her, Fulmer Hold a proud crown upon the peninsular. She smiled, even as pain seared her heart.

'It's like seeing an old friend.'

'One that has missed you,' her mother said softly.

For a moment Kesta wondered if the Icante had meant to make her feel guilty, but one look at her mother's face told her otherwise. Kesta and Dia both raised their hands, shooting a ball of flame into the sky. Moments later, an answering fireball acknowledged their signal.

'I'm nervous,' Kesta admitted. 'I don't know why.'

Dia drew in a breath. 'It's always hard to know what to say to someone who is facing death. You want to take it away from them, but you can't, and no words are enough, not even the words of a bard.'

Kesta turned back to her sharply. 'Did Temerran try?'

Dia's poised expression didn't falter. 'Of course, he did.'

Kesta swallowed, looking up at the high walls of the hold. Several warriors patrolled there, and she recognised the elegant figure of the *walker*, Everlyn.

They dropped anchor in the bay, Jorrun helping both Kesta and Dia into the small rowing boat. Vivess and Eidwyn took up oars alongside Gilfy and another warrior. As they made their way to the beach, three other boats headed out to the longship to bring in the rest of its crew. Two people waited on the sand; the broad-shouldered but one-armed man unmistakable. The hair of the woman beside him had dulled a little over the years, but it still shone with a burnish like brass.

'Uncle Worvig!'

Jorrun reached out to grab her arm and stop her, but Kesta stood and leapt out of the boat, wading through the surf to meet her uncle. He wrapped his arm around her, hard enough to bruise her ribs, and kissed her forehead. He didn't say a word as they struggled out of the water together, and Milaiya hurried to hug her despite the fact her clothes were soaking wet.

'Kesta, how are you?' The woman who had long ago been a slave in Chem winced and closed her eyes briefly. 'I'm sorry, that was a stupid thing to ask.'

Kesta shook her head. 'No, it wasn't. I'm hurting, I'm scared, but my health is good.'

Worvig cleared his throat. 'The children both well?'

'They are.' Kesta squeezed his arm.

'Catch.' Kesta turned just in time to grab the bag Jorrun threw at her, before it hit her in the chest. Her husband held out his hand to help Dia out of the boat, then did the same for Eidwyn and Vivess. Heara sprang out unaided, landing with the surety of a cat.

'How is he?' Dia asked Worvig at once.

'He's having a good day,' Worvig replied, although there seemed to be no relief in his eyes.

Dia nodded and forced a smile.

Kesta's hand went to her mouth. She suddenly felt sick. Jorrun placed a hand against her back, rubbing gently before taking her hand. Steeling herself, Kesta compelled her feet to follow behind her mother as they made their way up the beach to the coast path. As she crossed the narrow causeway, Kesta couldn't help but recall the time she and her father had held off the Geladanian raiders together, side by side.

She'd feared losing nearly everything she loved that night, but her father had made her strong.

Warriors greeted them as they entered the hold, addressing Kesta as Silene, although she rarely carried out the duty of advisor and chieftain to the Icante these days. She squeezed Jorrun's hand tighter as they came to the longhouse and the doors were held open for them. Kesta blinked in surprise.

A feast was underway. Two musicians were playing a reel and voices were raised in raucous conversation. Smoke from the central pit was drawn away from the high chimney and toward the open doorway; the smell of roasting meat turning Kesta's stomach again.

She caught sight of Everlyn, and a smile rose from Kesta's chest. The woman whose face had been scarred in defence of Arridia and Joss was glowing with happiness. A man more than ten years her junior was showing her small pieces of intricately carved wood, which she turned over in her fingers. They'd been married less than a year. In fact, the wedding had been the last time she and Jorrun had visited the Fulmers together. Calbri was a clever and quiet young man, who could make masterpieces of art from anything, and he worshipped the courageous *fire-walker* he crouched beside.

Kesta tore her eyes away to search the room. She almost missed her own father. Arrus had always been a bear of a man, even six months ago he'd still carried his muscular bulk. The man sitting at the high table was thin, his face gaunt, his skin more grey than olive.

Blood drained from Kesta's body and she swayed a little; then drew herself up, preparing to move.

Heara beat her to it, striding across the hall and bellowing. 'Arrus, you old fraud! The minute we leave, you're out here feasting.'

Arrus grinned, pushing himself up from his seat. 'Less of the old, woman!'

Heara slapped a hand to his cheek and kissed him on the mouth. Beside Arrus, Heara's long-time lover, Merkis Vilnue, merely raised his eyebrows.

Dia followed her friend at a more sedate pace.

Kesta took in several breaths to compose herself and force a smile. She freed her hand from Jorrun's as she made her way around the central firepit. Her father saw her, and he came to meet her, leaning on the table.

'My sea urchin!' He grinned and held out his arms.

Kesta broke into a run, people hurrying out of her way. Her father felt so small. She fought to hold in her tears, her throat aching. She sniffed, stepping back to thump him carefully on the chest. 'What have you been doing? Eating green foods?'

Her father chuckled. 'Well, your mother has been nagging me for years to eat that goat fodder.'

Dia tutted. 'Come on, let's exchange news in our room.'

'Don't fuss, love,' Arrus replied kindly. 'Let me enjoy the days I have.'

Dia glanced away, but she drew herself up and nodded.

'Jorrun!' Arrus thrust out his arm. 'How are your books?'

Jorrun grasped Arrus's wrist. The Fulmer warrior had never cared about books and could only read enough to decipher messages, but Jorrun didn't break the polite pretence. 'I'm still working my way through Farport's library.'

Arrus narrowed his eyes. 'I'm starting to suspect you conquered Chem just to get at their dusty old tomes.'

Jorrun laughed and winked. 'You might be right.'

Arrus turned to look for a chair, and Vilnue quickly moved one toward him. Dia flinched as he shakily sat, desperately wanting to help him, but mindful of his pride.

'Be a mate and grab my beer.' Arrus waved a hand at Heara.

The formidable woman rolled her eyes and huffed, but she did so at once.

'Any news?' Arrus asked his wife seriously.

One warrior who'd been keeping Arrus company offered Dia his chair and discreetly wandered off to get food.

'Just a few things, hopefully of no consequence,' Dia replied as she sat.

Kesta took a moment to survey the room again as her mother caught Arrus and Vilnue up on the goings on in Elden. Kesta recognised most of the faces in the room but was startled to see there were some islanders she didn't know. Vivess was with the musicians, and she joined her compelling voice with the ballad they played. Kesta knew little about her mother's new apprentice and promised herself she would show more interest.

Eidwyn had left the hall, catching up on reports on Dia's behalf. With a heavy heart, Kesta realised the young woman had taken the place she had once held. She glanced at Jorrun. She had few regrets, but losing her place here in the Islands was one of them. With all her responsibilities to the Ravens, it was unlikely Kesta would ever be Icante.

Everlyn excused herself from Calbri and joined them, standing close to Dia.

'So, my grandchildren are off on a quest, and the boy volunteered.' Arrus grinned. 'There'll be a woman he's trying to impress then. I'd bet a barrel of best beer on it.'

'What? No.' Kesta drew herself back to the conversation. When she looked at Jorrun, her husband appeared suspiciously sheepish. 'Jorrun?'

He shrugged with a glance at Arrus.

Kesta narrowed her eyes. 'He just likes adventure and doing the right thing,' she insisted.

Arrus laughed, but it died quickly, his face growing pale.

Dia snatched up his hand and crouched at his side. 'My love?'

'It's only a little pain.' He patted her arm and forced a smile. 'I'd probably better lie down for a bit though.'

Kesta had experienced helplessness several times in her life but forcing herself to stand aside while her father staggered away on her mother's arm was excruciating. Someone held a glass of wine out in front of her and she took it, twisting to meet her uncle's eyes.

'He tried to do too much today,' Everlyn whispered. 'It's the only way he has to fight his illness, to defy it.'

'He doesn't want to die in his bed,' Worvig said.

Kesta's jaw trembled as pressure built behind her eyes. She quickly gulped down half the wine. In her mind she was racing from the hall, tearing across the causeway to the high cliff path; but her body didn't move, and she held her dignity together.

'Your old room is ready,' Milaiya smiled kindly.

It was Jorrun who replied. 'Thank you, we'll settle ourselves in.'

'Shall I send food to your room?' Milaiya asked.

Kesta straightened herself up. 'No, thank you, we'll come out here to eat later.' She finished the rest of the wine and placed her hand briefly on her uncle's shoulder before hastening to the doors at the back of the great hall. Jorrun's quiet steps followed behind her up to her old room. She almost laughed when she saw Heara had taken up her accustomed position outside the Icante's room. Then Kesta froze.

'Heara, why do you need to guard my mother?'

Heara shrugged, playing with the end of her grey-streaked plait. 'I didn't like that talk of unknown magic back in Elden.'

'No,' Kesta murmured. 'Neither did I.'

'Come on.' Jorrun gave her a gentle push from behind.

With a scowl and a shake of her head, Kesta opened the door to her room. So much of it was familiar, but it lacked any personal touch, any sign of ownership. It even somehow smelled empty and neglected. She sat on the bed and Jorrun sat beside her, his leg touching hers. It was a while before either of them spoke, although the silence was far from uncomfortable.

'Are you hatching a crazy plan?' Jorrun asked.

She laughed, a tear slipping from her eye as she turned to hug him. 'I wish. But this is my father's battle, it's for us to follow *his* plan.'

Jorrun leant his cheek against the top of her head. 'I'll try tomorrow.'

She nodded but couldn't bring herself to reply.

***

Kesta and Dia sat beneath the long window. Arrus lay on the bed, his breathing hardly perceptible, until a snore shook him and Kesta couldn't help but giggle. Her mother reached out and squeezed her fingers, a smile on her own lips. Jorrun's forehead creased in concentration, his hand flat across Arrus's chest. Kesta could feel the magic flowing from her husband, but there was no way of knowing if it was working. She'd seen him heal many physical wounds, watched as the flesh knitted back together; but there was no change to her father's appearance.

Jorrun's shoulders drew in; his worry lines deepened. Kesta's breathing quickened, and she curled the fingers of her free hand into a fist, trying to will what could not be.

Jorrun leaned back, his spine sagging. Kesta didn't move until he opened his eyes, whereupon she almost threw herself across the room to sit beside him on the edge of the bed. It was Dia who Jorrun turned to.

'I'm so sorry.'

Kesta bit hard on her thumb, watching in admiration as her mother slowly stood and stepped across the room to touch Jorrun's cheek. 'Thank you for trying.'

'Did it do anything?' Kesta dared to ask, her eyes wide.

Jorrun winced. 'His body took my power. I repaired some damage done by the illness, but as always there was a cost to him and to my power. His body just doesn't have the reserves. I couldn't stop whatever's killing him.'

'But you could keep him alive?' Kesta grabbed his hands.

'I could—'

Arrus stirred. 'No, son.'

Dia hurried to assist him, placing two pillows behind his shoulders to help him sit up.

Arrus held a hand out towards Jorrun, and Dia moved aside so he could take it.

'I've had a good life, son, the best. Let me enjoy my last days. There's no point prolonging it if I'm left too weak to have any fun.'

'Do you feel worse?' Jorrun asked in alarm.

Arrus shook his head. 'Actually, I hurt much less, but I'm very tired.'

Jorrun's muscles relaxed a little, and Kesta leaned against his shoulder to peer at her father. His eyes were already closed, but his breathing seemed easier.

'We'll leave you in peace,' Jorrun told Dia.

Jorrun got to his feet, and Kesta stood with him. 'Would you like me to stay, Mother?'

Dia shook her head. 'No, you go on.'

Kesta swallowed, leaving reluctantly. She couldn't face the great hall. Even at this time of morning it would be busy with people using the large fireplaces for cooking, or the tables for teaching the younger children. Even the thought of her room made her feel trapped.

'I'm going to walk down to the beach,' she told Jorrun.

'Do you want time alone?'

She gazed into his pale-blue eyes, so full of pain of his own. She kissed him. 'No, come on.'

They passed through the main hall to get outside, and Kesta braced herself. Worvig and Milaiya were sat waiting with Heara and Everlyn. Her uncle stood at once on seeing them, but Jorrun shook his head. Worvig sank back down.

'We'll talk later,' Jorrun said.

Heara opened her mouth but bit her tongue. Worvig nodded.

Guilt stung Kesta, and her feet faltered. They should probably explain, but Jorrun put his arm around her. 'Take care of yourself for now,' he said softly. 'Then we can support them.'

Kesta couldn't help but feel all eyes were on them as they passed between the neat houses of the hold. The gates stood open and the warriors on guard politely acknowledged them.

It wasn't that cold, but Kesta shivered. The smell of wood smoke mixed with the briny scent of seaweed brought to them on the wind from the beach down below. The gulls seemed gratingly loud, circling high as though something had disturbed them. As they made their way down the coast path to the reed-covered dunes, they heard raised voices. Two islanders were struggling to land their small boat; both were in the water, muscles straining to get it out of the surf. Even with her *knowing* closed down, Kesta sensed their panic.

She broke into a run, calling power.

The waves were colliding unnaturally, crashing together to form almost triangular peaks. 'Leave the boat!' she yelled. 'Get on land!'

The startled men scrambled and waded for shore. Kesta skidded to a halt, spraying up sand, the lacy edges of the sea close to her feet. Jorrun was beside her in an instant, a shield raised and expanding to take in the frightened men. The boat was suddenly thrown up in the air as a jet of water shot up. As the spray subsided, it formed into the shape of a large woman, her aquamarine hair a constant, moving flow.

Kesta gasped. 'Water-spirit!'

The two fishermen threw themselves onto the sand, scrambling back out of the way. Their boat had smashed down on the beach with a crunch of splitting wood.

'How can we assist you?' Jorrun called out, his voice calm and commanding.

The sea-spirit answered in sibilant hisses. 'I am here to assist you! I have a warning, I brought it for the Icante, but it concerns you even more, fire-priestess.'

Kesta turned cold. There was only one people who referred to the *fire-walkers* as priestesses.

'They are coming,' the sea-spirit said. 'The whales sing of it in the deep ocean. Ships from the south.'

Jorrun's voice was strained when he asked, 'How many?'

The sea-spirit's burning blue eyes held his. 'About a dozen.'

The ground spun away from Kesta and she raised her hands to steady herself, barely able to catch her breath. Jorrun was silent, his skin pale.

'How far?' Kesta took a step towards the water.

'We will not be captured.' The spirit's eyes blazed, and its hair flowed faster. 'We go to the deeps.'

Without allowing them any time to protest, the spirit melted away, and the sea calmed.

As Kesta turned to Jorrun, something caught her eyes. High on the causeway was the unmistakable figure of the Icante, but she wasn't alone. A bright, fiery shape hovered above her shoulder.

Kesta drew in a sharp breath. 'Siveraell.'

Chapter Fourteen

Catya; Free City of Navere

Catya leaned back in her chair and let Cassien finish his rant, watching calmly as he strode up and down the room.

'You haven't changed, Catya, you're still using people. And as for filling your son's mind with that foolishness—'

'Is this how you speak to King Bractius?'

'What?' Cassien spun on his heels to glare at her, his face reddening.

'You never used to stand up to me like this, I like it.'

Cassien's mouth opened and closed, and Catya turned her face to hide her amusement. She drew in a breath and said seriously, 'It isn't foolishness, Cass. Edon Ra is a seer.'

'I can't believe you would trust in that nonsense.' He shook his head.

'It's not a matter of belief.' She sat up straighter, holding his gaze. 'It's a matter of knowing. Edon's abilities are real.'

Cassien slumped into a chair. His silver eyes still angry. 'Why have you kept him hidden all this time?'

'Because our enemy mustn't know of him.'

'Our enemy?' Cassien's eyebrows drew together.

'Jderha. Edon Ra will help us against her.'

'Jderha? We haven't heard from Geladan in fourteen years!'

Catya folded her hands together and leant toward him. 'We're about to, but we'll get to the Fulmers in time.'

Cassien scowled.

'Look, Cass.' She got to her feet and crouched before him. He moved away. His distrust and suspicion stung her, although she knew she deserved it. 'I'm sorry, okay.'

'Sorry?' He spluttered.

'Yes, Cass, I'm really sorry for the way I treated you. I was selfish. I didn't let myself consider what I was doing to you. You were my... you were my security blanket. I expected you to always be there, no matter what I did to you. I didn't set out to be cruel, it just happened.'

He stared at her.

Feeling suddenly uncomfortable, she got up and retreated to her chair. 'I took you for granted, because I could get away with it, until the day you hit me with the truth.'

They both sat in silence. Catya's gaze travelled across the familiar study, lingering on the portrait of Osun. She'd been a child still when Cassien's 'master' had died; the same year she'd made her first kill, stabbing the powerful Chemmish sorcerer, Inari. She shifted in her chair.

Cassien sighed. 'When do I get to meet your Rakinya?'

'Tomorrow, when we sail. And he's not *my* Rakinya, it's more like I'm *his* queen.'

Cassien tilted his head to regard her.

She shook herself. 'I'd best get back to Merin and Dys.'

Cassien didn't stop her as she left the room, and it surprised her at how much that rankled. As fickle as she'd been, he'd been her first love.

She dawdled down the familiar corridors to the rooms they had given her, rooms that had once belonged to a necromancer of the Dunham Coven. When she opened the door, she found Dysarta sitting up waiting for her. Catya's heart expanded at the sight of her beautiful wife. Dysarta had saved her in so many ways, pushing back the darkness within Catya, making vulnerability feel safe.

'I got Merin to go back to bed,' the red-haired sorceress told her.

'Thanks.' Catya sat slowly beside her, leaning her head against the taller woman's shoulder.

'How did it go?'

Catya cringed. 'It wasn't the most pleasant conversation I've had. As we expected, he doesn't believe the prophecy could be real.'

'He will.' A huge shape detached itself from the wall, its fur changing slowly from the dark burgundy of the wallpaper, to a creamy-white. It still astounded Catya how these creatures of the north could alter the colour of their long fur with a thought. Only his face was bare, the skin almost scaly, and somewhere between human and cat-like in form.

Catya had ended a long war between the Rakinya and the Tribespeople of the north, both of whom fought for possession of a hidden sanctuary within the frozen mountains of the far north. The Rakinya were an ancient race, one which was inherently benevolent despite their terrifying appearance. Dysarta's people were the original inhabitants of Chem, decimated and chased into the wilderness by the coming of the Demons claiming godhood; and later the rise of the Covens. Survival had made them enemies, but had ultimately brought them together.

Edon Ra padded across the room to join them, his clawed feet made silent by long fur. 'You didn't believe either, to begin with.'

Catya smiled distractedly, momentarily meeting the Rakinya's very dark-blue eyes. As true as Edon Ra's predictions seemed to be, they often made no sense until after the event actually happened.

Dysarta gave her hand a squeeze. 'Are you going to get some sleep yourself?'

Catya looked out of the window; the sky was growing lighter. 'Not much point now. Edon, shouldn't you be on your way to the docks?'

'There are supply wagons being loaded with trade goods for the Fulmers. I'll go in one of them. Cat, I...'

'What is it?' Catya sat up straighter. Despite their friendship spanning years, it was often hard to read Edon Ra's expression. Even so, she could see he was reluctant to speak. 'Have you seen something bad?'

He nodded, scratching at his furry shoulder. 'It was confusing, unclear, but it made me feel so cold, and deathly afraid. There were two ravens, with feathers like flame. A creature rose suddenly up from the earth and bit one, and its fire went out.' Edon Ra shuddered.

Catya swallowed, scrabbling to find something witty to say, but it eluded her.

Dysarta rubbed her back. 'It could be anything, let's not worry over nothing.'

All three of them knew it wasn't nothing. Catya stood and reached out her hand to take Edon's huge, furry paw. He had long fingers like a human, but hooked claws grew from the tips rather than nails. She looked up into his eyes, small flecks of blue catching the light in his otherwise black irises.

'It will be okay,' Catya said, trying to force conviction into her voice. So much depended on their attempt to change Edon's vision of the future, not least the most precious thing in their lives.

Edon Ra nodded, though his shoulders remained tense. With a shake of her head, Catya stepped in to hug him, her arms not long enough to reach around the enormous beast.

'You are right.' Edon Ra sighed out the air he'd been holding in his lungs, blowing Catya's hair back from her face as she looked up. 'We are borrowing sorrow from tomorrow, which may never happen. I'll get myself down to the ship. Will you try to sleep?'

She chewed at her bottom lip for a moment. 'Let's pack and then pay the markets an early visit, I really want you to see the city, Dys.'

'And I would love to see it.' Dysarta leaned forward, wrapping her arms around herself. 'You must show me all the places where you fought to change Chem.'

Catya smiled, pride swelling her lungs. 'We'll start at the docks then, at the house in which Kesta and Jorrun hid before they took this palace.'

***

Although they were only just setting up, the stallholders in the markets were happy to trade, and Catya found a few modest gifts for Merin. Even with a tour for Dysarta thrown in, they got back to the palace in time for a late breakfast with Calayna and Rece; Catya realised she'd missed them.

Rece chattered about all the news of the city, its guilds, its trade, punishments for the breakers of the Raven Laws, and their most recent Raven trainees. Catya listened eagerly, surprised at how much her heart yearned after such small news. Often her eyes would travel over Calayna's now clear skin, and she would stop herself, trying not to be rude. A good friend of hers in the north had been tattooed after being captured by Chemmen. If they didn't fail in their mission, she hoped to have her healed and the marks of slavery removed as Calayna's had been.

Rece and Calayna walked with them when it came to time to embark from the docks. The ship they'd been supplied with was a Chemmish vessel, broader than the *Undine* on which Catya had served for a few months. Merin stood looking at it with wide eyes, and Catya smiled. Her son had never sailed before. She stroked his hair, then pulled her hand back, not wanting to embarrass him.

'Go on up.' Catya nodded toward the gangplank.

With a grin, Merin scampered aboard, Dysarta a protective shadow. Cassien hovered nearby as Catya hugged both Rece and Calayna goodbye.

'We'll talk soon about settling things properly between Chem and Snowhold.' She winked at Rece. 'I'm keeping my crown though.'

Rece laughed, and Calayna smiled, although she shook her head.

Cassien remained a step behind her as she boarded and glancing back, she saw he was scanning the deck; then she realised she was doing the same. Scouting was in their souls.

'Ready to meet Edon?' she asked him.

Cassien blinked twice. 'Of course.'

The fact his hand lifted towards his sword didn't escape her.

Leaving her son and Dysarta to explore the deck, Catya headed to the ladder that plunged down into the deep hold. A sailor moved to stop her, but a sharp look had him scurrying away. Catya snorted in amusement, then climbed rapidly down the wooden ladder, jumping the last four feet and landing elegantly on her toes. Cassien followed at a more sedate pace.

It took Catya a few moments to locate Edon Ra. With a few Chemmish sailors still tying down supplies, he'd camouflaged himself against some sacking in a dark corner. Catya looked around at the Chemmen, wary of them seeing her friend.

Cassien cleared his throat. 'Leave us, please, we'll finish stowing this.'

The Chemmen appeared startled but touched their foreheads and hurried away.

'They'll think we're having an affair.' Catya grinned. Cassien glared at her and she rolled her eyes. 'You haven't got your sense of humour back then.'

'That wasn't funny.' He almost growled. 'I'd never do anything to hurt Kussim.'

Catya let out a large sigh. 'I know. And I wouldn't hurt Dys, not for anyone. I nearly lost her once. I gained Merin by it, but it's not something I'd do again.'

Cassien looked horrified. 'You were with Dysarta when you… when Alikan…'

Catya gritted her teeth and let out a groan. As much as she knew she'd been very much in the wrong, Cassien's judgemental attitude was really grating. It was one reason… one of the reasons she'd left him for the seeming freedom of Temerran's company. 'Cass, not now, okay?' She gestured over her shoulder. Judging by the widening of Cassien's eyes, she guessed Edon Ra was altering the colouration of his shaggy fur.

'Hello, Cassien.'

Edon Ra perched on the edge of a crate, his eyes black in the hold's darkness. Even seated, Catya knew how intimidating the huge Rakinya would look to someone who didn't know him; Edon was nearly seven feet tall.

Cassien swallowed. 'Hello. I'm honoured to meet you.'

Catya couldn't help but smile warmly at his perfect manners. She slapped Cassien's arm. 'I've missed you.'

Cassien recoiled a little in surprise. He turned back to Edon Ra, straightening up and not turning away from the scary-looking Rakinya's scrutiny.

'Yes,' Edon Ra said slowly. 'Destiny swirls around you, as it does Catya. You are a changing point.'

'What?' Cassien gave his head a slight shake, a deep frown on his face.

'He means you influence history,' Catya explained. 'For example, the effect you had on Osun, the influence you had on me.'

Cassien opened his mouth and shook his head again. 'I hardly influenced you, Cat, no one could tell you what to do.'

'That's where you're wrong.' She looked up into his grey eyes. 'You're the most honest person I know. When you called me a monster, I knew it was true.' He protested, but she held up her hand. 'It turned me from an incredibly destructive path, and sent me north, where I became a queen.'

Cassien screwed his face up, still far from convinced.

Edon Ra slipped down off his crate, revealing his daunting height. Cassien didn't flinch. 'It doesn't matter if you believe me or not, what matters is that you are both in the Fulmers, and soon.'

'Well, I guess we'll see.' Cassien looked from Catya back to Edon Ra. 'Will you come up on deck, join us? You are welcome.'

'And you are kind, Cassien Raven,' Edon Ra replied. 'But Jderha must not know I exist. The longer I am hidden and can help you, the more chance we have of defeating her. I have to remain an unknown and random element in her future.'

Catya could see from the narrowing of Cassien's silver eyes he didn't believe a word of what they said but was too polite to say so. When Catya had first met him, Cassien had been in deep mourning, little more than a child, but having had to endure worse than most adults in a lifetime. Kesta told her that when she'd first met him, he'd never stopped asking questions; but Osun's death and his crushing grief had killed the spark in him, and his hunger to comprehend the world.

She touched his arm. 'I don't blame you for not trusting us, Cass. All we ask for now is that you let Edon stay safely hidden.'

Cassien regarded the large snow beast. 'I will see no harm comes to you.'

Edon Ra smiled sadly. 'That means a lot to me.'

Catya looked away with a glance at Edon Ra. They both knew it was a promise poor Cassien would be unlikely to keep.

***

Catya's stomach twisted into a tighter knot as they drew closer to the island, the high cliff line achingly familiar. Her eyes followed the silhouette of the peninsular and the dip in the hills where the small beach lay.

'Is that it, Mother?' Merin's fingers gripped the rail, and he leaned out to see past her.

Catya moved aside to stand behind him and pointed. 'Yes. Fulmer Hold is up there, high on the cliffs.'

'That's odd,' Cassien muttered from where he hovered a few feet away.

Catya followed his gaze. A Fulmer longship was moving toward them at speed. She glanced up. Their Raven banner was displayed prominently from the mast, yet the Fulmer ship seemed far from friendly. Catya placed her hands on Merin's shoulders.

'Go find Dys.'

'But, Mother—'

'Now.'

Merin peered up at her, then scuttled away. Cassien stepped up to her side, ducking his head a little to keep the sun from his eyes. 'They have archers poised and ready.'

Their Chemmish captain had been alerted, and he strode across to the rail, both his hands held high. 'We are a trading vessel from Chem! We carry senior Ravens to Fulmer Hold!'

Catya's mouth quirked up in a half-smile. 'He's making me feel old.' Despite her humour, her heart was beating faster, and her right hand rested against the hilt of her sword.

As the Fulmer ship drew closer, Catya scanned the faces of the men and women aboard. There were none that she knew, and her heart sank. The man at the prow straightened up on seeing Cassien, and lowering his bow, raised a hand.

'What's happened?' Cassien demanded, leaning over the rail and increasing the volume of his voice.

'Cassien, it's good to see you,' the Fulmer warrior shouted back. 'You will be most welcome at the Hold. We've had warning from the sea-spirits to expect attack. The Icante will explain.'

Cassien spun on his heels to face Catya, his skin deathly pale. Her heart clenched in sympathy.

'Takes the world out from under you, doesn't it?' she said quietly.

Cassien turned back to the warrior and waved his thanks, then nodded to the captain who shouted orders to make all haste to Fulmer Hold.

'It's just coincidence.' Cassien took a step away from her.

Soft hurried steps drew their attention, Merin almost ran to rejoin his mother, Dysarta following at a more dignified pace. Catya reached out her hand and Dysarta took it, while Merin brushed past Cassien to watch the departing longship.

Dysarta gazed into Catya's eyes with her beautiful green ones and gave her fingers a squeeze. 'It will be okay.'

Catya wished she could be certain. She'd avoided this meeting, this confrontation for fourteen years, refusing to leave Snowhold to visit the Free Provinces, only accepting delegations of Ravens she barely knew. Catya didn't expect a warm welcome. She knew she didn't deserve one.

They drew closer to the hold, its high walls coming into focus. Catya had never been a coward, but she found it suddenly hard to breathe.

'Cat?'

It was Cassien who regarded her with a worried frown.

She waved a hand at him dismissively and took in a deep breath.

'Drop anchor!' the captain yelled.

They'd come as close as they could to the beach, they'd have to row the rest of the way.

'What of Edon Ra?' Cassien asked in concern.

'He'll follow after dark,' Catya replied. 'When I've had time to warn everyone who needs to know.'

They lowered two boats over the side and Catya followed down a rope ladder, staying just a little ahead of her son so she could watch his progress. She took an oar herself, Dysarta taking Merin to the rear of the boat to sit out of the way. It had been a long time since she'd landed a craft, and she enjoyed the pull and strain on her muscles. Cassien was the first to jump out into the surf to help drag them up the sand.

Both Catya and Cassien looked up at the walls of the hold and the long, narrow causeway. Warriors lined the battlements, most gazing out to sea, and a small group stood guard at the top of the beach road. Six men and two women were making their way toward them through the dunes, two of them so familiar Catya's heart ached.

'Dys.' Catya waved at the sorceress to join her.

One of the women broke away from the group, tapping a broad set man on his armless shoulder as she quickened her pace.

'Well, look what the tide dumped on our beach!' Heara's grin lit her face.

Catya choked back a surge of emotion, resisting only a moment before hurrying forward to embrace her old mentor. Heara's long plait was no longer sleek and black but shot through with grey. Catya let it run through her fingers as she pulled away to look up into the muscular woman's hazel eyes. There were a lot of lines about them now, but they still shone with confidence and mischief.

'Heara.' Catya spun on her heels as she excitedly introduced her small party. 'This is my wife, Dysarta, and this is my son, Merin.'

Heara clasped Dysarta's wrist without hesitation, then placed her hands on her hips to look down at Merin. 'You any good with a knife, son?'

Merin blinked, perplexed, as both Heara and Catya burst into fits of wild laughter.

Worvig caught up to them, shaking his head and going to Cassien to take his hand.

'What's happening?' Cassien asked seriously.

Heara quieted immediately and indicated toward the hold. 'Let's go see Dia. Worvig, you got this lot?' She gestured at the Chemmen who were landing on the beach.

Worvig nodded. 'I'll see to them.'

Heara waited until they were on the sandy trail between the dunes before she spoke again. 'We had warning just a day ago, so I'm guessing you missed the message sent to Navere. Both a sea-spirit and Siveraell came to warn us that Geladan are on their way.'

Cassien halted abruptly, eyes wide. 'Geladan?'

Heara looked him up and down over her shoulder. 'Yes. Quite a number of them too. Seems like our time's up.'

Cassien turned to Catya, his mouth open. She shrugged.

'Me, I'm surprised they left it this long.' Heara continued up the path toward the causeway.

Several of the warriors on watch greeted Catya, but she recognised few of them. She looked around for Merin and took hold of his hand, shocked when – unusually – he didn't protest. As they passed through the gates to the outer hold, a woman stepped out to bar their way, one hand on her hip, the other on the hilt of her long dagger. Kesta narrowed her mis-matched green eyes to glare at Catya.

'You have some nerve showing up here.'

Catya swallowed but held Kesta's gaze. Dysarta moved protectively closer, while Merin gripped her fingers tighter.

'Cat.'

She turned to see Jorrun had appeared beside Heara. Seeing how much older he looked, how worried he seemed, sent a sharp searing pain through her chest. He held his arms out toward her, and she let go of Merin's hand to step into his hug.

'Welcome home, Cat,' Jorrun said into her hair.

Chapter Fifteen

Scarlett; Kingdom of Elden

Scarlett came to a halt outside her sister's rooms, her fists clenched. She gave a loud growl, pivoted on her heels, and marched back to her own room. She needed to calm down; needed to think clearly. As much as she wanted to rip Eleanor's hair out, she knew it wasn't the best way to approach things. She opened her door and her lady-in-waiting stood immediately. Riane was a nice enough girl, but Scarlett was all too aware she was a spy and chaperone working for her mother, and so had never allowed herself to make a friend of her.

'You were gone a while, Highness, I was worried.'

Scarlett placed a hand on her stomach. 'Bad guts. I need to lie down.'

Riane's eyes widened and her mouth fell open, but she didn't protest as Scarlett retreated to the privacy of her own room. She sat on the bed, but in a few moments was standing again. She was still furious, no matter how rational she tried to be about it. Both her father and mother managed to be calculated and unemotional; why couldn't she see past her feelings to come at this from a logical point of view?

'Why am I so angry at Joss, anyway?' She narrowed her eyes as she stared out the window at the cloudy sky. She was attracted to him without a doubt, she'd even harboured childish daydreams that he might be the one she'd marry one day, but in her position as princess daydreams were all she thought she'd be allowed.

'He thought he was saving me.' She placed her hands on the cold stone of the windowsill. Her heart swelled despite her attempts to be sensible, pins and needles racing through her veins.

'How could he not know it was me!' She slammed one hand against the wall, her palm stinging. 'We're completely different!' The anger of betrayal rose as heat from her toes to her scalp. He might not have meant to, but he had betrayed her, though not as much as her own sister had. Quiet, innocent little Eleanor.

Scarlett snarled.

She spun on her heels and marched out through her parlour and out into the hall. Riane gave a startled squeal and followed. Scarlett kicked her sister's door open and charged into the room. She stopped so abruptly she almost fell back. It was as though an invisible hand had planted itself firmly in the middle of her chest.

Eleanor paused, her needle hovering above the fabric in her left hand. 'Scarlett, whatever is the matter?'

'You know what!' Scarlett snarled.

Eleanor sighed and put down her embroidery. 'So, you found out already. He didn't waste any time. Eager for more, was he?'

Scarlett made to charge at her sister again, but her feet wouldn't move. Eleanor waved at Riane and her own lady-in-waiting. 'Leave us.'

'Shall I get the queen?' Riane asked timidly.

'No.' Eleanor stood. 'I'll deal with this myself.'

'Why did you do it?' Scarlett demanded, trying hard not to screech. 'Why did you pretend to be me?'

Eleanor raised a delicate eyebrow, not losing an ounce of poise. It struck Scarlett then how very like their mother Eleanor was. 'What's wrong, Scarlett? Jealous it wasn't you? Have you been dreaming about that pretty oaf?'

Scarlett's nostrils flared. Her sister had touched on a truth she'd never admit aloud.

Eleanor sighed. 'I pretended to be you because he'd never have said yes to me, well, not quickly anyway, and I was short on time. After years of covering for you, it was easy enough to pretend to be you.'

'Time!'

Eleanor rolled her eyes. 'Yes, time. Thanks to you, we're out of it. Father has a plan to secure the future of Elden, a plan you know of but didn't take seriously. He intends for Lucien to marry Arridia and bring magic under the control of the throne. He wanted one of us to marry into a Coven in charge of a Chemmish sea-port to give a strong foothold in Chem, and the other to take control of our own biggest harbour, Taurmouth.' She gave a shrug. 'I didn't fancy Taurmouth, or Chem. While you've been playing at being free, I've been planning to take power the only way we can. Joss is nice to look at, he's easy to manipulate. He would also mean I can stay here in Elden, close to the throne. And there's the bonus that our children will very likely have power.'

Scarlett realised her mouth was hanging open and closed it. 'Do you love him?'

Eleanor scowled. 'Of course not. Wait.' She regarded Scarlett, who felt her temperature rise and her skin tighten in a blush. Eleanor threw her head back and laughed. 'You do, though, don't you! You love that foolish boy.'

Scarlett bristled; her hands clenched into fists. Joss was a year older than them, hardly a boy, and Joss was brave and kind, not stupid. 'He'll hate you! What kind of marriage will that be?'

Eleanor smiled in a way that made Scarlett's blood freeze. This wasn't her sister, it couldn't be.

Eleanor's eyes narrowed. 'Oh, I'll turn that around easily enough. In the meantime, tell him he has two days. If he doesn't approach Father and convince him to allow our wedding by then, then I'll go to Father and tell him all about how Joss seduced me. If you or he cause me any trouble or try to get out of this, I'll tell Father Joss forced himself on me.'

'You wouldn't dare! Father will never believe it!'

Eleanor looked at her, her hazel eyes hardening. 'I have the bed sheets to prove it, and if that is not believed...' She ran a hand over her flat stomach. 'After the night we had, there'll be firm evidence soon enough.'

Scarlett gasped air into her painful lungs and stepped back. 'How could you do this?'

Eleanor's mouth quirked up in a smug smile. 'Oh, it wasn't as bad as I thought it would be. Quite enjoyable, actually. But to answer your question.' She leaned forward. 'Survival and power.'

'I hate you!' Scarlett lunged, but somehow found herself on her hands and knees on the floor. Her entire body flushed in embarrassment; she was never normally so clumsy.

Eleanor sniggered. 'Be a good girl, sister, go deliver my message to Joss. Two days.'

Scarlett scrambled to her feet. 'I'll find a way to stop you.'

'Oh dear.' Eleanor pouted. 'Then I guess Joss will say hello to the hangman.'

Scarlett was breathing hard. There had to be something they could do. An idea occurred to her, and a spark of hope straightened her spine. She backed towards the door. 'I'll tell him.'

'Good. Oh, and Scarlett, if I were you, I'd start looking for where you want to spend the rest of your life and act quickly. At the moment, your choices are Mendel of Taurmouth, or Chem.' She raised a dainty hand and examined her nails.

Scarlett pivoted to hide her snarl. She'd known all her life she'd be expected to make a political marriage, but until now she'd never quite believed it would happen. And if it did... She shook her head as she stepped out into the hall. What? Had she really hoped it would end up like Kesta and Jorrun, that by some mad coincidence she'd end up being forced to marry her true love?

Her feet faltered, and she leaned against the wall. Eleanor was right, her sister had been the smart one.

Scarlett hesitated outside her door, wondering if Riane had returned there. She checked both ways along the corridor; no one seemed to be watching her. Eleanor had told her to deliver her message to Joss. Did that mean she was being allowed to go where she wanted? Was her mother in on this? The king?

Scarlett shuddered.

'Scarlett!'

She jumped, spinning on her heels. She knew that sibilant voice. 'Doro?'

The fire-spirit made himself larger, trapped inside a lantern on the wall.

'Are you okay, Sscarlett?'

She gave a firm nod. 'Hey, were you spying on me in my sister's room?'

Doroquael deflated. 'Ssorry, Scarlett, Joss wanted me to make sure you were safe.'

She made a sound in her throat, pleased despite herself. 'I'll try to get to Joss's room.'

'Go to Arridia's,' Doroquael urged her, before vanishing.

Arridia. That meant she and Lucien must know. Scarlett winced.

Steeling herself, she hurried from the royal apartments. The two men who stood guard glanced up at her but did nothing to stop her. It made the hairs rise on the back of her neck.

When she got to Arridia's room, she knocked once, then raised her chin and turned the handle to walk in.

Arridia wasn't there.

Lucien was. Her brother sat in a chair by the desk under the window. Joss was sitting on the opposite side of the room, his head in his hands, his short hair ruffled. Alikan froze mid-stride, relaxing a little when he saw her.

'What's going on?' Scarlett asked, feeling the tension in the room.

Joss looked up, the area around one of his eyes was darkening with a huge bruise, the skin swelling.

'Joss!' She ran toward him, but Alikan stepped in the way, clearing his throat and glancing at Lucien.

'He's fine,' Alikan told her. 'And probably deserved worse.'

'Hey!' Joss protested.

Lucien's cheeks coloured slightly.

Scarlett gasped, stepping cautiously closer to her brother. 'Did you do that?'

Lucien didn't answer, but there was a rare anger in his soft brown eyes.

'What did you find out from Eleanor?' Alikan prompted.

'Didn't Doroquael tell you?'

'He's gone to find Riddi,' Joss mumbled.

Scarlett nodded. 'I need to sit down.'

Joss stood to offer his chair, but he backed down at once at one look from Lucien. The prince stood and pointed at his own chair. Sheepishly, Scarlett took it. Lucien was never angry at her, not properly angry like this. Alikan poured a drink and handed it to her.

'Well?' Joss prompted, not yet sitting down.

Scarlett swallowed. 'Eleanor planned this, all of it.' She told them what her sister had said.

Joss and Alikan both swore, Alikan quickly apologising.

'So, it wasn't my fault!' Joss looked from Alikan to her.

Lucien cleared his throat. 'Oh, I wouldn't say that.'

Alikan waved a hand. 'The thing that matters is what we're going to do about it.'

'I will not be blackmailed into marrying that... that—'

'Careful,' Lucien growled. 'She's still my sister, and a princess.' He drew in a deep breath and blinked up at the ceiling. 'But I don't want her getting away with this either. What worries me is how deep this goes.'

'Yes.' Scarlett took one of her brother's hands in both of hers. 'I thought that too. Was this Father's plan? Or Mother's? Or was Eleanor acting alone?'

Joss slumped back down in his chair. 'What a mess.'

Alikan and Lucien both glared at him.

Scarlett drew in a breath. 'I have a plan. Joss and I should leave. We should get to the Raven Tower and get messages to the Fulmers and help from Rosa and Tantony, then we flee to Chem—'

'No.' Lucien shook his head rapidly. 'You're not thinking, Scar. Consider the repercussions. And why would *you* need to run?'

Scarlett's cheeks flushed. 'To avoid being forced to marry a horrible old man, or should I do what Eleanor did?'

Lucien blinked rapidly, his own skin reddening.

She sat in her chair and looked down at the brandy in her glass, then took a big gulp. Lucien was right. She was thinking like a foolish love-struck girl, not like a princess, not like a leader. The diplomatic fallout would be a nightmare, not to mention the fact Joss would probably end up with a price on his head and her sister and family feel the embarrassment of disgrace.

She gasped in air, feeling her nose tingle and pressure build behind her eyes. She realised she was shaking.

'Scar.' Lucien spoke gently, crouching by her chair. 'The best option might be for Joss to do as Eleanor says.'

'No!' Both Joss and Scarlett replied at once.

Lucien looked from her to the young Raven warrior. He gave the slightest of nods.

'Look, we've got two days.' Alikan moved silently across the room to stand closer to Joss. 'That's time to find an answer.'

Lucien stood, placing his hand on Scarlett's shoulder. She stopped fighting and let tears fall down her cheeks. 'We can't let Eleanor do this to Joss,' she implored her brother.

Lucien regarded them all. 'Let's see what Arridia has to say.'

Chapter Sixteen

Arridia; Kingdom of Elden

Arridia stepped into the stables, pulse racing. Several of the busy grooms turned to look at her, none of them the man she was hoping to find. Her heart sank, her spine sagging. She called up a little of her power, reaching out her *knowing.*

Her breath caught in her lungs. He was here. She hurried toward Freckle's stall, a smile pushing up from her chest.

'Can I help you, Raven?' a groom asked.

'No, thank you. I'm just visiting my horse.'

Freckle looked up at her approach, as did the man brushing her down. 'Arridia.'

She lifted the latch on the stall door, reaching up to caress Freckle's cheek, sudden butterflies stirring in her stomach. 'I was worried I'd missed you. I only heard by accident that a groom from Northold had escorted Princess Scarlett here. Why didn't you come and say hello?'

Nip stopped brushing to hold her gaze. 'I'm just a groom, I had no right to be in the castle. And you were working.'

Arridia clicked her tongue. 'Nip, you've never been just a groom, you could have been a Raven. Why... why did you never join us?'

Nip looked away, his long boots disturbing the straw as he shifted his feet. 'My father's health was declining, and I had a duty to him. You and Joss were safe, and Northold is my home. I'm sure that sounds boring to you, but I had enough that was dear to me to protect without hunting abroad for it.'

Arridia breathed out slowly. 'Having a quiet home to protect sounds perfect.'

Their eyes met again.

Arridia swallowed. 'So, will you go back to Northold today?'

Nip smiled and shook his head. 'I figured I'd hang around. I didn't like the sound of witchcraft in Taurmaline.'

A spark of mischief crept into her own smile. 'I thought you didn't need to defend me and Joss anymore?'

'I'm here to guard the horse.' He reached up and stroked Freckle's neck.

'Hey,' Arridia grumbled.

'It's a good horse.' Nip's face broke into a grin and Arridia responded in kind with a shake of her head.

'Yes, she is.' She studied Nip's face. He was about eight years older than her, but lines barely touched his tanned skin. He kept his curly hair much shorter now than he had as a child. It was hard to resist the urge to touch it. 'Why did you never marry?'

A surprised laugh burst from him, and she blushed.

Nip shrugged. 'I was waiting for the right person.' His expression grew serious. 'I did have a relationship with a widow for several years. We filled a hole in each other's lives and I helped provide for her children. I cared for her but was never in love with her. We drifted apart, and she married again. A good man. I... I'm not sure if you knew that.'

She shook her head, prodding and exploring her emotions, not surprised when she stirred a touch of jealousy. Nip had always been very private, even when sparing time for an annoying child like her. 'I didn't. I'm glad you had someone though, while you were waiting for me to catch you up.'

His eyes widened, and her embarrassment deepened. What a stupid thing to say. She rubbed at her face, hiding behind her hand. As much as she understood of his feelings through her *knowing*, she knew how delicate emotion could be, how easy it was to ruin its song and send it into discord.

A flare of light heralded Azrael, and Arridia let the air out of her lungs. Her relief was short-lived. The little spirit's frantic loops suggested trouble.

'Arridia, Doroquael has been looking for you! Joss is in big trouble.'

'What kind of trouble? Is he hurt?'

Azrael pulsed. 'They need you to get back to your room.'

'Is Dierra there?'

'No.' Azrael dipped lower. 'She's out searching for you.'

Arridia felt a moment of guilt for having given her the slip. 'Tell her to meet me.'

Nip put away the brush and snatched up his sword, following Arridia out of the stable. Azrael vanished through an open window, but Arridia waited until she reached the courtyard before breaking into a run. She slowed to a more dignified pace as they reached the castle keep, Nip staying a respectful distance behind her. It really grated on her that he was acting like a servant. She reached her room at the same time as Dierra.

'What's going on?' her cousin demanded.

'We're about to find out.' Arridia tried the door handle and found it unlocked. Several scenarios had flashed through her mind on her way here, none of them had been what was before her. Scarlett and Lucien sat at her desk, the prince looking furious, the princess red-eyed and sniffling. Joss sat next to her bed, his face blackening from a hefty punch. Alikan stood at the centre of the room, arms folded, the two fire-spirits hovering behind him.

Dierra let out a laugh at the sight of Joss. 'Whose daughter did you get caught with...' Her words faltered as realisation dawned.

Joss leapt to his feet. 'Rids, before you get angry, let me explain.'

It wasn't anger she felt, just a deep, hollow disappointment. Joss saw it on her face, almost crumpling from man to boy before her eyes. He quickly recounted what had happened, Scarlett interjecting to back him up. Arridia kept glancing at Lucien. It was hard to tell what the proud prince was thinking, and with so much turmoil in the room, she dared not open up her *knowing*.

Dierra swore, tactlessly gawping at the royal siblings.

'What should we do, Rids?' Joss held his hands out towards her. 'Should Scarlett and I make a run to Chem? I was thinking maybe even Snowhold.'

'It's a shame you didn't think before,' Lucien muttered.

Arridia drew in a breath, projecting calm. 'Who else knows?'

It was Scarlett who answered. 'We can't be sure. Perhaps our parents, maybe mine and Eleanor's ladies-in-waiting.'

'I'd like to tell Temerran,' Lucien spoke up.

'He should know,' Arridia agreed. 'But he can't get involved.'

She felt everyone's eyes on her as she crossed to the window. No matter what they did, their parents were going to go mad. Eleanor had manipulated exactly the scenario their mother and father had warned them against all their lives. She regarded her brother and Scarlett. The two of them had their eyes locked across the room. Arridia tried to consider how her grandmother would handle this. She turned to Joss.

'First, what have you learnt from this?'

Joss sat back, his mouth open. It was their mother's favourite teaching tool, one that had worked throughout their childhood.

'Go on,' Alikan prompted.

Joss squirmed a little. 'To think with your head, not your—'

Alikan coughed loudly.

'Heart!' Joss glared at his friend, his cheeks flushing. 'I was going to say heart!'

'Nothing wrong with thinking with your heart,' Nip said quietly.

Arridia bit her lower lip, then shook herself and approached her brother. 'Your heart is a wonderful part of you, Joss, but you need to listen to your head. And to your sister.'

'I know.' He scowled. 'You warned me.'

Arridia held up a hand. 'That doesn't help. Tell me again, why did you offer to marry Scarlett?'

'To save her,' he answered at once.

'To save her.' Arridia's eyebrows drew together. 'How would that save her? You'd be taking her from a loveless marriage, but for what? Another of the same? She deserves better than that, as do you.'

'I... But...' Joss's mouth opened and closed. 'But I would treat her well.'

Arridia crouched before him and held his eyes. 'And would you allow her the freedom to love who she wished? Or would you keep her captive like a man of Elden? Think with your heart for me, Joss. Why did you ask Scarlett to marry you?'

'Because I couldn't bear for her to be unhappy. The thought of someone hurting her makes me furious! Because I won't let her be treated like property. Because she's clever, thoughtful, brave, beautiful, and I love her.'

The room was silent, but for a 'whoop' from Azrael.

Joss stared at her, breathing hard.

Arridia turned to Lucien. 'Does that satisfy you?'

Lucien nodded, although there was no smile. Beside him, Scarlett's eyes were bright.

Arridia raised her chin a little. 'Princess, does that satisfy you?'

Scarlett nodded, standing to rush across the room to Joss, but Lucien grabbed her arm to hold her back.

Arridia stood.

'What are we going to do about this mess, though?' Dierra asked.

'Joss.' Arridia regarded her brother. 'You are going to have to face the consequences of your actions.'

'He can't marry Eleanor!' Scarlett cried.

'I agree.' Arridia looked from Alikan to Lucien. 'But they have to take responsibility and deal with it. They should tell your father the truth.'

Joss choked. 'What? Bractius will kill me or make me marry Eleanor!'

Lucien nodded. 'Riddi is right. It's the best way.'

'No.' Scarlett rounded on her brother.

Arridia called power to her hands to quiet the room and get their attention. 'We tell Bractius the truth. But we offer him a solution.'

'What solution?' Joss demanded.

'Trust me and listen.' Arridia told them her plan. There were objections and a long list of concerns, but they all had to reluctantly agree. Arridia turned to Lucien. 'Will you get us an audience with your father as soon as possible?'

'Of course.'

Arridia stepped closer to Nip, stretching up on her toes to whisper close to his ear, 'Would you please go to the stables just in case? If Azra comes to you, have as many horses ready as you can.'

Nip gave a slight bow and slipped out of the room ahead of them.

Arridia's fingers curled into fists. Was she doing the right thing? It was hard to be sure. What she did know was her mother was going to go mad.

***

Joss's face was pale, and he didn't say a word as they waited outside the audience chamber. They'd gone to the private entrance, avoiding the gaze of the other petitioners who awaited the king. Scarlett played with the cuff of her sleeve, not looking at her brother who sat with his spine straight and stiff. Alikan stood beside Joss, occasionally rising onto his toes to stretch his calf muscles. Even Dierra had run out of small talk and leaned against the wall, frequently regarding Arridia.

This was going to change all their lives onto a path they hadn't intended.

The door opened, Joss and Scarlett both flinched.

'Stay out of sight,' Arridia warned the fire-spirits. 'I don't want the king to feel threatened.'

The steward invited them in, his eyebrows rose as he watched them troop past.

Bractius remained seated on his throne. He examined their faces, their posture, tilting his head to one side as he observed Joss's black eye. His eyes settled on his son. All of them took to one knee, heads bowed.

Bractius grunted. 'So formal, children. I take it you have come to ask that I let Joss and Arridia go to the Fulmers?'

'No, your majesty.' Lucien stood, and gestured for the rest of them to follow suit. 'We have something important, something bad, to bring to your attention.'

'Really?' The king leaned forward. 'Tell me.'

'It's a matter of utmost privacy.'

Bractius waved a hand and the steward and two guards bowed and left the room.

Lucien stepped aside. 'I will let Joss and Scarlett tell it.'

Arridia forced herself to breathe slowly. She opened up her *knowing* very briefly. The king was puzzled, intrigued, and only a little concerned. It seemed unlikely he knew anything of what his other daughter was up to. Arridia withdrew her *knowing* and met Lucien's eyes. She nodded ever so slightly, and he returned the gesture.

'What happened to your eye, boy?' Bractius asked with amusement.

Joss cleared his throat, and Arridia had to admire the way his gaze never wavered. 'His Highness happened to my eye, your majesty. And I thoroughly deserved it.'

Scarlett swallowed, lifting her fingers to her mouth as Joss told of what had happened on the night of their victory celebration.

'What?' Bractius bellowed, his face red. 'You defiled my daughter!' He leapt off the throne and grabbed Joss by the throat. Scarlett screamed. Joss didn't back away. He didn't call his power or even raise his hands to defend himself. A surge of pride ran through Arridia's fear. Alikan had his hand near his sword, his fingers twitching. Dierra's eyes were wide as she looked from the suffocating Joss to Arridia.

'Let him speak a moment, Father.' Lucien's voice was soft, but it contained the command of a bard.

Bractius slowly let Joss go and took a step back, rubbing at his greying beard.

Joss reached up to touch his bruised throat. His voice was hoarse. 'Your majesty, I acted like a fool without thinking, but my intention was only ever to protect Scarlett.' He got quickly down on one knee. 'Your majesty, I ask your permission to marry Scarlett—'

'Scarlett!' Bractius exploded, spittle flying from his mouth. 'Is one of my daughters not enough? You will marry Eleanor! It may very well have been some misguided trick, but you will not dishonour her further.'

Arridia forced herself to stay calm and calling her *knowing* projected it outward.

Lucien glanced at her. 'Father, please let Joss finish.'

Joss's chest rose and fell several times before he could speak. 'Your majesty. If you allow me to marry Scarlett, I will be yours. I will serve Lucien willingly as his sorcerer, as my father was yours. I'll reside here and be yours to command. I will devote myself to protecting your son, Scarlett, and Elden.'

Bractius narrowed his eyes, regarding Joss and then Lucien. Arridia felt her heart flutter. In saving her brother, she was chaining him, at least for the many years until Lucien took the throne.

The king shook his head. 'That's all very well, but what of Eleanor? No one will have her now.'

Arridia's nostrils flared, and she gritted her teeth, but her voice was pleasant as she stepped forward to speak. 'No one need know. And if she has fallen pregnant, then send her to Chem where such things do not matter. In fact, they highly prize a fertile woman there. You wanted one of your daughters here, to strengthen ties in Elden, and the other to give you a stronger foothold in Chem. Send Eleanor to your Merkis, Dalton, or to my aunt in Farport. She might find an excellent match in either place.'

A part of her couldn't help thinking it was better than Eleanor deserved.

Bractius lifted his chin a little as he looked down at her, holding her gaze. Arridia fought her desire to look away. Both Joss and Scarlett held their breath.

'Hmm.' Bractius turned and stepped slowly toward his throne. 'Your suggestion has merit.' He sat, his eyes travelling over them all, lingering longest on Joss. 'Very well. It shall be so.'

Scarlett gasped, then ran forward to kiss her father's cheek. 'Thank you!'

'Don't thank me yet.' Bractius glared at her and Joss. 'There will be punishments for your sister and for Joss.'

Joss swallowed but nodded.

'You may leave.' Bractius waved a hand toward them. 'But make sure you can be summoned to me quickly.'

They all bowed and retreated to the door.

'Lucien.'

The prince halted, and Arridia turned with him.

Bractius leaned back against his throne. 'Thank you for bringing this to my attention. You handled it well.'

Lucien bowed. 'Thank you, Father.'

Once outside, Dierra and Scarlett started talking at once, the excited fire-spirits flying out of a torch to join them. Scarlett hugged her bemused brother, smiling at Joss.

Joss didn't smile. He met Arridia's eyes. They'd saved him from marrying a conniving, dangerous girl, but he was no longer a Raven. He was the prince's sorcerer.

Chapter Seventeen

Dia, Fulmer Island.

Dia splashed water on her face to rinse off the oat and marigold scrub. She dried herself and sat staring into the soapy bowl, watching the few bubbles burst. She realised she was hunched over, and straightened up, twisting to look to where her husband slept quietly. He seemed more peaceful today.

There was a commotion out in the hall; raised voices.

'Woah, your mother's resting.' Heara was unusually firm, considering who she was talking to.

'I'll deal with this myself, then.' Kesta sounded furious.

With a sigh, Dia stood and hurried across to the door, Arrus stirred but thankfully didn't wake.

'What's wrong?' Dia asked as she opened the door.

Kesta waved a tiny message scroll. 'This has come from Alikan! He says Bractius won't let the children leave court to see their grandfather unless Jorrun returns there. Bractius is worried by this sudden appearance of witchcraft.'

'As am I,' Dia said quietly. 'But our message obviously hasn't reached Taurmaline yet. He may change his mind when he hears of Geladan.'

Kesta subsided a little, but her skin was still flushed. 'I'm going to *walk*, get word to Azrael, I should have done so immediately.'

Dia shook her head and raised a hand. 'Not until we've decided the best course of action.' She turned to Heara. 'Who are we waiting on?'

Heara raised her eyebrows. 'Chem and Elden. But it will be a while until they can get here.'

Kesta shifted her weight from one foot to the other, her jaw clenched.

'We can't wait,' Dia said.

Kesta's eyes lit at once.

'Heara, clear the great hall for a council, get together all the *walkers* and chieftains who have made it here. Vilnue can speak for Elden, Cassien, Jorrun, and you, Kesta, shall have to speak for Chem and the Ravens.'

While Heara rushed off to make arrangements, Kesta lingered to regard her mother. 'How are you doing, are you okay?'

Dia let some of the poise fall away from her posture. 'I'm managing, my honey. Let me just tidy my hair, then I shall be with you and we'll decide the best way to protect the children – and all of us.'

She stepped into the room and let the door close behind her. Arrus was sitting up in bed.

'I'm guessing you've already decided what to do.'

She smiled at him, leaning back in her chair at the dressing table. 'I have. But as ever, I need to hear if there is a better way.' She picked up her comb. 'I hope there is. Mine is not a good plan.'

The bed creaked as he moved to the edge of it and swung his legs out. 'Not good as in you don't think it will work, or not good as in it will be unpleasant to implement?'

Dia swallowed, and a little shiver of painful emotion ran through her body. He knew her so well. It was hard not to think of him no longer being here. She wanted desperately not to tarnish the time they had. She tensed. It was likely Geladan would make that time even shorter. There was more than a chance he might even outlive her.

'It will not be easy, or pleasant, to implement,' she said quietly. She ran the comb through her grey-streaked hair and Arrus padded over to stand behind her.

'Let me.'

It had been a long while since Arrus had arranged her hair for her, but his fingers were sure and gentle as he divided it into small plaits and pinned it into place. When he'd finished, he moved around to look at her.

'Beautiful, as always.'

Dia scowled and flapped a hand at him, although a little flush of pleasure touched her face. 'You'd better get dressed quickly if you don't want to be late for this council.'

It relieved Dia how easily Arrus dressed himself, though she helped him with his boots. When she handed him his sword belt, his eyes shone, and he buckled it about his thinning waist. Neither of them mentioned the fact Dia had bored another hole into the leather for him.

The great hall was a buzz of excited and concerned voices. Milaiya and Vivess were organising refreshments. Jorrun sat at the high table beside Worvig and Vilnue; Heara standing before them and gesticulating animatedly. Cassien was quiet at the head of a lower table with Catya and the red-headed tribeswoman, Dysarta. Dia hesitated at the sight of the monstrous-looking Rakinya. They'd exchanged a few polite words yesterday, her *knowing* showing her an honest and earnest creature with a deep capacity for empathy.

Her eyes met those of her dear friend, Everlyn, who sat among the other *walkers*, younger Eidwyn at her side. Everlyn gave her an anxious smile, and Dia nodded.

Her heart contracted at one significant absence; she knew she would miss Temerran deeply today. Sion of the Borrows was here for the northern islands. Once Temerran's second mate, he'd stayed in the Fulmers to be with a Fulmer woman of Seal Hold. Sion would have to do.

The talking in the room faded to just a few conversations as Dia approached her seat at the high table. Arrus pulled out her chair for her before sitting beside her, exchanging a nod with his brother.

'Where's Kesta?' Dia asked Jorrun in concern. She had visions of her daughter rowing herself across the sea to Elden.

'She's making another check of the Hold's defences,' Jorrun replied. 'She'll be but a moment.'

Milaiya ushered out the islanders who'd finished setting water and ale on the tables, then took her seat beside Worvig. Vivess took a last glance around and was about to close the solid doors, when Kesta strode in, Siveraell at her shoulder, the spirit's blue eyes large and fierce. Dia straightened up, blinking rapidly, her soul aching in her chest. Her daughter moved with determination, strength in every atom of her small frame. Kesta was fire, Kesta was the heart of the islands; if anyone could save the children, Dia was sure it would be her. Pride in her daughter made her raise her chin, and Dia stood as Kesta took her place beside Jorrun.

'My people.' She let her gaze travel around the room, meeting as many eyes as she could. 'My dear friends. As you know, we face a threat like never before. An army approaches with the capability of wiping out the islands, all our four lands. We have no choice but to face them. Today, we must decide where, and how.'

Dia sat, relaxing her muscles and opening her mind to possibilities. Several hands raised at once, and Arrus took on his role of selecting who would speak. When he grew tired, Worvig stepped in.

Kesta stood suddenly. Her face was pale, but there were red spots high on her cheeks. She looked down at Jorrun, and he reached out to take her hand. Dia clasped her hands together tightly in her lap. Her daughter was shaking, and Dia doubted it was from fear.

Kesta drew in a breath and bit at her lower lip before speaking. She addressed the entire hall. 'We are deeply touched, and grateful, that none of you have even suggested anything other than protecting our children. We realise that this is bigger than that, that Geladan and this Jderha won't rest until all *fire-walkers*, perhaps even all fire-spirits, are no more. However...' She turned to Dia. 'We can't expect so many to risk themselves in our fight.

'We fought hard to free Chem, to protect its people. The Borrows still haven't recovered from the devastation of the necromancer's attack years ago, but they have started to heal. Elden... well, Elden still has a little way to go. But we can't lose everything we have struggled so hard for. We can't see innocent people dragged into this fight.' She squeezed Jorrun's hand. 'We intend to go out to face the Geladanian fleet, with only those who willingly volunteer.'

Before Dia could respond, Catya leapt to her feet and slammed her fist on the table. 'Snowhold is with you.'

Both Cassien and Sion quickly followed suit.

'I'll go with you,' Cassien said.

'The Borrow fleet is yours,' Sion growled.

Worvig and Heara stood at the same time, Heara grinned. 'You're not leaving me out.'

Vilnue stood tentatively with a wince. 'I can't really speak for Elden, but this old sword arm is yours.'

There was a scrape of chairs and voices rose as those in the room offered their assistance. Dia sat with her head bowed. Slowly, she got to her feet.

'Silence!' Arrus bellowed. 'Be seated for the Icante.'

The room hastened to obey, Kesta the last to sit.

Dia took in a deep breath and let it out slowly. 'We cannot face the Geladanian fleet, not at sea.'

There were several cries of protest, Sion the loudest. They had spent the last fourteen years increasing and improving their ships, all four lands sharing knowledge and resources. A sea battle was what they'd all expected.

'Siveraell.' Dia gestured elegantly toward the fire-spirit.

Siveraell drifted closer to her, growing a little in size. 'The Icante is right. Meeting them at ssea puts you at a disadvantage on at least two counts. First, the sea-spirits have said they will not fight with you, they refuse to allow themselves to be held captive, but that doessn't mean Jderha does not already have many enslaved in her service. Even with powerful magic users, your ships could quickly be decimated and there would be no escape, save drowning. You would also make it difficult for your strongest allies to fight beside you.'

'Which allies?' a chieftain called out, clearly deciding whether to be offended or not.

Dia smiled to herself.

Bright light flared in the hall, several startled magic users calling up their power. Nearly a hundred fire-spirits emerged from the torches and fireplace, setting up a perimeter around the room.

'Settle down,' Dia told the humans. 'My daughter is right, we cannot allow innocent people to get caught up in this, nor undo the good work of years and the sacrifices made to get to where we are. But we cannot allow Geladan and Jderha to win. Of course, we will fight, but we will choose our battle ground carefully.'

'Where?' Chieftain Urcan asked.

'You mean to use Fulmer Island,' Jorrun said quietly.

Dia nodded. 'It is the only fair place to do so. The island will have to be evacuated, as many people and domestic animals as possible taken by ship to Chem. We shall also warn the wild animals to move as far from Fulmer Hold as they can.'

'Will they not attack the south coast of the island?' Vilnue asked.

'They'll head straight for the children,' Catya said with certainty.

'Fulmer Hold has the best defence,' Jorrun nodded. 'Although any who stood with us here would be trapped.'

'Fulmer Hold should be a retreat,' Heara said excitedly, leaning forward to catch Dia's eyes. 'We fight out on the island, set traps, keep the Hold for a last stand if we need it.'

Dia felt eyes on her, and she met the exceedingly dark ones of Edon Ra. She couldn't help the shiver that travelled her spine. 'I had hoped to spare as much of the island as I could,' Dia admitted. 'But that is an excellent option.'

'It gives us a chance to each play to our strengths,' Cassien agreed. 'Espionage, scouting, sailing, magic, or weapons. We fight together, but in our own ways.'

Several excited discussions broke out around the room. Vilnue raised a hand to get Arrus's attention, following proper protocol.

'Go on,' Arrus prompted.

Vilnue had to raise his voice. 'What of Elden?'

Dia met his eyes. Vilnue might, in theory, work for Bractius, but she trusted and relied on him more than many of her own chieftains. 'We assume the Geladanians will head for us, but we should take precautions in case that isn't so. We will of course provide them with magic users.' Kesta protested, but a look from Dia stopped her. 'Vilnue, you may not be aware that King Bractius has refused the children leave to come here unless Jorrun returns to him first. A harsh but defensive move on his part. I think when Bractius learns Jderha is coming for the children, he will change his mind quickly. We cannot expect Jorrun not to be with Arridia and Joss, but I will send the king someone strong and reliable in his place. We must also ask the Ravens to send who they can without leaving Chem defenceless.'

'I'll ask my sister,' Jorrun offered. 'Although she will want to come here.'

Dia nodded her thanks, then turned to look down at the table to her left. 'Everlyn, I would like you to go to Elden and protect its capital.'

Everlyn froze, her face colouring as she held Dia's gaze. 'No, Icante.'

Dia's mouth fell open a little. Everlyn had never said no to her before. 'Eve, I need someone strong, someone level-headed with experience.'

'I'm honoured by how much you trust me,' Everlyn replied. 'But I will fight here, for the Fulmers.'

Dia regarded her friend and fellow *walker*, not missing the scars that ran across her face and down her neck, scars she'd received defending the hold, defending her grandchildren. If anyone had earned the right to choose where to stand, it was Everlyn. 'Okay, my friend,' Dia said softly. 'Okay.'

'Should I go?' Eidwyn asked. Her voice was strained; she didn't want to go either, but the younger woman put her own desires aside. It was not a cowardly choice. If Geladan came to Elden first, she'd practically be alone against a goddess until help arrived from Chem.

'Yes, please.' Dia smiled at her. 'We'll get some of Joss's Ravens to stay in Taurmaline as well. Okay.' Dia raised her voice. 'Sion, Worvig, Cassien, and Vilnue, coordinate ships for an evacuation. I need each chieftain and *walker* to organise the holds. We'll leave a small defence at each initially, but every hold except Fulmer will be abandoned rather than lose lives unnecessarily. Heara, start getting word out to the villages and farms.'

'The drakes can help with that,' Siveraell offered. 'Kesta, would you like me to go to Elden to warn Arridia and Joss?'

'Please.' Kesta pressed her fingers to her mouth. 'I was going to *walk* and speak to Azra, but if you'd tell Bractius, there's no way the king will dare to say no.'

Jorrun frowned but said nothing.

'We have a few more things to sort out.' Dia sighed and turned to Catya. 'Catya, I'd like to see you and your wife, and Edon Ra, in my room. You also.' She nodded toward Kesta and Jorrun. 'And Siv, just for a moment before you go to Elden.'

Arrus pushed himself up, his arms shaking a little as he stood. As much as she wanted to help, Dia waited beside him until he was ready to follow, then headed out of the hall and up the stairs to her room. Despite the spacious size and the long window looking out over the sea, the room felt crowded, especially when Edon Ra ducked in beneath the stone lintel.

There weren't enough chairs for all of them, but Kesta and Jorrun sat on the bed beside Arrus. Dia pulled her chair around to face Catya, who had perched on her desk, her wife beside her. There was something very warm, earthy, about Dysarta, something compelling; Dia could see why Catya had been so drawn to the tribeswoman. Edon Ra sank to the floor beside his friend to sit cross-legged. The large *snow-beast* waited patiently as Dia studied his face.

'Can I get anyone a drink?' Arrus asked.

'I would very much like some water,' Edon Ra replied.

Jorrun rose to help Arrus, but the Silene waved him aside.

'I'm sorry I haven't had much time to converse with you since you arrived yesterday,' Dia turned from the Rakinya to Catya. 'But a lot has fallen upon these shores in the last turn of the world.'

'It is no coincidence that so much has come together here, at the same time,' Edon Ra said.

Dia narrowed her eyes and breathed out slowly. 'Forgive me, Edon Ra, but like many I am wary of the idea of prophecy. It infuriates me, the position my family has been put in because of the paranoia of a creature that thinks itself a god.'

'What is a god?' Edon Ra asked slowly, his large, dark eyes fixed on Dia. Siveraell drifted closer to Kesta. 'Each culture, each religion, has a different idea of what their god must be.

'In Chem, the land was once ruled by chaotic, powerful beings of an elemental kind, ones which you now know of as Demons. Legends of their deeds became legends of gods.

'In Elden, they sought for benign, distant creators to watch over them, to explain the unexplainable, to turn to when there was no hope or comfort. Both the Borrows and you of the Fulmers put your faith in what is real. The power of nature, of the elements, and of your own souls.

'In the far south, in Geladan, there is a being who lives forever, who judges, commands, creates... to them, a god. To you...' He shrugged. 'What is a god, truly?'

Dia chuckled. 'You are a philosopher, Edon Ra. But it does not make you a true prophet.'

Both Catya and Dysarta bristled, but Edon held up his hands. 'I only know what I see. I cannot say from whence it comes. And yes, many times it is vague and only makes sense when fitted to an event after it occurs. Perhaps we can all say that of our dreams. But we are here, Icante. We are here.'

Dia tried not to show the uncomfortable, sliding feeling deep in her gut, like a snake was rising to her throat. They were here, and just when they were needed.

'All I know of gods is that they can die.' Kesta's voice was tight, her fists clenched in her lap. 'They have threatened those I love before and paid for it.'

Dia steepled her fingers and put them to her lips. 'This Jderha has lived for many years. She's powerful. She may be conceited, but I find it hard to believe she is stupid. If she truly believes one of us will kill her, why come here? Why not stay where she is safe?'

'We don't know for sure she is coming,' Jorrun said. 'She could just be sending her army.'

'Oh, no.' Edon Ra shook his head. 'She is coming. She is coming because you have been betrayed.' He turned his gaze from Dia to Jorrun. 'Someone has betrayed you.'

Chapter Eighteen

Rosa; Kingdom of Elden

Rosa froze, eyes wide in the darkness. She strained her ears, peering across the ward. Nothing moved among the vegetable beds. The silvery light of the waxing moon was peaceful, enthralling. She'd been lucky it was at the right phase, though the day had passed slowly as she quelled her nervous impatience. Rosa forced her feet to move again, her fingers brushing the stone of the Raven Tower. She hadn't dared bring a light with her, no one could know what she was doing.

Rosa knelt awkwardly. Her aging joints protested as she located the spot she needed. She unhooked her small trowel from her chatelaine, digging at the stubbornly hard earth, and checked now and then with her fingers. She hissed when she discovered the first, bile rising to her throat. She drew her dagger from her boot to cut free both feet of the long-dead raven and tucked them into the pouch of her apron.

Jorrun was so sentimental, he always buried any of the ravens that died at the foot of the tower.

It took nearly an hour to get all the feet she needed, constantly stopping to look and listen, nerves on edge. When she'd finished, she hastily pushed the earth back into place with both her hands and the small trowel. Rosa followed the curved wall of the tower back to its arched doorway, feeling a little of her tension fall away in the safety of its torchlight and familiar stairway.

She headed up to Jorrun's supply room and tipped the raven's feet out onto the central table. The single lantern showed the other objects she'd gathered together. Tiny precious stones refracted the light. Amethyst, labradorite, amber, and… she smiled to herself, tourmaline. There were also piles of herbs, some fresh, some dried and taken from the jars that filled the room's shelves. Clove seeds, coriander, dill, and rosemary.

Rosa picked up one of the white velvet pouches she'd hand sewn that day and dropped each ingredient in. When she'd finished all the pouches, she set them in a circle on the table and, covering her face in her hands, breathed in and out several times.

Would it work?

Her hands slipped into her lap and she straightened her spine. It wouldn't work If she didn't believe. She drew in a breath and spoke the incantation, repeating it again and again, each time trying to draw strength from deeper within herself. She stood, breathing hard, and gathered the white pouches into her apron pocket. She picked up the lantern and descended the stairs, snuffing out the torches as she passed.

She glanced up at the hold. Light danced behind the leaded window of Tantony's study. Rosa swallowed, then grabbed up her skirt and hurried to the gates. The warriors on guard looked surprised but didn't hesitate to let her through. No one seemed to stir in the outer circle, and she didn't slow her pace as she approached the closed outer gate. As she drew close, the gates yawned open.

'Do you need an escort, my lady?' a curious guard asked.

'No, thank you.'

Rosa pulled the hood of her cloak up over her head as she hurried towards the small wharf. A man was waiting for her, and he stood at her approach, unwinding the rope that held the boat in place.

'My lady.'

'Kurghan.' She touched his arm as she passed him, stepping down into the boat and bracing herself as it shifted beneath her.

Kurghan released the last loop of hemp and pushed them away from the wooden pier. Rosa sat quickly and Kurghan placed himself on the seat opposite, taking up the oars. She saw the tension in the carpenter's muscles, in the set of his jaw. She looked down at her own hands, at the lines and wrinkles in her skin. They were not young anymore, but she refused to be old. Her fingers dug in her apron pocket and she took out a narrow jar.

'Um, I made this for you. For your joints.'

She didn't tell him she'd used witchcraft.

'You're very kind, lady Rosa,' Kurghan said as he rowed.

Rosa placed the jar down in the boat between them.

They made a little small talk, then fell into silence as Kurghan rowed her across the lake towards the castle of Taurmaline. Blue and red blossomed on the horizon as they drew close to the docks. Rosa straightened up, scanning the ships. The sleek *Undine* was easy to spot; it meant Temerran was still there, and the children were too.

Kurghan came up gently against the wharf and looped a rope around one of the posts, and another through a metal ring encased in the stone wall.

'Should I come into the castle?' Kurghan asked, his forehead wrinkled in concern.

Rosa shook her head. 'Best you not be associated with me.'

Kurghan's bearded face crumpled in concern, but he held out his arm and helped Rosa up onto the path. 'Take care, my Lady.'

Rosa nodded, checking the contents of her apron pocket before realising she was doing so. She made a quick scan of the docks. Already the fishermen were arriving, testing their tools and supplies before setting off for a long day out on the lake. Rosa wrapped her arms around her body, turning her gaze to the castle. There was no choice but to go in by one of the guarded entrances.

'You can do this,' she told herself.

The guards at the outer gate either recognised her, or didn't see her as a threat, barely glancing her way as she passed through the dock gates. She followed the winding roads between the houses, taking the steep steps up to the higher levels of the city where the castle stood.

For many years, including much of her childhood, this castle had been where she'd lived. Sometimes it had been a home, but in the later years, it had been a necessary shelter in which she had used what little skill she had to survive.

She headed for the kitchen entrance, knowing it was the way through which the most strangers went unnoticed. One of the kitchen maids halted to stare at her, before bobbing in a hasty curtsey. Rosa muttered a mild curse; she'd hoped to go unrecognised. She chose the servant's passageways rather than the main corridors of the castle, ducking out of the way in a luckily empty room when she heard someone else on the stairs. By the time she reached the guest rooms, her heart was pounding and her breath coming fast through her mouth.

Rosa steadied herself, her hand reaching down toward her apron pocket. She had no idea which room she needed. She swallowed, and let her emotions go, all her fear, all her anxiety, and frustration. She hoped she was loud enough.

'Arridia,' she whispered. 'Azrael, can you hear me?'

A torch guttered, and she drew in a sharp breath.

There was a scrape of a bolt being drawn back. The door creaked open just a crack.

'Aunt Rosa!'

Arridia stepped out into the hall. She looked tired, her young skin ashen rather than dark, her beautiful, mismatched eyes red veined, and her long black hair in wild disarray.

'Oh, Riddi.' Rosa's hand moved to her chest. 'I have something to confess to you. I've been very foolish.'

Arridia's eyes widened. 'Well, you're not the only one. You'd better come in.'

Rosa followed Arridia into the guest room, closing the door slowly behind her. Azrael flew toward her to say hello, before retreating to the window. A groan came from the far side of the room and Dierra turned over to rub at her eyes. She was sleeping on a small servant's cot; the curtains pulled back. 'What's happening?'

'Would you like some tea?' Arridia asked, knowing how much Rosa relied on warm herb infusions in any moment of crisis.

'Oh, yes, please.'

'You heard about Joss, then.' Dierra sat up, swinging her legs around to place her feet on the floor. She pulled a sword into her lap and Rosa's mouth fell open. She had learned to keep a dagger under the bed but sleeping with a sword seemed a bit extreme.

'No.' Rosa shook her head. 'What's happened to Joss?'

'A moment.' Arridia gave Dierra a withering look. She called power to her hand and heated the water in the small kettle, before pouring it into a teapot. 'Rosa, what's brought you to Taurmaline so early? Is Tantony well?'

'He is.' She sat on a chair, her hand moving down to the pocket of her apron. 'Arridia, my dear, what do you think of Eldenian witchcraft?'

'What do I think of it?' Arridia frowned. 'It is an ancient form of magic that harnesses nature and the power of the mind, particularly that of women. Why do you ask? Is this to do with the research you carried out with Scarlett and Nip?'

Rosa winced. 'In a way.'

'You're scared,' Arridia said suddenly, hurrying across to her with a mug of steaming tea. 'Has something happened?'

Rosa shook her head. 'Um, not as such. I... well.' Her fingers touched the velvet bags in her pocket. 'I was worried about you and Joss here with an unknown witch, so I've... well, I've been learning.' She drew out one of the velvet pouches. 'I've been learning witchcraft to better understand it, and to work against it. But of course, it's a banned magic in Elden – or was. I have no idea if these will work, but I've made you these for protection.'

Arridia reached out slowly, her fingers barely touching the white fabric. Dierra padded over to lean close.

'It's supposed to ward off bad magic and evil spirits,' Rosa hastily explained. 'Well, I remembered the amulet your father used to wear. He lost it before you were born. I'm probably daft thinking I could make one.'

'No.' Arridia glanced at her and slowly took the pouch. 'It was very thoughtful of you, and... there is power in it.'

'There is?' Rosa sat back, eyes wide.

Arridia smiled. 'There is.' She slipped the pouch into her pocket and handed Rosa her tea. 'I think you should continue to learn everything you can. We think whoever it is has been capturing earth-elementals, but we don't know who or why yet.'

'I don't imagine they have good motives,' Dierra muttered.

Rosa curled her fingers around her tea. 'I've made enough pouches for Lucien and the girls, and of course for the four of you.' She dug in her pocket with her free hand and pulled out a white pouch for Dierra.

'Wow, thanks.' Dierra took it at once, feeling the fabric. She grimaced, and Rosa guessed she'd found the raven claw. 'Not sure we should give anything to Eleanor, though.'

'Why?' Rosa looked from Dierra to Arridia.

Arridia paled, it was Dierra who told Rosa everything that had happened. The blood drained from Rosa's face and hands. She pulled her cup closer to her chest, drawing in the small source of warmth.

'Oh, that silly, kind-hearted boy,' Rosa exclaimed. 'What have your mother and father said?'

Arridia winced. 'Nothing yet. I'm hoping to persuade the king to permit me to leave for the Fulmers today to see grandfather; Lucien said he'd speak for me.'

Rosa snorted. 'He'll let you, or I shall speak to him. I'll remind him how much he owes your parents and the Icante. Mysterious witches or no, he has no right to keep you here.'

Dierra shrugged. 'He has some right according to the trade and peace treaties. And he is the king.'

Rosa and Arridia's eyes met, and they laughed, realising they wore the same expression on their faces.

'I was going to head straight back to Tantony,' Rosa said. 'But under the circumstances, I'll wait and see how you get on with Bractius today. Perhaps Kurghan and I can get a lift across the lake with Temerran.'

Arridia's eyebrows drew together in a frown. 'I was hoping Tem would stay, to help Joss and Lucien. Although they have Ali, I guess.'

Rosa felt a moment of deflating hurt. She might not be a warrior or powerful sorcerer, but she liked to think she wasn't useless; and old as he was getting, Tantony was still strong and clever.

Azrael flared suddenly, Rosa raised an arm, blinking rapidly to protect her eyes.

'Ssomething comes!'

Arridia shielded, Dierra called power to her hands.

A large fire-spirit emerged from the fireplace. Azrael gave a squeal and shrank back, making himself small in deference. Rosa dropped her teacup.

Only Arridia remained calm, a smile touching her face. 'Uncle Siveraell.'

'Dear child,' the elder drake hissed. 'I am sorry to say I come with dire warning. Azrael, go at once and fetch Doroquael and Joss. We must go to the king.'

Chapter Nineteen

Temerran; Kingdom of Elden

'Well, it's a mess and no mistake.' Temerran turned from the red sun that rose over the distant fields to regard Lucien. The prince was leaning on the stone wall of the high walkway, looking older than he was. 'Your sister has learnt all your mother's tricks, and then some.'

Lucien's face reddened, and he straightened, holding Temerran's eyes unblinking.

'I'm sorry.' Temerran held up a hand. 'I shouldn't speak so of the queen.'

Lucien sighed and deflated a little. 'No, you're right. I'm not blind to my mother's past, and my father isn't as ignorant of the truth as he pretends. I fear this... incident... has played into his hands and so Eleanor and my mother will get away with more than they ought.'

Temerran raised an eyebrow. 'Although the alternative would force Joss into marrying Eleanor, rather than Scarlett. I wish you had come to me, Luce.'

'Would you have done things differently?' Lucien asked in concern.

Temerran sighed. 'No. I think there was no escaping Joss being tied to Taurmaline and Elden after what he did. However, not allowing him and Arridia to visit their grandfather is inexcusable. Bractius is using this sudden emergence of witchcraft to tie a collar about Jorrun's neck. After all these years, I'd have thought your father would trust in Jorrun's friendship. I fear this will destroy it irreparably.'

'I don't think my father has ever trusted.' Lucien's brown eyes were sad. 'Were it not for you and our friends at Northold, I imagine I'd have been shaped the same.'

Temerran reached out and briefly lay his hand on the prince's shoulder. 'A crown is a heavy weight to bear, especially for any with a conscience.'

'And those who do not wish to bear it.' Lucien almost smiled, but quickly grew grave. 'And yet, there is a part of me that wants the position, if only to put things right. My father thinks a benevolent king cannot be a good one, that every kindness must be paid out for a calculated reason.'

Temerran grunted. 'There is something to that, I guess, anyone whose actions affect the lives of others should be wary of consequence.'

'Does the Icante work in such a way?' Lucien held Temerran's gaze, his eyes wide and hopeful.

'Is she thoughtful, careful, and clever? Yes, of course she is. But she is also kind for kindness' sake. And her friends are true ones, not because of her power and status, but because of who she is. But that, Luce, is why the decisions she makes are so painful to her.'

'Painful?'

Temerran nodded, his gaze going back out over the city to the fields beyond. 'It is harder to order a friend to their death, is it not?'

Temerran could feel Lucien studying his face, but he didn't turn or speak, letting the young man find his own thoughts.

'I'd best prepare for speaking to my father.' Lucien broke the silence. 'I'm determined to get Arridia at least to the Fulmers. Will you... are you going to take her?'

'That had been my intention.' Temerran frowned. 'But I'm loathe to leave you and Joss, and there is still our unknown witch. I think perhaps I should stay.' His heart clenched. His best friend needed him, he knew it, but he couldn't bring himself to abandon Lucien.

Lucien drew in a breath. 'I would appreciate it. Do you... If we can't persuade my father, should I use my voice to make him agree?'

Temerran turned around to face the prince, folding his arms across his chest. 'We have discussed the morality of using your bardic skills. Do you think this instance truly warrants it? And what will the consequences be to your father, what will he learn from it?'

Lucien's gaze fell to the flagstones as he considered. 'It would do little harm to him, overall, to let Riddi go, and it would go a way towards limiting the damage to his relationship with the Fulmers.'

'But?'

'But. He would have actually learned nothing himself. And the Fulmers would receive a false impression of who he is.'

'Good,' Temerran replied, then grinned. 'Though I doubt Dia has a false impression of him after all this time, but your thought process is excellent. In this instance, I would recommend persuading him with logic and a sound argument, rather than magic. I—'

Fire flared suddenly and Temerran stepped in front of Lucien, hand on his sword before he realised who it was.

'Azrael.' Lucien smiled. 'Is Riddi ready?'

'No, no, things have changed,' Azrael buzzed. 'You must both come immediately to the king's private audience room. Siveraell is here, there is terrible news!'

'Arrus,' Temerran demanded. 'Is he—?'

'No one is hurt, not yet,' Azrael replied quickly. 'But Geladan is on its way.'

Temerran didn't need telling twice. Not waiting for Lucien, he ran for the door into the castle.

'Get Scarlett!' Lucien ordered the spirit.

Geladan.

Temerran fought to catch his breath. Jderha had been a threat hanging over them for many years, although he had to admit the weight of oppressive danger had lessened over time. His own experience of the fanatical Geladanians had been an intimate one, having fallen in love with their most dangerous assassin. Her name came to his lips, feeling odd there.

'Linea.'

His chest tightened against the aching, hollow void that blossomed within him.

The scuff of a foot reminded him that Lucien was right behind him, and he held the door as they reached the stairs leading down to the more populated parts of the castle. This would change everything, and not in a good way.

Scarlett caught up with them, coming from the other end of the corridor as they approached the king's private room. Arridia, Dierra, Joss, and Alikan were all waiting outside; Joss arguing loudly with the two guards who barred their way.

The doors flew open, the king stood in the doorway, his face pale. 'Let them in and go fetch Merkis Shryn.' He backed into the room and Temerran saw Siveraell hovering above the king's desk, his flames blue-edged and fierce. The spirit wasn't messing about.

'How close are they?' Joss demanded as they crowded into the room. Temerran entered last, closing the door.

It was Siveraell who answered as Bractius retreated to stand behind his chair. 'They are still some days away across the sea, how soon they will arrive it is hard to ssay. We were given warning by the creatures of the deeps, including the sea-spirits.'

'How many ships?' Bractius demanded.

Sivaraell's reply was a quiet hiss. 'At least a dozen.'

Temerran's heart faltered.

Bractius swore and sat down. Scarlett grabbed for Joss's arm. Arridia and Lucien turned to look at each other. One ship full of the southern sorcerers had been terrible, a dozen would be... devastating.

'What's the plan?' Alikan asked.

'The Icante has chosen Fulmer Island as her battle ground. As many as possible will be evacuated.' Siveraell dipped lower, moving closer to Bractius. 'To ensure the Geladanians target the island, Arridia and Joss must be there.'

Bractius paused only a moment before he waved a magnanimous hand. 'Of course, they must be with the protection of their family. What of Elden? There is no guarantee the Geladanians will not attack here.'

'You are right, there is no guarantee.' Sivaraell's eyes burned a dark, almost invisible blue. It was a warning, Temerran hoped for his own sake that the king took it. 'But we will not leave you without protection. The Icante is sending you help from the Fulmers and from Chem.'

'That is kind of her,' the king said through a tight jaw.

Temerran heard Lucien growl quietly in the back of his throat.

Arridia raised her chin. 'May we go at once?'

'They *will* go at once.' Siveraell flared brighter.

'Of course, they must.' Bractius forced a smile. 'But, Joss, you must remember our agreement. As soon as it is safe to do so, you will return here, and marry Scarlett.'

Joss paled but gave a stiff bow.

'I'll arrange your passage,' Lucien offered, looking from Arridia to Alikan.

Temerran's heart constricted. 'Go on the *Undine*. Nolv will take you.'

Arridia pivoted to look at him. 'Nolv?'

Temerran nodded, begging her with his eyes to understand. 'I should stay here to assist his majesty until reinforcements arrive with stronger magical ability than I.'

Temerran didn't miss the narrowing of the king's eyes or the way he looked from his son to him. Was he jealous of their friendship, or threatened by it? Temerran was never sure.

'We must go,' Siveraell prompted.

'Shall I go to Nolv?' Doroquael offered.

'Yes please, tell him to ready to sail and I'll be there as soon as I can,' Temerran replied.

The door rattled open and a flustered Merkis Shryn appeared. 'Your majesty?'

Bractius stood, his poise and authority restored. 'Fetch my advisors, have them here at once.' He turned to his son. 'Say your goodbyes and be back here immediately.'

Lucien bowed, and Temerran stepped aside to allow everyone to exit the room, making sure he left last. 'Would you like me to attend your council?' he asked the king.

Bractius regarded him through narrowed eyes. 'I would welcome your insight. Get your ship underway and return to me here.'

Temerran gave a low bow and hurried to catch up with the others.

'Geladan!' Scarlett announced breathlessly, her arm still linked through Joss's. 'I never thought it would really happen. It was always like some scary old wives' tale.'

'Old wives are worth paying attention to,' Temerran said quietly.

'We must all go to my room briefly.' Arridia looked over her shoulder at them as Azrael streamed ahead. 'Rosa is there.'

They received several curious looks from those they passed on their way to the guest quarters, but with the fire-spirits in tow, no one dared waylay them. Rosa stood, her alarm growing as they all piled into the room.

'Whatever has happened?' she asked, blinking rapidly. 'What was the news?'

'Geladan,' Alikan told her.

'Oh, my goodness!' Rosa almost fell back into her chair. Arridia grabbed Rosa a glass of water, while Dierra filled her in. Temerran smiled fondly at how quickly Rosa gathered herself. 'Well then, we must stop off at Northold and let Tantony know. Oh! But should we go to the Fulmers, or are we needed here?' Rosa looked around at the young Ravens and the royal siblings.

'Rosa, tell them about the pouches while I pack,' Arridia suggested, waving at Dierra to grab her things too.

Doroquael quietly returned from his mission.

Rosa pulled out her velvet protection charms and quickly explained, handing them out to Joss, Alikan, Lucien, and Scarlett. She looked down at the last one in her palm, standing and pivoting in her sensible boots to face Temerran. 'I meant this for Eleanor, but it had best go to you.'

Temerran took it carefully. It tickled against his skin. A warmth came from it that reminded him of the scent of roses on a sunny day. It was as though Rosa had somehow placed some of her kind and loyal soul within. It was a rare a precious gift.

'Thank you, Rosa.'

Joss stepped closer, almost timidly. 'I'd take it as a kindness, Aunt Rosa, if you could watch over Scarlett for me and help her root out this witch.'

Scarlett's eyes glowed and her cheeks flushed. Rosa drew herself up. 'Of course, I will. I shall get straight back to my research and give the young princess all the protection I can.'

'I don't know.' Alikan shook his head. 'With everything else going on, maybe it's best to leave this witch be for now.'

'That might depend on the witch,' Temerran cautioned. 'She may not intend to let things be. Lucien has enough on his plate preparing for Geladan, but I think it prudent to monitor our Eldenian spell-caster and discover their intent. I'll guide and advise Scarlett and Rosa as best I can.'

Alikan didn't seem convinced, but he nodded. 'What of the Ravens at Northold? Should they come with us, or stay? They are mostly novices or inexperienced.'

'I think Faria should stay at Northold to look after the Tower,' Arridia answered quickly. 'The other four we should split between Lucien and Scarlett if we can.'

'I expect Father would rather they were assigned to him.' Lucien winced.

Rosa straightened. 'One of the girls could serve Scarlett as lady-in-waiting and give her both close protection and a confidante in her work.'

'Brilliant idea,' Dierra agreed. 'I'd have liked to have done that.'

'Quickly then.' Siveraell brightened. 'You must be away to Fulmer as soon as may be.'

'I don't like leaving Elden with little protection until others arrive.' Joss looked up at the bright spirit.

Temerran tried not to be insulted by the young man's lack of faith in him, especially knowing he'd been taught better than to judge strength by magical ability.

Siveraell pulsed. 'I will stay here for you, Joss, just for a short while. I travel quickly and can catch you up. But if these two fail and harm comes to you...'

Azrael and Doroquael swelled in size, Doroquael giving a little squeak.

Alikan slapped Joss hard on the shoulder. 'Pack.'

The two of them left the room with Doroquael and Scarlett in tow.

Arridia pushed some of her rumpled clothes into a bag, while Dierra folded hers with care. 'Azra, please tell Nip what's happened. If he can make arrangements for the horses to go back to Northold, he should meet us at the *Undine*, if not he should set out at once with them for Northold and we will pick him up there.'

'I'm not sure you have time to wait for Nip,' Temerran said. 'He'll understand.'

Arridia held his gaze. 'We have time to wait for Nip.'

Temerran gave a small bow.

It took all of ten minutes for Arridia and Dierra to be ready, and they waited impatiently in the hall for the others. From the colour on Joss's cheeks, Temerran guessed the young man had been saying goodbye to Scarlett in as private a manner as he could with Alikan present.

'Are you coming to the docks?' Arridia asked Lucien.

He nodded. 'Of course.'

Temerran realised he was still holding his protective charm. He pulled out the leather thong he wore around his neck, at the end of which was a black pearl in the embrace of a silver woman shaped like the figurehead of the *Undine*. He tied the ribbon of the charm securely to it and tucked it back in his shirt.

With Siveraell once again taking the lead, they made fast progress down to the docks and along the wharves towards where the larger vessels docked. Arridia slowed, twisting to look behind them.

'We're being followed. It's Adrin and another man.'

'Damn him,' Temerran cursed. 'What does he expect to see?'

Nolv was pacing anxiously on the gangplank. As soon as he saw Temerran, he hurried over. 'Captain, yon spirit told me we're t' sail without you to the Fulmers?'

Temerran placed a hand on each of his first mate's shoulders. 'That's so. Get the Icante's grandchildren safely to Fulmer Hold, then return if you can. If they need you there, I trust you to take care of my lady.'

'But, Captain!' Nolv protested. 'The *Undine* can't sail without you.'

'She can and she will.'

'Perhaps you should go.' Lucien's eyebrows drew together in concern.

Temerran's nostrils flared. He could see in the prince's brown eyes that he was trying to be noble, but fear danced there too. He couldn't leave him

Dia, I'm so sorry. I'll be there when I can.

'No, Luce,' he said aloud, watching as the young man's tense shoulders dropped a little. 'I'll stay.'

Azrael gave a squeal and turned a loop in the air. 'Nip made it!'

They spun to see Northold's newly appointed stable master hurrying towards them through the busy docks.

'You best get going,' Temerran prompted.

There was a rush of farewells, Joss giving Scarlett a self-conscious kiss, before shaking Lucien's hand. Arridia hugged the prince.

'I wish I was going with you.' Lucien smiled at her through his anxiety. 'I'd better see you again.'

Arridia nodded, her eyes filling as she cleared her throat and turned to Temerran.

'Give your grandparents my love,' he said.

Arridia reached up and briefly touched his cheek. The sympathy and understanding in her gaze was heart-rending. 'They already have it.'

Alikan gave Temerran a nod before ushering a reluctant Joss up the gangplank, Dierra was already aboard.

'Take care, Captain,' Nolv muttered, before boarding the ship.

Temerran tore his eyes away. There had been too many goodbyes, and he had a sickening feeling there would be many more. A part of him wanted to snatch Lucien and Scarlett up and take them away on the *Undine* with the others so he didn't have to divide his heart and his scant protection. Was he in the right place to make a difference? Only time would tell.

'We'd best get back.'

'Don't you want to see them away?' Scarlett asked in surprise.

'Lucien needs to get back to the king,' he replied.

The truth was, he knew he couldn't watch his ship sailing away without the tears he was holding back escaping.

Adrin had almost reached them, but Siveraell had divined the Merkis was unwanted and flew straight at him. Adrin ducked, crying out as he covered his head. Temerran couldn't help the welcome laugh that gripped him.

'I shall stay hidden,' Siveraell told them as he returned. 'But call me if you have need, and I will keep watch.'

Temerran bowed. 'Thank you, spirit.'

When they drew close to the castle, Scarlett gasped and started to point, but pulled her hand back. 'That's Eleanor and Mother, I'm sure they're watching us.'

Temerran followed her gaze and spotted the colourful cloth of the royal ladies' dresses up on one of the high walkways. It could be a coincidence that brought them out, but the queen would be aware by now that Geladan was on its way.

'What should I do?' Scarlett asked her brother as they approached the king's private audience room. 'I want to be involved in this, not shut away like some delicate ornament.'

'I'll keep you advised at the very least,' he replied. 'But it might serve our hunt for the witch if you seem unobtrusive and innocent.'

'Scarlett!'

They spun on their heels to see Eleanor bearing down on them in a rustle of linen and lace. Her face was flushed, her eyes sparked with fury.

'Scarlett! How dare you steal my future!' Eleanor almost spat her sister's name.

'How dare you try to trap a good man like a whore!' Scarlett snarled back.

Eleanor let out a shriek and flew at her sister, but Siveraell was quickly between them and Eleanor screamed.

'Sisters, enough please, not here,' Lucien implored, glancing down the hall to where two guards watched with open-mouthed intrigue.

'You'll pay for this.' Eleanor's lip curled as she regarded Scarlett. 'You and Joss.' She turned, grabbing up her skirts and fleeing down the hallway.

'You okay?' Lucien asked his sister.

Scarlett nodded, staring after Eleanor.

'I'm not sure what mischief the princess is capable of, but we best ensure Scarlett isn't left alone too much,' Temerran suggested.

'I'll keep an eye when I can,' Siveraell offered. 'In the meantime, I have a king to spy on.' The Elder spirit didn't wait for a reply but vanished at once into a torch.

Chapter Twenty

Kesta; Fulmer Island

Kesta blinked rapidly, the wind stinging her eyes as she searched the sea from the battlement of Fulmer Hold. Two longships moved away from her toward the horizon, their undyed linen sails raised, flying the twin flags of the Fulmers and the Raven. Only a handful of warriors went with the women and children to guard them, older men and young trainees who had swallowed their pride to leave the battle behind them.

Messages had gone out for ships and aid, as yet the only replies had come via the fire-drakes and the *walkers* whose spirits they carried with them through the flame. Kesta herself had used her magic to *walk* to the far off shore of Chem and give warning to Calayna in Navere.

'They will be fine,' Jorrun said beside her. 'Better than us.'

She frowned. 'I watch for ships coming to us, not those leaving.'

Jorrun turned towards her. 'It is too soon for any to reach us.'

She shook her head. 'Not too soon for ships from Elden. Especially the *Undine*. Why is Temerran not here with the children?'

Jorrun sighed. 'You know Bractius, he will most likely stall while the danger is a little way off, until he secures what he wants.'

'Even with Siveraell there?'

Jorrun snorted, his mouth curling up in a smile. 'Even with Siveraell there.'

Despite his reassurances, she was still uneasy, and she jumped at Worvig's raised voice as he loudly accused someone of being an oaf. It wasn't like her uncle to be so harshly vocal, and she turned to gaze down over the houses nestling in the fragile safety of the Hold.

Possessions were being carted off to be stored in caves along the coast, partially for the sake of the owners, but mostly to clear room for warriors and fighting. Flammable objects in particular were being removed, some houses given over as storerooms for food, water, and arrows in readiness for a siege. In reality, such a thing was unlikely, they were facing an enemy able to break the walls in moments.

As they shipped the residents of Fulmer Hold away a few at a time, those from the inner island were arriving; many with livestock. Pens had been set up along the cliff path and down on the beach in readiness for larger ships to carry them to safety. Even with the *walkers* calming them, Kesta could sense their anxiety. It was hard to fool an animal; they knew something bad was coming.

'May I intrude?'

Kesta turned to see Catya walking toward them, her movements cautious as though she were expecting an attack. Kesta had spent years dwelling on how she felt about Catya, and she'd gone through hurt, anger, worry, and even to an extent, grief. What she experienced now was wariness. Jorrun on the other hand stepped forward to meet her.

'You're not intruding.'

Catya glanced at Kesta as she briefly returned Jorrun's smile. 'I, um... I've come to apologise.'

Kesta opened her mouth, but Jorrun pre-empted her anger and placed a hand on her shoulder.

'Cat, I let you down.'

'What?' Both Kesta and Catya stared at him.

Jorrun's smile had vanished, his eyebrows drawn in tight over his pale-blue eyes. 'I saved you from your uncle, but then I abandoned you. I was too busy being the Dark Man; Bractius' tool. Then I was engrossed in Chem, in living up to my brother's legacy. I should have been a father to you.'

Kesta drew herself up, nostrils flaring. 'Catya made her own choices. She is responsible for who she is, no one else.'

She expected some kind of protest, but Catya looked down, showing none of her usual swagger. 'Yeah, I made my own choices. Most of them were pretty stupid.' She looked up at Jorrun. 'I clung to my right to be angry at the world, revelled in my hate. Cass forced me to see myself, and I didn't like it. Shame was what kept me away. Shame made me unable to see you. Both of you.' Water glistened in Catya's eyes and she sniffed, wiping quickly at her face with two fingers. 'Anyway, I decided to stop being a coward and come and face you.'

Kesta tried to cling to the last shreds of her anger until she realised doing so was exactly why Catya had taken the path she had. With a shake of her head, she blew air out loudly through her mouth and stepped forward to hug Catya. 'You put us through so much worry, so many sleepless nights.'

'Ow, are you trying to squeeze me to death?'

Kesta laughed, loosening her grip on the younger woman, her own eyes watering as she stepped back.

'We've missed you,' Jorrun said, hugging her in turn. 'Cassien told us most of your story.'

Catya rolled her eyes. 'He would.'

'A queen.' Jorrun laughed softly. 'Only you would have the audacity.'

Catya grinned. 'Hey, I'm not the first one who had the idea of conquering a land with just a handful of people.'

Jorrun narrowed his eyes and chastised playfully. 'You had more than a handful.'

'Well, yeah.' She cocked her head. 'So anyway, where do you need me?'

'At the moment?' Jorrun looked down at the hold below them. 'I think everything is pretty much in hand. I'd send you out to scout, but thankfully there's nothing to look for yet.'

'No sign?' Catya raised an eyebrow.

'Nothing yet.' Kesta let her arms drop to her sides.

'Not even from the whales?' Catya frowned.

'We'll have to take that as a good sign,' Jorrun replied. 'Even their voices can only be heard so far beneath the sea. If the Orcas here have heard no warning, then the whales have seen nothing close to the island.'

'Or they have been driven away,' Catya muttered.

'Sail!' A warrior called out.

Kesta's heart gave a lurch, and she turned to look north-eastward, before realising the man was pointing north.

Catya leaned over the stone wall, squinting at the glare from the sea. 'Chemmish vessel. Two of them.'

Kesta strained her eyes, frustrated and embarrassed that it was a moment before she could make out the ships. Her muscles relaxed a little. At least help was coming.

'Let's get down to the beach,' Jorrun suggested.

As they turned from the battlement, movement caught Kesta's eyes. A white gull flew toward them across the water, straight toward the Hold.

'A messenger!'

Instead of heading for the beach, Kesta hurried down the steps, almost running as she skirted the great hall to enter through the main doors. She met her mother as she stepped out of her room with Heara.

'What news?' Kesta asked breathlessly.

Dia's eyes travelled over Kesta's face before she replied. 'It is good news, not bad. As well as the ships just sighted, two more head our way from Parsiphay. From what the gull conveyed to me, the Borrows have mustered their fleet and will be here tomorrow. They'll take refugees, then stand by in case we call for their few warriors.'

'That's good.' Jorrun gave a curt nod of his head.

'Anything from the east?' Kesta asked.

Dia shook her head. 'I sent no birds east, with Siveraell there to report back any trouble I wasn't concerned.' She regarded her daughter. 'But you are, aren't you?'

'They should have been here.'

'Only if they left at once,' Jorrun reminded her.

Dia took them all in with a quick glance. 'I will ask three birds to go. In the meantime, Catya, will you help Cassien and Heara come up with ideas for hidden defences around the islands?'

'Of course.' Catya gave a very slight bow, which warmed Kesta and made her chuckle. Queen or no, Catya was still a Raven, and unintended as it was, it was to Dia the Ravens looked to lead them when crisis struck.

'We'll greet and organise those arriving,' Kesta offered.

'Thank you.' Dia reached out and touched her arm. 'I'll eat with our new guests this evening to welcome them.' She turned and re-entered her room.

Heara gave Catya a shove. 'Come on, let's see what evil tricks you learned in the north.'

Kesta looked at her mother's closed door. The Icante was not herself, but it was hardly surprising. Jorrun took Kesta's hand, and they wove their way back through the busy great hall. 'What is it?' he asked as they crossed the causeway.

She gave her head a shake and wet her lips with her tongue. 'I'm just worrying too much. I'll be happier when the children are here.'

He squeezed her hand. 'Me too, but we can trust Riddi and Ali to get everyone here safely.'

'Not Joss or the drakes?'

Their eyes met, and they both laughed.

'Their hearts are in the right place,' Jorrun said. 'Joss will find his wisdom.'

'And Azra?'

Jorrun clicked his tongue. 'Our Azra is clever in his own way, playful and childlike as he seems. He did encourage me to tell you how I felt all those years ago.'

'And how do you feel?' She twisted to gaze up at him.

He bent his head to kiss her. 'You are the fire in my heart that gives me courage and the strength to do what needs to be done.'

Kesta couldn't help the glowing warmth that spread through her. 'And you are my safe tower, my balance.'

Jorrun smiled and bent to kiss her again. 'Come on.'

Kesta couldn't help but stop at the animal pens to lend her calm through her *knowing*, adding it to that of her fellow *walkers*. Vivess was taking down details of each animal so they could return them to their rightful carer should they ever come back to Fulmer. The animals that could survive well enough without human intervention would only have a short trip to the smaller islands that were to be completely evacuated of Islanders, the rest would take the longer journey to Chem.

She tried to make herself busy as she impatiently watched the ships draw closer. They anchored where the sea was still deep enough and several small boats were lowered, rowers assisting the tide to bring them in.

Jorrun took in a sharp breath.

'What is it?' Kesta turned to him in alarm.

Jorrun blinked rapidly, his nostrils flaring a little. 'Look who has come.'

Kesta turned back to the boats, searching those within, and the air caught in her lungs. Among the warriors was Jagna, the Chemmish sorcerer who had long ago joined them to take Navere. With him were Beth, Jollen, and Rey, some of the first women they had rescued and who had fought with them many times over. And Rece. Her captain. Loyal, steadfast, and brave. But he had no power; he had nothing to offer but his sword and his body against a creature that was a god.

They hurried to meet them, helping to pull the boats up onto the sand.

Jorrun clasped Jagna's wrist. 'How are you here, and so quickly?'

Jagna tilted his head and gave a slight shrug. 'I was in Navere. I received a message some days ago that you needed me.'

'A message from who?' Jorrun frowned.

'It bore no name, only the Raven crest, though the raven was white.'

Kesta looked up towards the Hold. Even her mother couldn't have sent messengers so quickly, and before they knew they needed aid. There was only one who claimed to know they had such foresight. Kesta bit at her lower lip. Was it possible the Rakinya seer was genuine? And if that were the case, could Jderha also be more than a paranoid and fearful dictator?

The thought that the supposed God might see everything they would do before they did it drained the strength from her muscles. And yet... they had thwarted her before.

She placed a hand against Jorrun's back and said quietly, 'We need to speak with Edon Ra.'

He nodded. Although his focus appeared to be on greeting their friends, she could tell by the lines on his forehead he had the same concerns as she.

'Rece, thank you for coming.' Jorrun hugged him.

'You've saved my home so many times, I felt it was about time I returned the favour.' Rece's hair was all silver now, the skin of his face looser and lined with years, yet he still moved with the surety of a younger warrior.

Kesta greeted the women of the original Raven Coven. 'Come with us to the Hold,' she invited.

They caught up on news of each other's families as they crossed through the dunes and climbed up to the cliff path, leaving Vivess to organise the rest of their visitors from the Chemmish ships. As they strode across the causeway, Kesta spotted Eidwyn hurrying towards them. She looked pale; her eyes wide.

'Something is wrong,' Kesta hissed to Jorrun.

'Kesta!' Eidwyn called out. 'Your mother needs you.'

Father.

Kesta broke into a run as Jorrun excused them and tried to follow at a more dignified pace. She had to force the air into her tight lungs, her throat aching with her fear. He couldn't go now; not yet.

The great hall was busy, but there was no alarm, no grief, as Kesta wove her way across to the far doors. Milaiya and Worvig were welcoming the chieftain and *walkers* of Otter Hold. If her uncle were here, surely Arrus was okay? Kesta slowed a little, giving Jorrun a chance to catch up. One of Dia's personal guards, Gilfy, was waiting for them at the doors. He hurried up the steps in front of them, knocked once and entered.

The first thing Kesta noticed was her father sitting up in his chair, dark circles beneath his eyes, but otherwise alive and relatively well. Heara was also there, both hands on her dagger blades. Dia quickly gestured to them to come in, and Eidwyn caught up with them just before the door shut behind them.

Kesta sensed it at once. Power. Metallic, alien, the signature of a spirit; yet she perceived no fire-spirits within the room.

'Kesta, Jorrun.' Dia looked as tired as her husband, but she held herself straight. 'We have visitors.'

The air shimmered and brightened, revealing the shapes of two creatures about the size of a domestic cat. They were almost completely translucent, with four wings like that of a dragonfly. Their faces were relatively human, but elongated, their chins coming to a point. Unlike the fire-spirits, they had no tail, but elegant limbs.

'This is Aelthan and Eyraphin,' Dia said. 'They have come to offer their help.'

Kesta shook her head. 'Why would air-elementals help? Surely you can avoid any conflict between us and Jderha and fly where you will? The sea-spirits have fled. Why would you not do the same?'

Eyraphin's voice was like the tinkle of chimes and the soft susurration of leaves. 'Because if the Fulmers and Chem are defeated, there will be no one to stop Jderha. No one. And all the world will fall.'

Chapter Twenty-One

Arridia; Kingdom of Elden

'We'll get you there soon, miss.'

Nolv ducked his head and thumped his chest as he passed in a gesture of respect, as though she were captain. Arridia forced a smile. The first mate's anxiety thrummed through her, not helped by the muttering of the Borrow crew. The *Undine* felt wrong without Temerran, like a lady in mourning. There was speculation that Temerran had lost his heart for the sea. Arridia didn't know the details of the Borrow tradition around their Bard, but she did know that when one of them was considering giving up a life at sea, they chose an apprentice, a talented and trustworthy man to take his place. Temerran had no such person in training.

Or perhaps he did...

She straightened up, leaning away from the ship's rail, then shook her head. No, that would be impossible.

'We should make Taurmouth long before nightfall,' Joss said, stepping up beside her. He gripped the rail and looked down over the ship's side at the river as it sped below them. Alikan was using his magic to put wind in their sails, of all of them he was best at creating wind for sailing. He had the patience and discipline for it.

Joss growled in the back of his throat and turned to face her. 'Did I do the right thing, Rids?'

She regarded her brother; his blue eyes were wide, and he barely blinked as he waited for her reassurance. She couldn't say no, couldn't tell him there'd been no right thing from the moment he'd let Eleanor into his room. 'As long as you and Scarlett can find some happiness, then yes.'

Joss sagged, kicking at the rail with the toe of his boot. Arridia winced. 'Mum always warned us about Bractius, I guess I never really believed it until now. As for Eleanor and her mother, they're worse!'

Arridia sighed. 'It won't be easy at court. I'll be near when I can.' She glanced past her brother to where Nip sat on the deck reading aloud from a book. A small brazier stood beside him, above which Azrael and Doroquael hovered. She couldn't help but smile.

'Nolv!' Their lookout yelled from the crow's nest up above. 'Something's up!' The Borrowman pointed down river to the eastern bank. They were only five miles from Lake Taur. What trouble could there possibly be?

Arridia and Joss both hurried forward toward the prow, Nolv striding across the deck to join them, eyes narrowed as he squinted.

'A village,' Joss stated unnecessarily.

Arridia froze as the sound of screams came to them despite the direction of the wind. She called up her *knowing*, reaching out for the emotions of the people. Terror. Stinging, desperate fear. And the tang of elemental magic.

'They're under attack.' She spun around. 'Azra, go look, but don't engage.'

'Can't be raiders this far inland.' Nolv frowned.

'It's an earth-spirit!' Joss pointed, his mouth hanging open. 'In a clay trap like the other, look at the size of it!'

Arridia and Nolv twisted to see as Dierra and Alikan came running over. The clay monstrosity was at least a head bigger than the one they'd faced at Teriton. Its eyes blazed as it smashed at the wooden buildings.

Joss had already unbuckled his sword. 'I'll try to reason with it.' He jumped up onto the rail and dived into the water.

'Joss, no!' Arridia yelled. 'Wait!'

Alikan swore, handing his own sword and belt to Dierra. With an apologetic glance at Arridia, he vaulted into the river after Joss. Doroquael had already shot out over the water.

'Can you get us to shore?' Arridia asked Nolv.

The old warrior shook his head. 'It's too shallow just there.'

Arridia bit hard at her lower lip. She could swim, but not brilliantly.

'Lower a boat!' Nolv bellowed.

With a grateful nod, Arridia hurried to help the Borrowmen, while they dropped the *Undine's* anchor. She scrambled down the ladder, Nolv selecting warriors to go with them. Nip took a seat beside her, taking an oar. She stretched her back to see what was happening on shore.

Blackness burst behind her eyes, and for a moment time seemed to stand still. She felt them before she saw them. *Bad men.*

Fourteen years ago, she had experienced the same jolt of concentrated malice that now ran down her spine and turned her insides to ice. Fourteen years ago, assassins had come for her and Joss.

She forced herself to move, dragged air into her lungs to once again push unaccustomed volume into her voice. 'To shore, quickly! Geladan has come. Azrael, to Joss. Now!'

Dierra scrambled about in the boat, trying to stand and see. 'Geladan? How can it be?'

Nip briefly squeezed her hand, then put his back into rowing. Nolv, having heard her cry, had already ordered their other boat into the water. Arridia called her power, shielding everyone.

Familiar magical signatures flared up around her, searing her heart. Joss and Alikan were fighting.

Their boat bumped up against the shallows and she stood at once, Nip reaching up to steady her as the boat rocked. She scrambled inelegantly up the bank, grabbing handfuls of grass. Dierra landed beside her in a crouch, dagger drawn, flames in her left hand.

'Three men and a woman,' Dierra reported. 'The elemental is going for Joss, but... I think it's trying not to!'

Arridia gained her feet and looked, heart in her mouth. Alikan was shielding, bracing against the three men, all of whom threw fire. Both the fire-spirits were battering at the shields of the Geladanians, Doroqueal's face contorted in rage, and he'd grown large enough to swallow one whole. Joss stood behind his friend and bodyguard, the muscles of his body straining as he attempted to do as she had done and pull apart the spirit trap. The golem was dragging its feet, roaring as it flailed first towards Joss, and then toward the woman who trailed it.

'It doesn't want to fight,' Nip said quietly behind her. She heard the shivering ring of his sword as he drew it.

'Orders, lady?' One of the Borrowmen barked. She had to admire their discipline. If only Joss had listened.

She glanced at the warrior. 'Two of you see if any villagers are hurt and need help getting away. The rest hang back, don't fight them until I've depleted their magic.'

She called her power, her fingers contorting into claws. All her life she'd struggled with this. As powerful as she was, using her magic took a terrible toll. She felt the pain she inflicted, experienced every death she dealt. When her power ran through her, there was no shield between herself and the emotions of the universe around her. While most Ravens learned to conserve their energy, Arridia did not.

'Riddi?' Dierra's voice was strained. Her duty was to protect Arridia, but Joss was already struggling and even Alikan was giving ground.

Arridia drew more power, and more. 'Shield who you can,' she hissed, her teeth almost locked together.

Nip grabbed Dierra's arm and pulled her away, gesturing for the Borrowmen to spread out.

A thunderhead formed with uncanny speed. Lightning crackled around Arridia; her nostrils flared as she breathed in the smell of ozone. She lashed out towards the three Geladanian assassins, crying out in anticipation of their pain. Only one shield buckled, the man's skin blackening. She increased her power, desperately trying to make his death quick.

'Riddi!' Joss cried out. 'Please break the golem!'

With a glance at her, Dierra sprinted across to Alikan, adding her shield to his. Alikan reached down into the earth, ripping up rock. One of the Geladanians sprawled facedown and the fire-sprits leapt, dissolving him into ash.

Arridia drew more power, reaching out for the golem. The woman among the Geladanians turned to glare at her, making a quick gesture with her fingers.

Doubt ripped through Arridia, her heart twisting in anguish.

The remaining assassin sent a blast of freezing air towards Azrael and Doroquael, then ducked and rolled, coming up closer to Alikan. Dierra reacted, her legs carrying her across the space between with phenomenal speed. With her left hand she threw flame, with her right she threw a dagger before springing into a cartwheel that took her into the shelter of Alikan's shield.

Tears and blood burst from Arridia's eyes. The golem broke through Joss's shield, green light crackling across its clay prison. As its arm swung down at her brother, Arridia ripped it apart, shards flying out in all directions. Something sharp sliced her cheek as she dropped to her knees.

Dierra and Alikan threw flame and ice at the remaining assassin, the two fire-spirits darting in to engulf him. Nip put his arm under Arridia's shoulder and hauled her to her feet; she leaned against him, blinking at the smoke, breathing hard. Where was Joss?

The Geladanian woman lay upon the ground, her elegant form still, her dark hair covering her face. Joss crept tentatively toward her, a weak shield fluctuating around him.

A shiver ran through Arridia, her vision blurred; or was it the air that distorted?

'Joss, watch out!'

Her brother glanced at her but took another step toward the fallen woman.

She vanished.

Arridia's mouth opened, but she couldn't cry out. The woman was no longer on the ground; she was behind Joss, a dagger raised. Joss turned, eyes widening as the blade plunged down between his ribs.

Arridia screamed, pain tearing through her chest. Her feet went from under her, only Nip keeping her from falling. The Borrowmen surged forward, but Doroquael and Azra reached the woman before them. She died swiftly, a smile on her face.

'Joss,' Arridia gasped.

'Search the area!' Nolv bellowed. 'Make sure there are no more!'

Doroquael and Azrael started wailing, fluttering around each other in tight circles above the still body of her brother. Alikan threw himself to his friend's side, his face crumpling, the skin around his eyes and cheeks reddening. He looked up and met Arridia's eyes, and the pain of her brother's death ripped through her again.

She forced her feet forward and Nip let her go, staying close at her side with his sword ready. Dierra stood watching, her arms hanging loosely. She swallowed, then mustered her voice. 'I'll help Nolv, make sure there aren't more.'

Alikan moved aside to let Arridia drop to the ground beside her brother. Their adopted brother had been trying vainly to stem the flow of blood, his hands covered in it. Arridia drew in a sharp breath. Joss still breathed. His eyes were glazed, but they sought hers.

'I'm sorry, Rids.' He coughed, a little blood spilling from the corner of his mouth.

She placed a hand against his cheek and leaned forward to press her forehead against his, sending him calm though her heart raced, trying to take his pain although her own was unbearable.

He drew in a wheezing breath. 'Look after Scarlett for me.'

She closed her eyes tightly, screwing up her face to desperately hold in her grief. Her kind little brother, always wanting to rush in and protect everyone. Arridia forced herself to nod, though she wasn't sure it was a promise she could keep. She pulled away a little to regard his face, to draw in every detail to keep in her soul. He looked so vulnerable, so young; too young to die. He coughed again, small bubbles forming in the blood on his lips. Both the fire-spirits had grown silent, but she felt the heat from their closeness.

Arridia drew in a breath. 'What have you learned?'

Joss laughed, sending a spasm of pain through his own body and hers. Alikan looked away, tears falling freely down his soot-stained face.

Joss's expression grew serious, his blue eyes momentarily bright and clear. 'I should have listened to my sister.'

A sob gripped her as she laughed in return, her own tears landing on her hand resting on his shoulder. 'Yes, you should have.'

His body strained as he tried to drag enough air from his lungs to speak one last time. 'What have you learned, Rids?'

The pain in her heart overwhelmed her, her vision blurring. What had she learnt? That she needed to be more assertive? That she should have stepped up to lead?

She tensed her muscles. No, that wasn't it.

Joss's life – Joss's death – had more meaning than that. It had to.

She looked down at Joss, placing her hand against his cheek again. He was so cold.

Something stirred inside her, something that went deeper than anger, stronger than despair. 'I have learned what our parents taught us. Never give up. Never turn away from something that needs to be done even when it should be impossible.'

She twisted, placing both her hands against his wound and called up her magic.

'Help me, Joss, call your power.'

Their father had tried to teach them many times, but like all but their aunt Dinari, they had never grasped healing. Arridia tried now, pouring all her remaining power into her brother, feeling the excruciating flares of hope from Alikan and the spirits. She tried to force her power, her will, into his blood, into his tissue, to knit it together and speed its natural urge to repair. With it went her love, her exasperation, everything she felt for her brother. Blood vessels burst in her nose and she gasped air in through her mouth, closing her eyes. Her skull throbbed, her veins stinging like blisters as she tried to pull the last dregs of her power through her exhausted body.

'Riddi, stop!' Alikan cried out. 'Riddi, you're killing yourself.'

His voice sounded a long way away. She couldn't stop, she couldn't give up.

Warm arms enfolded her, and Nip spoke softly into her ear. 'Enough, Arridia. That's enough.'

She let herself fall away.

***

The smell of wood and pine tar seeped into her uneasy dreams. She was moving, or rather the bed beneath her was. From the dip and sway, she knew they were on the sea, rather than the river. Instinct prompted her to call her *knowing*, but fear gripped her, making her muscles weak; instead, she opened her eyes.

The room was dark, just a single lantern lit on the table at the end of her bunk, the candle low and flickering. She turned her head a little to search around. This was Nolv's cabin.

She sat up, her head immediately pounding with an intense throb.

'Riddi.' Dierra shifted on the floor next to her, scrambling onto her haunches. 'How do you feel?'

'Thirsty,' she croaked.

Dierra sprang to her feet and poured some water into a cup, her energy making Arridia wince. Arridia took it and drank it down quickly. 'What time is it? Where are we?'

'It's just gone midnight.' Dierra pulled herself up to sit on the edge of the bed. 'We're maybe halfway across the sea to the Fulmers.'

A wave of grief washed over Arridia and she hid her face in her hands, shaking with the sobs that spilled from her heart and squeezed her throat. Dierra shifted on the bed to rub her back, then hugged her. 'You're exhausted, poor thing, but that's hardly surprising. How did you do it?'

Arridia shook her head in confusion. 'Do what?'

'Heal Joss.'

Arridia pushed her away to stare at her. 'What? Say that again?'

Dierra's mouth fell open. 'You don't know? You healed Joss.'

Arridia couldn't speak. Her breath trembled.

'He's still pretty weak and not completely out of danger. He lost a lot of blood.'

'Where is he?'

'In another cabin. Ali and Doro are looking after him. Ali is still furious with himself that he couldn't protect Joss.'

Arridia looked around the room, feeling a need to pinch herself. Surely she was still dreaming? 'Where's Azra?'

'He and Nip are guarding the prisoner.'

'Prisoner?'

'Well.' Dierra pulled a face. 'He's not really a prisoner I guess, but everyone is a bit wary—'

'Dierra,' Arridia prompted with unaccustomed impatience.

'The earth-elemental,' she explained. 'The one you freed. This fellow stayed around, wanted to talk to us.'

'I need to see him.'

'The spirit?'

Arridia shook her head. 'Joss. But yes, then the spirit.'

'You might want to get changed first.' Dierra pointed to her tunic, and Arridia looked down to see it stained with her brother's blood. Dierra grabbed her bag for her, then helped her pull the tunic up over her head. Arridia's hands seemed much too heavy at the end of her strengthless arms.

Arridia staggered as she stood, swallowing her pride to accept Dierra's help to get across the tilting floor. 'Is there a storm?'

'The wind's up.' Dierra pushed the door open. 'But no storm.'

They didn't need to go far along the narrow hallway, Dierra knocked on the first door to the left. There was a muffled response from within, and Dierra didn't hesitate to go in. Arridia stepped in more slowly. The room was illuminated by Doroqueal's soft glow, the fire-spirit perched atop a fat candle in a storm lantern. He hummed on seeing Arridia. Alikan looked up, his amber eyes haunted, anguished. He stood, offering Arridia his chair.

220

'No, it's okay.' Arridia waved him aside. 'I'll only be a moment.'

Dierra pressed herself against the wall so Arridia could pass.

Even in Doroqueal's warm light, Joss looked pale, cold. Rather than relaxed in sleep, his forehead was furrowed. He seemed older somehow.

Alikan reached out and pulled back the blanket. 'It hasn't fully healed, but it was enough. We should get him to your father in time.'

The raised line across Joss's chest, a little to the right of his heart, was red and angry-looking, but didn't ooze blood. It looked as though the Geladanian woman had hit a rib and the knife had slid before going in deep.

'Has he woken at all?' Dierra asked.

Alikan shook his head. 'Probably for the best.'

Arridia reached across the bed to squeeze his hand. 'Call me if he wakes before we get to the Fulmers.'

He nodded, pressing his lips together in a forced smile. She wanted to reassure him, but only he could forgive himself.

She pulled the blanket back up over her brother, pushing against the bed to get to her feet.

'Are you going to see the elemental?' Alikan asked.

'I am. Have you spoken to it?'

'Briefly.' He glanced at Dierra. 'Enough to be sure it really meant no harm. Like the fire-spirits for many years, they want nothing to do with humans. They dislike us, for our thoughtless ways, for our destruction of the land. He liked the sound of the Islands though.'

'The earth-elemental?'

Alikan nodded. 'His name is Gorchia.'

The stairs up to the deck seemed dangerously steep, Arridia's knees reluctant to bend and lift. Even before she reached the open air, the wind whipped around her and took her breath away. There were no lights on the deck but for the bright shape of Azrael; there was too high a risk of a lantern falling and catching fire. Nolv himself stood at the prow rather than at the wheel, a second pair of eyes to supplement those of the lookout.

Arridia didn't move for a moment, finding her balance before making her halting way to where the rain barrels were lashed together. Nip and Azrael huddled on the lee side of them. The stable master's legs were crossed, and he rested his elbow on his leg, leaning forward in conversation. With his other hand he held tight to a small chest, stopping it sliding across the *Undine's* planks. Only when she got closer did Arridia realise the chest was full of earth. A wilting dandelion and a clump of long grass had been planted in it. A tiny burst of green foxfire revealed the shape of a small brown man no bigger than her hand.

'Riddi!' Azrael turned a somersault and came streaming toward her.

'How are you?' Nip held out his hand, and she took it at once. He helped her keep her balance as she joined him.

'Tired.' She winced; her gaze fixed on the small elemental as much as she longed to lose her pain in Nip's kind grey eyes. The shape of the earth-spirit's face was almost fox like, and two narrow, pointed ears stood up on top of its head. Its eyes were a bright glowing green, and it was dressed in a perfectly tailored suit of brown and green. Its skin had tiny wrinkles, as though made of the bark of a young tree. She gave a polite bow of her head. 'I'm Arridia.'

The earth-elemental tilted its head, then bowed deeply in return. 'I am Gorchia. I am – so it seems – quite literally at your service.'

Azrael made a displeased buzzing sound. Was the fire-spirit suspicious? Or jealous?

'So, what happened?' She looked from Azra to Nip, then back at the elemental. Dierra remained standing, surveying the darkness beyond the ship. 'How long ago did the Geladanians capture you?'

222

Nip shifted beside her, looking down at the deck.

'It wasn't what you call *Geladanians*. I was captured before they arrived and trapped in darkness, within that clay prison. I think possibly for a week.' He folded his arms and nodded towards Nip and Azra. 'As I told your friends, whatever summoned and imprisoned me, was born of this land, what you name Elden.'

Arridia frowned deeply. 'I don't understand.'

Azrael blazed fiercely. 'Witchcraft. The native magic of Elden, but not the kind, thoughtful type like our Rosa tried.'

'So how were the Geladanians there?'

'Betrayal.' Nip clenched his jaw, the muscles of his face moving.

Gorchia unfolded his arms to place his hands on his hips. 'Yes, betrayal. Some time after the spell gripped me, I was filled with a compulsion to find and kill Joss Raven. I was told he would come by river. I tried to fight it...' The little creature shook its head.

'We are grateful,' Nip encouraged.

Gorchia lifted his chin a little. 'The Geladanians knew. Someone told them I was compelled to find and destroy Joss, they used me to find him too.'

'Then our Eldenian witch is in contact with Geladan.'

'And on their side,' Nip breathed.

Chapter Twenty-Two

Scarlett; Kingdom of Elden

'Well?' Scarlett hurried along the battlement toward Temerran and her brother, glancing at the single guard on watch who took the hint and moved away.

Lucien gave a slight shake of his head. His cheeks were flushed, whether from the blustery wind or from emotion Scarlett couldn't be sure. 'Despite Mother's protests, Eleanor is now confined to her rooms. She'll remain so until Father feels it's safe enough to send her to Dalton in Chem. Father had his sights set on a match with Jorrun's nephew, now, and Navere itself.'

Temerran folded his arms across his chest.

'I don't like the thought of Eleanor plotting within the castle.' Scarlett shuddered. 'It's a shame we can't get her locked away in some remote tower somewhere.'

Lucien's jaw muscles moved as he clenched his teeth. 'Well, despite everything, she is our sister. It isn't safe out there right now, and she does still hold the rank of princess.'

Scarlett scowled at him. He wouldn't be so charitable if it had been his future Eleanor had been messing with and his life she was trying to steal. 'So, what's the latest? What are Father's plans regarding Geladan?'

'Mostly to hide in his castle and hope the storm hits the Fulmers rather than here,' Temerran said, his green eyes unusually hard.

Lucien drew in a long, slow breath and met Scarlett's eyes. 'He has beacons set on the coast for if the ships are sighted. He's recalled warriors who were assigned to Mantu to strengthen this castle. Supplies are being gathered from the farms and villages to be stored in fortified towns.'

Scarlett frowned, taking a few small steps along the stone walkway before pivoting to look up at her brother. 'From my history, didn't Chem take Mantu first when they tried to conquer Elden? Wouldn't it be better to leave the island keeps strong?'

Lucien cocked his head. 'Chem attacked from the north, we imagine Geladan will attack from the south, or from the Fulmers.'

'Hmm.' Scarlett tried to picture the maps she had seen and studied of the four lands. She sucked in a sharp breath. 'But when Geladan attacked before, they did so from within, both here and in the Fulmers? Their tactic seemed to be to infiltrate, or gain access by treachery.'

She saw Temerran blanch, and she bit her lip in sympathy. The bard had been a victim of Geladan's sneaky tactics.

'What are you saying?' Lucien folded his arms across his chest, mimicking the bard. 'That we're wrong to put our strength here and on the coast?'

'Oh.' Scarlett was momentarily flustered, she'd assumed that her father had laid out the plans and dictated them, she hadn't thought her brother had had input into it. 'Well, I guess not, but...'

'No, go on,' Temerran urged her. 'What were you thinking?'

'Well, that's just it, we need to think differently.' She glanced at Lucien and plunged on. 'For most of our history, our enemies have been those who come by sea. Borrow raiders, and Chem. It's only in the last thirty years that Chem was strong enough magically to change the way they raided and fought, and, well, Thane Jorrun and Kesta changed the way we defended.'

'They defended by going to Chem and destroying their power there.' Temerran frowned. 'You are right, Scarlett, this won't be like a Borrow raid, but we can't go to Geladan and destroy their god.'

Scarlett sagged. 'I know. But... but it's no good just having beacons on the coast.'

Lucien scratched at his cheek. 'I could suggest to Father that we place the beacons on every high point across the land rather than just running in a line from the coast to here. The problem with that would be if every beacon were lit, it might be harder to determine from where the threat comes.'

'I hadn't thought of that.'

Temerran rubbed at his mouth. The usually neat bard had let stubble grow on his face, Scarlett had never noticed it before. His hand moved down to his chest. 'As for detecting any ill intent from infiltrators or sneak attacks, it is *walkers* who are best able to pre-warn of such things, if only a short warning. Unfortunately, there are presently none at the castle.'

'And I'm also at a dead end finding our witch.' Scarlett growled in frustration. 'Since I don't have any magic myself, I'm at a loss. No one has been up in that tower that I can see.'

'Have you tried tracking the materials?' Temerran asked her. 'The herbs used are relatively easy to find, but a crystal is a rarer and more expensive item. There's also the clay. Where did that come from, where was it stored?'

'And where was the golem made?' Scarlett nodded enthusiastically. 'I'll look into it.'

'Carefully,' Lucien cautioned. 'Take Kistelle with you. Father has agreed to let her be your new lady-in-waiting, but she is to report to him twice a day.'

Scarlett's eyebrows rose. 'That's a wonder. Okay, I'll wait. Where's Siveraell, has he left already?'

'I don't believe so.' Temerran's red brows drew together.

'He was at our meeting in Father's study,' Lucien confirmed. 'Where he has gone now, I couldn't say.'

Scarlett glanced toward the guard, then looked out toward the lake. 'Joss and the others should be near Taurmouth by now.'

'The *Undine* will see them home safely,' Temerran reassured her.

Lucien cleared his throat. 'We should meet again tomorrow, but somewhere different.'

'The servant's stairs,' Scarlett said at once. 'Where it accesses the royal ladies' quarters.'

'I know it,' Temerran said with the ghost of a smile. He gave a curt bow, then hurried to the door into the castle.

Lucien shifted his feet. 'I'll pass on your concerns to Father.'

Scarlett snorted. 'It would be better if he took me seriously and listened to them himself.'

Lucien winced. 'I don't disagree, Scar. If I'm ever king, things will change, I promise.'

She stared at her brother. 'What do you mean by 'if'?'

He gave a shrug but wouldn't meet her eyes. 'Things change. Geladan is coming. Be careful, Scar.' He turned on his heels and hurried to the door which had swung shut behind Temerran.

The wind pushed against her, making her feel more vulnerable now she was alone. She pulled her shawl in tighter and strode toward the exit at the other end of the battlement. Clay. She had no idea where it came from or where it might be purchased. There was so much missing from her knowledge. Scarlett snorted; she used to think she was well educated, but she probably knew less about the real world than a commoner.

An idea occurred to her, and she pivoted.

'Excuse me.'

The guard straightened up, his eyebrows raised as though startled by her address, or perhaps her politeness. He gave a quick bow. 'Highness?'

Scarlett licked her lips. 'Um, where would one buy clay?'

'Clay?' The guard frowned at her. 'Do you mean for making pots? Or for moulding tiles and building?'

'Either. Um, brownish clay.'

The guard scratched at his beard. 'Cheap pots and building bricks are made from redder, darker clay. You'd find that mostly near the south gate.'

'Thank you.' Scarlett gave a curt nod and hurried back to her rooms. Two guards were standing outside her sister's quarters, both straightening up to salute her without making eye contact. A deep ache came from nowhere within her chest. As different as they were, Eleanor was her twin. The betrayal stung, but losing her sister left her with a larger pain.

She opened the door to her parlour and gasped. A woman stood there dressed in green trousers and a long tunic, daggers at her hips. As the woman turned, Scarlett let the air out of her lungs and relaxed.

'Raven Kistelle?'

The woman bowed. 'At your service, Highness.' She had blonde hair, braided in a single plait and pinned in a coil at the back of her head, but the darker skin of the Fulmer islands.

'We've got a mission.' Scarlett strode to her bedroom, taking some trousers and a shirt she'd borrowed from her brother. She struggled out of her dress, slightly perturbed that the Raven Scout didn't come and help.

'Ah.' Kistelle rocked forward onto the balls of her feet and back to her heels. 'Your father gave me instructions not to let you leave the city.'

'What?' She turned, buttoning up her shirt. 'Oh, for goodness' sake. He won't let me into any of his meetings, and now he refuses to let me do anything useful!'

Kistelle hooked a thumb into her sword belt, transferring her weight to one hip. 'He said I could teach you anything you wanted to learn, as long as it's nothing dangerous.'

'Really?' Scarlett froze, her head tilted to one side. Was this some kind of concession from the king? 'He'll let me learn Raven skills?'

Kistelle nodded.

'Great.' Scarlett grinned. 'We can start with tracking.'

'Tracking what?'

'Clay.'

***

They passed through the city's main market square, Scarlett pulling her hood down low over her face. Most eyes turned to Kistelle. Even in this day and age an armed woman in what was considered male garb, was an unusual sight in Elden. Most Ravens conformed to Elden dress standards when visiting court, except Kesta, who delighted in upsetting the queen.

They paused at two pottery stalls, but these were expensive items, made of a fine, white clay.

The south side of the city mainly housed the labourers, those who left during the hours of daylight to work the fields, chop and shape wood, slaughter animals, and tan hides. Scarlett had never set foot in this part of the city before, and she fell back beside Kistelle rather than taking the lead. The smell was awful, stinging the back of her throat. The houses were small and uneven, built mostly of wood and white plaster with narrow, dark windows. Women sat on their doorsteps, their feet placed over the filthy gutters as they sewed, carded and tatted lace, making the most of the light. A wave of guilt swept through Scarlett. She knew nothing of life, nothing of the people who called her *princess.* Her feet almost faltered.

'There.' Kistelle pointed.

Scarlett followed her gaze. A high wall surrounded a large work yard, the painted sign hanging from a post depicting three roof tiles. 'Yes, let's try here.'

Excitement overrode her doubt as they walked in through the open gate, Kistelle moving ahead to scan the yard. Piles of different coloured muds, clays, and sand stood to one side of the yard, segregated by log walls. Large stacks of firewood and tinder were to the right alongside an open-fronted shed filled with roof tiles. In the centre of the yard was a huge stone oven around which a heat-haze shimmered.

Several men and boys worked in the yard, most giving them no more than a glance. A large man with a black beard straightened up and approached them, looking Kistelle up and down and deciding to be polite.

'Help you?'

Scarlett cleared her throat. 'Do you sell clay here?'

The man scowled, wiping his face with the back of his hand and leaving more mud there. 'We don't sell clay. We sell roof tiles.'

Scarlett looked around the yard, shifting her feet. She dug her nails into the palms of her hands; this was no time for her to lose her confidence. 'Have you sold any clay to anyone recently, though?'

'Look, lady, I don't have time for this. What do you want?'

Kistelle straightened up, her hand going to her dagger. 'We are Raven's, *sir,* and here on the king's business. Answer the question.'

The man's eyes narrowed, but he answered. 'I don't sell clay. I've never sold clay. It would be pointless since it's cheaper for anyone to get it from the same place I do.'

Kistelle raised an eyebrow. 'Which is?'

The man huffed. 'There's a big clay works at Anim, where the river is more of a bog. Otherwise, you can get it shipped via the Taur from all 'round the country.'

'Thank you.' Kistelle relaxed her posture a little.

Scarlett's eyes were drawn to the large firing oven. 'Um, I don't suppose anyone has asked you to fire anything unusual, like, er, a statue?'

'A statue?' The man screwed his face up. 'I don't do statues, just tiles.'

'Do you know who else has an oven as big as yours?'

'Anim. They make a lot of their own stuff on site. There's plenty of places further away though, I'm sure.'

'Thank you.' Scarlett's hand moved to her belt, her face reddening when she realised she hadn't brought a purse. Kistelle rolled her eyes and handed the man a coin.

'Where's Anim?' Kistelle asked as they left the yard.

Scarlett sucked in a breath. 'It's only about eight miles from here, along the Taur to the south.'

'So… near Teriton then.'

'Exactly.' Scarlett's pace quickened as she headed back towards the central city and the familiar shadow of the castle. She halted abruptly. 'Oh, but Father will never allow me to go. Would you do it?'

Kistelle hesitated. 'I'm not sure I should leave you and the king until stronger reinforcements arrive from the Fulmers and Chem.'

Scarlett ground her teeth in frustration. Then the answer hit her, and her mood immediately brightened. 'I know exactly who to send. I'll get a raven sent to Northold as soon as we get back.'

Kistelle smiled and nodded, moving slightly ahead as they arrived at the busier streets to keep a path free for the princess.

As they reached the castle, Scarlett noticed a tension in the air. The guards at the gate were alert and upright. Several pigeons flew out and away from the scribe's loft.

'Something's happened.' Scarlett increased her pace, trying to retain her dignity and not break into a run. Her eyes caught the red of Temerran's hair up on the battlement. He raised a hand, and she nodded.

Scarlett tried the throne room first but was told her father wasn't there. Temerran caught up with her in the corridor leading to her father's private audience room. 'What's happened?' Scarlett demanded.

Temerran took her aside, away from the guards who stood outside her father's door. 'It seems Geladanians have snuck their way into Elden. We're not sure how, since we have seen no ships.'

'They're here?' Scarlett looked up and down the hall, her knees going weak.

Temerran shook his head, reaching out to take her elbow gently. 'Not here, but close. They lay in ambush for Joss and Arridia—'

'Joss!' Scarlett's hand flew to her mouth.

'They're both okay. Joss was hurt. But they're back underway to the Fulmers. A pigeon arrived a while ago from Northold, and a rider from the village that was used for the ambush turned up less than an hour ago. The chap was quite happy to talk in exchange for an ale and some food.' Temerran smiled grimly.

'We must find out what's being done.'

Temerran went to stop her, but she spun on her heels and marched to her father's door. The guards glanced at each other, one of them putting his arm across the door as she reached for the handle.

Scarlett stared at the man in open-mouthed affront.

'Sorry, Highness,' the man muttered. 'His Majesty said no one else was to enter.'

'I need to see my father!'

The guard actually had the audacity to look to Temerran for help. Scarlett felt her temperature rise.

'Highness,' Temerran said slowly. 'We'll get news from your brother. In the meantime, there is something more I must say. In private.'

Scarlett glared at the guard but gave in and let Temerran lead her away down the hall, Kistelle shadowing.

'What is it?'

Temerran's gaze was earnest as his green eyes met hers. 'The Geladanians were following a golem. The witch is in league with them.'

Scarlett swallowed, her eyes widening. She grabbed Temerran's wrist without realising she'd done so. 'We have a lead. A small one. I can't go myself, but there is someone who can.'

Temerran tilted his head. 'Who?'

'Lady Rosa.'

Chapter Twenty-Three

Cassien; Fulmer Island

'It would most likely be a suicide mission, destroying their ships.' Heara leaned back against the tree and crossed her long legs in front of her.

Catya grunted but didn't disagree. They'd moved outside to clear their heads, walking a short way into the forest. So far several of their plans and proposed traps had been discarded because of their potential impact on the lives of the animals on the island, which had pleased Dysarta, but frustrated both himself and Catya. Cassien glanced at the red-headed tribeswoman. He was liking Dysarta more and more. She was warm and compassionate, patient, and insightful. She could also gently put Catya in her place.

'It's likely.' Cassien fiddled with the twig he held in his hands. 'Especially if Jderha stays on the ships and doesn't come ashore.'

'And they could just take the Fulmer vessels, anyway.' Dysarta pointed out. 'So, you'd have to send your own ships away.'

'We'd be as stranded on the islands as they are.' Cassien agreed with a nod.

'But the point is, they would be trapped here,' Catya said earnestly. Her son, Merin, leaned against her shoulder, taking everything in with his wide, amber eyes. Cassien still seethed that she'd brought him here into danger on the word of her northern creature. 'Even if we can't finish them off, others can try after us, and the Geladanians can't go invading anywhere else in the meantime.'

'There's a good chance sea-spirits will guard their ships, sorcerers certainly,' Heara pointed out. 'And they'll anchor a way out from the island so approaching them might be impossible.'

'I guess we won't know until we see them.' Cassien put down his twig, regarding them all. These wonderfully strong women weren't afraid to show their fear, but they would never let it stop them. It made him feel safe to speak his mind without reservation. There was no need for false bravado here. 'Obviously a night attack would be best, and swimming better than taking a boat, so we'd have to pick excellent swimmers.'

Heara gave a shrug. 'I managed it years ago when Dia took out Adelphi Dunham's ships on Lake Taur. I was younger then, mind you. We fired the ships, trapped men below decks, but their sorcerers put out some of the flames.'

'Black powder,' Catya said firmly. 'Our best bet will be to blast a hole in their ships they can't fix.'

'But if you swim with black powder, it's going to get damp.' Cassien threw aside his twig and sat up straighter.

'And it will take quite an amount to blow a hole in a ship that can't be repaired.'

Cassien shook his head. 'Not if you use fine grains in the right container, it burns faster, explodes with more pressure.'

'Really?' Catya cocked her head. 'I didn't know that.'

'But wouldn't you have to set it deep within the hold?' Dysarta's brows drew together in concern. 'There are too many problems, too many variables. It might be better just to send one or two strong magic users who can swim. Or warriors with axes.'

Catya visibly paled. 'You mean someone like you.'

Dysarta held her gaze.

Cassien cleared his throat. 'Well, it's something to consider. I wish Rothfel were here. There is no one better than him when it comes to things like this.'

Catya leaned forward, dislodging her son. 'Are you not his apprentice?'

Cassien smiled as fond memories crept into his heart. 'I was for a few years, but they needed me in Caergard and I had my family.'

'I know Rothfel,' Merin spoke up. 'He does tricks with coloured fire.'

'He does.' Catya smiled down at her son.

'We, er...' Heara looked around as though fearing to be overheard. 'We might consider destroying the causeway with your black powder to keep those within safe. As a last resort.'

The air froze in Cassien's lungs, but he forced himself to nod.

'Right then.' Heara uncrossed her legs and stood, brushing down the back of her trousers. 'I'll report our ideas to Dia, and we'll meet again later. I need to lug heavy stuff about and shout at people.' She didn't wait for a response but strode away toward the Hold.

Cassien got slowly to his feet. 'I'd best make myself useful too.'

Catya looked disappointed as he walked away, but his steps didn't falter, nor did his heart. Long ago Rothfel had said Cassien was a person who thought he needed a master, and to an extent the old rogue had been right. He'd been a faithful hound to Osun, the loss of whom had ripped his world apart. He'd tried to latch on to Jorrun, but the Thane and sorcerer only urged Cassien to seek his own path.

Catya had been easy to follow at first, so passionate about life, so sure of herself against Cassien's own uncertainty. But of course, she had also been cruel, deliberate or not, and he had almost lost himself, lost who he was. Rothfel had made him search inside himself, made him value his own thoughts and opinions. Rothfel had lifted him from slave to master of himself. It had led him to Kussim, and a marriage of respect and equality.

'I need to write home,' he muttered to himself as he crossed the causeway. His feet faltered, and he walked to the edge, leaning over to peer down. It wouldn't be possible to destroy the whole causeway, not with the little black powder he had; and there was no time to make more. But... they could make a sizeable hole in the path, perhaps, to hold back raiders. It would be a desperate move.

A shudder ran through Cassien's soul. He had a horrible feeling they would be more than desperate before the end.

He looked up and saw the familiar figures of Rece and Worvig on the battlement, the two men deep in conversation. Worvig raising his remaining hand to point southward across the island. Cassien quickened his pace, nodding to the warriors who stood guard at the gate. Inside the walls, the last of the families who were to be shipped north to Chem gathered beneath temporary shelters. He was impressed, amazed by their calm. There was no complaining, no crying, only determination.

He took the steep steps quickly, joining his friends to gaze out over the forest whose shade he had just recently left.

'Cass.' Worvig gave him a nod. 'What diabolical plans has Heara come up with?'

Cassien grinned, although his heart sank at the truth he had to tell. 'The plans are more desperate than diabolical. We've come up with a lot of options but... well, they'll have to be fluid. Too many of them hinge on 'ifs'.'

'Fluid is fine.' Worvig leaned against the battlement, his eyes narrowing. 'Rock cannot break water, but water breaks rock.'

Rece nodded. 'That will be your strength.'

'We have many strengths. There is one you have all overlooked.'

All three of them spun around at the soft, warm voice that came from behind them. Dia looked tired, though her muscles were relaxed.

Rece tilted his head, Worvig straightened up; Cassien gave a slight bow. 'What have we missed, Icante?'

'You have missed the *fire-walker*.' A slight smile played across Dia's lips and she moved elegantly to lean against the stone battlement.

'Magic users vary from continent to continent because their magic is tied to the land from which they grow. In Chem, their magic is in their blood. In Elden their magic was of the mind, and of the plants of the land. It is of spirit, voice, in the Borrows. Here in the Fulmers...'

Cassien held his breath.

'In the Fulmers we brought with us magic of the heart, magic of the elements. Elemental magic is common to all lands, but our ability to walk the flame with our soul is unique, something gifted to us for saving the fire-spirits. We are also cursed – or blessed – with the capacity to feel the emotions of others.'

'You have plans to use those gifts,' Cassien said, his hope rising, his heart beating just a little faster.

'We would be foolish not to use every advantage we have. Siveraell once carried my daughter far over the sea to spy for Chemmish ships. If there are spirits brave enough, we will do the same again.'

'What would happen if they capture a spirit bearing a *walker's* soul?' Worvig asked, his voice deep.

Dia looked down at the busy hold below. 'We do not know. Nothing good, that is certain.'

Worvig shook his head but offered no argument.

A drop of rain hit Cassien's arm, and he looked up. The clouds had thickened and darkened to grey, but a silvery light still shone through here and there. The rain increased and both Rece and Worvig made excuses to get on with tasks elsewhere, but Dia showed no inclination to move. Cassien placed a hand on the slick stone and followed her gaze out over the treetops to the south.

'I have empathy for the old Covens of Chem.'

'What?' Cassien pivoted to face her, blinking droplets from his eyelashes.

Dia's face was tilted up toward the sky, her eyes closed, her expression peaceful. 'These islands were not ours, but many years ago we made them our own, bent the land to our will in as gentle a way as we were able. But it's our home.' She opened her eyes, one blue, one brown, and smiled at Cassien. 'Now we fight to live, to save our way of life. Just as the old Covens did.'

Cassien scowled. 'But that was different. Their way of life was vile.'

'In our opinion.' Dia turned her gaze back to the forest. 'The Geladanian's think us vile.'

Cassien shook his head vigorously, his wet hair ticking his face. 'There is good and there is evil, it's as simple as that.'

'You have a kind heart, Cassien.' Dia unclasped the large brooch she wore to hold her cloak together. She pinned it to his chest, touching his cheek briefly before grabbing at her cloak to stop it falling. 'You never let what happened to you blacken it.'

'Some people think I'm naïve.'

'Some people see no further than the wall they build around themselves with lies. Look.'

Cassien looked to where she pointed. The clouds were breaking apart and shafts of sun hit the trees, refracting off them so it seemed as though they bore jewels instead of leaves. A rainbow appeared even as a single rumble of thunder cracked and rolled above the sound of the surf. Cassien let his fingers explore the brooch, glancing down to see it bore the design of two dolphins, nose to tail, in a stylised circular pattern.

Dia raised her chin. 'We do not have many hours left, Cass. We should hold a feast, sing, celebrate who we are and what we are fighting for. I've had to sacrifice much as the Icante, including those I love. This will be the last gift I can give my husband. The last of the time I have to give him.'

Something burst inside Cassien's chest, his vision blurring. For a moment all words fled and Dia stepped away, making for the stairs and the great hall. Cassien forced out a small sound and he hurried after her, smoothing down his shirt before kneeling in front of her on the wet stone – though part of him felt like a fool.

'My sword is yours, Dia Icante. If I can buy you more time with Arrus, I will.' He swallowed.

Dia lay her hand on his head. 'Cass, your place is at my side, not at my feet. Come on.'

She held out her hand, and he took it, surprised by the strength of her grip. He scrambled to his feet; his limbs lighter as he walked with her toward the great hall.

These won't be the last hours of the walkers. He swore silently to whatever gods would listen, clenching his fists. *It won't.*

Chapter Twenty-Four

Rosa; Kingdom of Elden

Rosa took another hasty check around her. She heard the voices of the men a few feet away but could catch no glimpse of them between the trees and the tall ferns. Lifting her skirts, she rubbed the brown salve into the joints of her hips and knees, letting out a long breath as a soothing tingling warmth entered her muscles. She placed the small jar in her pocket and hurried to rejoin the others. Tantony was looking out for her, his dear face relaxing in relief at the sight of her.

'Ready to move on?' he asked.

Rosa nodded. 'I really hope there will be a time when everyone just behaves themselves. I'm getting too old for this.'

Tantony snorted in amusement, helping her up into her saddle before struggling into his own, his damaged knee reluctant to bend.

With no prompting, two of Tantony's men moved out onto the path ahead, the other two taking up position behind. Rosa groaned inwardly as the bruises that had quietened were reawakened. She'd never been much of a horsewoman, and these days it was rare for her to ride at all. For at least the last two hours, she'd been regretting insisting on going with Tantony to Anim.

They'd set out early, following the lake road until they came close to Taurmouth before turning eastward. They'd considered staying in an inn within Taurmaline and going on again the next day, but Rosa had been concerned about their mission becoming known. As they came out of the small copse and back out into the open, her eyes were drawn towards the distant city and the plumes of smoke that rose from it.

'Thinking of a soft bed?' Tantony asked, following her gaze.

She winced. 'Thinking of sitting on something that doesn't move.'

Tantony's eyes grew distant. 'It's been a while since I rode out on any kind of adventure.'

Rosa hoped it wouldn't be too much of an adventure, although a rebellious part of her delighted at being called upon again by the young princess. Her hand moved up to where she wore her protective pouch beneath her blouse and bodice. Tantony had scowled and declined to wear his, so she'd sewn it inside the lining of his favourite old jacket. Her husband was still convinced whoever had been capturing earth-spirits was a Geladanian who had somehow snuck here with the others, or before, but an unexplainable doubt ate quietly at the back of Rosa's mind.

The sun was getting low as one warrior twisted in his saddle to inform them, 'That's it.'

Rosa held onto the front of her saddle, straightening her legs to stand a little in her stirrups and peer ahead. There were a few houses clustered closely, then some larger buildings further south. Withies were tied in bundles and leaned together in stacks. Reeds lay on racks, a grubby-looking family replacing the dry ones with freshly cut stalks. As they passed one of the houses, an old woman with wrinkled skin hanging off her bones gave them a malevolent hiss, slamming the door on them.

'There's your witch,' a warrior muttered. His fellow gave a laugh, though it ended on a nervous note.

Rosa and Tantony glanced at each other. She'd started reading Jorrun's books on the old witch trials of Elden, and what she'd seen within the pages had chilled her to the bone. Magic users of Elden had been hunted down and murdered, but so too had many innocent women, and some men. The last thing they needed was another wave of such murderous paranoia. The sooner they got to the bottom of this, the better.

Rosa jumped when Tantony called out to the family. 'Excuse me, where is the clay merchant?'

The woman in the group grabbed her closest daughter, yanking the girl behind her. She raised a dirty arm and pointed. A large barn with a tiled roof, but walls made of straw and clay blocks, stood perhaps a quarter of a mile further down the path. Several wagons were standing outside, none of which had horses hitched to them.

'My thanks.' Tantony gave a nod of his head.

The family stood completely still, their eyes glued to them until they passed, not a single word uttered.

Rosa shuddered. 'I've never seen such fear in an Elden village.'

'Nor I.' Tantony scanned the surrounding area. 'Be ready.'

As they approached the clay works, a scrawny-looking man spotted them and called two of his fellows over. One of them carried a nasty metal tool for cutting the thick clay.

'What do you want?' Scrawny demanded.

'Clay, of course.' Tantony swung himself down off his horse. All three men took a step back. The horse snorted, shying a little.

Rosa noticed a large stone kiln beyond the storage barn, its metal door closed and a bar across it. She sucked in a breath; why would they need to stop something coming out of a kiln? This was the place; she just knew it.

'What type of clay you after?' Scrawny tilted his head. 'We mostly sell rough stuff, for building and cheap pots.' He turned a little to look Rosa up and down. 'We don't do any delicate work here.'

Rosa straightened in her saddle. 'Neither do I, young man. You've taken on some odd work lately. Statues.'

The men glanced at each other. One of them made a gesture with his hand and two others appeared from where they were hiding within the barn, both armed with serviceable swords.

Tantony raised his hands. 'We don't want trouble. Just tell us who got you to make and fire the statues, we'll leave you out of it.'

'She'll know!' one man wailed, his fellow shoving him hard in the chest to silence him.

She.

'Look, trust me.' Tantony kept his hands up and away from his sword, though his warriors fidgeted in their saddles. 'You don't want to get dragged into this business any more than you already have been. Tell us who, we'll deal with her, and you'll be safe.'

The man with the cutting tool sprang, swinging it toward Tantony. Rosa let out a startled scream. Her horse stepped back, rearing slightly. She leaned forward, pulling the horse's head down and looking up in time to see Tantony's sword sweep out and catch the long pole of the cutting tool. The two men with swords also went for Tantony, but one warrior urged his horse forward to cut them off, another vaulting down to join his Merkis.

Scrawny and the other unarmed man realised at once the odds weren't in their favour and made a run for it.

'Don't let them get to the marsh!' Tantony yelled as he hacked again at the swinging pole.

The remaining two warriors set their horses after the fleeing men. Rosa groaned, she was no help to anyone, but the men seemed to have it all in hand. Movement caught her peripheral vision. The old woman from the village had approached, coming up behind Tantony. She raised her hand, revealing a black powder in her palm, and dipped her head to blow.

'I curse you!'

'No!' Rosa urged her horse forward, causing the startled woman to stagger back. She dragged her leg over, her skirt catching and riding up as she jumped down from the saddle. The old woman hunched herself, making herself smaller or preparing to spring. Her small watery eyes glared at Rosa as she drew her hand towards her mouth.

Rosa hesitated only a split second, then swore and swung her arm, punching the old woman in the face. She crumpled in a heap of rags.

Rosa put her hands to her mouth. 'Goddess, forgive me.'

A shout made her pivot on her heels. Tantony had stabbed his attacker through the chest. The two men armed with swords were also down. One of Tantony's warriors had a small gash on his arm that didn't seem serious. Tantony made a quick check that Rosa was safe, then ordered his men, 'Check the barn for anyone else.'

They obeyed at once, while Tantony took several hurried steps towards the marsh, squinting to see what was happening.

'Did they get them?' Rosa asked, holding her breath.

'Aye.' Tantony smiled grimly. 'Looks like they did. Is that our witch?' He gestured toward the old woman.

Rosa winced. 'I don't think so.' A little flush of shame burned her cheeks as she turned back to check the woman's pulse. It was faint, but steady. Rosa carefully knelt, her knees protesting abdominally. The old woman's fingers were curled, but Rosa carefully pried one away to examine what remained of the powder. It looked to be nothing worse than wood ash.

Grunting and cursing brought Rosa swiftly to her feet. The other two warriors were returning. One had a man draped across his saddle, the other was dragging Scrawny behind him, the man's hands bound by a rope.

Tantony placed the tip of his sword against Scrawny's throat. 'Okay, we asked the nice way. Now I'm not asking, I'm telling. You'll tell us who had you make and fire clay men.'

Scrawny cast his eyes around looking for help; they fell on the old woman. 'It was her!' He pointed. 'That evil old witch! We were too afeard before, but now she's out, we can burn her quick!'

Rosa frowned and shook her head slowly. 'I don't think it is her, Tantony. She didn't seem powerful to me, just scared.'

'Scared she'd been found out!' Scrawny blurted. 'You should kill her before she wakes.'

'No!'

Rosa and Tantony both turned to look. The filthy woman who'd been tending the reeds stood in the road, hands held out imploringly.

'Who is this woman?' Rosa asked gently.

The filthy woman's eyes welled up with tears. 'She's my mother.'

'She's a witch.' Scrawny spat.

'Aye, she can be an evil cow,' the woman nodded rapidly. 'But she ain't the witch.'

'You shut up,' Scrawny threatened.

Tantony pressed his blade harder against the man's throat, making him gurgle and choke.

'Please tell us.' Rosa stepped closer to the woman. 'I'm Rosa of Northold. I work for Thane Jorrun and Lady Kesta, we can help.'

The woman's eyes widened a little. She glanced at Scrawny, then took a step toward Rosa. 'She has my daughter. Took her to work for her, took her as a hostage. She's a lady-in-waiting at the castle.'

Rosa blinked in confusion. 'Who is, the witch?'

The woman shook her head. 'No, my daughter is a lady-in-waiting. But... but really a hostage.'

'To who?' Tantony demanded.

Scrawny struggled, grabbing the blade.

'It's her.' The woman sobbed. 'It's the queen.'

'What?' Rosa's mouth fell open. 'Queen Ayline?'

Tantony withdrew his sword, shaking his head with a snarl at Scrawny. 'If I see you again, I won't give you a second chance.' He turned to his men and Rosa. 'Get on the horses.'

Rosa took a step toward the woman. 'You're telling the truth?'

She nodded, her fingers clutching at the front of her filthy dress.

'Rosa, come on,' Tantony urged. 'We have to get to the castle. Now.'

Chapter Twenty-Five

Kesta; Fulmer Island

Kesta couldn't relax, much as she wanted to; it felt as though something heavy had settled inside the top of her skull. Vivess was singing, her rich voice somehow earthy. It was an old ballad with just a touch of humour, but also of sadness. Her father's laughter made her heart ache, but she forced herself to smile. He was exchanging tales with Heara, the two of them trying to outdo each other on who had performed the most dangerous deed. Dia played with the stem of her wineglass, a smile ghosting her lips, her soul in her eyes.

'Hey.' Jorrun reached out and touched Kesta's wrist.

'I'm okay.' She turned her hand over, lacing her fingers between his. Siveraell had returned but an hour ago with the alarming report of a Geladanian attack in Elden, and that there were rumours Joss had been hurt. It had taken a lot of persuasion for Jorrun to prise her away from waiting on the beach. Only for her father's sake had she done so.

An impromptu tug of war broke out in the hall, causing people to move chairs and benches out of the way. Heara clapped her hands together with a grin and springing from the high table hurried down to join it.

'Brother.' Arrus gave Worvig a shove that lacked any actual strength. 'Go stand in for me.'

Milaiya protested, but with a roll of his eyes Worvig strode down to take the opposite side to Heara. The still burly warrior took up the rear position, wrapping the rope around his one arm.

Edon Ra stood out among the guests, his size and oddness making him hard to miss. The Rakinya was deep in conversation with young Merin. They were playing a strategic game of some sort involving coloured pebbles. Beside them, Catya and Dysarta laughed at the tug of war, siding with Heara's team. The looks they shared filled Kesta with warm hope.

'She really loves her.'

'What?' Jorrun followed her gaze. 'Yes, I think she does.'

Kesta drew in a long breath and sighed it out. 'I'm glad.' She looked across to the opposite side of the room to where Cassien sat with Rece and Jagna among the other Ravens. Cassien straightened his spine, his eyes on the doors of the great hall as they opened. Everlyn stepped in, gracefully weaving past the still battling warriors; Heara's team were just edging ahead. Kesta stood, waiting with every muscle tensed as the *walker* reported to Dia.

'Icante, Kesta, a ship has been sighted. It's the *Undine*.'

'Go on.' Dia looked from Kesta to Jorrun. 'But be calm, don't alarm the hall. I'll have the storeroom doors unbarred to allow you some privacy when you come back in.'

Jorrun nodded his thanks.

Kesta needed to run, but she calmed her shaking breathing and bowed to her mother. She offered her chair to Everlyn, then waited as long as she could endure before making her way down through the hall, Jorrun at her side. Worvig's team were taking back ground and Kesta cheered on her uncle before slipping outside.

The cold air hit her, and she moved closer to Jorrun, hastening to keep up with his long stride. Both of them paused automatically on reaching the causeway to look out to sea. Even in the darkness of a starless night, the *Undine's* wood glimmered as it cut through the waves. Kesta's heart gave a leap inside her chest as a flare went up from the dark deck, signalling a *walker* was aboard.

'Come on.' She grabbed Jorrun's hand and started to walk, but he held her back, his gaze still on the ship. 'What is it?'

Another flame had shot up, this time changing direction and coming straight for them. 'A fire-spirit.'

Kesta reached out her *knowing* and sucked in a sharp breath. 'It's Azra!'

It took only seconds for the little drake to reach them. 'Jorrun! Jorrun. Kesta. Jorrun.' He turned crazy loops around their heads like a mad, illuminated wasp. 'Did you see? I came across the sea to you! I flew over the sea!'

'Azra calm down,' Jorrun held a hand up. 'Bug!'

Azrael halted abruptly, the light of his bright flames catching the moisture in Jorrun's eyes.

'I'm very glad to see you, Azrael,' Jorrun said. 'Please give us your report.'

Kesta realised she was squeezing Jorrun's hand and loosened her grip. She blinked rapidly to dislodge the tears from her own eyes.

'We are all ssafe.' Azrael pulsed a little brighter. 'Joss is hurt, but will be all right. Jorrun, Kessta, our Riddi healed him!'

Jorrun froze.

Kesta's eyes widened. 'With magic? Do you mean with magic, Azra?'

'I do.' He turned a loop.

'Tell us everything,' Jorrun demanded. 'On our way to the beach.'

Azrael did so, Kesta's body changing from hot to cold and back again as the fire-spirit's tale unfolded. She pressed her hand against her stomach to stop the nausea. She looked up, meeting Jorrun's frightened eyes.

Geladan was already here.

When they reached the beach, two boats were landing, assisted by the patrolling Fulmer warriors. Doroquael was hovering above the second boat, illuminating the faces of Alikan and Nolv, the *Undine's* first mate. Her eyebrows raised a little when she saw Nip scramble from the first boat, turning to help both Arridia and Dierra before picking up a small chest. At the sight of her daughter, emotion surged up from Kesta's chest.

'Riddi!'

Arridia looked up before Kesta spoke her name, moving away from Nip to hurry across the sand. Kesta reached out and her daughter fell into her embrace, shaking as she clung to her. Kesta fought to bring herself back to calm for her daughter's sake, grateful for Jorrun's warmth as he briefly placed his arms around them both, kissing the top of Arridia's head before striding across to the boats to assist. Alikan and Nolv were lifting out a stretcher with the help of some Borrowmen.

Arridia stepped back a little, looking down at her mother. 'Did Azra tell you?'

'I did!' Azrael flew around them.

'He did.' Kesta reached out and wiped the tears from Arridia's cheeks. 'We'll talk about that later, my honey. Let's get you safe in the hold. You'll be wanting to see your grandfather.'

Arridia sniffed and nodded, twisting to look over her shoulder. Kesta rubbed her back, then moved away to join Jorrun. Despite Doroqueal's anxious squeaks and fluttering, Joss didn't look too bad. His eyes showed pain and tiredness, but they were open. Jorrun placed a hand against Joss's cheek, then bent to kiss his forehead.

'You'll be well,' Jorrun breathed. 'You're home, son.'

Kesta took Joss's hand and kissed it, before beckoning the loitering Fulmer warriors to take over carrying the litter. 'In through the hall's supply door,' she instructed. Kesta gave Dierra and Nip a quick hug, then turned to Alikan. The boy she had raised alongside her own children tensed as she held him, avoiding her eyes as she tried to study his face.

'Ali?'

The young Chemman shook his head, blinking rapidly. 'I failed. I let you down.'

Kesta tutted loudly and punched him in the arm. 'Don't talk nonsense.'

His amber eyes widened in shock.

'I've fought Jderha's assassins,' she reminded him. 'You did brilliantly to defeat them all and lose no one.'

'We only didn't lose Joss because Riddi saved him.'

Jorrun joined them, placing his hand on Alikan's shoulder. 'That's as may be, but you are all here, and that's all that matters. Come on, son, let's get in the hold.'

'It's not just the Geladanians though—'

Arridia gave a hiss and Alikan clamped his mouth tightly closed.

'What?' Kesta looked from her daughter back to Alikan. Her eyes narrowed. 'What's going on?'

'Not here.' Arridia met her mother's eyes, her gaze steady. She straightened up and turned to Jorrun. 'In private. When you're sitting down.'

Jorrun frowned but nodded.

'Humph.' Kesta regarded them all. 'Come on, then.' She glanced around, making sure she had everyone, then noticed there was a significant absence. 'Where's Temerran?'

'He stayed in Taurmaline,' Arridia told her. 'He was concerned about Lucien and Scarlett.'

A deep uneasiness settled in Kesta's bones. The Bard of the Borrows had such a strong friendship with her mother it seemed odd that he wouldn't come here. Odder still that he would leave the *Undine*. She regarded her daughter and Alikan, before shaking herself and turning back to the present moment. She looked around for the *Undine*'s first mate.

'Nolv, you'll come with us to the Hold? Bring some of your men and eat with us, I'm sure my parents would love to see you.'

Nolv gave a stiff and awkward bow, using just his shoulders and neck. 'Thank ee, ma'am.'

Jorrun hurried to catch up with Alikan and the stretcher bearers, Azrael flowing after him. Dierra walked just ahead of Kesta and Arridia, her head turning as she instinctively checked the area. She wasn't the strongest of Jorrun's nieces, but she was a competent Raven. Kesta bit her lip hard when she realised it was only chance and circumstance that had brought Dierra here to face Geladan rather than any of her sisters.

'Mumma?'

Kesta linked her arm through her daughters. 'Just thinking too much, you know what I'm like.'

Arridia nodded, a slight smile coming to her lips.

They made their way up to the Hold, Kesta aware of the curious glances and the murmurs of the waiting refugees.

'What's happening?' Arridia demanded. 'Is everyone taking shelter here?'

'No. We'll explain it all when we're inside.' Instinctively she drew on her calm again in case her daughter needed it.

'It's very different to how I remember,' Nip spoke up behind them.

'How so?' Arridia twisted to look over her shoulder at him.

Lines formed around Nip's grey eyes as he gazed up at the walls. 'It seems smaller.'

'You haven't been back here since you were a child, though,' Kesta said. 'What were you, thirteen? Fourteen?'

'Yes, about that.'

'What do you have there?' Kesta nodded toward the small wooden chest he carried. Nip wasn't the sort of man who would concern himself with treasure.

Nip's mouth curled up in a smile. 'I carry a friend, but he is wary of people. When it's quiet, I'll introduce him.'

Kesta looked from Nip to the chest and back again, intrigued, but she didn't press him.

Everlyn waited for them at the storeroom doors. They were solidly made, redesigned by Everlyn's husband, with two layers of planks; some vertical, some horizontal. A set of steep stone steps led down into the large space beneath the great hall, at the centre of which was a broad rectangular pillar of stone supporting the firepit in the hall above. A second sturdy door stood at the bottom of the steps and four warriors waited on guard. The noise from the hall was loud, the thudding of feet mixing with laughter and song.

'Eve, would you kindly show Nolv and his men into the great hall?' Kesta asked her mother's friend.

'Of course.' Everlyn gestured for the men to follow.

Kesta led the rest of them up to hers and Jorrun's room, and the warriors placed Joss carefully on the bed before retreating. Kesta spotted Nip slipping out after them.

'No, Nip, stay. You're family.'

Nip's eyes brightened, going straight to Arridia, whose cheeks coloured slightly. Kesta narrowed her eyes. Was there something going on there, or was she imagining it?

Jorrun regarded them all. 'Sit down.'

Arridia, Dierra and Kesta all sat on the bed. Alikan offered Nip the chair by the desk, himself leaning against it while the two fire-spirits patrolled the window and door.

'Kes, why don't you fill them in on what our plans are while I heal Joss some more,' Jorrun suggested.

'It's okay.' Joss tried to sit up. 'We need to tell you something.'

'You're gonna go mad,' Doroquael muttered.

Azrael flew at his fellow Drake and shushed him.

Kesta folded her arms, looking around at their guilty faces. 'Okay, what's going on?'

Dierra shifted on the bed. Only Arridia and Nip would meet Kesta's eyes.

Arridia opened her mouth to speak, but Joss interrupted her. 'No, Riddi, I should tell it.' Kesta watched her son as he visibly gathered himself. He tried again to sit up and Jorrun slipped an arm under him to help him. Joss swallowed, looking up at his father as the safest option of his two parents.

'Okay.' Joss looked from Alikan to Arridia, before turning back to Jorrun. 'You know how you always warned us about King Bractius and his plans to bring magic into his bloodline?'

Kesta's nostrils flared, but she waited for him to go on.

'Well, it turns out his daughter has learned a few tricks and ambitions from her parents.'

'Scarlett?' Kesta gave a puzzled shake of her head.

Joss drew in a deep breath. 'Eleanor.'

He told them what had happened. Kesta's fingers slowly curled into fists, her teeth were so tightly clenched together she thought they might break. Jorrun's eyes had grown hard, almost wild. There was a stillness about him that was frightening. Kesta leapt up off the bed and Dierra gasped, shrinking back.

'Mumma.' Arridia's voice came out in a harsh whisper.

Kesta felt the pressure building inside her. How dare he! After everything, Bractius still connived to control and own Jorrun! And now their children. She would rip the man apart.

'Told you,' Doroquael muttered smugly.

'Kesta.' Jorrun stood in front of her, his hand held up palm outward between them. 'My love, not now.'

She met his eyes, the hardness gone, only concern and sadness there now. She glanced around quickly. Dierra was almost curled up on the bed, her knees drawn up to her chest. Arridia was staring at her, eyes wide and tear-filled. Alikan had crumpled in on himself, his eyes tight shut. Joss was breathing hard, his face pale but for two red spots on his cheeks.

Nip was on his feet, a determined expression on his gentle face, and he reached out to take Arridia's hand. Kesta's anger flew away from her, leaving her light-headed. Did faithful Nip really think he had to defend Arridia from her wrath?

Her hands flew to her mouth, then she held them out. 'Oh, my honeys, I'm sorry. I'm not angry at you, not at all.' She quickly crouched beside Joss, smoothing back his hair. 'It's Bractius and Ayline I'm furious with. I wish you'd waited, come to us, but it's done now.'

Jorrun drew in a breath and let it out slowly. 'We're upset we didn't do better at protecting you all.'

'But you have.' Arridia scrambled off the bed to hug her father. Jorrun rested his cheek on the top of her head, letting go of her momentarily to place his hand on Alikan's shoulder.

Nip cleared his throat. 'Shall I get us all something to eat and drink?'

'Please.' Jorrun gave him a nod, a smile softening his face.

'I'll help.' Dierra crawled across the bed and followed him out.

Jorrun reluctantly let go of Arridia. 'Let's get you healed, Joss, then we'll see if Arrus is still up and well enough to join us.'

'Thank you.' Kesta whispered as her husband knelt beside her. She pulled her *knowing* in tight despite her need for connection. It was rare these days she let her anger get the better of her, but Bractius could wait. She wouldn't forget, though, and there was no way she was going to let the sneaky, plotting throne of Elden steal her son.

Chapter Twenty-Six

Temerran; Kingdom of Elden

With a nod at the steward and the warriors on guard, Temerran slipped quietly into the back of the throne room. He froze. Eleanor sat at a table near to the king, as bold as a gull on a fishing boat. She was dressed in a demure, dark-blue dress, her hands folded before her. A stern-looking woman hovered behind her, and Temerran guessed she must be some kind of chaperone.

He drifted further into the room, rolling his eyes when he saw Adrin. What would it take for the king to get rid of the awful man? Merkis Shryn was standing below the throne, along with Jarl Hadger of Taurmouth. He wondered if the old lecher knew his son had lost out on a prestigious marriage.

The queen sat to Bractius's right on her smaller throne and unusually, Lucien had been allowed to join them. He looked small, pale, and exceedingly young, seated in the stark black chair once occupied by Jorrun. Temerran's heart constricted, and he ducked his head to hide his wince. If only Bractius could see the boy's worth, rather than constantly measuring him against himself and finding him wanting. It made Temerran's blood boil.

Scarlett was also in the throne room and appeared to be welcoming a group of nobles. Kistelle hovered at a discreet distance, observing the hall. Temerran recognised the Jarl of Southport and his wife, and frowned. Surely if they were expecting an attack from the south, the Jarl should be in his castle to defend his people? He didn't know the other man and woman with the group, but Scarlett spotted him and beckoned him over. Temerran loosened his muscles, allowing his most charming smile to come forth.

'Temerran, may I introduce my father's distant cousin, Kelinde, and her husband Jarl Medwyn of Roughton. This is Temerran, Bard of the Borrows.'

Temerran gave an elegant bow. 'An honour.'

'The bard!' Medwyn raised his eyebrows, a genuine smile on his face. 'We've heard so much about you over the years but have not had the pleasure of being here when you have.'

'Then I must sing for you later, if the king permits.'

'That would be wonderful.' Kelinde's cheeks dimpled with her smile. She had the same tinge of pale red to her hair as Bractius, the same brown eyes.

'So, what has brought you to Taurmaline at such a fortuitous time?' Temerran asked innocently.

'Well, in times such as these, his majesty has gathered those who need protecting to the safest place,' Kelinde replied.

Temerran glanced at Scarlett, sure he must have the same shocked expression on his own face. Putting all those of value in one place was the worst thing the king could do. He shaped a pleasant smile. 'I do not know Roughton, is it a coastal land?'

'Not at all.' Medwyn shook his head. 'We are a lake city much like Taurmaline and in the central southeast. You must visit us, Temerran, we would love to have you at our hall.'

'You are kind.' He gave another bow, hiding his discomfort. This was no time for polite invitations. Did these people not understand the danger they were in? He exchanged a longer look with Scarlett before surveying the room again. 'Where are ambassadors Dorthai and Finian?'

'Oh, did you not hear?' Scarlett took an excited step toward him. 'A messenger came from Taurmouth. A Fulmer longship is on its way with *walkers* and Ravens to protect the castle. They should be here soon, around sunset. The ambassadors went down to the docks to meet them.'

A servant offered Temerran some water, and he took a cup with barely a glance.

'It will be a relief to have them here,' Medwyn chattered. 'I can't believe Thane Jorrun has left us at a time like this, he shows a distinct lack of loyalty to his king.'

Temerran almost choked on his water, wiping his chin and apologising quickly. Scarlett raised her eyebrows at him and steered the subject safely away. Temerran winked at her, then took a step back, noticing a frown on Kistelle's face. He followed the scout's gaze. She seemed to be checking out one of the servants. With a jolt Temerran realised the man had darker skin than that of an Eldeman, more like an islander. He snorted out loudly through his nose, shaking his head at his own paranoia.

He clenched his teeth, bracing himself, before approaching Adrin. The man was so narcissistic he was usually easy to tap for information, but it also took Temerran closer to the thrones.

'So, you and your men are to defend the king rather than the coast?' Temerran ensured the tone of his voice implied a compliment.

Adrin's chest swelled as he lifted his shoulders back. 'Well, of course his majesty would want his best to stand by him and his family.'

Temerran let the man run his mouth while he himself observed the room. He caught Eleanor's chaperone watching him. The dour woman looked quickly away. The Jarl of Southport and his wife had joined Eleanor at her table and the princess was smiling politely, if without any warmth.

An uneasiness spread down Temerran's back. He couldn't put his finger on it, but there was a tension in the hall which didn't seem to come from any of the guests. He nodded distractedly at something Adrin said, his gaze wandering to the thrones. The queen's eyes met his and held, her chin lifting. Temerran bowed deferentially, and Ayline gave the slightest of nods in response.

She had been obsessively ambitious when he'd first met her, but also blindly naïve. Over the years Temerran had watched as the young woman had learned to better cultivate the little power she was allowed, learning subtlety, honing her skills. She was intelligent, and she was cold. Not that she lacked passion, on the contrary, Temerran suspected she hid a fire she'd never been able to explore; but she could manipulate a man's death and not bat an eyelid. With a wince he wondered if he'd made a mistake in not trying to befriend the queen, but he'd been too wary, too unforgiving, since she'd attempted to hang Dia all those years ago.

Lucien shifted uncomfortably in his black chair, his focus on his father as the king instructed Merkis Shryn. Two of the Ravens Joss had left in Elden stood either side of the door behind the thrones where they could observe all the room. Something prickled on the back of Temerran's neck, and he rolled his shoulders, trying to dislodge his unease.

Murmurs broke out behind him and he pivoted on the balls of his feet as the steward announced the delegation from the Fulmers. He smiled on seeing Eidwyn, some of his tension falling away. He knew the pretty *walker* well, intimately in fact, they'd had a brief relationship on one of his visits to the Fulmers. She hadn't renewed their relationship on his next visit, which had disappointed him, but not broken his heart. She was young still, and he couldn't blame her for wanting a man who would stay around and offer her a family. Though perhaps... he smiled to himself. Perhaps here in Elden she would enjoy his company.

There were two *walkers* with Eidwyn and a further four Ravens. Temerran turned to see the king's reaction. Considering what the Fulmers was facing, Dia had been generous in her protection of Elden. Or in sending Eidwyn here, had the Icante hoped to save a friend?

'Welcome, welcome.' Bractius smiled warmly, then rose and made his way down the two steps to meet them. Lucien quickly pushed himself up and followed. The queen remained where she was, showing her disdain for the people who had come to keep her safe. 'We are grateful that you came.'

'It's an honour.' Eidwyn gave a curtsey. 'If it is not too abrupt of me to ask, there was rumour on our way downriver of an attack from Geladan?'

'We dealt with it. Come, take some refreshment, be welcome in my hall.'

Temerran slipped away from Adrin, who was appraising the *walkers* in a way that made Temerran want to break his nose. Temerran took a sip from his cup, stopping to stand side by side with the prince.

'Your father puts all his eggs in one basket.'

'What?' Lucien blinked at him in momentary confusion. 'Oh, yes. He still thinks the Geladanians will have to hit the coast first.'

'Hmm.' Temerran raised an eyebrow. 'Well, we've seen that isn't the case.'

'You think there are more?'

Again, a feeling of dread swept through Temerran and he shifted his feet. *I know there are.* His instincts screamed of it. 'Be on guard.' He briefly touched Lucien's arm. 'Stay close to a Raven.'

Temerran continued to circulate around the room, exchanging news and concerns with Dorthai and Eidwyn. At a word from the queen, more servants came in, carrying food and wine. Temerran rubbed at his stubbled chin. Something was niggling again. He glanced around. The strain of wearing a smile and being polite was fraying his patience. For a reception it seemed longer than usual, surely a formal greeting followed by allowing the guests to settle and be later welcomed at a feast was the norm here at Taurmaline? Was this a slight of the queen's against the Fulmers?

There was a commotion at the door as the steward tried to stop someone entering. Temerran straightened up, lowering his cup. Tantony and Rosa.

Rosa looked pale, frightened. Tantony's face was red, his mouth fixed in a firm, thin line. The man was furious.

The steward hurried to King Bractius, who nodded, and the steward gestured for the Merkis and his wife to approach. Rosa spotted

Temerran and veered toward him to grab his wrist with both her small hands. Her voice was breathless. 'Temerran, you'd better hear this.'

He nodded, following her to catch up with Tantony as he reached the king.

The old warrior bowed stiffly. 'Forgive the intrusion, majesty, we have a matter of dire urgency.' He glanced around the room. 'But we should speak in private.'

'You have my ear.' Bractius looked him up and down, and moved away toward the back of the room. Ayline stood as they passed.

'Perhaps in your study,' Tantony persisted.

'Whatever is it, man.' Bractius gave a bemused shake of his head. 'Just spit it out.'

Tantony swallowed, checking to see who was in earshot. He lowered his voice. 'Majesty, I don't know how to tell you this, but we have discovered who the witch is.'

'Well, that's splendid news!'

Tantony hissed at Bractius's booming voice, then winced when he realised he'd shushed his king. 'No, your majesty, it isn't. We... it...'

'It's the queen,' Rosa blurted.

Bractius laughed, throwing his head back.

A deep cold gripped Temerran's bones. He turned and looked at Ayline, who met his eyes, her gaze unwavering.

'Have you been drinking, Tantony?' Bractius slapped the Merkis hard on the shoulder. 'Ayline has no power.'

The queen's lips twisted up in a snarl and she strode toward her husband, whose eyes widened in shock.

'No power!' She curled her fingers into claws. 'Oh, I have power. You'd give me none of the respect I'm owed, so I found power of my own.'

'Witchcraft?' Bractius spluttered. 'How could *you* learn such a thing?'

Temerran's heart gave a lurch, and for a moment the floor seemed to vanish from beneath him. He knew exactly from where. He'd brought the treacherous Geladanian spy here himself fourteen years ago, and she and the queen... she and the queen had become firm friends.

'Linea.'

'What?' Bractius shook his head.

Ayline took several steps backward, straightening up, seeming to grow as she went. Temerran felt the drawing of her power like a dark, icy wind rising from the earth. Ayline spun about to face the hall. Her voice was strong, unwavering.

'Listen to me. While your king has been wasting his time with weak alliances and Fulmer whores, I have saved us all. Yes, we are safe. Geladan will not attack us. Jderha is our friend.'

Bractius's mouth fell open. He leaned forward, but his feet didn't move.

'What have you done?' Temerran demanded. 'What have you done?'

'A simple exchange.' Ayline's mouth quirked up in a smile. 'I sent my own delegation to make a treaty, offering friendship and a truce.'

'In exchange for what?' Temerran roared.

Ayline tutted and raised her perfect eyebrows. 'They get the Fulmers. I get the throne, and Eleanor after me.'

'You would take my throne?' Bractius finally moved. 'You?'

Ayline lifted a finger. 'Uh, uh. I wouldn't lay a finger on me if I were you.' She turned to look down at the throne room. Most people had frozen where they stood, but Kistelle had called up a shield and pulled Scarlett toward her brother. Ayline reached out her hands, palm upward in a welcoming manner. 'Come forward, my friends.'

Several of the servants put down or dropped what they were carrying and moved toward the thrones. The two warriors who were guarding the doors closed them and put the bar across.

Ayline turned to her husband. 'Our guests from Geladan.' She sauntered toward him, triumph in her eyes. 'That crown's mine.'

As she reached up to snatch it, Bractius's hand flew up, his dagger catching the light. Ayline had time only to gasp in a breath before he plunged it up to the hilt in her throat. Scarlett screamed, a sound that was echoed by her twin across the room. The Queen of Elden crumpled to the floor, Bractius stepped over her as though she were already only a rag.

'Kill them!' he bellowed. 'Kill the Geladanians!'

Temerran closed his eyes.

Chapter Twenty-Seven

Joss; Fulmer Island

Joss found it hard to keep still. His wound tickled and itched, his father's magic giving him a floating sensation as it flowed through his blood. Slowly his vision focused, and he blinked, realising his father's power had withdrawn. He reached up to touch his bare chest, his fingertips finding the small ridge of a scar.

'How is he?' His mother sounded worried.

'He'll be fine.' His father's long fingers brushed across his forehead. They were warm and calloused. 'Arridia, you did really well. I've been thinking. The first time I was able to heal I was in a traumatic situation, in genuine fear of losing a good friend.'

'Rece.' Arridia's voice came from further in the room behind his parents.

'Yes.' Jorrun nodded, twisting to look over his shoulder. 'But your aunt picked it up with relative ease. She still believes the magic has something to do with intent, but I wonder now if emotion somehow plays a part.'

Kesta made a sound in the back of her throat. 'There could be something to that.'

Joss pushed himself up on his elbows. The room was lit by a single candle and by Azrael and Doroquael who floated before the window. They had moved him onto the bed and his father perched on the edge beside him. His mother had pulled a chair close to watch over his healing. Arridia and Dierra sat together on the carpet in the corner.

'What time is it?' Joss demanded. 'Have I missed grandfather? Where's Ali?'

Jorrun smiled, and Joss relaxed at the calm warmth in his father's pale-blue eyes. 'It's only been an hour, son. Ali and Nip are taking our plates out to the hall. We'll let your grandfather know you're ready.'

'I'll go!' Doroquael offered at once, vanishing into the candle flame.

Joss touched his scar again.

'Does it still hurt?' Kesta asked in concern.

'Oh, no.' Joss shook his head. 'It's just, well, I still can't believe I'm alive sometimes.' A lump formed in his throat.

There was a soft knock at the door, and it opened at once. Joss scrambled to sit as his grandmother entered. His grandfather was behind her, leaning on Worvig's arm.

'What's this I hear my grandson has won himself a princess?' Arrus grinned.

'Father.' Kesta tutted.

Arrus gave Joss a wink, and Kesta moved aside to let him sit down. As exhausted and emotional as he felt, it was a tough fight for Joss not to let his shock and grief show. His grandfather had always seemed like a boisterous, friendly giant to him. This wasted old man was a stranger. Even Dia looked different. She was still calm and poised, but something had gone from her strength. She didn't look like the Icante; she looked like... she looked like a grandmother. Worvig gave him a nod and quietly left the room.

'My honeys.' Dia kissed Dierra on the cheek, hugged Arridia, then held Joss as lightly as though he were a wren's egg. 'You have been through so much,'

'What news is there?' Joss asked anxiously.

'You should rest,' Kesta urged.

'No, Mum, I can't rest until I know.'

'Briefly then.' Dia sat on the bed on the opposite side to Jorrun. Nip and Alikan slipped quietly back into the room as she explained the basics of their plan. Several times Joss met his sister's eyes. It was his father who noticed his unease.

'What is it?'

Joss shifted on the bed. 'All this because of me and Rids. Perhaps we should get Nolv to take us on a long voyage on the *Undine*.'

Kesta protested at once, but his grandmother smiled and lay a hand on his arm. 'Tomorrow I'll introduce you to someone. He's a kind of expert on prophecy.'

Arrus chuckled. 'An overgrown bear with too sharp a mind is what he is.'

Dia's smile widened, and she shook her head at her husband.

Joss wanted to feel their humour, their familiar love, but he couldn't get past the squirming unease in his body and his soul. His grandmother seemed to realise and took hold of his hand.

'None of this is down to you, Joss, nor Arridia.' Dia drew in a deep breath and glanced at Kesta and Jorrun. 'Call it what you will, fate, bad luck, paranoia, prophecy. We have the misfortune of Jderha picking now, and she has found someone to fit a dream steeped in fear and anger from decades ago. If it hadn't been you and Riddi, it would have been someone else. That's probably no comfort, but I hope you understand that you are not responsible, and by no means should contemplate sacrificing yourself to make amends for something that is not your fault.'

Exhaustion swept through him and a light, floaty relief. His thoughts went immediately to Scarlett, to her fragile bravery. He suddenly missed her with an intensity that floored him. 'Is there any news from Elden? Any news from Scarlett?'

'Nothing,' Dia replied. 'Which we have to take as good.'

'Come find me tomorrow.' Arrus gave Joss a light thump on the shoulder with the flat of his hand. 'I'll give you some tips on how to be a good husband.'

Dia covered her mouth with her hand, but her eyes shone as she looked at Arrus. 'Well then. It's late and I still have work to do. We'll let you all settle.'

Nip took a step forward. 'If you'll excuse me, while you are all here, may I have a moment?'

Dia straightened up and tilted her head to regard him. 'Of course.'

Nip turned to Arridia, and she picked up the chest beside her on the floor and handed it to him. Joss had heard all about the earth-spirit, but having been confined to his bed on the ship, he hadn't seen the creature. He pulled himself up against the headboard to see past Arrus and his parents.

Nip took in everyone in the room, his dark-grey eyes earnest. 'I'm going to introduce you to Gorchia. He's an earth-spirit of Elden who was trapped by a witch and turned into a golem.'

'The one who attacked Joss?' Arrus asked.

'The one.' Nip nodded. 'We have talked a lot. The earth-spirits hate people—'

Azrael gave a hiss.

'—because of their destructive disregard for nature, but the people of the Fulmers and especially *walkers* intrigued Gorchia. He is native to Elden, but he has conversed with earth-spirits of Geladan. He knows some were loosed here on the island when the high priestess was destroyed. Because we freed him from the golem trap, and because he thinks he will like the Fulmers, he has agreed to come and talk to those spirits. They may be reluctant to help, but they might at least be able to offer insight into their erstwhile captors.'

'The islandss are fire islands,' Azrael muttered. Arridia shushed him.

'Can we see him?' Joss asked eagerly.

'I would love to meet him,' Dia said politely.

Nip reached for the lid of the chest and slowly opened it. Joss leaned forward. He'd only glimpsed the spirit at Teriton, and this one was startlingly different. He'd assumed earth-spirits were as similar to each other as fire-spirits; but then he'd always somehow been able to tell them apart. The bark-skinned elemental gave a low bow, his ears folding over his face.

Nip introduced everyone, and Dia took a step closer around the bed. 'On behalf of the Fulmers, I welcome you and thank you for your offer of help. It is a risk for you to come here.'

Gorchia folded his arms and leaned his weight on one leg. 'It is, *fire-lady*. But everywhere is a risk these days it seems.'

'That is sadly true.' Dia raised her eyebrows. 'Is there anything you need? Anything we can do to help you in your endeavour?'

'Nip has given me food and water and earth from my home. If I may have your permission, I shall seek the native spirits.'

'We're the native spirits,' Azrael grumped.

'Actually.' Jorrun turned to his oldest friend. 'You're from Chem.'

Azrael flared and spluttered, but he couldn't disagree.

'Don't be jealous, Azra,' Arridia told her guardian gently. 'You know we love you.'

Azrael continued to blaze silently but didn't interrupt again. Joss twisted to look at his own spirit; Doroquael was watching Gorchia but didn't seem perturbed.

Dia's eyes flickered from her daughter, to Jorrun, then to Nip, before she nodded at the earth-spirit. 'You have my permission.'

At once, foxfire flared up around the small elemental and his body appeared to burst into several small spiders. Nip flinched just a little as they scampered out of the chest and dropped to the floor. Dierra let out a startled scream. Every little spider had a green glow in its myriad eyes as they vanished between the floorboards.

'Well.' Dia broke the silence. 'This time we really must rest.'

All of them stood politely as the Icante left with Arrus, except Joss, who could only sit up straighter. The door had barely closed before Kesta was organising them.

'Riddi and Dierra, my honeys, Heara and Vilnue have kindly given up their room so you can stay nearby. Heara intends to sleep outside my mother's door. Joss and Ali, you have the small guest room down in the stores, although if you want to remain here tonight—'

'It's okay.' He gritted his teeth and swung his legs off the bed, his eyes widening when there was no pain in his chest muscles. In all honesty, he needed some quiet time and a moment to think. His gaze travelled to his sister, and she gave a small, thin-lipped smile of understanding.

'Do you need help?' His father asked.

Alikan stepped forward. 'I got this.'

Alikan held out his arm and Joss clasped his wrist, using his brother's strength to stand. Dierra passed Joss his shirt and Jorrun opened the door to let them through. Doroquael took the lead, making himself large as he floated down the steps to the corridor behind the great hall. There was a lot of noise coming from behind the solid door and Joss stopped to listen.

His childhood had been full of exciting visits to Fulmer Hold, and on more than one occasion he'd snuck out here to sit on the stairs and listen when he should have been in bed. His grandfather's loud, rolling laugh had always made him feel safe. Sometimes Temerran had visited, and he'd learned a lot about the different lands from the songs the bard had sung. Joss smiled. He'd learned something of romance from those songs too, and that not all tales had a happy ending.

'Joss?' Alikan asked in concern.

'Let's pop in the hall, just for a minute.'

Joss quickly smoothed back the longer hair on the top of his head and opened the door. Two warriors who stood on guard stepped aside, giving Joss and Alikan a nod, their eyes following Doroquael, who pulled a scary face on entering the hall, just in case. Joss recognised two chieftains from Dolphin Island, sitting beside the large fireplace, their feet up on stools. Many of the small alcoves around the hall had their curtains closed so the guests within could sleep with a modicum of privacy. Worvig was talking with a small group of men, his wife Milaiya having gone to bed.

Alikan gave a sharp intake of breath, and Joss turned to look at him. His friend's skin had paled, and his amber eyes were wide as he stared unblinking. Joss followed his gaze to a group of three people farther back in the hall. A tall woman with fiery red hair sat close beside another woman dressed in similar black leather armour with a white fur trim. Both were heavily armed. The redhead was pretty, but it was the other woman who drew Joss's attention. She was pale with blue eyes, her hair plaited and drawn back into a tail at the nape of her neck like a Borrow warrior. She was animated as she spoke, showing none of the tiredness of her companions. The third of the group was a young boy, about seven or eight. For some reason, Joss thought he knew him.

'Who's that?' Joss nudged Alikan.

It was a moment before Alikan replied. 'That's Catya.'

'What? You mean Mother and Father's Catya? The Queen of Snowhold?'

The blue-eyed woman saw them and froze. She said something quietly to her companions and stood before strolling over. Alikan took a step back as she approached.

'Catya.' Doroquael bobbed politely.

'Hey, Doro, how are you?' Catya cocked her head slightly to regard the fire-spirit, then she looked up at Alikan. 'Alikan.'

Alikan swallowed. 'Catya. Your Majesty.'

A little of Catya's swagger seemed to fall away, and she tore her gaze from Alikan to study Joss. 'You must be Joss? You were so small when I last saw you. I can see both your parents in your face.'

Joss held his hand out, and she clasped his wrist like a warrior. 'I've heard so much about you. Heara is always saying you were her smartest pupil.'

'Really?' Catya brightened.

'Have you... have you come to fight for the Fulmers?'

She gave a firm nod. 'Of course. But...' She paused and turned back to Alikan. 'I have also come to introduce my son to his father.'

Alikan was breathing hard, like a trapped animal. The glare he was giving Catya was almost murderous. Joss had never seen his friend so angry. Joss looked past Catya to the redhead and the boy. They were both watching avidly, the boy's eyes wide.

Those eyes.

Joss's mouth fell open. He couldn't help himself, he laughed.

Alikan turned on his heels and headed for the doors.

'Ali, hold up!' Joss called after him. He winced at Catya apologetically before hurrying after his brother. The doors to the hall almost swung back into Joss. A grin was still trying to break out on his face. After all those years of lectures, it turned out perfectly behaved Alikan wasn't so well behaved after all. 'Ali.'

Doroquael gave a squeal when he realised he was being left behind and shot after Joss to fly at his shoulder. Alikan took the stairs down two at a time, ignoring the startled guards and striding to the last door on the left.

'Hey, come on, Ali.' Joss's chest had tightened, and he breathed through his mouth to fill his lungs. 'I'm sorry, okay.' He followed his friend into the small guest room. A bed stood on either side of the room with a single washstand between them. Alikan stood with his back hunched, facing the wall. There was no window, but Doroquael chased back the darkness.

Joss attempted some humour. 'Hey, I only managed a princess, you bagged a queen.'

'Seriously?' Alikan spun to face him. 'Have you learned nothing, Joss?'

Joss took a step back, his face falling. 'I... Sorry.'

'This isn't funny. There's a child involved for the gods' sake.'

A little touch of nausea settled in Joss's stomach. He'd never heard Alikan swear by the Chemmish gods before.

Alikan sat heavily on the edge of the bed. 'She didn't even have the decency to let me know.'

Joss crept across to his own bed and sat down opposite his friend and brother. 'Was it, um, serious between the two of you?'

Alikan shook his head, his long ponytail falling from where it had snagged on his shoulder. It was a moment before he spoke. 'I was young. Younger than you. It was when I was apprenticed to Rothfel for a few months, and went with him on one of his visits to Snowhold. You stayed in Navere with our parents. I've told you of what it was like there, the fierce and mysterious Rakinya, serene but wild tribespeople. I didn't tell you much about the queen.

'Catya, she's, well, she's compelling. She has such an aura of confidence about her. I was... enamoured.' He sighed loudly and looked up. 'I was a stupid boy trying to be a man. A couple of glasses of wine and some flattery and the next thing I knew I was in her bed. I thought it was the best night of my life until early morning when Dysarta burst in on us.'

'Dysarta? She had a wife at the time?' Joss swore.

'She nearly didn't.' Alikan rubbed at his forehead with his hand. 'Dysarta was furious, understandably. Luckily, she didn't blame me, but she did leave the castle and headed back to her home in the far north. Rothfel took us all out of there quick as he could and back to Navere. I never went back.'

'And no one ever told you about the boy?'

Alikan lay back on his bed. 'No.'

Joss breathed in. 'His eyes, though. What are you going to do?'

Alikan stared up at the ceiling. Doroquael bobbed silently, dulling his flame. 'The first thing I'm going to have to do is apologise. I really hope the boy knows my reaction wasn't for him.'

'Hey.' Joss sat up. 'Does this make you a king?'

Alikan turned his head to glare at Joss.

Joss grinned. 'Only kidding. Seriously, Ali, I know I'm an idiot sometimes, but if I can do anything, well, you know?'

Alikan rubbed at his eyes. 'Yeah, I know. But don't be offended when I go to our father for advice rather than you. Get some sleep.'

Doroquael settled on the candle in the washstand, and Joss undressed and climbed into bed without protest. Part of him still couldn't help the small surge of mirth that wanted to well up in him. Another part of him felt sick for his friend's shock. The nausea increased, and he swore silently. He hoped there would be time for Alikan to know his son.

He sat up and swore again. He'd been ridiculously careless with Eleanor. There was every possibility he might have a child himself.

Chapter Twenty-Eight

Dia; Fulmer Island

Dia watched as Arrus's breast rose and fell. Far below the window the surf shushed, growing and retreating. It was a clear night and stars glimmered beyond the horizon, their silver light comforting, but at the same time, taunting. The night sky seemed infinite, and yet here before her was proof that life was not. An unbearable ache grew in her chest, but she didn't fight it. Life was pain, love was loss. She had no regrets.

There was only one task left to do.

The candle flame flickered, and she turned, seeing the tiny blue eyes within. Siveraell unfurled, detaching himself from the wick but not increasing in his intensity, mindful of Arrus.

'You should sleep, Dia, bright soul.'

She turned to the spirit and smiled through her hurt. 'There is no time left for sleeping, there is no time left at all.'

'You have served our people well, no one better.'

Dia looked down at her hands. 'Perhaps, spirit.'

'There is no perhaps. Yours is the heart that binds the land beneath the sky. Yours the blood that heals the lands. Your daughter, your granddaughter, bear fire in their souls, but there is a greatness of wisdom in you that is rare beneath the sky. Long ago, love saved the fire-spirits; love saved the priestesses of the flame. We gather now in love, to save the Fulmers.'

Dia leaned her forehead against her hand. Siveraell meant well, but she was tired, her soul exhausted. Although she held out hope for her family, for the Fulmers, she had left none for herself. Despite the heavy ache in her bones, she drew in a deep breath and sat up straight. 'Dawn is coming. We have work to do.'

'We do. Where would you like to start?'

Dia turned her gaze back to the window. 'Would you take me to the beacons in the south?'

Siveraell folded in a bow.

Dia knew the elder spirit had already taken Kesta out over the sea the evening before, and other *walkers* had watched through the night, but there was no substitute for seeing for yourself. She placed a cushion on the floor and settled on it. Siveraell hovered in front of her, closing his burning blue eyes so he wouldn't distract her as she concentrated on the flickering of his flame. The meditation used by the *walkers* to ready their mind to *walk* was a simple one, though a closely guarded secret. First, she reached her consciousness down through the floor, imagining she had deep roots that plunged into the ground. She expanded her awareness, reaching out, connecting to the life-force of the island.

'Earth beneath me.'

She breathed in deeply, picturing the infinite sky beneath which all things lived. As her lungs expanded, she invoked the benign power of the universe.

'Sky above me.'

Around her she imagined a ring of flames, warming, protecting, keeping all bad things at bay.

'Fire around me.'

Last of all she turned her thoughts inward, to the blood running through her that carried power, to the liquid that sustained her body and gave her life.

'Water within me.'

She flexed the muscle in her skull and triggered the magic that allowed her to leave her body, opening her soul's eye to find herself inside the fiery vortex that was Siveraell. They plunged down, deep into the earth to the fire-realm, the colours searingly bright and dizzyingly fast. It was an almost unbearably long time before she looked through the fire-spirit's eyes and saw the sea before them. Behind were the walls of Eagle Hold, sparsely manned. Arrows and spears stood in stacks and small catapults waited within the courtyard, just strong enough to hurl clay pots filled with oil should any ships come close enough. One man on watch saw Siveraell and pointed, but no one interfered. They knew he was an ally, and likely carrying a *walker*.

'We'll go out a way,' Siveraell offered.

She felt his anxiety. Even this powerful and brave elder spirit feared the deep ocean where he was cut off from the fire-realm. It had never stopped him though, not since the first time, years ago, when Azrael had sought his help to take Kesta north, hunting for necromancers. It had been blood magic they'd feared then, binding magic, the type wielded by Jderha.

A sudden terrible thought came to her. *Can the Geladanians use necromancy?*

Siveraell answered slowly, reluctantly. 'I have heard it said that Jderha and her most powerful priestesses have done so. Not on the scale used by Dryn Dunham, but as a vile punishment. She kills those who offend her the most, then resurrects them, to be killed again and again at her leisure.'

If Dia had her own stomach, she was sure she would have vomited.

'Steady,' Siveraell warned.

Light was growing in the east and they paused over the sea, looking south. As much as she imagined them, there were no sails.

'Sheerwater and Otter Hold?' Siveraell offered.

Please.

Siveraell flew back to the coast and into the beacon, diving once again into the fire-realm and emerging at the watch post on Fulmer Island's southwestern-most point. Again, they moved out across the sea, again they saw nothing. At Otter Hold the two *walkers* left to guard it were standing on the cliff edge, the rising sun casting long shadows before them. They bowed on seeing Siveraell and one of them called out.

'No news!'

'And none with us,' Siveraell replied.

Dia and the elder spirit remained with them for several minutes and they fed each other courage, before Siveraell headed back to Fulmer Hold.

Dia phased back into her own body, sharp pain greeting her, and she rubbed at her forehead. 'They cannot be far,' she whispered, more to herself than to the spirit.

'Sadly, you are right.' Siveraell dulled his flame to spare her eyes.

Dia moved her stiff joints, twisting to ensure Arrus still slept, before pushing herself up onto her feet. She crept to the door, glancing at her husband before leaving the room. Heara lay across the doorway in the hall, and the old warrior opened her eyes at once. She stretched her long limbs. 'Do you need me?'

'No news.' Dia sighed. 'But let's look over our preparations again. We may think of something new.'

Heara stood, fully clothed and armed, and kicked her blanket out of the way.

As soon as they entered the great hall, Nip got to his feet, climbing over his bench to meet them.

'Icante.' He gave a bow.

'No need to be so formal, my honey,' Dia replied.

'I have news, but I didn't want to disturb you.' He turned and picked up his wooden chest. 'Gorchia is back.'

'I would love to see him.'

Out of the corner of her eye, Dia saw Heara's hand move to a dagger hilt. Nip held her gaze with his soft grey eyes for a moment, before lifting the lid. Gorchia got to his feet, his tiny hand brushing a leaf of the dandelion. The little elemental gave a deep bow.

'Fire lady. I have spoken with my kindred here. They will help you against Jderha.'

Dia took a step back, breathing in and out to steady herself. She didn't dare let herself hope against the odds they faced, and yet, she did. 'Those saved from the priestess?'

'No, lady.' Gorchia smiled, showing tiny white teeth in his fox-like mouth. 'All of them.'

Siveraell flared brighter and hummed in approval. Dia placed her hand on her chest. 'We are honoured. I thought you did not like people?'

'We do not.' Gorchia folded his arms, then immediately unfolded them. 'But I have spoken much with Nip, and he has given me hope that there are some who still honour nature, and life.'

Dia regarded the young man. Nip had always been quiet, but never shy. There was a comforting solidity about him that encouraged trust.

'Well, then I thank you both,' Dia said. 'From the bottom of my heart. Heara, could you please tell Nip and Gorchia of our plans, I think the earth-spirits will be invaluable to you.'

Heara shifted her weight to one hip, hand still on her dagger. 'Welcome to the team.'

'If you'll excuse me—'

'Icante, if I may.' Nip's eyes were wide. 'I, um, need some advice.'

'Of course.' Dia frowned. 'What is it?'

Nip started to put Gorchia and the chest down, then thought better of it and straightened up. He drew in a deep breath. 'In Elden, the tradition is for a man to ask a woman's father for permission to marry. But, well, in the Fulmers you should obviously speak to the woman first.'

Heara laughed out loud, slapping Nip's arm.

A tingling, healing pins and needles stirred in Dia's chest. 'No matter where the woman is from, ask her first. But it would mean a lot to Jorrun if you spoke to him after.'

Nip's cheeks and neck coloured ever so slightly.

'You give me hope.' Dia rubbed her chest with her hand. 'On a day when I thought I'd find none.' She looked from Nip to Gorchia. 'Look after each other.'

Not waiting for a reply, she continued out of the hall and made her way up onto the battlement. Worvig was consulting with the warriors on watch, instinct causing him to turn on her approach. Or perhaps he'd caught Sivaraell's brightness.

'Dia.' He hurried toward her, pulling at his greying beard. 'Three ships are approaching from the north. Two travel together, flying the flags of Parsiphay and Farport.'

Relief swept through her. These ships brought both help from the Ravens and a means to evacuate the last of the people of the Fulmers. 'The third ship?' She prompted.

Worvig frowned. 'See for yourself. It comes from the northwest and flies a Raven flag, but its sails are unusual. They are black but show a large white raven, wings spread.' He turned to look out across the sea.

'Snowhold.' Dia told him. 'That's the emblem of the Queen of Ice.'

Worvig raised his eyebrows. 'Well, all help is welcome.'

'Very much so.' Dia faced Siveraell.

The spirit flickered. 'Perhaps it is time to introduce the children to Edon Ra.'

Dia looked back out to sea and sighed. 'I'm not sure, spirit.'

'Neither am I,' Siveraell admitted. 'But I think he can take the weight and burden from their hearts, and they need it. They have been through much, but their souls are young still.'

Dia nodded. 'Very well.' She kissed Worvig's whiskery cheek and made her way back down to the houses that surrounded the great hall. Someone's home had been given over to Catya and her family and Dia approached it, only mildly surprised to find the furry Rakinya waiting for her on a wonky chair outside.

'Icante.' He rose, his huge limbs unfolding. 'You needed me?'

'As I need all true hearts right now.' She looked over her shoulder at Siveraell, and the spirit dipped in acknowledgement before shooting away. 'Did you know it?'

Edon Ra offered his chair, but Dia declined. 'Much of prophecy is not knowing but feeling.' He regarded her with his midnight-blue eyes. 'Which you would understand.'

Dia narrowed her eyes but nodded. 'You realise I do not entirely believe.'

Edon Ra blinked. 'And you are right to be wary. Prophecy is a tricky thing, even to those who are genuine. When you dream, most dreams are random, fleeting things. Some are brighter, some stay with you long after waking. Most are only your soul's way of telling you what is wrong in your life, what troubles and obsesses you.'

'Yes, I have such dreams.'

'The dreams of prophesy are different; even so, they contain frustrating symbolism, your mind's own code. You learn over time to understand the meanings, but too often the true meaning isn't understood until after the event.'

'Then what is the point of it?'

Edon Ra smiled, showing his long canines. 'That, I do not know. There have been times when a dream of mine has saved a life or changed the course of a people.'

'You speak of Catya and the Rakinya?'

Edon Ra nodded. 'And others. You may find it strange that I am wary of my own "gift".'

'Not at all, all power comes with responsibility. Tell me though, Catya felt you could help us against Jderha.'

Edon Ra turned away, his eyes growing distant. 'I have an understanding of how her mind might work, but I might also see things differently to her, in a way you might use.'

'Like ensuring the right people are here?'

He smiled, although he looked sad. 'Indeed.'

'But?'

'But.' He took in a deep breath. 'Every action we take changes time. There are some things more inevitable than others. Some events are set in stone. A single deed can alter a rare few. Others take a million small deeds to shift it off its path.'

'Jderha must realise this. If she's truly a god, if she has lived these hundreds of years, she must know prophecy is a fluid thing.'

'Oh, she knows. But like all creatures that need absolute power, she is plagued by paranoia, fear, and jealousy.'

'Jealousy?'

'She has adoration of a kind from her people, but mostly she has subservience through terror. She claims immortality yet lives in dread of it ending. What was it that brought her fear to the fore? It was love, loyalty, the truest of friendships between a priestess and her fire-spirit.'

'That's an interesting observation,' Arridia said from behind them.

Dia twisted her spine to see her granddaughter accompanied by Azrael, Siveraell, and Dierra. Joss, Alikan, and Doroquael weren't far behind them. Dia smiled at her family but turned back to the Rakinya. 'She was afraid that the bond between her priestesses and the fire-spirits would be stronger than their fear of her.'

'I wasn't there, of course,' Edon Ra said. 'But that is how I see it. Ah. Arridia and Joss. It is good to meet you.'

Joss caught up with them and held out his hand to the immense creature, meeting its deeply dark eyes as they shook.

'Can I...?' Arridia bit her lower lip. 'I hope I'm not rude, I sometimes can't help my *knowing*. You feel different from a person, almost like a spirit.'

'Go on,' Edon Ra encouraged. 'Tell me how.'

Arridia glanced at her grandmother. 'Elemental spirits feel strange, like an odd note, or a distinct vibration. You feel similar, like a plucked bowstring, but not as discordant as a spirit.'

'That's intriguing.' Edon tilted his furry head. 'It would be interesting to know if it is a thing of race, or a thing of power.'

There was a moment of contemplative silence, which Alikan interrupted. 'Is there any news?'

'Our last ships are on their way,' Dia told him. 'We should be able to finish our evacuation by this afternoon.'

'But nothing of Geladan?' Her adopted grandson frowned.

Dia shook her head. 'Although it cannot be long before we see their sails.' She turned to Arridia. 'Have you seen Nip this morning?'

'I have.' Arridia's eyes brightened at once. 'And heard Gorchia's news.'

'Earth, air, and fire,' Dierra said. 'If only the sea-spirits hadn't been such cowards.'

Dia's thoughts shifted to Temerran. If anyone could have persuaded the volatile spirits it was he, but her friend had chosen to protect a lonely boy, and in doing so avoid her pain. There had never been any jealousy between Arrus and Temerran, yet the bard had foolishly worried his presence was now somehow an intrusion. She had a horrible feeling they'd miss the bard and his unique powers before long.

She would certainly miss his company.

She brought her mind back to the present and regarded her grandchildren. 'I wanted you to meet Edon Ra, so he can explain a little of prophecy and take away any erroneous feelings of guilt or responsibility you may be carrying.'

'Prophecy is real then?' Joss asked.

'Well, now.' Edon Ra sat, and Dia wondered if the gigantic creature was trying to make itself less intimidating. 'Prophecy is mostly guesswork, but there is a little skill involved. Where it comes from, I could not say. We Rakinya don't believe in gods, but in an intelligent energy if you like, a life force that connects all things.

'Let me give you an example of prophecy. A short while back, I was warned that you, Joss, would die, but there was also a clue that you would cheat death which I did not see. My mind has shaped the essence of you and your sister into twin Phoenix, the legendary elemental bird who dies to rise again.'

Joss's mouth fell open. 'Are you saying we're immortal?'

Arridia and Alikan both turned to glare at him.

'What?' Joss mouthed at them.

Dia hid a smile, and Edon Ra chuckled. 'No. What I am saying is that prophecy is often useless, often only a guess. This god, Jderha, some three hundred years ago dreamed a dream which caused her to attempt to annihilate an entire branch of unique magic users and those spirits who would protect them. Her fear, her wrath, based on symbols she believed she knew the meaning to.'

'A guess.' Joss shook his head and took a step back and gestured wildly with his arm. 'You mean all this is a guess.'

Edon Ra raised a furry eyebrow. 'And sheer coincidence. Temerran unknowingly took word of the existence of the Fulmers to Geladan. Geladan's spies found someone to fit Jderha's prophecy. Tales of Dia and your parents' power would have shaken them, and her.'

'I don't understand.' Joss screwed up his nose. 'You're saying prophecy is both real, and nonsense?'

Edon Ra laughed, but Dia raised her hand. 'What he is saying, Joss, is they fit the prophecy to you, to us, because they wanted it to fit. But it could just as well have been anyone else. It was pure bad luck that brought them to us now. So, you mustn't think it's the two of you who have to challenge and fight her. It is not on your shoulders alone to save us.'

Arridia held her gaze and gave a single slow nod.

The door to the house opened suddenly, and a boy peered at them before stepping out. Both he and Alikan froze as their amber eyes met.

Edon Ra reached out to touch the boy's shoulder. 'I'm sorry, did we wake you, Merin?'

'His name's Merin?' Alikan took a step forward. He crouched but thought better of it. 'I'm Alikan. I'm... Gods, I don't even know if she told you.'

'You're my father.' Merin blinked up at him.

Alikan's shoulders sagged a little. 'Listen, Merin.' He said the name slowly, as though tasting it. 'I'm sorry that you haven't met me before, but I didn't know about you. And I'm sorry I ran off last night, but I was shocked and angry. Not at you. I was angry at your mother.'

Merin gave a shrug. 'Everyone gets angry at Mother.'

Alikan's eyes widened, but Edon Ra laughed.

'Look at this!' Merin took a step toward Alikan and held out his hand. A small flame appeared on his palm.

'You have power?' Alikan knelt swiftly, supporting the boy's hands gently with both of his.

'Dys has taught me a bit, but Mother wanted me to learn from you, to be fostered out and trained in all the lands like a Raven.' Merin chattered, unaware of the moisture gathering in Alikan's eyes. 'She wants me to be a great king.'

'I don't know how to be a king,' Alikan replied. 'But I hope I might show you how to be a good man.'

Warmth and pins-and-needles spread from Dia's heart as she watched the exchange. It was the Fulmer way to always be completely honest with children, even when it came to the hard things in life, and it was clear some of Kesta's parenting had rubbed off on Alikan. She gestured to the others.

'Come away, let's give them some privacy.'

Arridia nodded and ushered Dierra and Azrael to go ahead of her.

'Do you want me to stay?' Joss asked his friend.

'Oh, yes, please.' Alikan got to his feet and quickly introduced Joss and Doroquael to the boy.

With a smile at Edon Ra, Dia turned and followed her granddaughter, Siveraell hovering at her shoulder.

The fire-spirit made a deep, buzzing sound. 'Dia, do you intend to challenge Jderha, to sacrifice yourself to save your grandchildren?'

Dia glanced over her shoulder, Edon Ra was watching them. 'Of course, I do, spirit.'

'Life will go on, even when you lose Arrus.'

Dia clicked her tongue. 'I know that, spirit. I'm not some foolish girl.'

'But you have a heart, Dia Icante, and it is breaking.'

For a moment, Dia's calm facade cracked, pain leaking from her vulnerable, faltering heart. She refused to reply, but took in a deep breath and held it, straightening her spine. Grieving or not, she was the Icante, and the Icante was shield to the Fulmers.

'Something comes.' Siveraell made himself larger and up ahead Azrael gave a squeal and halted abruptly, shooting back a few feet towards them.

The air shimmered, little patches like heat haze solidified into the shapes of the two air-elementals, Aelthan and Eyraphin.

'We have news,' Aelthan said, its dragonfly wings a blur of motion. 'It is not good news, but it is what you have been waiting for.'

'The ships will be here soon,' Eyraphin said, its voice a deeper timbre.

'When?' Dia demanded.

Aelthan fluttered before her face. 'Before the sun sets tomorrow.'

Chapter Twenty-Nine

Scarlett; Kingdom of Elden.

Scarlett's eyes met her sister's across the room, her scream echoing her own. Their mother lay unmoving, blood spilling out over the floor. There was so much of it. Scarlett didn't even have time to take in a breath before Kistelle grabbed her arm to yank her to the back of the hall, the Raven calling fire to her free hand as she retreated. Temerran, Lucien, and the king drew their swords. Rosa reached for the dagger in her boot but stumbled as her husband pushed her toward Scarlett and drew his own blade.

'Stand down!' Temerran's voice carried over the expanse of the hall. 'The queen is dead, but we can negotiate.'

Eidwyn was backing slowly toward the high dais. The other *walkers* were with Dorthai and Finnian far across the room. Scarlett forced herself to take in the scene before her. Most of those in the throne room were unarmed, only those on the dais and the Ravens had weapons. Temerran was right, fighting wouldn't get them out of this. Nausea rose from her stomach and she clutched at her chest.

It was Eleanor who replied. 'There will be no negotiating. The throne is mine. Surrender, or die.'

Bractius laughed at his daughter, and a deep dread swept through Scarlett, clenching her heart. 'Eleanor, my dear, this is foolish. Your mother has twisted your mind—'

'Kill them all,' Eleanor snarled. 'No prisoners.'

Shock ran through Scarlett, and she gripped Kistelle's free hand tighter.

The Geladanians called power, their first attack aimed at those standing by the thrones. The two Ravens who'd stood guard at the back of the room ran forward, shielding the king just in time. Fire and ice hit their barrier and within seconds one of the Raven's crumpled. Eidwyn leapt onto the dais and into a cartwheel, adding her own shield.

In the hall below, the two *walkers* worked together, one defending as the other attacked. Dorthai armed himself with a meat cleaver and a long carving knife, holding back behind the protection of his people. Adrin picked up a chair and hurled it at one of the Geladanians, before diving beneath a table which exploded into splinters as the man retaliated. Scarlett felt a moment of rage. Why on earth didn't the stupid man have a sword? Surely Adrin at least should have come ready to defend his king, not dressed to flirt and feast?

A strangled cry made her catch her breath. One of the Geladanian assassins chose to go for the easier targets first. Both Kelinde and Medwyn were lost in a billowing tower of flame that left the walls and ceiling black. Scarlett's hand flew to her mouth. The smell was unbearable. The Jarl of Southport made a run for the barred doors and received a sword in his belly before he made it. His wife collapsed to the floor but saw no mercy. A Geladanian grabbed her by the hair and slit her throat.

'To me!' Temerran bellowed. 'To the king!'

Adrin made a run for it, Jarl Hadger and his wife on his heels. The elderly couple weren't fast enough, both were swept up in a freezing wind and crushed against the walls.

'We have to do something!' Lucien glanced at Temerran as he danced from one foot to the other, his sword gripped uselessly in his hand.

Adrin scrambled onto the dais and into the shelter of the magical shield. Scarlett could see the strain in Eidwyn's shoulders. The Raven beside her was shaking. Kistelle sent balls of flame hurtling toward the woman who had escorted Eleanor, distracting her enough that the four Fulmer Ravens made a bit of ground, coming precious inches closer to the thrones.

'Anything I sing affects us all.' Temerran clenched his teeth in frustration. 'If our side comes under my enchantment first, we're dead.'

Scarlett turned her wide eyes back to the hall, flinching as a cascade of flames hit Eidwyn's shield. She gasped as the *walkers'* sudden combined attack took out one of the assassins, crushing his ribs as well as his shield.

But there were still so many.

The Ravens on the lower level emulated the tactic of the *walkers*, concentrating on a combined barrage. One of the Geladanians fell, but it cost the Ravens dearly. As soon as they weakened their shield, three of the assassins blasted them with flames. Two of the Ravens combined their shield in time, but the other two were incinerated. Kistelle gave a cry of anguish, the skin of her face creasing as she drew more power to send everything she could against one of the Geladanians. He stumbled back, then his shield buckled, and his body exploded outward, showering the hall in blood and bone.

Movement caught Scarlett's eye. Merkis Shryn built up the courage to move. Unlike Adrin, he did have a sword, and he sprang out from under a table, swinging his blade at the back of one of the Geladanians. Distracted by the *walkers*, the man didn't turn in time and Shryn severed his spine. He had no time to flee. The female assassin incinerated both him and her dying compatriot.

'We can't survive this,' Temerran warned.

The two remaining Ravens on the lower level tried to move toward the *walkers*, no longer attacking but putting all their remaining power into shielding. With a signal from the female assassin, the Geladanians concentrated all their strength on the Ravens. Eidwyn seized the chance and let go her shield to attack, taking out first one, then two of the Geladanians. For a moment hope surged in Scarlett's chest, only to be brutally ripped away when the two Ravens were torn apart only two feet from the *walkers.*

'We can't win this.' Temerran stepped up behind the king, speaking close to his ear. 'Your majesty, we have to get out of here.'

Lucien was shaking his head in denial, but even as he did so his feet were taking him several steps back. Tantony touched his wife's arm and pointed. With a nod, she hitched up her skirt and hurried for the door.

Scarlett scanned the hall, spotting ambassador Finnian dead behind a bench. She turned in time to briefly catch Dorthai's eyes. She'd known the man since she was born. He whispered something to the *walkers*, then ran out from behind them, leaping a table and seeming to fly through the air with his borrowed weapons. The *walkers* made a run for the thrones, Eidwyn, Kistelle, and the last Raven all blasting fire out across the hall. Fire curled up to meet Dorthai, but with inhuman strength the ambassador didn't stop, charging the hall to embed his carving knife high in the chest of a Geladanian before he collapsed to the floor.

The two *walkers* almost made it, almost; but one assassin created a vortex that lifted several tables, which he slammed into the women. Scarlett turned away, eyes tight shut. She was sure she heard the cracking of bones.

'Go!' Temerran gave Lucien a shove toward the door, then snatched ungently at Scarlett's arm. There was fury in his green eyes, colour high on his cheeks.

'This is my throne,' Bractius roared. 'I'll not give it up!'

All the remaining Geladanians turned their power against those on the dais. Eidwyn cried out, blood bursting from her nose as she held her shield. She glanced at Kistelle, warning the Raven she couldn't hold on.

It was young apprentice Raven Gret who fell, shards of ice piercing his body and eye. With his shield gone Scarlett was suddenly exposed. Fire roared toward her, unfurling like a rapidly growing rose. She couldn't breathe. She couldn't move. Death came for her in a swirling ball of bright reds.

Her father sprang, filling the space left by the Raven's shield with his own body. Scarlett screamed. Tantony grabbed her about the waist and hauled her backward toward the door. She tried to fight her way free; she had to see.

'Father!' Fire danced in Lucien's eyes as he watched the King of Elden burn. Temerran lowered his shoulder and forced the prince – the king – back.

'Go!' Kistelle yelled.

Eidwyn fell back behind the Raven's shield, Kistelle remaining in the doorway as they all fled through it. The door slammed shut and Scarlett turned the moment Tantony dumped her on her feet, realising the Raven was on the wrong side of it. She tried to scream the woman's name, but it caught in her throat and choked her. Something tickled her face, and she touched her cheeks to find them wet with tears.

How could this be real?

'Where?' Tantony demanded.

'Servants' stairs,' Rosa panted, taking the lead.

Rosa ran ahead of them, Tantony falling back to take up guard at the rear, Temerran supporting the struggling Eidwyn. Rosa hesitated at a door, then pulled a bunch of keys from her chatelaine and picked one.

'Sorry.' She glanced at Lucien. 'I never got around to handing them back.' She pushed the door open and ushered them through, swiftly closing the door behind them and locking it again.

They were plunged into darkness.

Eidwyn called up a weak flame.

'No,' Temerran told her softly. 'Save your strength. Rosa, how well do you know these passages?'

'Not well,' she admitted. 'I used them a bit, but it wasn't really seemly for a lady-in-waiting.'

'I know the way,' Adrin muttered. 'Where do you need to go?'

Scarlett didn't want to ask why the Merkis knew his way around the passages, but she had a good idea.

'Somewhere near a quiet way out of the castle, but we must think about what we're going to do and where we're heading for.'

'We can't just abandon the people here,' Scarlett cried.

'We need to move,' Temerran prompted. 'Now.'

'This way.' Adrin pushed past them and set off at a jog, taking a sharp left where the passage ended. He descended a flight of steep steps, and Scarlett's dainty court shoes slipped on the stone. She flung her arm out to grab for the wall, but Temerran snatched a handful of the back of her dress to stop her falling.

'Thanks. Now I know why Lady Rosa always wears boots beneath her dresses.'

Adrin slowed, then halted. 'We must leave the corridors briefly, cross over to another section. Do you have your key Mistress Rosa?'

Rosa fumbled at her belt and found it. Adrin unlocked the door and opened it just a little, then wider.

'You there!'

Scarlett held her breath, hand over her mouth.

'Did you know the castle is under attack?' Adrin continued. 'Well, it is, and the king is dead. Best get yourself and the others out of here, fast as you can.' He turned back to regard them all and shrugged. 'Might buy us a minor distraction to hide our movements in.'

Temerran raised an eyebrow and nodded.

Adrin stepped out into the hallway and gestured for them to follow. Scarlett found herself in a dark stone corridor with no carpet on the floor and only two torches burning on the walls. 'Where are we?'

Adrin broke into a run, then stopped and pointed at another door. As Rosa hurried to open it, Temerran asked, 'Where are we heading?'

Adrin drew in a breath. 'There's a small iron door on the west side of the keep, where they take prisoners in and out quietly and down to the dungeons. It's a bit of a way from there to any gate from the ward, but I thought it would be less obvious than the kitchens.'

Temerran nodded. 'Good thinking.'

Rosa got the door open, and they hurried back into the darkness of the passageways. They only went a short distance before they came to another door.

'That's it,' Adrin told them. 'There's no more passage from here.'

Temerran waited for Rosa to unlock the door, then slipped out in front of her, drawing his sword. 'Which way?'

'Right,' Adrin said.

Like the other long hallway, this one was also bare stone, but at the far end Scarlett could see the studded iron exit. Just to the left of it, a door stood partially open. Temerran turned to look at Adrin.

'The guardroom.' Adrin nodded toward it. 'It's normally locked.'

Temerran held up his hand for them to wait, and he crept forward. Scarlett glanced behind to see Tantony had turned, ready to face anything that came at them from the other direction.

'There's no one here,' Temerran called. 'They must have fled. We can secure this door from the inside. We'll rest here a moment.'

The room was filthy, but Scarlett was too exhausted to care much. There was a single bed against the wall and a table with four chairs. A chamber pot stood in the corner. Tantony was the last to enter, and he barred the door, standing with his ear close to it and shifting his weight onto his good leg.

Eidwyn sank into the chair nearest the door, sitting sideways and leaning her head against her arms on the chair back. From the shaking of her shoulders, Scarlett knew she was crying. Rosa screwed up her nose, but perched on the edge of the bed, Adrin had no qualms about taking one of the other chairs.

'Go on.' Temerran offered the remaining seats to Scarlett and Lucien. The bard himself sank to the floor.

A chill swept across Scarlett's skin, and she moved her chair close to her brother. Without a word, he held out his arms, and she hugged him hard. He felt hot, his heart racing as fast as her own. She hid her face, wanting to be strong, but her pain was overwhelming. 'I thought he didn't like me.' A sob broke out, loosening her tight throat. 'I thought he didn't care about anything more than his throne.'

Lucien didn't reply, and she felt the tension in his muscles. Pulling back and sitting up, she saw her brother's hard eyes fixed on Temerran. She turned to the bard; he looked broken. His cheeks were flushed, and a tear slipped from the far corner of his green eyes.

'You didn't even try,' Lucien growled at the bard.

'What?' Scarlett straightened up.

'You did nothing,' Lucien accused, pulling his arm free from Scarlett to ball his fingers into a fist.

Temerran didn't move, neither did he look away. He spoke softly. 'You know my powers better than anyone, your majesty. I cannot shield. If any of them had been immune to my words and all of our side immobilised by them, we would all be dead. I have my limits.'

'I'd say he saved our lives,' Tantony muttered.

'They decimated us in minutes,' Temerran continued. 'We had seconds more, your majesty.'

Lucien leapt to his feet and snarled. 'Stop calling me that! I don't want to be king.'

'Then let your sister have the throne,' Temerran replied calmly.

'I can't let Eleanor and the Geladanians have Elden!' Lucien's eyes filled with water.

Temerran drew in a breath. 'Did I say Eleanor?'

Lucien stilled, blinking once.

Scarlett realised her mouth was open and hastily wiped the snot and tears from her face with her sleeve. A sick dread seeped out from her chest at the same time as... what? Hope, pride? She shook her head. She wasn't her sister; the throne was Lucien's.

'We're all exhausted and grieving.' Rosa spoke up. 'Let's rest and think. Catch our breaths. Then we can talk about what to do next.'

There was no argument. Adrin stood and pushed his chair toward Tantony, who still listened at the door, then he settled on the floor with his back to the table leg. Eidwyn didn't stir, and Scarlett wondered if the *walker* was already sleeping. With a glance at her brother, Scarlett folded her arms on the table and leaned her head against them, closing her eyes.

The image of her burning father was there to meet her in the darkness, and she drew her arms in tighter around her head in a vain attempt to keep it out. The smell of smoke was in her clothes and she screwed her face up, clenching her teeth against the wave of grief. She breathed out, giving in to it and letting her pain flow out with her quiet tears.

***

She woke slowly, voices breaking into her foggy mind. Scarlett hadn't meant to sleep, but her body had apparently had other ideas. She stretched her aching muscles and blinked to clear her eyes.

'They'll expect us to head to Northold,' Temerran was saying. 'And knowing the *Undine* will be on her way back makes me want to make for the lake and the Taur, but I wonder if we wouldn't be better off heading south, or across country to Burneton.'

'We can't leave Elden.' Lucien shook his head, the skin around his eyes was very red. 'We have an obligation to our people.'

'Elden isn't actually in immediate danger.' Scarlett turned to see Tantony on his chair in front of the door, his head leant back against it. The grey bearded Merkis raised a hand to bid Lucien wait as he explained. 'The Geladanian force that took the castle was deadly, but small. They were relying on Ayline to take the throne and hand them the obedience they required. Instead, they have a girl. Either way, Elden will accept no one on the throne without support from the Jarls. Without their cooperation, it will be impossible for Eleanor and these Geladanians to control all Elden. They might very well wreak havoc in the castle and city, but on the whole the people of Elden are safe a while longer.'

'Tantony is right,' Temerran agreed. 'Your safety and Scarlett's are what we must prioritise, Luce. The question is, do you hide out in Elden and wait for a chance to do something, or do we send you to Chem?'

Lucien narrowed his eyes. 'You say that as though… as though you mean us to go without you.'

Scarlett stared at the bard who held her brother's gaze. 'When you are safe, I will do what I can here.'

Lucien shook his head, his eyes widening. 'I didn't mean what I said earlier. You were right, there was nothing you could do.'

'But there will be when you are safe,' Temerran persisted. 'If I can catch each of the Geladanians alone within the castle, I might take out more of them.'

Tantony cleared his throat. 'I think our best choices are Burneton, or head east then north and row out to Haven on Mantu.'

'The tricky bit is going to be getting out of the castle and city,' Temerran mused. 'We might be best waiting for nightfall.'

'We—' Tantony froze and held up his hand.

All of them stared at the door, Scarlett's heart was pounding so hard she could see her chest rise and fall in her peripheral vision.

There was a scuffle of feet outside. Adrin scrambled up off the floor.

'Power!' Eidwyn cried out in warning, drawing up a weak shield.

The door exploded inward, hurling Tantony across the room. Rosa screamed. Scarlett ducked, shielding her face with her arms.

'Kill her.'

Scarlett looked up at her sister's voice, in time to see one of the Geladanians who accompanied her break Eidwyn's shield in an instant and crush her ribs. Scarlett screamed again.

'You evil bitch!' Temerran drew his sword.

'And him.' Eleanor pointed at Adrin.

The man didn't even have time to protest before the Geladanian sorcerer threw him against the wall and roasted him.

Temerran tipped over the table and moved swiftly to place himself between Lucien, Scarlett, and the door.

'You know, you were surprisingly hard to track down.' Eleanor tilted her head, looking directly at Scarlett. 'I couldn't find any of you in my scrying bowl, not until I thought of trying Adrin.'

Rosa gasped, her hand going to the charm beneath her blouse. Tantony stirred beside her on the floor.

'You haven't been trying a little witchcraft yourself, have you, sister?'

Scarlett shook her head.

In front of her Temerran's breathing was slowing, each breath seeming deeper and longer.

'What do you want done?' One of the Geladanian's asked, the one who had killed Eidwyn.

'Hmm.' Eleanor settled her weight onto one hip. 'They will make useful tools against the Fulmers. We'll flay the bard alive and send a piece of him at a time to the Icante—'

'I'll kill you!' Lucien bellowed, trying to push past Temerran.

'Oh, but *you'll* have to die, dear Luce.' Eleanor's mouth curled up in a smile. 'You still stand between me and my throne. Kill him.'

Chapter Thirty

Catya; Fulmer Island

Catya leaned against the tree, the bark rough against her cheek. The sea seemed traitorously calm, but as yet its surface was empty. Behind her, she heard the low voices of her team and the snort of a pony. Only seven equines remained on Fulmer Island to be used by those who needed to move quickly. Her own ship had brought them swiftly south around the island before retreating; not back to Snowhold, but just beyond the northern horizon to be called upon as a last chance for evacuation. It had been against Dia's wishes, but Catya wanted to keep their options open.

She had her own people in the north to think of.

'Still nothing?' Heara called up from the forest below.

Catya leaned out from her branch to look down. 'Still nothing.'

Aelthan and Eyraphin had found them only an hour before, warning not of the ship, but of elemental scouts heading for the island. Eyraphin had gone on to Fulmer Hold, leaving Aelthan as their messenger.

'No, wait.' Catya held her breath, straining her eyes toward the far horizon. Her pulse quickened. 'Sails.'

'How many?' Heara demanded.

Catya watched as more slowly came into view. 'Too many.'

She swung her legs over and dropped, catching the branch momentarily with her fingers before landing lightly on her feet.

'Okay.' Heara strode down to their camp. 'They're on their way, keep watch and stay out of sight.'

'Anything?' Catya asked Aelthan who'd been watching for enemy spirits.

The hovering air-elemental shook its oddly shaped head.

Catya looked around at their small group, catching Tyrin's eyes and exchanging a smile. He and Mayve had arrived on the ship from Parsiphay, and having worked with them before, Catya grabbed them to join her. Their faces had lost the softness of youth in the years since she'd last seen them, Tyrin now wore a red beard cut close to his jaw.

Dysarta and Cassien were standing side by side, looking toward Eagle Hold, which stood less than half a mile eastward along the cliffs. Nip was soothing one of the anxious ponies, Gorchia perched on his shoulder. The stable master was wearing supple leather armour and unlike the rest of them bore only a sword.

Amongst the forest undergrowth and high within the trees, Catya caught the glimmer of the eyes of her Rakinya, their fur rendering them almost invisible.

'The Hold has seen them.' Cassien twisted to call over his shoulder. 'And they're shooting arrows at something.'

'Air-elemental scout,' Aelthan whistled.

Dysarta sucked in a breath. 'The two *walkers* are attacking. It seems to be retreating.'

Catya and Heara exchanged a glance. Those in Eagle Hold had only one purpose, to draw the ships in, then try to survive. Catya moved back to the cliff edge and settled in the grass. It was an uncomfortably long time until she could be sure the ships were heading towards them and a buzzing anxiety grew in her chest, refusing to dissipate.

'Well, so far so good,' Heara whispered behind her.

'It will only take one of their scouts to spot us and it's all over.' Catya chewed at her bottom lip, shifting her position a little as her muscles cramped. Each ship bore only one mast, and she could make out the oars that bristled from them.

'How many?' Cassien asked, joining them.

Catya drew in a breath. 'Fourteen.'

Heara swore.

'That's a lot of people.' Cassien crouched beside her.

'I'd say about seventy crew including the rowers.' Catya moistened her lips with her tongue. 'But on such a long-distance voyage they wouldn't be able to carry a huge number of warriors and feed them. I'd make a guess at a hundred and fifty per ship at most, but that's still...' She tried to get the numbers to sit still in her head.

'Two thousand, one hundred.'

They all turned to look at Nip. The stable master shrugged.

'How many of them are going to be magic users,' Heara murmured.

Their attention went back to the ships, no one saying a word as boats were hoisted over the side. The ships had anchored too far out to swim to, or even row to unnoticed. Catya counted silently. There were a dozen rowboats. Good. They knew Eagle Hold was weak. Two of the warships broke away from the others and continued westward.

Catya clicked her tongue behind her teeth. 'Damn it. Now that we didn't need.'

Heara gave a shrug. 'It was never going to go completely to plan.'

'Shall I follow them?' Aelthan asked.

'No,' Catya and Cassien replied at the same time.

They turned to each other and smiled.

'Dia will have to deal with them.' Heara shifted her weight to one hip, her hands going to her dagger hilts. 'We need you here.'

'Movement at the Hold,' Dysarta called out. 'I think the air-elemental is back.'

'What's it doing?' Tyrin asked, standing up.

Dysarta gave a slight shake of her head. 'Harassing the battlements. The *walkers* are responding.'

Catya grimaced. 'It's wasting their power.' A thought occurred to her, and she stiffened. 'Aelthan, can you speak to it? Find out all you can? Presumably it's working under duress. If it is attacking willingly, just get out of there, but head away, not back to us.'

The air-elemental's wings seemed to miss a beat, but it dipped and flew away.

Nip moved to the edge of the cliff, staying within the shadow of the trees. Gorchia was no longer on his shoulder but sitting in his hands.

The rowboats were coming closer, the faces of those within becoming discernible. Nearly all of them had olive skin, like the people of the Fulmer Islands. 'I see six staffs,' Nip said.

'Six or six-hundred.' Heara put her hands on her hips. 'I'm sending as many as I can to their afterlife.'

Nip gave a nod.

'Hey.' Heara placed a hand on his shoulder. 'We'll get you back to Riddi. And just think of this, nothing is going to be as scary as asking Kesta for her daughter.'

'What's this?' Catya raised her eyebrows.

Nip didn't respond, but Heara grinned.

A swish and hum came from the Hold, and they all turned. The catapults were slinging clay pots of flaming oil at the oncoming rowboats. Most missed, falling harmlessly into the sea, those that hit were quickly extinguished by Geladanian magic users. Screams and the scent of burning flesh were brought to Catya on the wind. Bright balls of flame rose from the Geladanian boats and hurtled toward the Hold. Once again, she held her breath. As the captive fire-spirits reached the Hold, others shot upward, enveloping them and dragging them down through the earth to the fire-realm to hold them prisoner until they could be freed.

'Any chance you and Aelthan can do that with the earth and air-spirits?' Catya turned to Gorchia.

The earth-spirit's brows furrowed. 'An interesting idea. I do not know. Nip, pop me down.'

Nip crouched and let the elemental hop onto the ground. Its fingers elongated, looking like rapidly growing roots that burrowed into the earth. He closed his eyes.

'Aelthan,' Dysarta warned from where she kept watch on the Hold.

The air-elemental came skimming across the ferns, wings whirring. 'You were right,' it fluted. 'My kin was bid harass the Hold to distract and drain their energy. He was not commanded to kill, so it will do what it can within the bounds of its instructions. It was also able to tell me Jderha is on the central ship anchored before you.'

Coldness rose through Catya's bones, but she forced herself to breathe slowly. 'Thank you, Aelthan. Can you take a message to Dia for me?'

'Should I not wait to report what happens here?' the spirit asked anxiously.

Catya shook her head. 'This is too important.' She gave the elemental her message.

Dysarta laughed, turning from her post. 'I love your mind.'

'Only my mind?' Catya grinned.

'We're up,' Nip said quietly.

They all turned back to the sea. The rowboats were close to beaching on the stretch of sand between them and the hold.

'Eagle Hold is evacuating,' Dysarta whispered.

Catya leaned forward to look. The air-elemental was still buzzing about, occasionally blasting away a bit of the battlement despite the fact it was no longer manned.

'I hope we can free that spirit,' Cassien said. 'It deserves it.'

The shadows of the trees stretched out, the sun a red giant dipping between the trunks of the forest. Nip hurried back down to the ponies to steady them and keep them quiet. The next two hours were agony. The Geladanians stormed Eagle Hold, ripping down its walls. Catya didn't stop the tears that fell for the proud southern home of the *walkers* as their enemy swarmed into it. Forty warriors and one priestess remained with the Geladanian boats below, setting up camp on the beach. Catya narrowed her eyes as she watched them.

There was a sudden, loud, rolling boom.

A ringing sound filled Catya's ears as she clenched her teeth and raised her fists to the sky in triumph. Several of the ponies screamed, and Nip hastened to quiet them. Catya turned to Cassien, who crouched at her side.

'Thank the universe for Ignaya,' she said.

'And for Rothfel.' Cassien clasped her wrist and gripped it hard.

'It's taken about half the hold,' Mayve reported, blinking as the smoke and dust reached them.

'Time to move.' Heara stood, turning to regard them all.

Catya drew in a breath. 'Go.'

She felt the air stir as the almost invisible Rakinya passed her, throwing down the knotted ropes they had ready to scramble down the cliff. Gorchia dissolved into his myriad spiders and scuttled toward the beach. Catya met Dysarta's eyes, taking the briefest of moments to hold them in her heart, before swinging out over the edge.

Muffled cries sounded in the darkness, followed by yells of alarm. Catya drew her throwing knives, picking out the Geladanian warriors. A left-handed throw took one through the throat. The right-handed embedded her knife through an eye. The Rakinya cut through the camping warriors, dropping small bundles into the boats as they went.

Bright light flared up. The priestess called power and several fire-spirits flew from her staff, all of them snatched from the air and dragged down at once by free spirits. The priestess let out a screech of fury, sending a burst of flame toward one of the Rakinya, whose fur ignited.

Catya roared.

An answering blast of cold air hit the priestess and saved the Rakinya. Dysarta stood on the edge of the surf, her red hair refracting rainbows in the light of her power. The Geladanian priestess fell suddenly, a swarm of scorpions surging up her robes, green foxfire in their eyes. Cassien darted in, grabbing her staff and smashing it against the side of one of the boats again and again.

Heara appeared from the darkness, her blade catching the light as she slit the priestess's throat. 'Fire the ships!' she yelled. 'Fire the ships, then retreat!'

Mayve and Tyrin sent flames rolling out towards the boats. Catya pushed herself off the sand and sprinted for the cliff, finding the end of a rope as behind her their black powder ignited. Pressure exploded in her ears and she hit the side of the cliff hard. She took three rapid breaths and felt again for the rope, hauling herself up. Her eyes were sore and gritty, but she looked to her left and saw Dysarta ascending not far away. She paused, hanging for the briefest of moments to let relief wash through her, before she forced her muscles on.

She'd barely gained the top of the cliff before Nip was forcing reins into her hands.

'Thank you,' she panted. One of the Rakinya pulled itself up beside her. 'Go on.' She gestured southward. 'Keep going.'

Nip helped her up into her saddle, then ran to untie another two of the frightened ponies from their picket. Both Tyrin and Mayve had reached the line and were fumbling to get their own mounts. Catya twisted in her saddle, holding her breath, only releasing it as she saw Dysarta's beautiful red hair as she made the top of the cliff.

'Dys!' Nip drew the sorceresses' attention, throwing her the reins. His wide grey eyes scanned the cliff top, his shoulders dropping slightly as Heara appeared.

Cass.

Catya's heart thundered, then an arm appeared over the edge and Cassien hauled himself up.

'Okay!' Heara called out. 'Make for the next muster point.' She snatched her pony from Nip, swinging up and galloping away without a backward glance.

Cassien staggered toward them, shaking his head. Catya guessed he'd been closer to the blasts than her. 'Cat.' He said a little too loudly. 'I'm going to stay and watch. I might see something useful.'

Catya shook her head. 'That wasn't the plan. You need to get back to Fulmer Hold. Merin is there.'

He held her gaze, his grey eyes like flint. 'If your seer is real, then I will be there when I need to be. Someone needs to ascertain what we've gained, and what their next move is.'

Nip stooped, letting Gorchia run into his hands, and then up onto his shoulder.

'Go on,' Cassien urged them.

Nip hurried to untie his own pony, then waited, his eyes fixed on Catya. With a cry of annoyance, she turned her mount, leaning low. 'I'd better see you again soon, Cass.'

She kicked her heels and set her pony southward.

Nip didn't follow.

Chapter Thirty-One

Kesta; Fulmer Island

The explosion shook the night, and Eagle Hold momentarily stood in ruined silhouette against the horizon. Kesta counted her heartbeats until a second series of blasts rent the air further to the west. It had been a hard march through a night and a day and back into darkness, her heart a knot in her chest at the gamble they were taking. She felt only the slightest of triumphs that their plan so far seemed to have worked.

The flashes of fire faded, and silence gripped the island. Kesta held her breath. Jorrun stepped closer, putting his arm around her. She didn't move, letting the air out of her lungs and breathing hard as though she'd been running. Arridia stood just to her left, her skin pale despite the glow of Azrael's fiery body, and Kesta had to force down her need to send her daughter back to Fulmer Hold. To Jorrun's right, Jagna shifted, his eyes firmly fixed on the south although it was now too dark to see. Behind them, Dierra cleared her throat, but said nothing. Kesta glanced over her shoulder, catching Jollen's eyes and sparing a quick smile for her, Beth, and Rey.

Kesta felt the approach of power, calling up a shield before she recognised the signature. The air rippled and Aelthan materialised before them.

'What news?' Jagna demanded.

'They have taken the boats out,' the spirit told them. 'But the enemy only brought a dozen ashore. Two ships head west, but we have been advised Jderha is with those anchored south. There were five priestesses at Eagle Hold, of sorcerers and assassins we do not know. Um...' The spirit fluttered its wings. 'Catya bid me bear a message on to the Icante.'

It told them.

Jorrun's eyes widened. Kesta swore. Both of them turned to look at Azrael. The spirit shot back a little way, not quite hiding behind Arridia. The idea was simple, and typical of Catya's sharp mind. If they could implement her plan, it might change everything.

'Go on to Dia,' Jorrun said. 'Tell her we'll deal with Catya's plan if it comes to it.'

Azrael gave a slight squeak.

Arridia looked at them, her mis-matched eyes large in the darkness. Fear for her daughter squeezed Kesta's heart, but she forced a smile to hide it.

Aelthan dissolved into the night, his vibration fading as he sped away. Jorrun turned to Azrael and Arridia. 'We'll talk about it, but let's deal with this first.'

Sounds came to them through the forest. The shush of brushed undergrowth, the snap of twigs, then the pounding of running feet and the harsh, desperate breaths.

'Give them light,' Kesta said quietly.

She and Jorrun raised their hands, calling up flame. Their companions swiftly followed, fire-spirits rising out of the earth. Several warriors burst into sight, some of them halting, others pushing past behind their lines. One man skidded to a halt, seeing Kesta and hurrying over to her.

'The Hold has fallen,' he panted. 'We didn't lose many.'

'And the Geladanians?' Kesta asked.

The man winced. 'I didn't stop to see.'

'Go on,' Jorrun said kindly. 'You did a magnificent job. Get yourself to Fulmer Hold.'

The man nodded, then with a glance at Kesta, broke into a jog to follow his fellows.

Jorrun turned to Kesta. 'Ready?'

'Let's do this.'

They advanced slowly, extinguishing their flames, all the fire-spirits but earthbound Azrael vanished into the ground. Azrael whimpered as he forced himself to fall back so he wouldn't give them away.

They'd decided to separate the children, to give Jderha two targets. With Arridia better fitting the parameters of the prophecy, it was more likely the god would come for her, and they were knowingly using her as bait to draw Jderha to where they wanted her. Kesta glanced at Arridia. Her daughter had plaited her hair and bound it about her head to keep it out of the way. The muscles of her face were relaxed but for a line of tension between her eyes. Kesta drew in a long breath and let it out slowly, trying to quell her anxiety.

Ahead of them, the trees opened up to a wide stretch of meadow. A few small fires still burned in the distance against the skyline where resolute Eagle Hold had stood for many years. Kesta couldn't help the wave of grief and regret that washed through her.

'I hope it was worth it,' she said under her breath.

'Okay.' Jorrun spoke softly, but somehow his voice carried. 'You know what to do. Take down as many of them as you can, then get yourselves back to our meeting place. If you are injured, head for Fulmer Hold. If you don't think you can make the Hold, hide.'

He stepped out into the open, and Jagna accompanied him. Kesta couldn't help reaching out to take Arridia's hand briefly as they followed. They broke into a jog, the magic users staying together as the warriors and scouts surged ahead. An enemy lookout on the remnants of the Hold's walls cried out, spotting their movement, or perhaps the glimmer of metal in the firelight.

The Fulmer warriors ran on another few paces, then let their arrows fly at the battlements. They fell back instantly, not waiting to be roasted by the retaliating flames of the two Geladanian sorcerers who were first to respond. As the warriors passed them, the magic users ran forward, raising their shields. A handful of Fulmer warriors weren't quite fast enough, and Kesta closed her eyes from the terrible sight, gritting her teeth against the unbearable screams. Light flared behind them and to the left, Azrael came streaking from the forest trailed by several fire-spirits.

Jorrun pointed and Kesta's group all drew their power, only Jagna and Beth shielding for the moment. The rest of them went for the figure on the right of the battlements from which the flames had come. Foolishly unprepared and standing alone, the Geladanian didn't have a chance. Azrael's group attacked the other visible sorcerer whose shield withstood for what to Kesta felt like an excruciatingly long time before they reduced him to ash, his staff tumbling to the ground below.

The Geladanian's retaliated. Two bright jets of ice blasted up from the ward below, and fearful squeals burst from the fire-spirits.

Arridia's hands flew to her mouth. 'Oh, Azra, get out of there!'

The fire-spirits dived into the earth. Kesta held her breath.

'He's okay.' Arridia almost sobbed.

'Riddi.' Jorrun turned to his daughter. 'Close off your *knowing*. Now.'

Arridia's face flushed a little, but she nodded. Kesta swallowed, her husband was being the Dark Man for the first time in many years. Had to be, to get them through this.

'Come on.' Jagna shifted his weight from one foot to the other. 'Show yourselves.'

Jorrun shook his head. 'We must draw them.'

'Plan three?' Kesta looked up at him. He met her eyes and nodded.

She, Arridia, and Jorrun all raised their left hands, creating a bright blue flame in their palms to signal their intent, while their friends around them all added strength to their shield. They counted to five, then recalled their power, all of them heading toward the centre of the meadow. Half of them, including Kesta, closed their eyes to save their night vision, allowing the others to guide them. The warriors who had retreated surged back, at the same time the fire-spirits rose from within the hold, making themselves huge and bright. The warriors let fly their arrows, one volley, two, taking out the Geladanian warriors who stood out in silhouette against the flare.

The fire-spirits didn't wait, streaking off eastward.

'Open,' Arridia said.

Kesta opened her eyes and let go of her daughter's arm. She blinked at the Hold, scanning the earthworks for any sign of movement. It seemed the Geladanians hadn't manned all the defences, and she frowned; perhaps they hadn't felt they needed to. She looked quickly at her friends, following Jorrun's gaze to the battlements.

'There!' Jorrun pointed.

Three air-elementals flew up over the inner wall and dived at them. It was what Kesta had dreaded, having to kill innocent creatures through no fault of their own.

'Shield,' Jorrun said calmly. 'Stick to the plan, engage the captors, not the spirits.'

They pressed on toward the hold; the gates standing open for them, having been blown apart by Catya's group and the fire-spirits. All of them shielded, though both Kesta and Arridia held back their power, conserving energy for a much tougher battle yet to come. Unlike her daughter, Kesta stretched out her *knowing* to give them early warning of attack and – more importantly – feel for either reinforcements, or Jderha herself. It was hard to filter out the emotions of those around her, and the air-elementals were like huge distracting bluebottles.

A flare of sharp emotion made Kesta's heart leap. Not wasting words, she drew up her power, reaching down into the earth and pulling upward. There was a shriek as a woman robed in gold-trimmed purple was thrown onto the path before them, another woman and several warriors running to her aid. Jorrun created a vortex of air to snatch the staff from her hand, but with a snarl the woman tore it apart.

Jorrun raised his eyebrows, then glanced over his shoulder. 'Rey, with me. As we planned, everyone.'

Rey stepped forward, dropping her shield to draw all her power to the fore. Kesta closed down her *knowing,* concentrating on adding to their protection. A bead of sweat trickled down her back.

Rey and Jorrun went for the warriors first, and they were merciless; the Geladanian magic users made no attempt to defend them. Obviously recognising them as islanders, they aimed their counterattack not at Jorrun but at Kesta and Arridia. Kesta had no choice but to increase her power to the shield, muscles straining, blinking rapidly at the flames that roared only inches from her face. The air stirred behind her and Azrael appeared between her and Arridia, boosting their strength.

Jorrun called up another vortex, Rey adding flames to it. With his right hand, he reached out and tore stone from the ravaged wall. The weaker Geladanian fended off the tornado but didn't see the masonry coming. It stoved-in her skull and ribs, pinning her crumpled body to the ground.

At once several elementals exploded from her staff, but Kesta's heart sank as she watched them flee rather than aiding them.

The last priestess didn't run, instead she advanced. She pointed her staff at Arridia, who reacted instinctively, lashing out with lightning. The bright flashes illuminated the shock on the woman's face, but she didn't relent.

Kesta turned to Jorrun. Plan or no, if he couldn't do it, she'd have to.

Several fire-spirits launched themselves at their shield, and Kesta glimpsed at least two earth-spirits as they fell from the staff and broke apart to burrow into the ground.

'Shield below!' Kesta warned Beth.

Jorrun drew more power, then more, his tendons straining through his skin, his pale eyes wide and wild. He dragged air from two directions, pressing inward. The priestess's shield buckled but wouldn't break. She still came on, blasting more fire at them. Jagna groaned, staggering back. Jorrun shook his head, his nostrils flaring. He stepped forward, drawing out his sword and calling up a shield of his own. Kesta cried out.

Flames engulfed Jorrun as he swept up his sword and charged, but they didn't touch him. He took off the priestess' head.

The fire subsided; the attacking spirits halted, then sped away into the night.

Jagna dropped his power, bending over with his hands on his knees, gasping for air.

Jorrun cleaned his sword and sheathed it. He was breathing hard.

'Father?' Arridia called out worriedly.

He hurried back to rejoin them, meeting Kesta's eyes as he placed a hand on his daughter's shoulder. The high-priestess had been a match for all of them, and there would be others like her.

Kesta quickly reached out her *knowing*. 'There are a few Geladanians left in the Hold.'

'I think we need to go.' Arridia's eyes were huge and round.

Kesta and Jorrun looked at each other and nodded.

'Back to our meeting point,' Jorrun instructed breathlessly. 'Keep your shields up if you can until we get back under cover of the trees.'

Kesta reached up to place her hand against his cheek. 'Are you okay?'

He nodded, but there was worry in his eyes. 'Come on, let's get away from here before more ships land.'

Chapter Thirty-Two

Dia; Fulmer Hold

The air-elemental's wings whirred. 'Catya's group have achieved their goals. When I left, Jorrun was about to take back the Hold. He… bade me pass on a message Catya gave me. She says we must find a way to tell the captive spirits to work against any command given to them. They must try to fight with us where there are any loopholes and join us once they are freed. Although there will be some who will think only of their own escape, there will be many who will want to kill the Geladanians.'

'Thank you, Aelthan.' Dia bowed her head toward the air-elemental. 'Would you seek Kesta and Jorrun to let them know Joss and his party will meet them at the appointed place?'

'Of course.' The elemental dipped, then swooped away through the window.

'Joss and his party?' Siveraell flared at her.

Dia sighed, glancing at Gilfy who stood guard inside the door, and then meeting Everlyn's eyes. 'Eve, I can't leave Fulmer Hold with two ships still on their way.'

'Icante.' Everlyn leaned forward. 'We'll need you against Jderha. If the Hold falls, so be it. We have sacrificed Eagle Hold. We will do the same here if we must.'

Worry lines creased Dia's forehead, and she folded her arms tight around her body. 'And yet it is the best place for us to make a last stand when it comes to it.'

Gilfy shifted his feet, clearly not liking the certainty in her statement.

'Worvig.' She twisted in her seat to address her brother-in-law. 'Get everyone underway. Tell them I will follow. Chieftain Redick and

Walker Mimeth must take command until that time, or until I join them.'

He stood slowly, but left without protest.

'I'm sorry, Icante,' Siveraell hummed. 'I am not sure this is wise.'

Dia looked down at her hands folded in her lap. 'And yet I need to keep paths open while I may. Catya's message has given me an idea.' She rose suddenly and Gilfy straightened up. 'Siveraell, if you would be so kind, can you send some of your spirits to watch for the ships' progress?'

Siveraell appeared to subside a little, the flames of his body rolling more slowly. 'Of course, I will.'

'Eve, Gilfy, please follow me down to the beach.'

Everlyn stood at once and Gilfy opened the door, while the elder spirit vanished into a candle flame. Dia blew it out, then stepped out into the hall. It felt wrong not finding Heara there. She prayed her friend was safe.

She took the stairs down quickly, Gilfy moving ahead to open the door to the great hall for her. Arrus sat in his chair at the top table, Milaiya next to him with the boy, Merin, between them.

'Everything all right, love?' he asked Dia.

She screwed her nose up a little. 'Not quite, but I have a plan.'

He smiled at her and nodded, turning back to the boy.

'Do you need me?' Vivess hurried over from where she'd been readying bandages at one of the long tables with another apprentice *walker* who was to stay in the Hold.

'No.' Dia shook her head and touched the girl's arm. 'Would you try to get Arrus to eat, though? Maybe sing something for everyone?'

Vivess looked sad, but she gave a slight bow and walked across to where food was being kept warm at the large fireplace.

Siveraell rejoined them as they crossed the causeway. Dia couldn't help her eyes searching for the fuses put there by Catya and Cassien. In the cracks of the rocks below, they'd placed black powder brought by Catya's ship. Cassien had warned it was unlikely to do more than take the sides off the walkway and possibly collapse the escape tunnel below, but it might just give those within the hold the slightest of chances.

When they reached the beach, Dia took off her shoes and waded out into the water. Gilfy and Everlyn looked at each other but said nothing. Siveraell followed her out a short way.

'My friend, would you hold back a little?' She twisted to look up at him. 'The sea-spirits are offended enough by me. It would be as well they do not see you.'

Siveraell buzzed. 'They fled.'

Dia smiled to herself. 'We'll see.'

Siveraell reluctantly moved away as Dia knelt in the water, the waves coming up to her chest as they rolled past her. She reached out her *knowing*, sending out not just emotion, but also the memory of the call of her beloved whales. She closed her eyes. It was almost ten minutes before the water rose around her with a surge of power.

'You said you would leave.' She opened her eyes slowly.

Two aquamarine figures with constantly flowing hair and bodies as clear as the ocean emerged a few feet from her. 'If you believed that, why did you call us?'

'You would not go without being sure your bard was safe.'

'We won't risk our freedom for you.'

Dia nodded. 'That's fair enough. But I hope you can help even so. The song of the whales, it carries far. Do the Geladanians and their god understand it?'

One of the sea-spirits made a loud shushing sound like the crashing of surf. 'Only you, fire-woman, make such an attempt to know the creatures of the deeps.'

Dia drew in a breath and held it. 'Two ships travel this way. I will attack them from above, but it is from below I hope to destroy them. Would the whales do it? I do not think the Geladanian sorcerers would look or feel for them, and Jderha is away to the north. If the whales were quick and dispersed at once, they should come to no harm.'

'There will probably be captive spirits guarding those ships.' One of the sea-spirits darkened.

'Yes.' Dia winced. 'Drowning the priestesses should free them, but they might be instructed to hurt any who attack. The key is in the wording of what they are commanded. Can you sing in the whale's tongue for your sisters to resist in any way they can? Avoid harming the whales?'

One spirit reared up, but the other subsided. 'No promises. But we will try.'

Dia stood quickly as two enormous waves towered over her, holding her breath just in time as they broke. Her feet went out from under her, but strong fingers grabbed her arms and hauled her up.

'Thanks, Gilfy.' She wiped the brine from her face with her hands, blinking rapidly. 'They do always have to make a point.'

'Without Jderha there, it might work,' Siveraell hummed, joining her as she staggered through the surf and sand toward Everlyn.

'Eve, I shall start the storm, but you must take over, I cannot wait here too long nor use too much power. Bring Worvig and a handful of warriors west along the coast, but don't stray too far. You are the Fulmer's last defence.'

'Yes, Icante.' She nodded in a bow and took two hurried steps toward the Hold before halting and turning. She strode back to Dia and hugged her hard, then headed off again without a word.

Dia watched her go for a moment, her throat and chest tight and painful. She touched Gilfy's arm and waded back into the water, stretching out her *knowing* again. There was a subtle vibration of power that told her the sea-spirits had moved away, but not yet left. She closed her eyes and reached out her power, sending calm and affection. She felt rather than heard the distant reply of her beloved orcas, whom the Islanders called magpie whales; then from further out the deep reverberation of a pair of blue whales. She sent them images, the water a conduit for her power.

She smiled and staggered to her feet.

'Icante?' Gilfy regarded her hopefully.

She gave a firm nod. 'They will try.'

They hurried over the dunes toward the cliff path, Dia's wet clothes chaffing her skin, and she cursed under her breath. She didn't want to go back into the Hold and have to say goodbye, but she couldn't make a long trek across the islands as she was. Praying she wouldn't regret the use of power, she used her magic to warm the fabric and dry it.

Dia waited on the high cliff, above the waterfall from which their escape tunnel emerged. Her team had already headed north, disappearing into the forest. Worvig and Everlyn hurried up behind her with their warriors.

'Okay.' Dia swallowed as she regarded her friends. 'If this doesn't work, just do your best to defend the hold for us. Blow the causeway as a last resort to keep yourselves safe. If we defeat Jderha...' There was a tremble of doubt in her voice that she hoped they didn't hear. 'We will come back to you. But keep the way open for as long as you can for those who retreat from the south.'

'We will do what we can,' Worvig replied.

Dia moved away, calling up her power and heating the air, condensing moisture to form a fast moving, billowing thunderhead. She built the pressure, adding energy, and the sky darkened to the colour of a deep bruise.

'There.' She stepped back, breathless, as lightning struck down at the cliff-side to the west of them. 'Eve?'

Everlyn took her place, her greying dark hair blowing loose about her face as she reached up for the storm.

Dia backed away further, then turned to Gilfy and Siveraell. Without a word, she set off toward the forest.

Chapter Thirty-Three

Cassien; Fulmer Island

Cassien lay flat to the clifftop, the long grass tickling his cheek. A few Geladanians had survived their attack on the beach, most of them fleeing toward the Hold, only to come running back as the magical battle broke out there.

He watched the sea.

With his night vision ruined by the still burning fires and the flares of light from the east, he didn't see the new arrivals until they were landing.

Three more rowboats, all of them containing men dressed in mottled dark colours.

Assassins.

'What's going on?' a voice demanded. A tall, bearded man climbed out of one of the boats. He carried no staff, but from his rich robes Cassien guessed him to be a sorcerer.

He couldn't make out the reply from the man who had his back to him, but moments later the tall, bearded man gestured to the assassins. Most headed toward the Hold, but some fanned out across the beach, looking for a way up the cliff.

Cassien was about to draw back, when a bright white light caught his eyes far out to sea. His eyes widened and his muscles froze, the air catching in his lungs. The tumble of a loose stone below broke him out of his shock, and he silently pulled himself away from the edge before standing and running down the slope to the ponies.

'Thanks for waiting.' He climbed into his saddle and took the reins from Nip.

'What is it?' the younger man asked.

Cassien turned slightly, mouth open. He blinked and shook his head. 'Something I won't forget in a hurry, even if I want to. I'll tell you as we move.'

Nip nodded, getting into his own saddle and following the fast trot Cassien set through the dark forest.

'I think I've seen her,' Cassien said after a few moments. 'Jderha.'

Nip didn't press him but waited patiently for him to find the words and go on.

'She was coming ashore, but not by boat. She... she froze the sea.' He twisted to look over his shoulder to catch Nip's pewter-coloured eyes. 'She just made a path of ice and started walking. Even from that distance I could see that, well, she's big. Not giant big, but taller than Jorrun, I'd say. I don't know Nip, she... she stole the courage right out of me.'

'I don't see anyone running away,' Nip replied steadily.

Cassien snorted. 'We probably ought to. Nip, you fought their assassins when you were a boy and survived it. What can you tell me?'

'That I was lucky,' Nip retorted. 'It was Heara who fought them, really, and Kesta. Heara, well, you know Heara, she's amazing. But they were fast. I mean, really fast. But even though they tore her up, Heara wouldn't stop. All I did was get a stab in here and there. But it wasn't just Heara. Rosa fought one off with just a bedwarmer until Azrael roasted him.'

'She did, didn't she.' Cassien screwed his face up, glancing at Nip again. 'Would you say that although they are strong in magic, they don't tend to use it at first?'

'What are you thinking?'

'That because they're assassins, they hold back on their power. Magic can be detected. It gives them away. They use it when attacked by someone with power, but otherwise stick to stealth. If they have been sent to scout inland, they won't want to get caught.'

Nip drew up his pony. 'I thought eliminating any scouts was the next job of the Rakinya, Ravens, and earth-spirits?'

Cassien turned his pony around to face him. 'Then why have you stopped?'

Nip shook his head, but the stable master smiled.

'Besides,' Cassien reminded him. 'I am a Raven, and I believe that's an earth-spirit sat on your shoulder there.'

Nip looked down at Gorchia. 'You up for this?'

The tiny elemental shrugged. 'Why not?'

Cassien had hoped setting himself a task to focus on would settle his rattled nerves, but they still buzzed, and he jumped as a dark bird landed on a branch above him.

'Is that one of Dia's?' Cassien wondered aloud.

'That one's mine.' Gorchia showed his sharp little teeth in a grin.

'Okay.' Cassien lowered his voice. 'We won't be stupid about this. We'll try to take out two or three, then get out of here. If the first proves too tough, just go, Nip.'

The stable master narrowed his eyes slightly and slipped down from his pony. 'Will you track them, or let them track us?'

'That's not a bad idea.' Cassien thought for a moment. 'We could draw them in with the ponies.'

'Or with me.'

Cassien regarded him. 'I don't know, Nip. If they choose to just blast you with magic, you can't shield.'

'Neither can you.'

'I can,' Gorchia pointed out.

Cassien shook his head. 'No, it's too risky. Stay hidden a short way from the ponies. Gorchia, stay close too, take out any I miss.' He drew a long knife. 'I'll go back along our trail, see if anyone is following.'

'Listen for my crow,' Gorchia said. 'It will caw when it sees one.'

Cassien swallowed, his stomach still unsettled. He thought for a moment of Kussim, Raith, and Enika, closing his eyes.

He breathed in deeply, then headed into the darkness of the trees.

Cassien placed his feet slowly, using his ears more than his eyes, moving brambles and low branches with care. Something caught his attention off to the left and he crouched, waited. It was several heartbeats before he was certain it was just a fern being moved by the wind, and he let out the breath he was holding. The moon briefly flew clear of the clouds and Cassien froze again, shrinking back against a tree. He scanned the forest floor, seeing the tracks of his companions who had headed north earlier.

A crow cawed once and Cassien lifted his head, turning toward the sound. The light crunch of a dead leaf helped him pinpoint the direction. A darker shape in the shadows swayed closer. Cassien felt the tree behind him with his fingers and inched around it, ensuring his boots didn't clip any roots and give him away. With a wince he realised he should have done as Catya used to and cover his face in mud or ash. He drew two knives from their leather sheathes on his wide belt.

The shadow came on. Cassien barely breathed, keeping the trunk of the tree between himself and the assassin. The man's tread was soft, but not silent. As he passed the tree, Cassien spun, pushed himself off the ground with one foot and plunged his daggers into the man's lungs. Cassien let go of the left dagger and snatched at the man's hair; he withdrew his right dagger and sliced deeply across the assassin's throat from ear to ear.

Cassien gritted his teeth as he took the man's weight, letting him down to the forest floor slowly. He retrieved and wiped clean his daggers.

He waited and listened.

A twig snapped some distance off to his left, but the crow made no sound. Cassien wriggled his toes in his boots and headed that way, anyway. A short, sharp cry cut the air suddenly and set Cassien's heart pounding. Silence followed, seeming to press in from all around.

The crow landed with a clatter in the tree above Cassien, then sprang back into the air, heading toward where the cry had come from. Cassien screwed up his nose, shook his head, and followed.

He found the source of the outcry a few yards away. An assassin hung from the trees by one ankle, snared in ivy. A branch plunged in through the man's chest and blossomed on the other side. Cassien glimpsed small bright eyes peeping down at him from above. The creature blinked, there was a slight flare of foxfire, then it was gone.

The crow muttered in the back of its throat, then fluttered westward.

Cassien tried to ease the ache in his tense muscles. The bird was taking him further from Nip than he was comfortable going. It cawed suddenly and Cassien stopped dead, his heart banging against his ribs. He strained his ears but could hear nothing. He crouched, making himself small, and heard the swish of a bent branch returning to its place. A pale glow filtered through the trees, showing him a man studying the ground, power oozing from his hand.

Cassien wet his lower lip and raked his teeth over it. It would be hard to catch him up without creating a sound.

The wind stirred and Cassien moved, stopping again as the trees hushed.

The man had straightened up, losing stealth to move faster. What had he seen?

The wind picked up again and Cassien ran, taking several wide leaps to land on tree roots or what looked like bare patches of ground. A twig snapped beneath him and he clenched his jaw, freezing where he stood. He let out his breath when the Geladanian pushed on.

Cassien continued his pursuit, using every surge of the wind to gain ground. He was almost upon the assassin when the man drew power, his curled fingers filling with flames. A Rakinya reared up out of the darkness and the assassin drew back his hands to strike. Cassien let his daggers fly, the first bounced off the man's skull, the second embedded itself in his back, just below the ribs. His flames went wide. The Rakinya lashed out, ripping off the assassin's face.

Cassien retrieved his weapons.

'You okay?' he asked the Rakinya.

'I am. My thanks. They track well in the dark.'

'Too well.' Cassien raised an eyebrow.

The creature nodded and slipped away.

Cassien took a moment to be sure of his bearings, then cut through the forest back toward the ponies and Nip. A small jolt ran through his body as he heard an indistinct murmur off to his right. He used the wind again to hide his movements, but the swaying trees and undergrowth made it harder to pick anything out in the shifting shadows.

The crow gave a harsh croaking sound, then cawed twice. Cassien hesitated, pressing himself up against a tree. Did the crow mean to tell him there were two of them, or three? Or did the number of sounds mean nothing at all?

He moved anyway, a knot forming in his chest. Not far away he heard the snort of a pony. The wind died down again, and he waited, muscles poised to move. When the wind stirred, he ran, drawing his daggers.

Flames came roaring toward him and he dived aside, his shoulder hitting the ground first before he came back up onto his feet in a crouch. The ponies screamed. Cassien ran, finding the cover of a sturdy beech tree as flames came at him again. An unearthly screech cut through the night and the burning tree shivered and groaned, leaves raining down. Cassien crawled away rapidly on his hands and knees, breathing hard. A chilly wind howled above his head, sending a shiver down his spine, and the flames flickered and died.

Cassien didn't move.

The terrified ponies snorted, and he glimpsed them through the trees, pulling at their tethered reins.

He slowed his breathing and closed his eyes to help restore his vision. Shifting into a crouch, he turned his daggers so they lay back across his wrists.

Movement to his left.

He stood and leapt, landing on his left foot and spinning, letting fly his dagger from his right hand. The assassin shielded, batting it away. Cassien landed on his right foot, letting his knee buckle to spin low to the ground, and he hurled the dagger in his left hand. Again, the assassin knocked it aside. There was a green glow, and tiny dark shapes crawled up the assassin's shield. The man cried out, swatting at the spiders before recalling his magic.

Cassien whipped out his sword and was on the Geladanian in three strides. His blade caught in the man's spine as he hacked at his neck. He yanked it free as the assassin toppled. The spiders scuttled away as fast as they'd appeared.

The crow cawed.

Cassien dived for the cover of another tree. The ground heaved. He rolled aside as roots came alive to snake beneath him. He snatched in a breath as an assassin loomed from nowhere and twisted his spine to launch himself onto his feet. Fire swelled in the assassin's hands, but Cassien swept his sword around and severed the man's wrists. The Geladanian's eyes widened, and he staggered back, his bloody stumps held before him. Cassien thrust forward, the point of his blade embedding in the man's neck.

A guttural cry made him crouch and turn. Another assassin had come up behind him, but a tree root had accelerated upward, exploding from the man's chest and open mouth.

Bile rose to Cassien's throat, and he retched.

The ponies screamed again, rearing to tear themselves free. The crow cried out, rending the air. Cassien turned and turned again, trying to see where the danger was coming from. Light flared. Power surged toward him. He dived to the ground, bramble thorns tearing through his skin.

Silence.

Heart racing, lungs heaving, Cassien lifted his head.

The assassin stood frozen; his mouth contorted. A plain, serviceable blade withdrew from his chest. The Geladanian collapsed to the ground, revealing the sturdy figure of Northold's stable master. Nip reached out a hand and helped Cassien to his feet.

'Well.' Cassien panted as he caught his breath. 'Not the best idea I had.'

Nip grinned, and Cassien returned it.

'We've covered our tracks a bit,' Nip conceded. 'But at the same time...'

'We have rather drawn attention to ourselves.' Cassien nodded.

They approached the ponies, Nip smoothing their noses and necks to calm them. He untied Cassien's and handed him the reins.

'Gorchia?' Cassien asked in concern.

'I'm here.' Green fire crackled at Nip's feet, and he bent to allow the fox-faced elemental to clamber into his hands and onto his shoulder.

'Let's catch up with Catya,' Cassien said as he swung up into his saddle.

Nip looked down at his feet, then lifted his eyes to face Cassien. 'I have another place to be.'

Cassien regarded him for a moment, his breathing slowly steadying. He nodded. 'Take care of yourself.'

'And you,' Nip replied.

Cassien set off into the dark forest alone.

Chapter Thirty-Four

Azrael; Fulmer Island

Azrael tried to keep his flames small as he hovered over their camp. So far there had been no sign of pursuit, but even so Kesta was only willing to give them an hour to rest. He gazed at Jorrun. His dear friend's eyes were downcast, his shoulders tense. Sometimes Azrael wished he wasn't made of fire and could touch people.

'Jorrun,' he hummed. 'What's troubling you?'

Jorrun looked up. There was pain in his eyes. 'Catya's message has been troubling me.'

Azrael dipped lower, but it was Kesta who spoke. 'It's a good observation, and it worked for her.'

'It's like the golems.' Arridia's eyes were bright where they reflected Azrael's flames. 'They obey a command to the letter, but as we've seen, they will try to resist in any way they can. If we free them, they might join and strengthen us.'

Jorrun frowned. 'But so far, the spirits have not joined us, just fled. Catya is right, we need to communicate somehow with those still captive, give them hope and bring them over to our cause.'

Kesta shifted to face him fully. 'You've thought of how, haven't you, but you don't want to do it.'

Jorrun looked up at Azrael and a flicker of unease ran through the little drake.

'Is it me, Jorrun?' Azrael asked. 'Do you need me?'

Jorrun swallowed, looking down at his hands. 'We should wait until there's an opportunity.'

Azrael flared at him. 'No, what was the plan you were thinking? The one that's upset you.'

Jorrun glanced at Kesta and met Azrael's gaze. 'That you and the other drakes seek captured spirits and see if they can spread the word somehow. But it's too risky, I won't risk you being caught.'

'I should try it though,' Azrael buzzed.

'He might not need to.' Kesta sat up straighter. 'Some drakes captured imprisoned spirits and took them down to the fire realm to hold. We could just ask them.'

Jorrun shook his head. 'We killed those holding them captive, they will be free now and probably unwilling to risk themselves again.'

'There was at least one sorcerer or priestess we missed.' Kesta reminded him. 'It's worth a try.'

'I'll ask at once!' Azrael brightened and calling up his power he dived into the earth.

The world about him changed to one of colour and light, the earth he passed through rough and ticklish. He imagined it would feel like sliding down a scree slope on a hessian sack to a human. Deeper he travelled, until brightness exploded around him. He floated on the edge of a molten universe, keening at the painful desire within him. He knew if he pressed forward, the fire-realm would push him out. He belonged in the realm of men now, a soul for a soul. Whispers came to him, the susurration of distant conversation.

'Hello?' he called out, trying not to get impatient and irritated. 'Someone talk to me!'

Almost at once, a spirit emerged, its body stretching forth from the greater fire. Not an ancient spirit, nor even an elder like Siveraell, but a young spirit like himself.

'The captive spirits brought here from Fulmer above,' Azrael asked urgently. 'Are any still bound within a trap?'

The spirit shrugged.

'Will you find out?'

The other spirit rolled its blue eyes.

Azrael made himself huge, pulling a fearsome face and stretching out his tongue. The other spirit retaliated, matching Azrael's size and making several faces rapidly in return. Azrael's anger blossomed; he had no time for this. He made himself even bigger and roared.

'Find out, now!'

The other spirit snapped back to its normal size and vanished with a squeal.

Azrael returned slowly to himself, mourning the drain on his power. He might very well need it later.

'Azra.'

The voice was like the whisper of leaves, impossible in this place far below the realm of earth. It cut his fiery heart in two.

'Naderra?'

'Dear Azrael.' A shape emerged, not the tailed teardrop of a spirit, but the lithe flowing form of a human, her hair ablaze.

He wailed, letting out his grief and joy.

'Dear Azra, it is good to see you. Is my boy well?'

Azrael quailed a little. 'He is well, but he is in danger.'

'You protect him still?'

'Always. Always. His children too.'

'How fare my grandchildren?'

Heat rose through his fiery form. 'Joss and Arridia are brave and kind.'

Naderra closed her eyes, the only part of her that was not flame. 'What aid do you require?'

'I need to speak to any spirits that are being held here, but still bound in a trap. Some useless fellow went to ask for me.'

Naderra's shape wavered. 'There are none, dear Azra, those held are now free.'

He'd failed! It was no good. Azrael fell. Naderra plummeted with him, reaching out to merge her flame with his, her warmth restoring his own.

'Do not despair, Azra, you are the bravest spirit I know.'

He hummed miserably. He wasn't brave, only when he had to be because he couldn't bear for his humans to be hurt or sad.

'You can do it,' Naderra urged. 'Keep my boy safe.'

'I will.' He didn't know how, but he would try his hardest.

The spirit he'd spoken to a moment ago emerged, and Naderra withdrew. Azrael keened, then flared at his fellow spirit and shot up and up, back through the rock, avoiding the water, to shoot out of the ground between his human family.

'Azra?' Jorrun rose to his knees.

Azrael let himself drift slowly down. Jorrun's eyes were wide, hopeful. Azrael couldn't help but make himself small. He longed to tell Jorrun his mother's spirit still lived within the flame, but he'd promised, and he had to keep his promises. 'There are no sspirits held by Geladan in the fire realm, Jorrun.'

He closed his eyes briefly. 'Not to worry, Azra. Thank you for trying. We'll watch out for opportunities.'

Azrael hummed, though his little heart was fearful. 'I don't think we should wait, Jorrun.'

Jorrun's fists clenched for a brief moment. 'Well, you cannot go, it won't be safe for you alone, and your job is to protect Arridia.'

'He might not have to go alone,' Kesta murmured.

'What do you mean?' Jorrun's eyebrows drew in tight together. It had taken Azrael a while to recognise human expression, but he knew very well that his Jorrun was scared.

Kesta opened her mouth and drew a breath before speaking. 'Years ago, when I first *walked* with Siveraell, I was able to control and use my magic while with him. If I *walk* with Azra, I can help defend him if he gets in trouble.'

Jorrun shook his head vehemently. 'I don't want to risk either of you, never mind both.'

Kesta lay her hand on his arm. 'We are all going to have to take risks if we are going to survive this.'

'I don't like it.' He held her gaze. 'I wish I'd kept quiet.'

'It might be enough to tip things in our favour,' Kesta urged. 'We have to seize every advantage we can get.'

'Perhaps I should do it,' Arridia offered.

'No.' Both her parents replied at once.

Jorrun took Kesta's hand and held her gaze. 'If you're caught, there is a chance we might free Azra, but we have no idea what would happen to you.'

'We won't go near any people,' she assured him. 'I can use my *knowing*. We know they don't have amulets like the Chemmen did.'

Jorrun looked from her to Azrael, who immediately blazed brighter.

'No risks, and I mean it. We need you both against Jderha.'

'You know I'll do everything I can to get back for the children.' Kesta held his gaze.

Arridia looked away from them and up at Azrael. He loved her pretty human face, her violet eye most of all. It made him think of raindrops on flowers. He'd crossed the sea with her so many times now it hardly frightened him at all.

'All right.' Jorrun sagged, though anxiety radiated from him.

Kesta reached up to touch Jorrun's face, then shifted away, making herself comfortable. She gave Azrael a warm, encouraging smile that made him tingle before she relaxed, mouthing the words to fall into her meditation. To Azrael it looked as though she grew, stretched out of herself, before her body darkened like an empty lantern and a bright spark merged with Azrael's heart, before shifting behind his eyes.

Where shall we go? he asked her.

South, her thoughts replied. *But slowly, Azra. Give me plenty of time to adjust and reach for other life.*

Azrael kept as low as he could, weaving between the trees.

It was always an odd sensation for him to carry someone else in his head, but he'd only ever conveyed Kesta, Riddi, and Naderra, and he trusted them implicitly. As he chased away the shadows, he found Kesta's presence comforting, and he had to bite back on his desire to hum. For some reason he thought of oat biscuits. He didn't need fuel, he just wanted one.

Are you sure you want to do this? Kesta asked.

He realised she was experiencing his anxiety, and he puffed himself up, before remembering he was meant to be being cautious, and quickly made himself small again.

It's fine, Kesta. I just worry we won't be able to save the islands.

So do I. Careful now, I sense something.

Azrael slowed, burning a fierce blue to make himself as dark as possible.

It's okay. Kesta's relief was his own. *It's one of our rear-guard scouts. Give her a wide berth, we don't want to give her away accidentally.*

Azrael did so, relaxing and letting his flames flow normally to conserve his energy.

They didn't go much further before Kesta flinched. Fear gripped her and rippled through his flames before she gathered herself, forcing calm.

'Kesta?' he squeaked aloud.

There is such an overwhelming sense of anger and malice coming from the south.

Azrael shuddered at her words.

Azra, my honey, there is something up ahead to the left, it feels like a spirit. It's scared.

He braced himself and burned a fierce blue again, dropping to skim the forest floor. He saw the shimmer of the almost invisible air-elemental and rose upward, making himself brighter.

The spirit gave a spark of alarm and fled.

'No, wait!' Azrael called out. 'Pleasse! We don't want to hurt you, only talk. We want to free you!'

The spirit halted abruptly, spinning to look at them from within the branches of an ash tree. Azra could almost taste how frightened it was on his tongue.

Kesta subtly sent out calm and Azrael closed his eyes to absorb it, even though it wasn't meant for him.

'I'm Azrael. We want to try to free you all, all the trapped spiritss.'

'You want to kill Jderha,' it whistled.

'Not really.' Azrael pulled a face. 'We'd rather she shoved off and left uss alone.'

The air-elemental gave a shiver of understanding.

Ask it what its precise instructions are.

'Tell me.' Azrael drifted closer. 'What orderss were you given?'

The spirit of air hesitated only a moment, and Azrael guessed it was exploring the bounds of its confinement. 'I was ordered to watch for enemies and report back if I see any.'

Azrael brightened in delight. 'Well, that's okay then, because I'm a friend, so you don't have to tell anyone anything.'

The elemental darted sideways in alarm. 'You are right!'

Azrael felt Kesta's humour and affection, and pride thrummed through him.

'Do you undersstand?' Azrael urged. 'There are ssmall ways to resist. Small wayss to help us so we can free you. Are you able to tell others? Get them to try too? And when we free you, will you please stay and join us? Fight with us so all spirits can stay free?'

The air-elemental's wings whirred. 'I can try.'

Azrael hummed. 'That's all we ask.'

He means it. Azrael could almost feel Kesta's smile. *He will try.*

There was a sudden rush of air, an immense force threw Azrael back and the air-elemental came tumbling after him. A brief gale howled through the trees, bending them and stripping leaves.

Azrael wailed.

What is it?

'What isss it?'

The wind died as suddenly as it had come.

The air-elemental fluttered just a few inches from them. 'It's Jderha. She's coming.'

Azrael didn't wait to be told, he sped back towards their camp.

Chapter Thirty-Five

Temerran; Kingdom of Elden

'You will not harm Lucien!'

Temerran put all of his powers of command into the words.

Eleanor spun about to stare open-mouthed at her Geladanians, whose arms had dropped to their sides. She turned back to Temerran and snarled; her small nose wrinkled. 'The first thing I will have sent to Dia is your tongue! Your magic doesn't work on me, bard, I'll despatch my brother myself if I have to.'

Lucien raised his sword, but didn't move. His eyes were wet with disbelief and pain.

'She must have an amulet,' Scarlett whispered, glancing at Rosa.

Tantony stirred, but Rosa placed a hand on his arm to still him.

Eleanor glanced at the sorcerers. 'If the bard so much as opens his mouth, silence him.'

Temerran clenched his jaw, judging the distance between himself and the men at the door. His fingers tightened around his sword hilt. He'd never reach them before they called up their power.

Lucien drew himself up. 'You will harm none of us!'

Temerran sucked in air through his teeth. Lucien's words had been too fraught with emotion to carry the magical tones. Eleanor pivoted to glare at her Geladanians. One of them raised a hand.

A brutal force hit Temerran hard in the chest, slamming him against the wall and knocking the wind out of him. For one terrifying moment, he couldn't draw in a breath. Pain rippled across his back.

'Oh, brother.' Eleanor laughed. To Temerran, her voice seemed to retreat and return. 'Did you think you had power? It seems not.'

'What's happened to you?' Scarlett implored tearfully. 'You're our sister. Just let us go. You can have the throne, Luce never wanted it anyway. Elle—'

'But you do, don't you?' Eleanor's voice lowered. 'You were always scampering after Father, trying to be noticed, trying to be good enough. While you were wasting your time amusing him with your poor attempts at being a warrior, Mother was teaching me actual power.'

Temerran tried to pull himself up against the wall. Lucien glanced at him but stayed close to Scarlett.

'What do you want done with them?' one sorcerer asked impatiently.

Realisation struck Temerran. The throne wasn't Eleanor's, not yet. The bargain must have been the Eldenian throne in exchange for delivering the Fulmers. They still had time; the Islands hadn't fallen yet.

'We're near the dungeons.' Eleanor sighed. 'Put them in a cell.'

'Just let us go, Elle,' Scarlett tried again, her cheeks red.

'If they resist, kill Rosa.'

Rosa gasped, her hand going to her mouth, and Tantony dragged himself up.

Temerran raised his hands. 'We'll go with you to the dungeons.'

Scarlett stared at him, mouth open, but Lucien reached out his hand to help him up.

With a shake of her head, Scarlett moved to help Rosa with Tantony.

'Leave your weapons,' one of the Geladanians commanded.

As they left the room, Temerran couldn't help his eyes going to the broken form of Eidwyn. The brave, loyal, and kind-hearted *walker* had deserved so much better. He felt sick with anger.

A chill ran over his hot skin.

I should have thought of something, saved her.

'Which way?' a sorcerer asked.

It was Lucien who pointed and pushed forward to take the lead.

Tantony glanced up, briefly meeting Temerran's eyes. He at least still had faith the bard had a plan.

It was a shame he didn't.

They descended the cold stairs to the level below the castle. Temerran flexed his shoulders against the aching pain in his chest and back.

Two wide-eyed guards stood outside the bolted door.

'Open up,' Lucien told them. 'Then do as Eleanor says.'

'Highness.' One of the guards gave a swift bow as the other drew back the bolt. 'What's happened up there?'

As soon as they were all through, the Geladanians turned and killed the unprepared guards.

Temerran closed his eyes, his fingers curling into fists.

'They were your subjects!' Lucien almost roared at his sister.

Eleanor shrugged. 'We couldn't have them letting you out the minute we turn our backs.'

'Princess,' one of the Geladanians spoke urgently under his breath. 'Magic. Upstairs, not ours.'

Eleanor's eyes widened, Temerran felt a surge of hope.

'In there!' She pointed at an open cell, herself slamming the door shut and drawing the bolt across.

Lucien kicked futilely at the door.

'What now?' Scarlett demanded.

Temerran drew in a breath which sent stabbing pains through his lungs. 'We're alive, and we have time.'

'Who was left?' Tantony asked. 'Who was left that has magic?'

Temerran frowned. 'No one else that I can think of. Only myself, Luce, and Rosa.'

'Who is upstairs then?' The Merkis wondered aloud.

'Are you badly hurt?' Temerran asked him.

'No, you?'

Temerran shook his head, although it was too dark to see much. A little light came in through a small, barred window from a single torch somewhere in the corridor.

'Was it a lock or a bolt?' Rosa asked, stepping forward.

'A bolt,' Lucien replied. 'Why?'

Rosa sagged. 'I just had a silly idea that I could pick the lock.'

'You can pick locks?' Lucien asked in astonishment.

She shrugged. 'I learned all sorts from Kesta and Catya.'

Tantony snorted. 'Sadly, jailors have learned over the years that the type of people they lock up, tend to know how to get in and out closed doors.'

'I wonder if I might reach the bolt, though.' Scarlett stepped forward; the small window was at eye level. 'Can someone lift me up?'

Lucien begrudgingly did so, and with a lot of huffing Scarlett squeezed her arm through. After a while, she drew it back, rubbing at the reddening bruises.

'It's no good.' She shook her head at them.

The cell shuddered and a loud boom sounded distantly above them. Dust rained down and Temerran instinctively shielded his face.

'What was that?' Scarlett demanded, grabbing her brother's arm.

'Magic.' Temerran said.

'It has to be someone come to fight the Geladanians.' Scarlett looked around at them hopefully.

'Maybe fire-spirits,' Lucien suggested.

Temerran shook his head. 'Other than Siveraell, fire-spirits are unlikely to attack without a *Walker* in case they're trapped.'

'Maybe one survived...' Scarlett stumbled to a halt. They'd seen the *walkers*, there was no doubt they were all dead.

Temerran caught his breath as his heart tore again. Eidwyn had deserved so much more from life...

'Well, we'd best just rescue ourselves.' Rosa began unlacing her bodice.

'What are you doing, woman?' Tantony stared at her wide-eyed.

'I'm going to make a little noose. Perhaps Scarlett can loop it about the bolt.'

With a loud sigh, Tantony got onto his hands and knees to allow the princess to stand on his back. He winced as Scarlett caught one of his many bruises.

She tried for some time; her face screwed up in concentration. 'It's no good. I don't even know if I'm anywhere near it. If its flat to the door, I won't be able to get it, anyway. If only I could see it.'

'Shall I try for a bit?' Lucien offered.

Temerran didn't miss the expression on Tantony's face.

All of them froze as another tremor went through the foundations of the castle.

'I'll keep trying.' Scarlett turned back to the window, grunting as she twisted her arm through. Her breath caught loudly. 'I think I have something!'

'Gently,' Temerran urged, not allowing himself to hope. 'Try to pull the noose tight around it.'

'I've got something,' she said, her face pressed up against the door.

'If we ever get out of this, I'm going to have to make some changes to the dungeons,' Lucien muttered.

'Especially when you're surrounded by devious women,' Tantony retorted. His voice strained as he continued to take the weight of the princess.

Rosa folded her arms, but she smiled at her husband.

Scarlett let out a hiss. 'It's moving.'

Temerran took a step forward, sudden energy flooding his muscles.

'It's stiff.' She adjusted her position and footing. Tantony closed his eyes, his face reddening, his arms shaking.

'Got it!'

They all heard the scrape as it slid back. Scarlett jumped down and Tantony got unsteadily to his feet.

Temerran crossed to the door to open it. He expected to see a sorcerer, but the narrow corridor was empty. Obviously, none of the Geladanians were willing to lower themselves to guard duty.

'Okay.' He turned to regard them all. 'We need to decide. My instinct is to get you all to safety and then come back and see what's happening. But this is Elden, and I am not the king.' His eyes met Lucien's. The young man didn't look away, although he swayed slightly.

Lucien swallowed. 'Many good people have died because of my family's treachery. If more have come to fight for us, then I have to fight with them.'

Tantony didn't look happy with Temerran, but the Merkis kept his thoughts to himself.

'Very well. We'll grab our weapons and make our way up, go back through the passages. Scarlett and Rosa, perhaps you should find somewhere to hide out until we know it's safe—'

Scarlett made a disgusted sound in the back of her throat. 'I don't think so.'

Rosa merely raised her eyebrows.

Temerran grinned. 'Come on, then.'

They retraced their steps, Temerran taking the lead and Tantony bringing up the rear. The castle seemed deserted. Temerran hoped it was because its residents had fled.

As they drew close to the throne room, there was a strong smell of burning. Temerran tried the servant's door and found it unlocked. He opened it a crack. Smoke drifted past down the corridor. He held his breath, stepping out a little way.

The carpet was scorched, the walls and ceiling blackened, though the fire that had ravaged this part of the castle had been extinguished. A charred body lay on the floor and Temerran stooped to examine it. From the remnants of the clothing, it seemed to be a Geladanian.

He still refused to let himself hope.

He stopped outside the king's entrance at the back of the throne room, hovering his palm just above it to check for heat, then pressing an ear to it.

Nothing.

'Be ready.' He glanced at the others. All of them held their swords ready, bar Rosa, who clutched her knife to her chest.

Temerran opened the door, his muscles tensing as he expected a blast of magic.

There was only an eerie silence.

Nothing moved in the throne room, but it looked different to when he'd fled it. For a start, the body count had increased. He spotted a smouldering Geladanian. It was the woman who'd appeared to chaperone Eleanor. Close to her lay a man Temerran knew, a man who shouldn't have been there.

'Udiss!'

'What is it?' Tantony demanded, stepping up behind him.

'One of my crew.' The muscles tightened above Temerran's nose, a prickling sensation pressing at his eyes. 'The *Undine* is here.'

Tantony grunted. 'I didn't think your men were sorcerers.'

Temerran turned to face him. 'They're not.'

The sounds of fighting came to them from beyond the open double doors which hung from their hinges.

'Careful, then.' Temerran made his way slowly across the long room, stepping around the bodies and raising his sleeve to his nose to try to block out the awful stench of burnt flesh that caught in his throat.

Scarlett cried out, spotting the remains of her parents.

'Come away, my honey,' Rosa urged her, pulling her close. 'Don't look.'

Lucien quickened his pace to walk beside the bard. Temerran didn't stop him, although every instinct wanted to put himself between the young king and harm.

He stepped out into the ornate corridor. No guards in brightly polished armour lined the way, only corpses piled outside the door. He didn't want to, but he had to search for the faces of his own men.

Fire roared past the main doors out in the courtyard. There was a scrape behind him, and he turned to see Rosa picking up a discarded bow and quiver of arrows. He crept forward, blinking at the light of day.

He caught his breath at the scene before him. His men own were backed against the high wall of the ward, weapons held at the ready, along with Chemmish guards in the green uniform of Farport. The sight of Nolv alive, if dishevelled, made him want to weep. Before them stood a solid shield of Ravens, Dinari at the centre, her daughter Ylena at her side. He recognised Ovey and Meric.

Free Chem had come.

He turned to see who they faced. Only three Geladanians remained, two high priestesses and a sorcerer. It was a moment before he spotted the would-be queen, huddled against the stone of the castle to his right.

Temerran gestured for the others to get back against the wall. One of the Geladanians glanced up and saw him but was too busy holding off the Ravens to worry about a lone man with a sword. Lightning flashed and the sky rapidly darkened, both Dinari and Ylena feeding it. The energy of the storm filled Temerran with an overwhelming urge to sing, but he clenched his jaw tight.

Lightning forked down, the thunder echoing through the empty corridors of the castle. Ovey sent a small tornado spinning toward the Geladanians from the left, Meric did the same from the right. Water erupted up through the cobblestones and Temerran had to shield his head with his arms. Eleanor screamed as blinding lightning lashed down again and again, hitting the wet cobbles.

The Geladanians' shield collapsed, and the Ravens tore them apart.

There was a pattering of falling stones, and then silence.

The crew of the *Undine* let out a roaring cheer. Temerran took a few staggered steps forward into the courtyard, then meeting Dinari's eyes, he swept his arm out and gave a low and elegant bow.

'Temerran.' The Lady of Farport hurried to meet him. 'We thought we had lost you all.' She looked over the ragtag group behind him, then held out her arms for a hug.

Temerran shook his head, his stubble catching her hair. 'I had to run. We had no choice.' Shame washed through him, flushing his skin.

Dinari stood back and looked at him, her blue eyes wide and honest. 'You survived, the king's children too. That's all that matters.'

'Stay where you are!' Lucien roared.

Temerran closed his eyes and groaned. The young king's magical command had rooted almost everyone to the spot, everyone but the most powerful Ravens, those who wore Rosa's amulets; and the one person he had intended to stop.

Eleanor was making a stumbling run for the gate. There was a swish and a hum. Eleanor skidded to a halt with a squeal as an arrow cut in front of her.

'He said don't move,' Rosa called out calmly. 'Next time I won't aim to miss.'

'You can't touch me,' Eleanor snarled, fists clenched. She gasped in shock when Lucien did just that, grabbing her by the arm and feeling around her neck. His fingers found a cord, and he tore it from her, dropping the array of amulets and crystals to the floor.

'Unfortunately for you, Elden is served by a good and true-hearted witch. Eleanor of Taurmaline…' Lucien's fingers dug into his sister's arm as she tried to pull free. 'You are guilty of treachery, of betraying your country, and causing the death of the king.'

Dread left Temerran's muscles suddenly weak, but he pushed himself to move, taking swift strides towards the young king, his hands outstretched. 'Lucien. Luce, do nothing you'll regret.'

Lucien drew himself up. 'Eleanor, I sentence you to death.'

'No!' Scarlett screeched. 'Lucien, no.'

Eleanor collapsed to her knees, clutching at his shirt with her free hand. 'No, no. Lucien, Mother made me.'

Lucien let her go and drew his sword, not even hesitating as he swept it around. It sliced through the arm Eleanor raised, catching partway in her neck. Temerran cried out in alarm, blood draining from his face and hands. He bent over, turning his head away. A sickening sound followed, then a soft thud.

Scarlett's wail of despair rang through the otherwise silent courtyard.

Lucien dropped his sword and ran for the castle door. Temerran cursed and ran after him, catching up in time to see the King of Elden fold over and vomit on the floor. Lucien collapsed, curling in a ball, his face caught in the rictus of a mute scream as tears coursed down his red face. Temerran's heart constricted, his pulse slowing, and he sank to the ground beside the distraught boy.

Temerran gathered Lucien into his arms and held him, rocking him. 'I have you, Luce. I'm here. I have you, son.'

Lucien shook, a moan escaping from his tight larynx.

'Hush now,' Temerran soothed. 'I am here, always here. My boy.' He kissed the top of Lucien's head. 'My boy. The son of my soul. I'm always here for you.'

Chapter Thirty-Six

Joss; Fulmer Island

The storm lit the sky to the north as they marched southward, cutting through the trees that had often been the playground of Joss's childhood. Every rumble of thunder set his heart beating faster. At Eagle Hold, his sister and his parents were already engaging the army of Geladan. Behind him, his grandmother was attempting to secure their retreat.

When he'd heard confirmation the Geladanians had landed on their southern shore, his mouth had gone dry. Then a second report had come to say Jderha herself now walked their beloved Island. Anxiety had gnawed at him ever since, despite his attempts to find his courage. He realised he'd reached up to touch his light armour above where his scar sat, and he quickly let his arm drop.

They set a fast pace; there were several miles to cover to reach their meeting point, the place at which they intended to challenge Jderha. Joss frequently glanced behind to see if there was any sign of the Icante, until he tripped over a tree root and nearly went flying.

Alikan grabbed his arm, ensured he had his balance, then set off again.

His friend hadn't laughed at him. Joss's anxiety blossomed outward.

'She's here,' Doroquael buzzed.

Joss's heart flipped painfully in his chest, taking time to slow and calm even after he realised the fire-spirit had meant Dia, not the Geladanian God. His grandmother moved up through the warriors with Gilfy at her side. She looked determined, serene, and Joss felt a moment of despair. Was he a coward to feel fear like he did?

'Mimeth' Dia greeted the *walker* she'd left in charge.

'The ships?' the younger woman asked.

Dia shook her head. 'I don't know. I couldn't afford to wait. Everlyn will handle it.'

Joss tensed his muscles, angry at himself. 'Pull yourself together,' he muttered under his breath.

The sounds of the storm faded behind them, though the wind picked up, conspiring in the leaves and swirling the undergrowth.

There was no talking, no banter. This was so unlike any mission Joss had run as a Raven. There was no excitement at a challenge, only apprehension.

'We'll take a quick break,' Dia announced.

Joss guessed they must have covered about eight miles. He peered up through the leafy canopy. There were a few clouds, but the stars were bright between.

'Rest.' Alikan had already sunk to the ground, and he gave Joss's trouser leg a tug.

Joss sat reluctantly, turning at every sound from the surrounding forest.

'What's up?'

He realised Alikan was watching him.

'Oh.' He shook his head. 'Just a bit on edge, I guess.'

'Must be odd,' Alikan said slowly, his amber eyes still regarding his brother in all but blood. 'All those years living with the threat of a monster under your bed, and now here she is. Real.'

Joss shrugged, desperate for a clever quip that wouldn't come.

Doroquael blazed brightly, quickly dulling again when Dia cleared her throat and gave him a glare. 'I'll scare her off,' Doroquael whispered. 'Just like I always did.'

Joss smiled at that. There had been many times in his childhood when the fire-spirit had chased shadows from the corner of the room or checked under the bed for monsters.

Alikan reached out and briefly gripped his arm. 'We're gonna be fine, Joss.'

'I know.' He screwed his face up, as though Alikan was the one being daft.

His grandmother was speaking so softly to Mimeth Joss couldn't catch her words. The Icante was without all her usual close protection, except Gilfy. Heara was off doing what she did best. Arrus and Worvig were behind at the Hold. Joss's eyes widened when he realised the Icante had set out for battle without a single one of her Silenes with her. She was even wearing just a simple blouse and jacket with her long boots and green trousers. Why was his grandmother facing a god with no armour at all?

Dia stood. 'Time to move on.'

Joss cleared his throat. 'Any news from the others?'

His grandmother shook her head. 'Walk with me for a while, Joss. You too, Ali.'

Joss brushed himself off. Doroquael flew at once to Dia's shoulder.

Joss sucked in a breath. 'Where's Siveraell?'

'Gone ahead to find Kesta and Arridia.' His grandmother looked up at him, her mismatched eyes warm and calm. 'I'm scared too, you know.'

Joss's feet almost faltered. His grandmother was the strongest person he had ever known.

'We all face our fears differently,' she continued. 'Your mother gets angry. Your father becomes the Dark Man. Your grandfather laughs. I...' A slight smile played about her mouth. 'I have my own way.'

Joss frowned. 'I don't know what my way is.'

Alikan gave a snort. 'You just charge straight at whatever's scaring you without stopping to think.'

'I do not!' Joss protested.

Dia squeezed his arm.

Joss glowered at his friend and protector, who was trying not to grin.

But some of his anxiety had eased.

The night wore on and they gained more miles, leaving the shelter of the forest to cross open meadow and farmland. Light seeped into the sky, and now and then a flare of magic would illuminate the horizon, the source of the battle hidden by the rise of the hills.

Two foxes broke cover, not running from them, but at them. Dia crouched, and they ran straight to her hands. Joss watched in open-mouthed awe, feeling the tingle of his grandmother's magic. Dia stiffened, but she thanked the foxes as they slipped away.

'Everyone down!' she commanded in a loud whisper. 'Do not move, do not react, no matter what. Stay hidden.'

Joss got down on all fours, then lay flat in the long grass; his armour and weapons digging into him. Doroquael vanished into the earth.

It was only a few heartbeats before two figures appeared before them. A female Fulmer scout supporting an exhausted Raven. They stumbled together up over the rise, then came hurrying down toward the hidden watchers.

Fire flared up behind the hill, momentarily lighting several Rakinya in silhouette. Many had bloodied or singed fur. Four more Fulmer scouts appeared, two jogging, one somehow finding the energy to sprint; the last barely able to walk. Joss groaned, unable to breathe, his muscles itching for him to leap up. A Rakinya, almost invisible against the grass, scooped up the struggling scout and threw him over his shoulder with barely a pause. Joss's hand flew to his mouth.

Several more of their people appeared in ones and twos, fleeing the sparks and blasts of magic.

The first Scout and Raven reached them, almost falling to the ground when Chieftain Redick called out. 'You are safe, what's happening?'

The Raven gasped out his reply. Joss suddenly realised it was red-headed Tyrin behind the blood and dirt. 'They sent out assassins to scout, but we took most of them out. Then they sent two sorcerers and several warriors around Kesta and Jorrun's group, possibly to cut them off from you. We've taken out as many as we can, but Heara ordered a retreat.' Tyrin shook his head. 'We were losing too many.'

'Heara?' Dia asked sharply.

Tyrin found the Icante in the darkness. 'She is covering our backs with Cassien, Cat, and Dysarta.'

Joss's nostrils flared. Only one magic user against the oncoming Geladanians? His grandmother had to help.

'Go on,' Dia urged. 'You have a long way ahead of you yet, but get back to the Hold.'

Tyrin pushed himself up, reaching out his hand to pull up the Fulmer scout who had supported him. They set off at a fast walk northwards. The other fleeing scouts passed them, Joss feeling the brush of a Rakinya's fur as it leapt over him and away. For a moment, the hill before them was empty, dawn touching its summit. Joss turned to look at his grandmother; her eyes were wide and bright, a tear catching on her eyelashes before falling.

Then three figures appeared, stepping backwards as they rose against the skyline. In the centre was Heara, taking up her familiar fighter's stance, a long dagger in each hand. To her left, the fire-haired sorcerer from the north let fly a blast of ice at some unseen foe. To their right, Cassien twirled his sword in his hand, bracing to fight.

Where was Catya? Joss glanced at his friend; Alikan was gripping the grass before him with both hands.

Cassien pivoted and ducked. From nowhere Catya leapt, her foot hitting Cassien's back as she launched herself into a high backflip. She tucked, then straightened, landing behind two oncoming Geladanian warriors. Her left hand plunged a knife into the back of one, as her right swung out her sword to take out the throat of the other who turned to fight her.

Cassien came up at once to engage a knot of three swordsmen. He parried, ducked, and spun, his sword flashing as it caught the rising sun. Dysarta sent out another blast of magic and another, a retaliating surge of flames curling around her shield that encompassed the four defenders of Fulmer. Two enormous men came at Heara, but she didn't hesitate, dancing aside from the sweeping hacks of their broadswords. She lured them closer, then stepped in to plunge her knives into one man's throat and heart at the same time. She hooked his ankle, pulling him down to use as a shield against the other man whose sword caught. Heara rolled free and onto her feet, her knives somehow still in her hands.

Catya threw her dagger; and it thudded into the neck of Heara's attacker. The Queen of Snowhold then sprang at the last man who faced Cassien; Cass having somehow already dispatched two. Heara pulled Catya's knife free and threw it back to her, before moving to stand ready at Dysarta's side. Faster than a snake, Catya forced her dagger up into the last Geladanian warrior's kidney as Cassien thrust his sword into his belly.

They all turned to face southward, backing slowly down the slope of the hill. Something was still coming.

Joss clenched his fists tight and groaned, pushing himself up and drawing up a knee ready to spring to his feet.

'No,' Dia said sternly. 'You must learn this lesson, Joss, it was the hardest one for me. If you survive this, you will be advisor to the throne of Elden. To protect the land, you will have to send people you love to die.'

Joss shook his head incredulously, turning back to watch the meadow before him. As the four defenders retreated, another figure appeared against the skyline, a woman with a headdress like the rays of the sun.

'We have to do something,' Alikan urged.

'Wait,' Dia ordered.

'Icante.' Joss felt sick. He looked from his grandmother to the advancing priestess of Jderha.

Dysarta sent out a devastating explosion of cold air and ice shards. The north-woman was incredibly strong, but the priestess withstood it, countering with an attack of her own. The four defenders didn't increase the pace of their retreat, their backward steps slow and steady.

It struck Joss suddenly. Was that what his grandmother had seen? They weren't afraid. Did they have a plan? Or did they believe they could win? Hope welled up within him.

The priestess attacked again and again, hot wind whistling over the heads and backs of those who lay hidden in the meadow below the hill. Dysarta didn't respond, only shielding. Was she running out of power?

Then the answer rose out of the grass, towering over the priestess. Edon Ra reached out his huge paws and ripped the priestess's head off.

One of the waiting Fulmer warriors started to cheer, but quickly cut himself off.

Dia raised an eyebrow, then stood and gestured to Joss and Alikan.

Catya gave them a cheerful wave, breaking into a trot to reach them ahead of the others. 'We've cleared out most of their scouts to the west, Icante,' she panted. She looked Alikan up and down and nodded. 'But we can't guarantee none got through. How Kesta's team have fared against them, I cannot say.'

Heara caught up with her, throwing her arms around Dia in a hug before moving to stand at her side. 'Those earth-spirits were pretty handy, quite inventive when it comes to killing, too.' Heara pulled a face.

Catya grinned.

'Icante.' Cassien bowed politely. 'You should be clear to your meeting point. Aelthan and Eyraphin are keeping an eye.'

'Thank you.' Dia regarded them all. 'What you have done is amazing. Now get yourself to the Hold.'

All of them hesitated, even Dysarta shifting her feet. Joss could understand these fighters not wanting to back away from the big confrontation.

'Go on,' Dia prompted. 'You have assignments to fulfil there.'

Catya suddenly laughed. 'Okay, I'd say Icante outranks queen, especially on her own turf.' Her face grew serious. 'Good luck. Take care of yourselves.'

They said their swift goodbyes, Heara and Dia holding each other's wrists, their gazes unwavering, until Heara slipped away.

Joss swallowed the lump in his throat.

Dia cleared hers, her eyebrows raised at the Rakinya who remained where he stood. 'Edon. Are you not following your queen?'

He folded his huge, furry arms. 'I know where I am meant to be.'

Dia made a quiet snort. She turned to regard her small, waiting army. 'We still have a few miles to cover. Let's go.'

Joss drew in a deep breath and followed his grandmother.

Chapter Thirty-seven

Scarlett; Kingdom of Elden

Scarlett wiped at her sore nose with a washcloth. Her cheeks were puffy and her throat raw. Everything around her felt oddly far away. Her parents were dead. Her sister was dead.

There was no news of Joss.

'Here.' Rosa pressed a cup of steaming tea into her hands. 'Valerian and passionflower. I added nettle and chamomile to make it taste a little nicer.'

'Thank you.' She glanced up and forced a smile.

The bed gave as Rosa sat beside her. 'Will you not talk to Lucien? He's very upset.'

A wave of anger washed through her, and she shuddered.

'I think you should,' Rosa persisted gently.

Scarlett gazed down at the carpet, letting her eyes unfocus. She didn't want to have to think about anything.

Rosa stood suddenly, her hands on her hips. 'Well, you have a lot to grieve for, that's for certain, but you are a princess, young lady, and you have responsibilities.'

Scarlett stared at her, wide-eyed.

'Tantony is out there with Dinari trying to restore the castle. That should be you. You want to lead? Then show them you have what it takes.'

'I can lead,' Scarlett protested.

'Then talk to Lucien, show a united front even if you don't want to, and start getting our country back on its feet. This isn't over yet.'

Scarlett held her cup tighter. Rosa was right. She had to put her duty first, no matter her own feelings. She gasped, looking up at Rosa's brown eyes.

Duty first.

It was what Lucien had done, slaughtering their sister to protect Elden. A decision even Bractius had not been able to take regarding their treacherous mother.

She gulped down some of the hot tea, even though it scorched her mouth, then rubbed at her face and smoothed back her hair. She took in a deep breath. 'Okay. Let's start by seeing Luce.'

Rosa opened the door for her, but Scarlett hesitated, pivoted on her heels and gave the older woman a big squeeze of a hug before heading out. A man stood outside her door. He looked to be about thirty and had curly brown hair and brown eyes like a Borrowman. He smiled and gave a small bow, his cheeks dimpling.

Rosa's forehead wrinkled. 'Meric?'

'I am, Lady Rosa. Your highness.'

'Forgive me.' Rosa blushed a little. 'You were much younger when you apprenticed at Northold.'

'I was.' His smile broadened. 'May I escort you somewhere?'

'To my brother, if you please.' Scarlett's fluttering nerves began to settle, although she wasn't sure if it was Rosa's tea, or knowing that the Ravens were watching over them.

'My honour.' Meric inclined his head and strode along the corridor.

Another Raven stood outside Lucien's rooms, a little younger with strawberry-blonde hair.

'Have you met Ovey?' Meric turned to ask.

'I have.' Rosa smiled fondly at him.

Scarlett cleared her throat. 'Not yet, but I am delighted. Thank you for coming to our aid.'

'We're Ravens, Highness,' Ovey replied with a shrug.

Meric knocked at the door, and there was a muffled response. He opened it and stepped aside with a bow.

'Scar!' Lucien almost leapt from his chair, his eyes wide and hopeful.

Temerran was seated by the window, Lucien's lute cradled in his lap.

Scarlett's face crumpled at the sight of her brother, her eyes watering again although her body felt as dry as ashes. They met mid-room, Scarlett holding her brother as hard as she could.

'I understand.' She hiccupped. 'You had to be the king.'

She felt him nod. 'I couldn't leave a threat to Elden. We both know the stories, that before we were born Mother was in league with those who would destroy us, but she claimed she'd been bewitched. She'd planned this for the last fourteen years, Scar.' He stepped back to look down at Scarlett, his eyes red veined. 'Father made few mistakes, but he always underestimated Mother. I couldn't afford to do the same with Elle. And I couldn't leave it to weigh on your shoulders. I had to bear the burden.'

Scarlett shook her head in confusion.

Lucien stepped back. 'Are you all right?'

She took in several breaths and nodded. 'Rosa has reminded me I have a duty to perform.'

'As has Tem.'

The siblings regarded their friends. Rosa blushed, Temerran leaned back in his chair and raised his red eyebrows.

'Okay.' Lucien drew himself up. 'Where do we start?'

Scarlett placed her palms together and pressed her forefingers against her lips. 'Well. We must get word to all Elden that the castle is saved, but that the king and queen are dead.'

'And we must advise the families of those who died,' Lucien agreed.

'We will need to appoint new Merkis as advisors.' Scarlett let her arms fall to her side, but her left hand rose to rest on her hip. 'If I were you, I'd ask Tantony to stay and be your chief advisor.'

Both Scarlett and Lucien turned to regard Rosa.

'Oh.' Rosa looked from one to the other of them. 'I'm sure he will. At least... well, for a while.'

Brother and sister turned back to each other, holding each other's gaze.

'Rosa.' Scarlet raised her chin. 'Merkis Rosa. You must also stay to advise us.'

Rosa's eyes almost bulged from their sockets. 'Eh?' The older woman swayed on her feet and Temerran leapt up to take her arm.

Lucien smiled and laughed, although pain still haunted his dark eyes. 'Yes, Rosa, you shall be Elden's first lady Merkis. To be a Merkis, you need to lead a hundred men. From what I recall you led almost as many women and children with bows once, in defence of Northold. We shall have to create you another such band of archers.'

Rosa flapped her hand in front of her face, while Temerran kissed her cheek.

'You have a place to start.' Temerran stepped away from Rosa and regarded the royal siblings. 'Take control. Stand together. Be decisive. What is best for Elden, may not always be what is best for you.'

Scarlett and Lucien both nodded.

'Oh.' Rosa flapped her hands in front of her again. 'When Tantony and I hunted for the witch in Anim, a woman there said her daughter was being held here as a hostage, as a lady-in-waiting. If you wanted more answers, you might start there. And let the poor lass go home.'

Lucien turned to Scarlett. 'Do you want to handle that?'

She straightened her spine. 'I will.'

'Thank you. I'll get messages out and get a report on the castle's status from Dinari and Tantony.'

Temerran regarded them both. 'Your majesty, your highness. Now I feel you are safe, I must go.'

'No,' Lucien said at once. 'I mean... we might still need you.'

Temerran looked to the carpet, brushing his red curls away from his face. 'Myself and the *Undine* are long overdue in the Fulmers.'

'But...' Lucien clenched and unclenched his fists.

Temerran placed a hand on his arm. 'Luce, I will come back, you know it. Dinari is an excellent woman and powerful, and you are in safe hands with Tantony and Rosa. In the meantime, you must decide between your heart and your conscience.'

Lucien nodded. Scarlett felt an unsettling flutter of dread. There was something unspoken that she'd missed.

'The girl from Anim,' Temerran prompted.

'Of course.' Scarlett gave a firm nod. 'Good luck, Luce, I'll see you soon.'

She pivoted on her heels and headed out the door, Rosa close behind her. She considered her mother's ladies-in-waiting, trying not to let images of her mother come to mind, nor grief swallow her heart. All the women had good connections and were from prominent families; as was her sister's lady.

She gasped, her hands going to her mouth. 'Oh Scarlett, you absolute idiot!' She spun to face Rosa, seeing the man, Meric, followed discreetly behind.

'Whatever is it?' Rosa asked.

'My own lady-in-waiting, Riane. She has only been with me five months, and I never much had anything to do with her as I guessed she spied for Mother. My previous lady was suddenly called home to be betrothed. It's her, it must be!'

Scarlett hurried for her room, then remembered she'd dismissed the girl again the last time she'd seen her. Usually, Riane went to Eleanor… but likely she had fled with most of the castle's population.

Scarlett's heart quailed, first at how blind she had been to the poor girl's plight right under her nose, and more so at the thought of entering her sister's rooms.

Rosa waited patiently while she plucked up the courage to move.

She reached tentatively for the door handle, then pushed it open and strode in.

The small parlour was empty. Her sister's embroidery lay upon the table, the box of threads still open. Scarlett rocked on her feet, her vision blurring.

Rosa closed the box. 'Would you like me and Meric to check the other rooms?'

Scarlett stirred herself and shook her head. 'No. Let's go together.'

She checked the lady-in-waiting's room and the larger sitting room. Everything was surreally untouched and normal, just achingly empty. Scarlett couldn't help but wonder; if she had been closer to her sister, would their mother have been less able to pull her into her mad plans? Or would Scarlett have been drawn in too?

There was but one area left to check. Scarlett listened for a moment at the bedroom door, before cautiously pushing it open.

The room was also empty. Several dresses lay across the bed, all of them far finer than anything Scarlett owned. Eleanor had obviously been preparing to take her seat on the throne.

There was a muffled sob. Scarlett's eyes widened, and she pivoted to look at Rosa. The newly made Merkis reached down to take her knife from her boot, wincing and putting a hand to her hip as she straightened up.

Meric drew power, treading silently on the thick carpet as he moved toward the source of the sound; one of the extensive wardrobes. Scarlett tensed as the Raven pulled back the ornate wooden door.

There was a scream, quickly stifled as the girl buried her face in one of the fine dresses.

'Riane.' Scarlett dropped to her knees and shuffled closer to her lady-in-waiting. 'Riane, it's me. You're safe. The castle has been saved.'

The girl continued to huddle beneath the clothing, but she turned to peep at the princess.

'I know who you are,' Scarlett said softly. 'My friend here, Rosa, she visited Anim, she spoke to your mother.'

'Is Mother safe?' Riane straightened up, pulling aside the clothes to look cautiously at Meric and Rosa.

'She was safe when I left her,' Rosa confirmed. 'Oh, my.'

Scarlett turned back to see what had alarmed Rosa. Riane had a nasty bruise blackening on the left side of her face.

'Who did that?' Scarlett demanded.

'Princess... the queen... I mean to say, your sister.'

Scarlett hid her face momentarily behind her hand, then steeling herself, reached out to the girl. 'Come out, Riane, it's safe now. Eleanor is dead. Luce... the new king had her executed for treason.'

'Oh, but what of me?' Riane almost wailed.

'We know you only worked for the witches under duress,' Rosa reassured her. 'Come on, I'll make us all some tea. And I'd best check in my books and see what I can do for that bruise.'

Scarlett bit at her lower lip. That was something she and Lucien would have to consider. Their Lady Merkis was also – as far as they knew – now Elden's one and only witch.

'So, they took you from Anim,' Scarlett prompted as she helped the girl out of the wardrobe. They headed for the parlour, Meric making a quick check of the hall outside while Rosa heated water.

Riane nodded. 'The queen stopped by on her way to visit her family. She was interested in the kiln. I didn't see or hear much as we were to go inside so we wouldn't offend her majesty with the, well, the filthy sight of us. But then a man came in the house and dragged me out. The queen said I would do. She told my father if anyone mentioned she had been there, or what work they did for her, I would die. Then she would come for them.' Riane shuddered. 'I believed her.'

Rosa poured them all some tea. Meric smiled and nodded, leaning against the door to sip his.

'And once here, she gave you to me.'

'She did.' Riane met Scarlett's eyes. 'I was just to watch you and tell everything to your sister. At first, they were cross that you kept sending me away, then they... they didn't seem to care. I don't think they thought you were doing anything of interest until you examined the tower. After that day, they started doing their magic right here.' She pointed back towards Eleanor's bedroom.

'I'll have a look around later,' Rosa said. 'Make sure there is nothing of concern left here.'

'Oh, be careful!' Riane looked wide-eyed at them all. 'There are all sorts of potions, even a scent that makes you fall in love.'

'Really?' Scarlett stiffened. Had her sister used it on Joss?

'Oh, my.' Rosa paled.

'What is it?' Scarlett asked.

Rosa winced. 'Well, Linea taught the queen...'

Scarlett gasped. 'And poor Temerran fell in love with Linea. Should we tell him?'

Rosa's nose wrinkled at the thought of it. 'Let's keep it to ourselves for now, the poor man blames himself enough.'

Scarlett fiddled with her cup before meeting Riane's eyes again. 'Riane, I'm very sorry I didn't bother to get to know you. I was so focused on my own life. I used to think I was so clever, that I knew so many things. Lately I learned I know absolutely nothing.'

'You know how to get out of a dungeon,' Rosa pointed out.

Scarlett laughed, the tension in her muscles easing a little. 'Yes, I do know that. And we might have a need of those dungeons. Riane, do you think you'd be able to describe or point out those who worked for my mother?'

Riane straightened up. 'I can try, highness.'

***

It was late when she went in search of her brother, Rosa yawning at her side and Meric still watching their backs. The new king was in their father's — his — study with Tantony. Ovey was outside the door. Lucien looked flustered, Tantony was calm, but there were shadows under his eyes.

'Good evening, your majesty.' Rosa gave a curtsy. 'Merkis.'

Tantony gave a loud huff of a sigh. 'Good evening... Merkis.'

Rosa smiled, her cheeks flushing.

'How's it going?' Scarlett asked.

'We have the castle as secure as we can.' Lucien told her. 'Dinari and Ylena have just gone to bed to get some rest. I've been inundated with pigeons carrying panicked messages, but people have started to make their way back to the city. I've recalled some of our warriors who were sent to the south coast. If there is another attack from anywhere, it will come from the direction of the Fulmers.'

Scarlett sat down heavily in a chair. 'Has there been any word?'

He shook his head. 'Not from the Islands.'

Scarlett sucked in her bottom lip, her heart aching for Joss. She prayed he was safe.

'I hear you've been arresting people.' Tantony regarded her from under his bushy eyebrows.

'Only two. I think most of Mother's supporters died or fled, but we've made copies of names we know and descriptions to circulate just in case. Did, um... has Temerran gone?'

Lucien looked away. 'He has. The *Undine* sailed a few hours ago. Um, Scar... there's a duty that needs doing, which I haven't plucked up the courage to deal with yet. I wondered if you could do it?'

She leaned forward. 'What is it?'

Lucien swallowed and glanced at Tantony before opening his mouth to speak. 'Those who died have not been moved, they lay still where they fell.'

'Oh.' Scarlett shrank back. 'Oh, well, they must be dealt with. Leave it with me, Luce.'

'Thank you.' His brown eyes were sharp with pain.

Scarlett stood quickly, moving around the table to give him a brief hug, before heading to the throne room.

'We will need help,' Meric said as he followed. 'Shall I find you some volunteers?'

'Oh, yes please,' she said over her shoulder.

'I'll be but a moment, please stay on guard.' The Raven slipped away.

Rosa hurried forward to proceed Scarlett to the throne room. Only four torches burned on the long walls, leaving most of it in darkness. Four warriors stood guard at the broken main doors, all of them shifting uneasily.

'Shall we have some light?' Rosa suggested. 'There will be candles all over the floor.'

Scarlett nodded, unable to find her tongue.

By the time they'd set several candles on the few long tables left standing, Meric rejoined them. He brought a mixture of people with him. Servants, warriors, Ravens, and Thane Vedun of Haven who was alive only because he'd been laid up in bed with gout.

'Your orders, highness?' Meric gave a polite bow of his head.

Scarlett rubbed at her chest, then drew in a breath. 'We need sheets or curtains to cover and carry the dead. Put the Geladanians out in the courtyard. Lay all our people around the edge of this room until we have time to sew shrouds, then we can seek their families' wishes.'

'And... the late king?' Rosa asked, her hands folded before her.

Scarlett's chest tightened. 'Place my father in his bed. And my mother and sister in theirs. I will wash them myself.'

The small group quickly got on with their grizzly task, Scarlett not shirking from moving and carrying the sticky and charred bodies. She paused to stand before the throne, her eyes travelling over its emptiness, its loneliness.

She shuddered.

Chapter Thirty-Eight

Arridia; Fulmer Island

'This is it.' Kesta slowed, taking two cautious steps beyond the trees.

Arridia looked around at the wide clearing. The sun moved in patches over the grass, shorn close by the sheep who were now safely across the sea. Bees hummed as they worked, but the birds were eerily silent, sending a shiver down her spine. The hill sloped gently upward facing the north, but it was sharp and steep on its southward side. The area of forest they had just passed through was narrow, but beyond the hills it stretched for almost a mile, large enough for those fleeing to lose their pursuers if they needed to.

'Riddi?' Her father placed his hand on her arm.

It was time. She gazed up at his worried blue eyes before closing her own and reached out her *knowing*. She could feel the deep thrumming of the trees, but none of the sharper emotions of mammals. It was hard not to be distracted by the people and spirits around her. She straightened in relief as she touched on what she was looking for.

'They are a way away yet.' She turned to her father. 'But grandmother is drawing close.'

Jorrun raised his voice. 'Take your positions! You all know what you must do.'

Arridia was about to clamp down on her *knowing* when she felt a presence that both shocked her and made her heart ache.

'Nip!'

'Nip?' Jorrun followed her gaze towards the forest on their left.

Eyraphin trumpeted a warning, causing several of their magic users to call up shields, including Dierra who stood at Arridia's back.

'Hold!' Arridia held up a hand, trying to shut out their panic. She forced herself to breathe slowly, though she dreaded what was to come. She had never faced battle on this scale, and even a small conflict left her raw and battered by emotion. 'It's a friend.'

Moments later she saw movement in the shadows and a pony trotted out from the undergrowth. Arridia held her breath. The stable master looked relaxed in his saddle. She could see no sign that he'd been hurt. A brief flare of green fire revealed the small elemental perched on his shoulder. She let the air out of her lungs.

Azrael gave a spluttering snort.

'Azra.' Jorrun chided. 'What do you have against that earth-spirit?'

'Nothing.' Azrael buzzed.

Dierra laughed. 'He thinks he'll lose some of Arridia's attention to it when she and Nip get together.'

'I do not!' Azrael blazed.

Arridia's face burned, and she looked up at her father.

'Arridia and Nip, eh?' Jorrun said slowly, his eyes hardening.

'Come on.' Kesta gave Jorrun a soft shove. 'We're meant to be getting into position.'

Arridia spared both Azrael and Dierra a glare, before heading not where she wanted to go, but up the slope behind her parents. Nip found them anyway, swinging his leg over the pony's back to jump down. 'Did Catya's message reach you?' he asked Kesta and Jorrun.

'It did,' Jorrun nodded, a small line of anxiety furrowing his forehead above his nose. 'Did you see how our scouts fared.'

'Some of it.' Nip winced, his dark-grey eyes growing momentarily distant. 'Cassien and I lingered at the beach. Cassien saw Jderha.'

'Tell me,' Kesta demanded, taking her husband's arm and leaning against him.

Arridia folded her arms across her stomach. She wasn't sure she wanted to know.

'I didn't see her myself, but he said she was big, larger than a normal woman. He said... well, he believes she has four arms. And she froze the sea to walk ashore.'

Her mother's face paled, but her father just nodded. 'It's no more than we expected.'

'Arridia.' Nip's voice softened as he turned to her. 'Would you be kind enough to tell my pony to return to the Hold, or perhaps just head north out of the way, once I have stripped it of harness?'

'Of course.'

'Shouldn't you be heading to the Hold yourself?' Jorrun frowned at the younger man.

'No.' Nip didn't flinch from the Dark Man's gaze.

'Very well.' Jorrun turned on his heels and stalked off to see that everyone was positioning themselves as they should be. With a warm smile at Nip, her mother followed.

'How was it, really?' Arridia asked as she helped him remove the pony's saddle.

He stroked the animal's neck, then slipped off its halter. 'The hardest thing for me was standing by, knowing there was little I could do.'

'But you stood there still.' She met his eyes and smiled. 'And you have an uncanny habit of being in just the right place when you're needed.'

Nip smiled in return. 'We shall see.'

'There are spirits coming from the south,' Gorchia warned, shifting on Nip's shoulder to look behind them.

Arridia quickly turned her attention to the pony, using her *knowing* to send it warning that danger came, and it should head toward the sea and the Hold to the north. With a nudge at Nip, the pony trotted away down the slope of the hill, breaking into a run to weave between the warriors.

'I'd better get into position,' Arridia said. The anxiety of the people around her was hard to close out, but she focused on the solid calm of the man before her. 'What will you do?'

Nip narrowed his eyes a little as he made a quick survey of the area. 'I should retreat into the trees with the warriors and scouts, though Gorchia will be of use to you here on the hill. Perhaps he should remain with you?'

She laughed. 'Azra will go mad. No, stay together. I have no doubt I will need you soon.'

Nip nodded. 'We will be there.' He reached out to touch her cheek, then strode away after the others.

'Riddi!' Azrael came flying toward her erratically. 'Over here.'

Wishing she could slow the pounding of her heart, Arridia followed the fire-spirit to where her parents waited with Dierra. Several flames blossomed in the trees and a dozen fire-spirits streaked toward them, led by Siveraell.

'They come,' the spirit confirmed in answer to their worried faces. 'Their scouts and assassins have been dealt with, along with a strong priestess she ssent after Catya's party. We lost an earth-spirit and two of fire obtaining the following information.'

Azrael made a small keening sound and Arridia rubbed at her shoulder, trying to subdue the ache in her heart.

'I mourn the loss of our friends,' Jorrun said quietly.

'Jderha lingers still at the ruin of Eagle Hold,' Siveraell went on. 'But she hass sent a large party against you, mostly warriors, but led by five priestesses and three sorcerers. We susspect there is one among them who is a bard. He wears a suit of crimson.'

'Is everyone ready?' Jorrun asked.

Arridia swallowed, looking from her father to her mother, taking courage from theirs.

Kesta nodded, glancing quickly to the forest behind them. 'The warriors and spirits are in place. We just need to get ourselves into our groups.'

Both her parents regarded her. None of them wanted to speak the word 'goodbye,' but they all knew this was what it might be. Arridia was surprised at how steadily her heart beat, though each thrum was loud in her ears.

'Come on.' Dierra broke into the awkward silence, taking Arridia's hand and pulling her away. Arridia let herself be dragged, her feet seemed heavy and clumsy.

Her parents stood together at the summit of the hill with Siveraell; their aim to take the full focus of Geladan's attack if they could. Behind them were Jagna, Beth, Jollen, Rey, and *walker* Tarlos of Eagle Hold. Arridia's group gathered several yards to their left. With herself, Dierra, and Azrael, were Perta, Charis, and Vorro of Chem; also *walker* Dinai of Dolphin Hold.

Arridia couldn't help looking northward, although she refrained from letting loose her *knowing*. Her grandmother and brother's positions to their right as yet stood empty.

The wind played through the trees below them, blowing the branches in sporadic ripples. Arridia held her breath as two figures, then two more, appeared between the trunks. Scouts, both Fulmer and Raven; the last of their rear guard. Spotting Kesta and Jorrun, they made their way to them to report.

'What are they saying?' Dierra demanded.

Arridia gave a shrug. She couldn't make out the words, but their fear was sharp.

The air distorted, small patches of rainbow hurtling toward them. The final warning.

'They come!' Aelthan whistled.

'Hold steady,' Vorro said behind her. Arridia didn't look around, her focus on the forest.

Darker shapes moved within, here and there a garish colour. Her eyes sought the bright blood red of the bard.

The Geladanians halted inside the treeline. Their warriors wore a uniform armour of black with iron plate across their chests, most of them olive skinned and dark-haired like Arridia herself; like her Fulmer family. She wondered how many of them really wanted to fight. She bit down hard on her temptation to stretch out her *knowing* and find out.

The crimson bard moved, a smile on his face as he stepped forward into the open.

Kesta and Jorrun drew power, the rest of them only a moment behind. Every magic user on the hill blasted the man with flame; they couldn't give him the chance to speak. He was incinerated before the Geladanians could react; a cry of outrage shuddered through the forest.

'There will be no surrender.'

Arridia drew in a sharp breath at the familiar voice. Her grandmother was making her way up the hill to take her position further to the right. Her own party of magic users trailed a respectful distance behind, only Gilfy at her side.

'There will be no negotiation.' Dia's voice was clear and calm. 'You will leave the islands. If you do so, we will never come after Jderha.'

'Be silent, slave!' One of the priestesses roared. 'You will kneel or die.' Her face was incredibly pale, and Arridia guessed she must use some kind of powder for that effect, as she'd also rimmed her eyes with red like a Borrowman's battle mask.

'Ready,' Dierra said unnecessarily, bracing herself as they all called power. As the next to speak, the priestess had marked herself as their new target. Again, the magic users on the hill struck out, although this time some of them shielded, including Arridia and Azrael who were to conserve their power. Astoundingly, the High Priestess's shield held.

'Attack!' she cried out.

The Geladanian warriors surged forward, and several spirits came flying from the priestess's staff. Dierra laughed aloud as the spirits shot not toward them, but back towards the warriors. The priestess's too unspecific command had played right into their hands.

Arrows whistled over their heads as the Fulmer archers stepped out of the woods, sending three swift volleys into the ranks of the Geladanians. A bright wall of flame followed as the fire-spirits rose out of the earth, setting warriors ablaze before vanishing just as quickly. Arridia caught the cries of the Geladanians who were last out of the trees; the earth-spirits were taking out any stragglers in their diabolically inventive way.

The high-priestess's shield still hadn't folded and now the other's added their attack, flame and ice slamming against Arridia's shield; and warriors still came on, closing the ground between them.

Movement caught Arridia's peripheral vision. She dared not look to be sure, trusting that their own warriors must now be charging in from left and right as planned, braving the magic of their enemy to stop them reaching those on the hill.

She recognised her father's signature as a strong wind ripped across the grass and finally the high-priestess fell.

Arridia could feel nothing but despair. They still faced at least seven Geladanian magic users and Jderha herself, and already they were using too much of their limited power.

Vorro stood to Arridia's right, he called out suddenly, 'Sorcerer just ahead to the left!'

They all took him as their next target without question, Arridia still concentrating on shielding with Azrael and Dinai the *walker*. She had to close her eyes briefly as again the fire-spirits shot up, this time only feet from them, to try to halt the warriors who still came on. They vanished as quickly as they came, leaving several Geladanians screaming in agony. Several of the fire-spirits were hit by the priestesses and sorcerers, and Azrael let out a desperate wail.

"Ware!' Dierra cried suddenly, drawing her sword. She sprang forward, engaging the blade of a warrior.

Others reached them and were blown apart by Charis and Perta. Fire struck Arridia's shield from two directions and she stumbled. 'Dierra! Dierra get back.'

Dierra's own shield held, but she didn't withdraw, instead fending off two more warriors who'd reached them at the same time as sending a vigorous attack against the sorcerer. Another blast hit them and Dierra vanished from view, Arridia wasted power to sweep the flames aside, to try to see her cousin. She staggered as her shield was struck again and again, debris and smoke darkened the sky.

'Dierra!' Arridia screamed. She was breathing hard, eyes wide despite the stinging smoke.

The air cleared.

Dierra lay still upon the scorched grass, her body blackened, her chest ripped open.

For the briefest of moments, time stood still for Arridia. The only sound was the thunder of her heart and the incredulous whimper that rose from her chest.

Arridia tried to run, but Vorro grabbed her arm and held her back.

'Let go!' She struggled to free herself. 'I have to heal her!'

'No, Riddi, sstay back!' Azrael wailed.

A blast of ice struck; the fire-spirit's flames wavered as he took the impact on his shield for all of them.

'You're not shielding,' Vorro shouted in her ear, his grip tightening as she continued to struggle.

'I have to heal her!' Her vision blurred, a sob shaking her body. Screams rang out around her, arrows whistled past. She tried desperately to find Dierra with her *knowing,* her chest tightened, her heart raced against her ribs.

Azrael made himself larger, drifting closer as his shield was battered again. 'Riddi. Riddi, I'm sorry, but Dierra is dead.'

His calm flowed through her like a welcome sun, easing aside the frost. An anguished cry rose from her lungs. She shook her head, her hands trembling as they pushed away the strands of hair that clung to her face. Sweat beaded her neck and back, nausea trying to rise.

'Riddi.' Azrael withdrew, his blue eyes coming into focus. 'Your friends can't hold their shield without you.'

Coldness struck Arridia. She straightened up, another cry escaping her lips. She drew up her power and turned back to the fight, her heart still screaming out her dead cousin's name.

Chapter Thirty-Nine

Joss; Fulmer Island

Joss followed Alikan as he wove through the undergrowth, picking his path as carefully as a cat. He kept glancing through the trees, trying to track his grandmother's progress as she made her way up the hill. His parents were visible in the distance on the summit, and he swallowed back the queasiness in his stomach. He wished he was stronger; he wished they didn't have to set their own lives as a shield for his.

Doroquael gave a sudden hiss, and they all froze. 'Scout,' the spirit whispered. 'I'll take him.'

Doroquael vanished into the ground. Moments later fire flared up between the trees, then went out.

'Okay.' Alikan nodded to himself. 'Come on.'

Joss turned to force a smile at the small group behind him, hoping they didn't see through his thin act. Belir, Sharne, and Holin had all served in the Fulmers, but he only knew the younger Holin well. Sharne was the strongest of the three and had been rescued from Uldren years ago. She and Belir both had dark curly hair which denoted some Borrow blood, but Sharne was paler with blue eyes.

Alikan picked up their pace, no longer worrying about making a sound. The crashing and snapping of twigs told him the Fulmer warriors who trailed them were doing the same. Joss flinched at the sudden barrage of power out on the hill, instinctively turning to run toward it to see what was happening. Alikan put out an arm to stop him.

'We have our own job to do,' Alikan said, not unkindly.

They passed the clearing, heading deeper south and leaving their warriors in position behind them. Battle broke out, magic thrumming through the air, blood and smoke a heavy choking tang in the back of Joss's throat even at this distance.

Alikan halted, gesturing for them all to get down. 'Their warriors have moved out. Let's pick a target.'

Joss crouched at his side, trying to look at the chaotic and heart-stopping scene before him dispassionately.

'It makes sense to take out the one nearest us and away from his fellows.' Joss pointed through the trees to a sorcerer who stood behind the partial shelter of an oak, sending flames toward those on the hill regardless of his own warriors.

Alikan gave a single, curt nod, then sprang to his feet and attacked at once. Joss enveloped the group in a shield, Belir and Doroquael adding their own power. Alikan held back his strength, but Sharne and Holin did not. Taken completely unawares, the sorcerer stumbled, losing his concentration, but sadly not his shield. He recovered, scrabbling about the tree to face them. From nowhere, a branch exploded out of his chest.

Joss gave a cry of disgust and retched.

There was a flash of green.

'On,' Alikan urged.

Doroquael took the lead, not going too far ahead and keeping his own shield tight. He paused on the edge of the clearing and gave a little squeal of alarm. 'Riddi is in trouble.'

'What?' Joss pushed past Alikan, leaning out to look. He couldn't even see his sister through all the smoke, flame, and magical distortions, she was too far away. His grandmother's group were holding their own; just beyond her, his parents were taking a battering. His heart constricted, a sharp pain shooting out to his shoulder. He looked down the treeline.

'That one,' he growled. Several air-elementals swirled about the high-priestess's staff, trying to resist whatever command she had given. 'Let's free those spirits. We'll go through every one of those Geladanians to get to Riddi if we have to.'

'Just remember to save your power,' Alikan warned.

Joss pulled a face behind his friend's back. Staying within the trees they crept closer, then on Joss's signal attacked.

As soon as she felt the flare of their magic, the priestess whirled about to meet it. She was younger than Joss had expected. From this distance it was hard to tell if her face was contorted in rage, or fear. He itched to attack, gritting his teeth as he held his shield steady against first flame, then ice. Sharne, Belir, and Holin all created fierce tornados, sending them at the priestess from all directions to batter her defence. Alikan followed with razor shards of ice. With a scream, the priestess fell, her own elementals streaming back to finish her.

Joss tensed his muscles to run, but Alikan stopped him again. Joss swore at him in frustration.

'I have my orders.' Alikan held his gaze with his amber eyes. 'Next target.'

They moved together, keeping low, Joss's anxiety coming in waves. The Geladanian warriors had been wiped out, but he dreaded to think how much of a toll it had taken on his family's power. Joss's eyes widened as he saw his father take out first a sorcerer and then a priestess. Had they given up hope of saving energy?

Another priestess fell to Dia's group. How many were left?

The ground shook.

And again.

An intense dread gripped Joss's soul, an odd light sensation bleeding from his heart outwards. His mouth opened, but it was a moment before he could get any words out. 'Get down, he hissed.'

His group obeyed, hitting the forest floor as shapes emerged from the south.

A second army.

They paused, some Geladanian warriors quickly moving aside as something came forth.

Joss's eyes widened; his heart flipped inside his chest. He wiped his clammy hands slowly down his trousers.

The woman was enormous, her presence somehow larger. Her dark hair plaited and coiled about her head. Four swords were buckled at her belt, one for each of her four hands. And her eyes, they were white, colourless, but for the wide pupils.

Jderha had come.

Chapter Forty

Dia; Filmer Island

Dia raised her chin.

So, this was the creature who thought she could hurt her family.

Power thrummed from the Geladanian's god. Dia reached out her *knowing* but was startled to find only emptiness. Either the Goddess was incredibly controlled, or she wore some protection against a *walker's* power. Or perhaps... perhaps gods felt no emotion at all.

'I have a question,' Dia called out. 'We had no awareness of you. You were never in any danger from us. So why come? Why provoke us?'

'Do not dare to speak to your God!' the priestess snarled. 'Get down on your bellies before her.'

Dia made a sound in the back of her throat. 'No. I think I'll stand.'

The priestess stepped forward, brandishing her staff. 'You are nothing but a slave! Nothing but dust—'

Dia drew herself up, her voice loud and true across the clearing. 'I am the Icante.'

The Goddess gave a barely perceptible start. She turned away from Kesta to regard Dia. 'I knew Icante. You are not her.' Jderha's voice was deep for a woman, but soft, soothing.

'I am her descendant I am led to believe.' Dia took another step forward, causing Gilfy to shift uncomfortably. 'Jderha, Goddess of Geladan, we had no wish to harm you. Will you not leave us in peace? We will never come to Geladan.'

The Goddess remained completely still. Dia had to force herself to breathe. The wind stirred in the trees, whispering its anticipation.

'No,' Jderha replied. 'No. Nothing changes. If Icante's treacherous blood lives, it can steal my immortality.'

Dia sucked in a breath. Her thoughts tumbled inside her in a rush of blood. Was that it? Was that the answer? And Arridia was so obviously the key. Third generation *walker* on her mother's side. Third generation *walker* on her father's, although it had skipped a generation with Jorrun himself. But how could she tell Arridia?

Her eyes widened. She had to take the risk. She called out loudly. 'What makes a *walker* unique? What is in their blood?'

Had Arridia understood? Had Kesta?

From the corner of her eye, she saw her daughter's head whip around, stepping back a little to gaze not at Jderha, but at her.

Kesta knew. Her clever daughter knew.

But then hope died.

Instead of answering, Jderha replied with brutal force. A shockwave exploded outward from the god, uprooting trees, killing some of her own men, but also sending all of those on the hill flying. The impact of the hit fractured several bones in Dia's body and stole the air from her lungs. For a moment she was endlessly falling, then she slammed to the earth and tumbled, clutching at the grass to try to hold on to the earth.

Only one withstood the blast.

Dia blinked at the brightness of the roaring flames, pushing herself up onto her feet despite the pain. Siveraell had made himself huge, a living barrier between the god and those who survived on the hill. The fire-spirit flew at Jderha, battering at her defences, spilling his energy, pouring his heart, life, and soul into his desperate, brave, but futile attack.

Jderha ripped him apart.

Dia fell to her knees, a silent scream of fathomless grief locked her muscles. It should have been impossible. It was incomprehensible. The elder spirit was gone.

Siveraell was dead.

Chapter Forty-One

Arridia; Fulmer Island

She felt his death.

She felt the ending of a great soul.

Arridia pulled herself up, her bruises raw and throbbing, her heart bleeding grief.

'Azra,' she cried out, looking around desperately.

Perta lay completely still, just several yards behind her. Beyond Perta, Vorro and Charis were staggering to their feet. *Walker* Dinai was on her hands and knees, shaking her head.

Nip… Where was Nip?

Her eyes caught sight of her parents. They stood together, shields raised, power drawn, already making their way back up the hill. Beth stumbled after them, blood trickling from her nose. Arridia shook herself, drawing up her own shield quickly.

'Azra!'

As she reached the summit, Kesta crouched, and Arridia sensed her mother reach down and down. A deep thrum came from far below, vibrating in an almost ticklish way through Arridia's bones. It was as though she felt her mother's voice.

Earth beneath me.

The sky darkened, clouds gathering at a phenomenal speed. The sun's light faded, everything cast in a strange purple-brown hue. Lightning struck down, illuminating the Icante standing alone but for Gilfy. Thunder cracked and rumbled above, rolling around the ravaged island.

Dia's voice rang out clear and strong.

'Sky above me.'

Light flared up and Arridia ducked away, shielding her face with her arms. A ring of fire-spirits rose about her and looking across she saw they also surrounded her mother and grandmother.

One spirit hovered before her, his fiery blue eyes filled with love.

'Fire around you, Riddi. Always.'

Azrael's image distorted as her tears overflowed. She blinked rapidly, peering down at her hands.

'Water within me,' she whispered.

The blood of a *walker.*

The blood of a *walker*, unlike any other, could draw in and send out emotion.

Arridia gasped in air, breathing hard as she made a quick scan of the hill and the forest. Water, and even patches of ice, still glistened on the grass.

'Are you ready?' Azrael asked.

There was an awful sensation of everything being sucked toward the towering god as she took power to strike again.

Arridia drew her own.

'Ready.'

The fire-spirits shielded. Dia brought lightning down on Jderha again and again. Kesta ripped upward, part of the hill caving in as first solid, then molten rock spewed upward. Jderha and the last priestess vanished from sight, but Arridia didn't pause to hope. She first cooled the ground, then drew a soft, warm wind across it just as her father had taught her. Mist rose.

With a roar, the Geladanian warriors came pounding out of the forest. Roots reached up, branches lashed out, some men collapsed, pulled down by spiders, scorpions, or bees. There was a whir of wings as Eyraphin and Aelthan led in the spirits of air, and more drakes leapt up to consume the men. Arridia's heart gave a small leap as arrows buzzed past her, left and right. Despite everything, some Fulmer warriors still lived and fought.

There was a boom as Jderha rose, face contorted, and struck at Dia. The fire-spirits held, though their flames dulled and flickered. Heart in her mouth, Arridia looked for her parents. Jderha twisted to send a barrage of ice at them, but Kesta turned it away, using the momentum to increase its speed and power to send it back against its creator. Her father... her father was creating mist! He'd seen her, trusted she had a plan and was helping.

'Okay, Azra.' Every inch of her body was trembling. She fed more power into her rising mist, thickening it. 'Burn hard and dark for me.'

Her circle of spirits made themselves small, burning as fierce a blue as their eyes. Arridia curled and uncurled her fists several times before she found the courage to move her feet. Around her, spirits and warriors fought. Magic raged between her mother, grandmother, and the goddess who had come to kill them all.

They moved through the mist, dark shapes looming close. Two Geladanian warriors came straight at them and the spirits flew into them, rapidly burning them from the inside out so they had no time to scream. Momentarily the mist was whipped away, but it closed back in quickly, coming from the forest. Joss and Ali? It had to be.

A small whimper escaped from Arridia's lips. All her life she'd fought to keep hold of her *knowing*, close it down. Now it was time to let it go.

Arridia stopped holding the tightly held knot within her, letting it blossom outward. She stumbled and cried out, clamping a hand tightly over her mouth. Pain ripped through her body from another's death, but she knew the pain wasn't real within her flesh and she forced herself to move on.

'You can do it; you can do it, Riddi,' Azrael urged.

She started there; drawing in the little spirit's love and fear to lie with her own. She grabbed for the hope and the pride of his fellows. She reached further, not evading the pain but embracing the horrendous rawness of it.

She touched her parents and sucked in their emotions willingly, desperately, expanding her awareness wider and wider.

Her grandmother's grief was an explosion inside her and her vision left her; but the images in her mind did not fade.

Dierra ripped open and beyond her reach to save.

Nip's face.

Where was Nip?

Her grandfather, haunted by his imminent death.

All those she loved that she might never see again.

Her heart was a rapid thrum within her, her fingers so cold despite the circle of fire-spirits. Still, she reached for more.

Except... except before her was a huge, numb void, a nothingness her *knowing* could not touch.

Touch.

It was the only way.

'We have to get closer, Azra,' she said through dry lips.

Azrael keened; the sound drowned by the roar of the magical battle that somehow still raged within the mist.

A ferocious gale battered them, some drakes clinging to each other so as not to be torn away. Arridia crouched on her knees, staggering up again as soon as it eased. Her own mist had long ago dissipated, but her father's and her brother's rolled in, mixing with the smoke of the burning forest.

They edged closer to the void, Arridia barely aware of her body now, gripped by a swirling, overwhelming cacophony of sensation. The drakes' shield was battered again and again as they were caught in the crossfire between Kesta and Jderha, until they drew closer to the forest and behind the god.

'Leave me now,' Arridia whispered.

'What?' Azrael squeaked. 'No, Riddi, never. I can't.'

'Yes, you can.' She couldn't help it, as defenceless as she was, she projected everything in her heart.

Azrael lost his shape, becoming just a long, flickering flame. He cried.

'She will see you all, I'll never get closer,' Arridia explained. 'Distract her for me, help my mother.'

'But who will shield you?' Azrael implored.

Arridia closed her unseeing eyes, both now glowing with an eerie, violet light. 'For once in my life, I will have to shield myself.'

The fire-spirits parted, Azrael remaining a moment longer than the rest, his eyes huge and round. Arridia took everything he gave her, wishing she could ease his brave little heart.

She drew up her shield, stretching out her senses to guide her to the emptiness that was the god. Her feet slid over the grass. It couldn't have been far, and yet it felt like a lifetime. The mist parted as Dia threw almost everything she had left at Jderha.

Arridia dropped her shield. She called every ounce of her power to her *knowing*.

She reached out her hand and grabbed for the bare arm of the god.

Chapter Forty-Two

Dia; Fulmer Island

The hill shook. Dia braced herself, calling down lightning as she increased the pressure of the storm. Her mismatched eyes widened just a little as mist rose to engulf Arridia.

Had she understood?

Kesta and Jorrun were both thrown off their feet as Jderha retaliated, the fire-spirits quickly rallying to form their shield again. Kesta didn't even bother getting up before she reached out again, turning an onslaught of ice back at the god.

Dia pulled down lightning again and again, but Jderha threw it aside. The high-priestess crawled out of the crater Kesta had made and Dia didn't blanch at finishing the injured woman off.

The mist increased, forming below Jorrun on the hill and curling down to meet Arridia's. Several of the fire-spirits joined Kesta in blasting Jderha, their rage, their bewilderment at losing Siveraell outweighing Dia's own. It was too painful, too huge to comprehend that the Elder spirit was no more. Taking their cue, Dia's own fire-spirits re-formed to fight, only to be hurled back and scattered by a freezing, momentary hurricane. The storm clouds above her parted. Her own shield held, but a moment of anxiety made Dia falter as Geladanian warriors broke through the defence of the spirits. Gilfy met them, felling the three men the Fulmer arrows missed.

Dia's body ached, her cracked ribs a distracting agony. She wanted to call a hurricane to add to her storm and draw it back but feared it would destroy her granddaughter's work. Her power was waning, and she knew she had little time left; but that scant time might just be enough for Arridia.

Kesta sent out a barrage of fire and Dia matched it, their flames curled up high as they caressed the edges of Jderha's shield.

Pressure built inside Dia's skull, several small veins bursting in her nose. Some of her fire-spirits tried to flutter back to re-form her protective ring, but Jderha struck at them again and again.

Dia's shield broke.

Red and black flared behind her eyes.

She turned to her young bodyguard as blood dripped down her cheeks from her eyes. 'Run, Gilfy.'

The Fulmer warrior straightened up, meeting her bloodied gaze. 'Never. It has been an honour, Icante.'

Dia drew the last of her strength, tearing down one last fork of lightning.

The mist parted.

For a moment the lightning lit the goddess, turning her skin silver. It also illuminated the desperate figure of the dark-haired girl who reached out her hand.

With a greedy rush fire flew from Jderha towards Dia and she closed her eyes, a smile on her lips.

'I will see you soon, Arrus.'

Something hit her hard, taking her down to the ground with it, its weight crushing her. She tried to breathe, but her lungs couldn't expand. The sickening smell of burning flesh and fur somehow reached her nostrils and the back of her throat. Her head pounded, her mouth open wide although the muscles of her chest and neck wouldn't move. Her heart thundered, drowning out the continuing sounds of battle beyond her tomb. Then her heart slowed.

Blackness swallowed the Icante of the Fulmers.

Chapter Forty-Three

Joss; Fulmer Island

'Just stay down,' Alikan hissed.

Joss followed the goddess with his eyes as she left the trees to confront his family. Two of the hundred warriors who accompanied her came very close and Joss slowed his harsh breathing, not daring to move.

Dia's storm sucked the light from the forest, lightning showing Jderha's odd, four-armed silhouette which stayed to float before Joss's retinas.

They all felt it, the drawing of the god's incredible power. Joss strengthened his shield as a tremendous force swept over his head. Several trees exploded into splinters, roots were ripped from the earth and they toppled, crashing into their neighbours. Geladanian warriors screamed as their own leader crushed or impaled them. Alikan leapt out of the way of a beech tree, Joss rolling aside just in time as it hit the ground, a sad tremor running through it. He scrambled to his hands and knees, checking on the others.

He heard the shiver of steel as Alikan drew his sword. Some warriors had spotted him as Jderha ordered her attack. Most of the Geladanians made a charge for the clearing, but almost a dozen chose Alikan as an easy target and moved to surround him.

Green light flared in the fallen trees, roots and ivy whipping out to puncture and strangle. Joss blinked as a black tide of tiny spiders with myriad green eyes enveloped a warrior. Whatever Nip had said to Gorchia to persuade the earth-spirits onto their side, the man deserved a stable made of gold in Joss's opinion. He drew his own sword, leaping up onto the uprooted beech to take off someone's head from behind before jumping into the fray beside his adopted brother.

Their three Ravens took their cue, using their weapons and conserving power. Belir held his left arm tight to his body and Joss guessed it was broken. Doroquael darted in, blazing through the bodies of two Geladanian warriors who collapsed with smoke rising from the holes in their chests.

'Siveraell, Siveraell, Siveraell!' The little spirit wailed. He made himself huge and roared, engulfing another warrior in his expanding mouth.

The ground beneath them trembled, and Joss braced himself, recognising his mother's powerful signature. Sharne finished off the last of the warriors, and Alikan snatched a belt from one of the fallen to strap Belir's arm against his body.

Joss made a quick survey of the battle beyond the trees to assess where they were most needed. He watched for several heartbeats, open-mouthed, as he saw mist gather and spread.

'What's happening?' Alikan demanded.

'Ali, we need to help them create mist, theirs is just being blown away every time Jderha strikes out.'

'I don't know, Joss, it seems like a waste of power.'

'Exactly.' Joss pivoted to face his friend; his left hand clenched in a fist. 'Our family wouldn't waste power for no reason. It's important.'

'All right,' Alikan agreed. 'Doro, save your power. The rest of you please shield us, we're likely to get caught in the crossfire.'

Joss led them closer to the battling god, his heart in his mouth. The first thing he needed to do was find a source of water. He looked up at his grandmother's storm. He reached for it, swirling air to separate some of the dark cloud and draw it down. Fat spots of rain splattered them, and Joss immediately set to cooling the ground. As they'd practised many times together, Alikan ran a warm wind over it, sending it gently toward the clearing.

Fire spewed up over Jderha's shield, catching within the branches of the few trees that still stood. The Ravens' shield took a battering but held.

'We need to move.' Alikan shook his head. 'Those branches are likely to come down, and our own family is going to accidently kill us in a minute.'

Joss gave a nod, clenching and unclenching his jaw. They picked their way through the ruin, keeping the fine balance of their power so the mist continued to flow. It was hard to see what was happening, but he could sense his grandmother's storm dying. He wiped his palms on his trousers, forcing himself to breathe more slowly and deeply. Then the mist cleared as Jderha swirled her power to strike at the Icante.

'No,' Joss cried out, freezing where he stood. His sister appeared out of the mist, reaching out to grab for one of Jderha's four arms. Even from here he felt the crushing turmoil of emotions Arridia carried, that she pressed into the god.

Jderha screamed. A sound that went on and on, shaking the forest, bursting painfully inside Joss's ears and leaving them ringing. Jderha flailed, two of her arms gripping her hair, the third snatching at the cloth at her chest. The fourth arm grabbed Arridia, flinging her high into the air.

'Riddi!' Joss bellowed. 'Riddi!'

Beside him, Alikan drew his power and attacked.

Chapter Forty-Four

Kesta; Fulmer Island

'Beth, stay down, stay where you are until you can slip away,' Kesta yelled over her shoulder.

'How much power do you have left?' Jorrun asked, breathing hard.

'Not enough.' She drew her daggers.

He raised an eyebrow and drew his sword.

'Shield us as long as you can,' Kesta told the drakes.

Fire billowed out from Jderha's hands, not coming at them but for the Icante. Kesta's eyes widened as she pivoted on her heels; a huge claw of pain stabbed into her heart and lungs, squeezing tight so she couldn't breathe. Her mother had no shield. The Icante of the Fulmers stood alone on the hill but for Gilfy. No armour, no magic, between her and death.

'No!' The word burst from her with all the frustrated rage within her, leaving her lungs heaving.

She spun to face Jderha, knowing there was nothing she could do, only to see her daughter flung into the mist like a broken doll.

Kesta roared, her anguish blending with the scream of the god. She ran, blind fury turning her vision red, her knives gripped in her fists. A warrior came at her and she ducked beneath his sword, coming up to rip out his throat with her knife, her teeth bared in a snarl. Two more appeared through the smoke and fog, the fire-spirits incinerated one, Jorrun took off the arm of the other then sliced through his belly.

'Kill her!' Kesta bellowed, pointing to the writhing shape of Jderha. 'Fulmers, Ravens, Spirits, to me!'

She drew on the last dregs of her power, sending fire. The spirits responded by joining theirs, and Jderha was momentarily lost to view. A chill swept through her. Where was she? Where was her daughter?

'Riddi!'

She couldn't help it, Kesta turned her feet from the god to run toward where Arridia had fallen. A horrible numbness spread through her limbs as she forced her legs to find more speed. Dark shapes moved, the winds of magic revealing agonising glimpses of the Geladanian warriors who stood between her and her daughter. So many still. Her mouth was dry, but she fought for more volume from her lungs.

'Riddi!'

Jorrun's long stride took him past her, and he swung his sword with both hands, taking off a head. Power came suddenly from within the forest, changing Jderha's scream to one of outrage. Someone had power left!

Hope swelled painfully inside her, catching in her throat to choke her. Heat and cold tore across her skin, reaching to rip at her soul.

'Riddi!'

Two men came at Jorrun. While he engaged their swords, Kesta danced past them to stab one in the back. His weight pulled her dagger from her grip as he fell, and she left it to run on.

The wind took the mist and smoke again and Kesta saw the scene before her clearly for a moment; a moment that stretched out for an eternity. The strength fled from her muscles and she dropped to her knees, tears streaming down her sore skin.

Too late.

Kesta swayed, pain digging deep through her skull, stopping her heart.

Too late.

Her hands gripped her stomach.

Only one figure remained standing. His clothes torn and bloodied, his shoulders heaving. In his right hand was his own sword, covered in gore. In his left hand, he held Arridia's thin blade.

Nip looked down, and Kesta followed his gaze.

Almost a dozen Geladanians lay dead around the stable master. Before Nip's feet was a tangle of tree roots, a shield of green fox fire flickering over it.

Jorrun skidded to a halt at Kesta's side. He reached down and grabbed her arm, yanking her up onto her feet. She let him drag her, her body loose, a horrible floaty feeling suffusing her. Her mother was gone. Riddi was gone.

'Nip.' Jorrun strode toward him, his voice hoarse. 'Son, are you hurt?'

Nip gave a shudder, his eyes focusing as he turned. 'No. I mean, nothing bad.'

Kesta became aware of a deep, penetrating, and foreboding silence. The air was still. The mist fading. No one was using magic. She spun about, turning full circle.

'Where's Jderha?'

Jorrun straightened up, searching the area with his own eyes.

Movement caught her attention and Kesta looked down. The strange cocoon at Nip's feet unfurled, revealing a body within.

For the briefest of moments, desperate grief ran through Kesta's body from her toes to the roots of her hair... but her daughter was breathing.

'Riddi.' Kesta threw herself to the ground as the tree roots withdrew completely. Her soul surged up from her chest in a convulsive sob, her eyes overflowing so she could barely see. Little Gorchia hopped out of the way towards Nip. Kesta smoothed back Arridia's hair, and kissed her forehead, touch like an anchor making everything blessedly real.

'Riddi, my honey.' Tears followed the drying blood down her cheeks.

'Where's Azra?' Jorrun demanded, his blue eyes wide. His face was pale, glistening wet tracks forming a pattern in the ash and dirt on his skin.

'I'm sorry, Thane.' Nip winced. 'He wasn't here when we got to Riddi.'

A fire-spirit came blazing toward them, flying joyous loops. 'You're alive!'

'Doro!' Kesta choked back a sob. 'Joss, is he—?'

'Here, Mum.'

Joss ran out of the trees, Alikan and three other Ravens just behind him. Kesta leapt up to hug Joss, while Jorrun clasped Alikan's wrist, pulling him close to hold him for a moment.

'Joss, can you help get your sister into the forest and out of the open?' Jorrun asked. 'Ali, search for survivors, get them all back here. Spirits, too. Doro, do you...' His voice faltered. 'Do you know where Azrael is?'

Doroquael gave a wail. 'No, Jorrun, I don't.'

Kesta stood, her body shaking. 'Mother.'

Jorrun reached out and touched her cheek. 'I'll go.'

She shook her head. 'I need to come too.'

Jorrun gave Joss and Alikan a nod. Kesta started to go, but Nip moved just a little faster, holding out Arridia's sword.

Kesta looked at it for a moment, then forced a smile and took it. 'Thanks, Nip.'

'Be careful,' Jorrun warned. 'This isn't over yet.'

Kesta let Jorrun lead the way, too exhausted to be proud. Her head throbbed with a deep pain. She rubbed at her nose and her hand came away bloody.

They found Beth first, huddled against the grass.

'Can you walk?' Jorrun crouched to touch her shoulder. The Raven groaned, but nodded, dragging herself up.

Not far from her, they discovered the ruined body of *walker* Tarlos. A weak, almost empty feeling washed through Kesta. So many *walkers* gone, and they were few to begin with.

'I don't see her.' Jorrun frowned, turning his head to survey the hill.

'What?' Kesta couldn't even shake her head, her neck and shoulders were so locked with tension. She spotted Gilfy, recognising him by the remnants of the clothes and armour he'd been wearing, most of his visible skin and hair was burned away. 'She must be close.'

Her eyes fell on an odd shape, a huge shape. Small patches of white fur had somehow survived. 'That's a Rakinya. I thought they'd all returned to the Hold?'

They walked cautiously toward it together. It had been so badly burnt that bone showed in places. It was curled up slightly, its arms over its head as though to protect itself. Or... Kesta's intuition prickled. Or someone else.

'Help me,' she cried to Jorrun, kneeling and gritting her teeth as she tried to lift the gigantic beast. Jorrun put down his sword to assist her, grunting as they finally lifted and rolled the Rakinya away.

Kesta gasped.

Her mother lay on the grass, her arms tucked in beneath her. Her mouth was open, her eyes glazed. Kesta shook her head, torn between hope and despair.

Jorrun reached out and placed his hands on the Icante's back, sucking in air sharply through his teeth as he tried to draw power.

Dia's ribs rose and fell. Then she gasped in a breath.

'Mother.' Kesta lay her head against the back of hers, holding her gently as she sobbed.

Jorrun stood, picking up his sword and sheathing it. 'I think it's Edon Ra.'

Kesta lifted her head to look, wiping at her nose and eyes. It might be the seer, but she couldn't be sure.

'We need to return to the others,' Jorrun warned.

Kesta moved aside as he picked up the Icante, staggering a little. She imagined he had no more strength left than she. He was breathing hard by the time they reached the forest and Joss helped his father lay the Icante down. Jorrun collapsed to the ground almost at once, and Kesta sank down beside him.

'Report?' Jorrun asked Joss.

Their son swallowed, his face pale. Kesta glanced around quickly. There were so few of them left. She could only hope that others had run north to reach the safety of Fulmer Hold.

Mimeth sat with her back to a tree, *walker* Dinai's head cradled in her lap. Mimeth was bruised, but Dinai's leg was broken. Nip was doing his best to splint it with what he had.

Beth was curled up within the roots of a tree, her eyes tight shut. Perta and Charis sat to either side of her, both battered but whole; Perta softly crying. Vorro sat close to Arridia, his cheeks reddening a little as he met Kesta's eyes, no doubt feeling unnecessary shame at not having protected her. Someone had sacrificed a part of their shirt to bind the bloody fingers of his hand.

Almost twenty Fulmer warriors had also made it. One of them sat wide-eyed and frozen as Gorchia directed several large spiders to bind up a jagged wound across his chest with web. A handful of other earth-spirits peeped at them from low branches, while little distortions and the whir of wings gave away the air-elementals. Fire-spirits were bright, reassuring, living lanterns although the darkness had cleared, and the sun had returned.

'Riddi hasn't woken,' Joss said. 'There's still no sign of Jderha. Aelthan and Eyraphin have gone south to hunt for her. We thought she might have fled back to Eagle Hold and her remaining ships.'

'She may well have.' Jorrun rubbed at his beard with both hands.

'We need to destroy those ships,' Kesta said firmly.

Jorrun pulled himself up a little. 'Spirits of fire and air, dear friends, would you do it? Can you destroy the ships? If they are too well guarded, come back. If you see Jderha, come back.'

'We'll go,' several air-elementals chorused. There was a whir of wings as they shot away.

Not to be outdone, several fire-spirits squealed and chased after them.

Kesta doubled over, one hand clutching at her stomach, the other covering her eyes. Losing Siveraell was still too raw, too hard to comprehend. She drew in a long, shaking breath, her hands trembling as she wiped at her nose and eyes and forced herself to straighten up.

'I think that's everyone.' Alikan joined their battered camp. Holin and Sharne supported a barely conscious warrior between them, Belir bringing up the rear, his face drawn in pain.

'Okay, we rest then,' Jorrun regarded them all. 'Tend to our wounds as best we can—'

He shot to his feet, pivoting to look north.

'What is it?' Kesta demanded.

A bright light was coming towards them, keening as it came. Her eyes widened, her heart expanding in joy and relief.

'Jorrun, Kessssta!' Azrael turned a somersault, then flew around and around them, dipping low over Arridia, flaring at Joss, before turning back to Jorrun. 'I followed her. Jderha. Riddi broke her. Joss, Ali, and usss spirits hurt her, she couldn't hold her shield. But she went north, and I followed. I...' He stilled, making himself small. 'I think she is going to Fulmer Hold.'

Chapter Forty-Five

Catya; Fulmer Hold

Catya halted, breathing hard. Relief flooded through her at the sight of the sturdy hold. She made a quick study of the walls; they appeared intact and islanders still manned them. Cassien stepped up beside her.

'No ships,' he said.

Catya nodded, narrowing her eyes a little as she scanned the sea herself. 'Looks safe, come on.'

Their band of scouts and Ravens followed, some of them limping, some dragged on litters by the strong Rakinya. Dysarta walked at the side of Mayve's litter, keeping the severely injured Chemmish Raven company through her pain.

As they crossed the causeway, the gates opened, and Worvig hurried out to meet them.

'What news?'

Cassien reached out to clasp the old warrior's wrist. 'We took out their scouts and assassins, then retreated as planned. We saw and heard signs that battle has begun. And you?'

Worvig grinned, showing his teeth through his grey beard. 'Eve saw off to of the ships with help from the creatures of the deep. A few Geladanians tried to swim ashore, but we filled them full of arrows. A dolphin even saved a couple of earth-spirits from drowning.' His grin faded. 'I imagine we lost a few of the poor critters who were trapped.'

'It can't be helped,' Catya said, although her heart and stomach constricted at the thought of it. 'Could you help us in with the injured? The Rakinya don't want to be caught within the walls of the Hold, they'll stay out in the forest.'

Worvig grunted. 'I don't blame them.' He turned and waved at some watching warriors to come and help.

'Where's Merin?'

Worvig tutted and shook his head. 'With my brother. The two of them are thick as thieves and full of mischief.'

It was Catya's turn to grin.

The houses of the hold were eerily empty, but the walls were busy with archers, both male and female, patrolling or looking outward. The doors to the great hall stood open and Catya's stomach gave a painful gurgle at the savoury smell of the food. It had been over two days since she'd eaten.

Inside the hall it was busy, but calm. Milaiya looked up from where she was helping with the food and called to Vivess.

'Welcome back.' The Chemmish woman greeted them with hope in her eyes. 'Bring your injured over here.'

Catya left Cassien to organise it, her eyes seeking for the most precious thing in her life. Merin leapt up from his chair at the high table beside Arrus and came tearing down the hall towards her, dodging Rece and Everlyn who had come to help with the injured. He didn't slow, launching himself into her waiting arms and knocking the wind out of her. Catya breathed in his smell, closing her eyes.

Merin broke away first to hug Dysarta.

'Where's Uncle Edon?' he asked, looking up at them with his innocent amber eyes.

'You know Edon,' Dysarta replied, with a glance at Catya. 'He's up to his own business.'

A sick feeling turned Catya's stomach. Edon hadn't told her why he'd insisted on shadowing Dia, but something in his midnight-blue eyes had really frightened her.

She forced a smile. 'I'm starving. Where's the best food?'

Merin took her hand and led her toward the fireplace. 'You'll have to come and eat it with me, next to Arrus Silene. He's been teaching me the greatest songs.'

'Has he.' Catya narrowed her eyes. She could well imagine what type of songs. Probably ones she chuckled at herself.

She picked a bowl and wooden spoon up off the table, dropped in a hunk of bread, then ladled hot stew over it. She caught Dysarta's eyes, and they both laughed. Catya had reason to both hate and love stew.

'It all seems so normal,' Dysarta breathed.

'It's Arrus's way,' Catya replied. 'But don't be fooled. As soon as an enemy is sighted, he'll be up on his feet with a sword in his hand, dying or not. Hey, Silene.' She kissed Arrus's cheek and dropped into the seat next to him.

'Cat.' He smiled. 'You have a very bright boy.'

'Too bright sometimes.' She ate a spoonful of the stew, closing her eyes briefly in appreciation. A yawn overtook her.

'Get some sleep,' Arrus suggested. 'We'll wake you if there's any news.'

Catya regarded him. He looked in need of sleep himself, though she could empathise with his desire to live every moment. There was pain in his eyes and dark shadows beneath them, his skin almost translucent. Even so, he smiled and there was a rebellious spark about him.

'Go on,' he urged. 'Just get me a beer before you go.'

She finished her food, letting Merin's chatter heal her heart as he caught up with Dysarta. Cassien had settled their injured comrades and was drinking steaming tea with Rece. She sighed. He was still the most loyal and honourable man she'd ever known. She pushed aside her guilt at what she knew was coming.

Catya stood, taking her bowl and dropping it into the barrel of hot water kept near the fireplace for washing. She picked up a pitcher of beer and crossed the hall to Cassien.

'We're going to get some rest,' she said.

'Good idea. I'd best do the same.'

She returned to Arrus, plonking the pitcher down before him. 'Merin's only to have a sip.'

'Mother,' Merin grumbled. 'I'm nearly eight.'

Arrus laughed out loud but turned to wink at Catya.

'Call us,' Catya urged. 'Any news at all.'

The Silene nodded.

***

Evening was closing in when a knock at the door woke Catya. She scrambled off the bed, grabbing for her sword. Dysarta groaned and rolled over.

Catya padded across to the door and opened it to find Milaiya there.

'I'm sorry to disturb you, but people are arriving who fought to the south. Jagna is one.'

'I'm on my way.' Catya grabbed for her jacket and quickly armed herself.

'What is it?' Dysarta mumbled.

Catya kissed her cheek. 'Sleep a little longer, we have a bit more time.'

Milaiya was waiting out in the corridor, and they hurried up the steps together towards the great hall.

'Jagna says they took back Eagle Hold, although it lies in ruins.' Milaiya told her. 'Then they confronted a large portion of Jderha's army. Jorrun sent Jagna and some others who were out of power or injured here to recover.'

'And Jderha?' Catya thrust open the doors to the great hall.

Milaiya shook her head and shrugged. 'No word.'

Catya made a quick scan of the hall. Vivess had joined Arrus and Merin, and she gave them a nod and a smile as she passed.

'Where are Heara, Cass, and Worvig?'

Milaiya gestured towards the doors. 'They went out to watch the walls.'

Catya wet her lips with her tongue, then clapped the former slave on the back. 'Thanks. If there's any sign of danger, give Dysarta a shout.'

She didn't wait for a reply but continued outside.

The air was cool, a few stars appearing as the sky darkened. She headed for the stairs near the main gate and jogged up them.

'What's our situation?'

Worvig was closest to her, and it was he who answered.

'A few survivors, though none now for a while.'

Everlyn stood beside Heara, leaning out over the stone of the battlement, and Catya wondered if she were using her *knowing* to feel for life. She called out to the *walker*. 'Have you recovered your power, if it isn't rude of me to ask?'

'Some,' Everlyn replied, her voice low.

Heara gave a growl in the back of her throat. 'I hate not knowing what's happening.'

Worvig harrumphed. 'Would it make you feel any better if I told you I have a creeping feeling in my gut that we'll know all too soon?'

'You probably ate a bad shellfish.' Heara grinned at him.

Catya turned her gaze to the only one in their group who hadn't spoken. Cassien barely blinked as he watched the forest. His left hand rested on the gap in the battlement's crenulations, his right held loosely to his sword hilt. A shiver ran through her.

'I'm going to check everything again,' Worvig announced, then squeezed past Catya to make his way around the walls.

Night deepened.

Three more warriors made it back to the hold, two of them carrying the other between them. They bore no news other than what they already knew.

Dysarta and Jagna joined them on the wall. Worvig returned for a while, but wandered off to check on his brother and pace the walls again.

'Has Merin gone to bed?' Catya asked Dysarta. They stood so close together, their arms touched.

'No, but he was curled up asleep in his chair. I think he gives the Silene comfort and strength.'

Catya swallowed, looking down into the darkness below the wall. She knew the tide was in from the swish of the waves.

'There!' Cassien cried out.

A fire-spirit shot up out of the earth close to the forest's edge and sped along the causeway. Catya held her breath as it hurtled closer, then propelled itself up the wall to float before them.

'I am Tyrenell,' it said. 'I bring dire news and warning!'

Everlyn held up a hand. The burn scars on her face looked alive in the spirit's flickering light. 'Tell us, dear friend, but slowly.'

Tyrenell darted about, then stilled. 'Our Elder, Siveraell has fallen.'

Everlyn swayed and grabbed for the wall. Heara swore.

'Jderha?' Cassien demanded.

'Arridia broke her defences, and we spirits, Ali, and Joss, hurt her.' Tyrenell gave a whoop, then made himself small. 'But she fled. She is coming here.'

'The Icante?' Heara held her hands out. 'Kesta? The others?'

The drake wailed. 'A long way behind her. Most of the spirits flew south to destroy the remaining ships.'

Everlyn and Dysarta regarded each other. As the strongest magic users, it would likely be down to them.

Cassien turned to regard them all. 'We need to make a decision regarding the causeway.'

'I don't know.' Heara screwed her nose up. 'Once it's gone, it's gone.'

Catya drew in a breath, holding Cassien's gaze. 'Time it right, and we could do Jderha some significant damage.'

'It would be hard to time,' Cassien replied.

She nodded. 'It would have to be short fuses.'

'You don't need fuses.' Dysarta placed her hand on Catya's arm. 'Eve or I could just send fire at the black powder.'

'And if Jderha shields or bats it away?'

Dysarta's shoulders sagged.

Cassien looked from Heara to Everlyn. 'Yes, or no?'

It was Heara who answered. 'Get down there, get it ready. Use your best judgement and we'll do our best to cover you from the walls.'

'I'll get the rest of the Ravens up here,' Jagna offered. 'Even a little power might make a difference.'

Catya gave Dysarta a quick kiss, before following Cassien down the stairs.

Warriors pushed at the gates and one of them called out, 'Do we leave them open for you?'

'Only a crack.' Cassien strode through without looking back. 'But if Jderha gets past our explosion on the causeway, close it, no matter what side we're on.'

Catya peered down the long length of the causeway. For many years, walking its smooth stone had meant coming home. They had left only four braziers alight, bathing the way in a red-gold hue. They worked in silence, lying on their bellies to lean out over the edge and check where the black powder had been wedged into imperfections in the high cliff wall, climbing down to where they'd placed it lower. Catya pulled herself up over the side and rolled into a crouch.

'You know none of it is deep enough.' She shook her head.

'I know.' Cassien looked toward the forest. 'It would have slowed an army. The god? I guess we'll see.'

'Let's shorten these fuses.' She didn't wait for a reply but hurried back along the causeway. The closer she got to the Hold, the shorter she cut the fuses. She noticed Cassien checking her work as they progressed, but she wasn't offended. Rothfel had taught Cassien. Most of her skills with black powder resulted from her own trial and error.

They finished and moved towards the brazier furthest from the hold. Several torches had been left there, and they took two each. Part of Catya marvelled at how in tune they were still after all these years; but they had always worked exceptionally well together, no matter what Catya had put the poor man through.

They turned to face the forest.

The surf below was deceptively soothing. Shadows moved as the wind teased the branches. Catya shifted her weight from one foot to the other.

They froze as a penetrating wail of despair emanated from the trees.

It made her hair stand on end.

The night was rent by the crack and groan of a tree falling and the rushing swish and snap of it hitting others. Every fibre of Catya's body was primed to run, but she held fast.

The light of the braziers caught the glint of gold thread, and the goddess stepped out of the forest.

She wasn't what Catya had expected.

Jderha's hair was in disarray, her white eyes wild. Her artfully applied cosmetics were running down her face with her tears. The goddess's mouth contorted into a grimace of despair.

For a moment, pity stirred in Catya's heart.

Cassien moved, plunging his torches into the brazier to light them. His breathing was unusually loud, giving away his fear.

She lit her own torches, and they backed to the edge of the causeway.

Jderha's attention seemed to be on the Hold. Light bloomed in two of her four hands and she hurled a ferocious blast of energy at the hold. It collided with the air and dissipated.

Catya swore. 'I was hoping she'd have less power left.'

'I was hoping for the last fourteen years she wouldn't come at all.' He braced himself to move. 'Good luck.'

Cassien made a sprint for the other side of the causeway. Jderha started to turn their way, but two fireballs came streaking over their heads from the walls.

Jderha batted them away with ease.

The goddess took a step forward, then another, building power again in her hands. Catya's heart raced; Dys was strong, but she couldn't last long against this barrage. Catya glanced down at her right arm; it was shaking. For all her confidence, she'd lived in fear of this juncture since the day Edon Ra had told her of it. She turned to look at Cassien, his silver eyes more like amber in the firelight.

'Merin,' she whispered.

Fire shot over their heads and she instinctively ducked, fearing for a moment that Jderha would accidently blow them all apart, but the flames rose up the invisible shield of the defending Ravens.

'You think you know pain?' Jderha roared. 'I'll destroy everything you love, child, everything.'

Catya's jaw dropped a little. Who was the goddess madly yelling to? Arridia?

It had to be.

Jderha threw more fire at the Hold, then ice. Fulmer Hold didn't retaliate and with a sick feeling, Catya guessed they were putting all their strength into shielding in the hope the black powder would work. Cassien shifted from one foot to the other, no doubt wondering like her if they'd have to be the bait to draw her onto the narrow walkway.

A freezing blizzard whistled overhead from behind, and Catya gasped as the torches flickered. She recognised the signature of her best friend and lover's magic.

'You dare defy me, slaves?' Jderha created a whirlwind to force aside the attack. 'I am your ruin, it is foretold!'

Jderha drew more power and took a step forward, then another; her momentum building as she came at the causeway.

Cassien touched his torch to a fuse and whirled to dip his second torch to another, Catya but a heartbeat behind him. Turn, dip, turn, they danced their way across the stone as the goddess bore down on them.

'Run!' Cassien warned.

Catya dropped her torches and sprinted for the gates. An explosion went off behind her, her ears bursting painfully and all sound dying but for a high-pitched ringing. She felt the next explosions, and she was lifted off her feet and thrown high into the air. She hit the causeway hard, curling up to roll and tumble. Emptiness was suddenly beneath her and she snatched for the edge, missing with her left hand but grasping at the stone with her right. Cassien appeared before her, sliding on his belly. He grabbed her left wrist, then the clothing on her back, and dragged her back up onto the causeway.

Catya spared a second to look behind. Only one brazier still burned, and it revealed a ragged, uneven pathway that narrowed to less than a foot across at one point. For a moment she thought Jderha might have fallen into the sea far below, but then she caught the movement of a large, white limb as the goddess pulled herself up.

Catya and Cassien didn't need any prompting, they scrambled to their feet and ran.

They squeezed through the gap in the gate, helping the warriors push it shut and slide across the two sturdy bars.

The gates shook.

One of the bars cracked.

Catya swore.

They scattered just in time as the gates exploded inwards. Jderha didn't follow. A barrage of power rained down on her from the wall as every magic user left in the Hold attacked. Jderha howled. Warriors moved in to fire arrows at the god, then dispersed swiftly at a warning from Everlyn.

The defenders' shield was failing.

But Jderha wasn't retaliating.

Catya straightened up.

With a roar, Jderha appeared through the ruins of the gate, summoning a last rush of wind to sweep several warriors aside and smash in the doors to the great hall. Everlyn and Dysarta threw flames at the goddess's back, though there was little bite left to their attack. Jderha's shield held, just, but she staggered forward over the threshold.

Catya could hardly breathe, but she forced her feet to move, skidding to a halt inside the great hall with Cassien at her side.

Some of those taking shelter within the hall had ducked beneath the tables, others pressed up against the walls. A few warriors stood with their weapons drawn, braced to fight.

At the far end of the hall, Arrus got slowly to his feet, his sword in his hand. Merin clutched at the back of the Silene's chair, his amber eyes wide.

Catya turned to Cassien. He held her gaze.

They both ran.

Chapter Forty-Six

Cassien; Fulmer Hold

Arrus didn't flinch as the crazed god drew her four swords and came at him, hurling aside the meat-spit and placing a huge dent in the copper chimney of the central firepit. Several warriors tried to stop her, each one was cut down, including Merkis Vilnue.

Cassien sprinted out into the hall. Catya was faster. She leapt onto a table and sped along it, vaulting into the air and twisting twice before she landed in a fighter's stance, drawing her own sword. It was her left hand that moved first, throwing a dagger, but Jderha knocked it aside with one of her blades. Inspired, Cassien drew two of his own knives, aiming them at her back. Impossibly, she twisted in time to bat one away as though she had eyes in the back of her head. The other caught between her ribs and she shrieked in rage.

'I will kill you all, slaves, and eat your bones!'

She turned her empty eyes toward Cassien, and his heart froze.

'You are mistaken,' Arrus called calmly. 'There are no slaves here.'

Catya darted in to engage the goddess. As swift as she was, ducking, dancing, weaving, Catya had no choice but to give ground or be impaled, Jderha getting closer and closer to her son. Catya was phenomenal, always had been, but Jderha, with her enormous advantage, was better. Cassien slid across the polished wooden boards of the hall, spinning on his heels to halt before her with his sword raised just as she lost patience and used the last of her magic to hurl Catya against the wall.

'Mum!' Merin cried out. Then, 'Cass!' The boy threw his small sword. It spun, and Cassien plucked it from the air, sweeping it up to catch one of Jderha's swords.

She was fast, but Cassien was faster.

The world around him faded away. There was only him, the eyes of the goddess, and her ferocious blades. Like Catya, he had no choice but to give her ground, holding one of her swords too long would allow another two to plunge or slice toward him. He caught one though, whirling aside and bringing down his other blade to hack off one of her hands at the wrist.

Jderha's mouth opened in a rictus of a scream, though no sound came out. Two of her blades swept around, the third stabbing towards Cassien, and he ducked, rolling out of the way and back onto his feet. Two warriors, then a third, took the chance of running in to help, but Jderha sliced them up in seconds, before rounding on Cassien again.

There was one way.

He saw it as clearly as though his old mentor Rothfel had drawn him a diagram.

A strange peace suffused him.

He ran in, engaging one of her blades. The other two came at him, but he didn't stop them. One blade struck the brooch Dia had given him, sliding up to cut deep across the top of his shoulder. He felt the searing, burning pain as her second blade broke his skin, cutting through his lower ribs and out through his back.

Somewhere, far away, Catya screamed.

Cassien met the god's white eyes, and he smiled. He thrust his second sword up into her heart.

He hit the floor. He knew he had, and yet he felt as though he were floating. His blood was hot as it seeped into his clothing.

He grunted as Catya landed at his side, her hands quickly exploring his wounds before bending over him, her face close. He focused on her eyes. She was crying, sobbing, the tears falling in rapid succession.

'I'm so sorry, Cass, so sorry. It had to be you. You were the only one fast enough, Cass. The only one fast enough to cheat destiny.'

He blinked; it was too much effort to speak.

'It was Edon Ra's dream.' She touched his face. 'He'd had it all his life. He dreamed he was a boy, a boy who saw the world with an amber light. A monster came from the sea, one with many arms. It came for him. In his dream, every time he dreamed it, the Raven girl...' She shook her head. 'Um, that's me. The Raven girl was never fast enough. The monster always killed him, and the world dies. I said we should just stay safe in Snowhold, but Edon told me that the monster would still come. But if she came to Snowhold, it would mean the Fulmers had fallen.

'So, we had to come, Cass, to save the Fulmers. And it had to be you.'

He nodded, concentrating on his breathing for a moment before squeezing out the words, 'Tell Kussim and my boys I love them.'

Another figure loomed over them. 'Get me some bandages,' Heara demanded. 'Quickly. We need to stop the bleeding. Out of the way, Cat, if you're not going to help.'

Catya shuffled back. Cassien grimaced in pain as Heara cut at the leather and cloth on his shoulder to get to the wound.

Catya's blue eyes didn't leave his; not until his sight faded away.

Chapter Forty-Seven

Dia; Fulmer Island

Sound seeped into her dream. A grasshopper chirred, there was wind in the trees.

She shivered, goosebumps rising on her skin.

Dia sat bolt upright, letting out a short whimper at the pain in her ribs. She was in a small clearing in the forest, night was setting in. Two fires had been lit and there were maybe forty people sitting or lying about her.

'I'm alive?'

'Mum.' Kesta hurried over to her. The tracks of tears marked her daughter's face. Dia reached up to wipe at Kesta's cheek, but her daughter took her hand and held it gently.

'What happened?' Dia looked up into her mismatched eyes. 'I... I was so sure I was about to die. I couldn't breathe. I should be dead.'

Kesta swallowed. 'Edon Ra saved you. He shielded you from the fire with his body. Between his weight and Jderha's flame stealing the air, it's no wonder you struggled to breathe.'

Dia stiffened, pain swelling to bursting in her heart. 'Gilfy?'

Kesta shook her head, glancing away. 'I'm sorry.'

Dia hunched in on herself, curling about the pain. 'But the children?'

'Oh, they're fine.' Kesta squeezed her hand tighter, sitting down properly to face her. A tear slipped from Kesta's red-rimmed eyes. 'But... we lost many. Siv... Siveraell is gone.'

The pressure building inside Dia's chest spilled out from her eyes, her daughter's image blurring with rainbow colours.

'Also, Dierra, Tarlos—'

Dia held up her hand, tensing her muscles, pulling herself together with a shudder. 'There will be time for grieving, but I fear it is not now. What of Jderha?'

'She got away. Arridia, she... she crippled the god, weakened her with her *knowing*. Joss and Ali attacked along with Azra and the spirits. They hurt her, broke her shield, but she ran.'

'Ran where?' Dia searched her daughter's face.

Kesta drew in a breath. 'North, towards the Hold.'

Dia tried to get up. 'Why are we still here?'

A hand landed firmly on her shoulder, pushing her back down. 'Because we need to heal and recover power, otherwise we are just wasting lives,' Jorrun said. Dia looked up at her tall son-in-law. He crouched and offered her some tea. 'Horse medicine.'

She took it tentatively, giving him a quizzical look.

Jorrun smiled, tilting his head to indicate to her left. She followed his gaze. Nip was sitting beside a warrior, checking his bandages.

'Nip's a healer,' Jorrun said.

Nip glanced up, his face colouring slightly. 'I'm a healer of horses. My dad taught me.' He shrugged. 'But a bone is a bone.'

Dia looked down at her tea, and Jorrun gave a soft chuckle. 'It's okay, it's only nettle, comfrey, and rue. We salvaged a few useful things from the farm nearby, including cups. The earth-spirits have been fetching us healing herbs.'

'We were deciding what to do,' Kesta broke in. 'Those of us who can need to get moving to the Hold. We're going to leave the injured here in the care of Nip and the spirits. It was just... you and Arridia.'

'Arridia should stay here.' Jorrun turned to the stable master. 'With Nip.'

Nip held his gaze, before turning back to his work. After a moment, Nip said, 'When Riddi wakes and recovers some power, she could call for the ponies left loose on the island. We'll try to catch up, at least get the injured to the farm and proper shelter.'

'That's a great idea.' Kesta seemed to breathe easier. 'Thank you, Nip.'

'How soon can you travel?' Jorrun asked Dia.

'Let me finish my horse tea, and I'll be ready.'

Jorrun nodded, then moved away to distribute the rest of the tea Mimeth was brewing. Dia sipped at hers. It was a little bitter but tasting bitter meant she was alive.

Her heart eased at every familiar face she saw. Azrael was hovering low over Arridia, who was wrapped in a borrowed blanket. The Ravens, Vorro, Perta, and Charis were sitting with Dinai at one of the fires, the *walker's* leg bound in a make-shift splint. Beth was curled up asleep. The young Raven scout from Joss's retinue, Sharne, sat beside her. Belir was propped up against a tree, his face pale, his arm strapped to his body. Jorrun took the young man over some tea, Nip joining him to drop powdered willow into the cup.

'Grandma?'

She twisted around to see Joss emerging from the darkening trees with Alikan and Holin, all of them carrying blankets and sacks.

'Dia!' Doroquael cried joyfully, whizzing toward her to fly about her head. 'Dia, you're awake!'

'I am, but you are making me dizzy.' She laughed.

Doroquael made himself small and still. 'Sorry, Dia.'

'Oh, no dear spirit.' She shook her head. 'Don't be sorry. I am very happy to see you too.'

Kesta got up to help the young men, draping a blanket over Beth and taking a sack of food to Mimeth. Joss put down everything he carried to hurry over to Dia, kneeling down to hug her. She cried out at the pain that rocketed through her ribs to her skull and teeth.

'Grandma?' Joss pulled back in alarm.

'It's okay,' she reassured him.

Joss studied her face, then stood. 'Nip, can you help a moment?'

Dia tutted. 'Joss, don't fuss.'

'What's up?' Nip hurried over.

'I'm just a bit battered,' she grumbled under her breath.

Nip knelt. 'Where?'

'My upper left arm, and my ribs.'

'May I check, Icante?'

'If you stop calling me Icante.'

A small smile brushed his lips. Nip carefully ran his hands down her arm, lifting it a little while placing a hand on her shoulder to perceive how the muscles and joint moved. She untucked her shirt and he reached under it, his hands calloused, but gentle. She sucked in air and jumped when he touched tender spots.

Nip withdrew his hands and sat back. 'Nothing is out of place, so no bad breaks. I think you have at least five fractures.'

Joss hissed in sympathy.

Nip turned to shout into the forest. 'Gorchia? Would you kindly get me some more willow bark? I promise to repay the forest.'

There was no reply, but Nip seemed happy enough. 'I have some left for now, but it will only take the edge off.'

Dia tilted her head. 'What was that about repaying the forest?'

'Oh.' Nip looked down at his hands, then met her eyes again. 'It's an earth-spirit thing. If you take from the forest with good intent, you must give something back. It keeps the balance, pleases the spirits. They, um, they will want to talk to you about that at a better moment, and um, sorting out some kind of truce with the fire-spirits.'

Doroquael flared. 'It's not me.' His blue eyes looked meaningfully toward the subdued Azrael.

Dia nodded. 'We'll talk later. I appreciate it, Nip.'

***

It wasn't long after night fell that they prepared to divide their small group and head to the Hold. Arridia still hadn't woken, but her breathing was deep and even.

'Are you sure you're well enough?' Kesta asked.

Dia turned and narrowed her eyes at her.

Kesta grinned. 'You're well enough.'

They chose Sharne and a few healthy warriors to remain and guard the injured. Vorro and Belir were to stay despite the fact they'd recovered some power. Beth was awake now, but wished she wasn't as the headache she had was unbearable despite Nip's best efforts; there was no way the poor woman could travel.

Azra had been terribly torn, wanting to go with Jorrun to the Hold, but unable to bear leaving Arridia. He'd made promises to protect both, but Jorrun calmly asked the spirit to take care of his daughter. The Thane approached Nip, who was still working quietly.

'We'll leave Eyraphin with you in case you need to send urgent word. If you hear nothing from us by tomorrow night, head for Seal Hold. It's sparsely manned, but they have a few fishing boats that could make the crossing to Elden.'

'Understood.' Nip gave a quick nod.

'Are we ready?' Jorrun looked around at those who were heading north.

'Ready,' Alikan called. He and Holin slipped into the trees with Aelthan to mark their path. Jorrun and Joss followed, Doroquael illuminating the way. The others fell in behind, Kesta staying at her mother's side.

'I thought you'd be the one to scout ahead,' Dia said to Kesta.

'I will later,' she replied, scanning the surrounding trees. 'I'll take over when night crosses towards dawn.'

It was a weary walk. Every step seemed to jar Dia's bones. Had they not been in such dire need of every ounce of power, she'd have begged Jorrun to heal her. They stopped to rest three times, Dia leaning against her daughter's back for warmth and support and taking a sip from the flask Nip had given her.

The island was horribly quiet.

When they set off again, Alikan and Holin stayed with the main group and Kesta vanished ahead, insisting on working alone. *Just like Heara.* Dia smiled to herself, then her face crumpled and her stomach churned with dread. She didn't even know if her friend was still alive.

Light began to seep into the sky. Here and there a bird started up its song.

Aelthan came skimming back to them, his wings catching in the shafts of the soft, low sun.

'What news?' Jorrun demanded.

'They blew the causeway,' the spirit whistled. 'Kesta is taking a closer peek.'

Jorrun picked up their pace, almost breaking into a run. They found Kesta on the edge of the forest, looking across to the Hold.

'What's happening?' Joss asked.

Kesta shushed him, then turned to Jorrun, a smile spreading on her face. 'The causeway is damaged, so they were attacked. The gate's been decimated.'

Jorrun shook his head. 'So why are you smiling?'

She grinned. 'Look at the walls.'

Dia took a step forward, her breath catching. Three unmistakable figures stood on the wall. Stocky, one-armed Worvig, slender Everlyn, and the polished-armoured and straight-backed ex-captain of Navere; Rece.

'They survived it.' Joss turned to grab Alikan's arm. He gave a whoop. 'They survived the attack!'

'Let's be cautious still,' Jorrun chastised him.

Even so, their hope and excitement didn't die down, even Dia finding the steps she took easier.

Kesta led the way, Alikan stepping up to walk protectively at her shoulder. Kesta called a little power, sending a ball of fire upward, signalling a *walker* coming home.

From the walls, Everlyn gave a fiery reply and Dia thought her heart would burst with joy.

The causeway was littered with rocks. Here and there a deep chunk was missing from the edge. Toward the middle only a narrow section of path remained, about a foot wide, with a sharp, jagged slope down to the cliff edge.

Worvig and Everlyn came out of the gates to meet them, while Rece called down a greeting from the wall above. Kesta hurried to hug her uncle; Dia took hold of Everlyn's hands and squeezed them.

'I'm a bit too sore for hugs,' she apologised. 'What happened?'

'Jderha attacked,' Worvig growled. 'But she was alone. She didn't seem to have much power left, but even so put up a fight. Thought she'd kill us all, truly, but then...'

'What?' Joss demanded.

'Young Cass.' Worvig glanced at Everlyn and shook his head. 'Offered his own life to kill her. Got close and stabbed her through the heart.'

'No.' The word burst from Jorrun, his face turning grey.

Kesta had completely frozen.

'Come on into the hall,' Everlyn prompted.

Dia almost didn't dare, there were too many faces she hadn't seen yet, too many more potential loses she didn't think she could face, but she followed the others in.

'It's so quiet,' Joss observed.

'Your grandad is asleep.' Worvig rolled his eyes.

As they stepped into the hall, Catya came hurtling towards them. She clutched at Jorrun's jacket, her cheeks and eyelids swollen and red, her body somehow finding the moisture to produce more tears.

'Oh, Jorrun, quick, it isn't too late.'

'Too late for what?' He placed a hand against her cheek and smoothed back her snagged hair.

Catya pointed.

Close to the high table was the body of the goddess who had come to destroy them all, Merin's blade still protruding from her rib cage. Arrus sat in his seat, a beer untouched before him, his head fallen against his chest. Beside him, Merin was curled up, his head cushioned by the warrior's arm.

Two yards from the felled god, Dysarta crouched at Cassien's head. They had placed a pillow beneath him. With a gasp, Dia realised he was alive.

'I thought he was dead?' Jorrun looked from Everlyn to Worvig.

'The minute we pull that sword out, he is,' Worvig replied. 'We're prolonging his suffering by not doing it.'

Catya almost snarled at him, then turned back to Jorrun. 'Please, you can heal him.'

Jorrun's hand moved to his mouth, and Dia could see by the pain in his eyes that Jorrun didn't have the strength left to do it. 'Of course, I'll try.' His throat was tight, making his voice harsh. He looked around at them all, his eyes lingering on Joss and Alikan.

'Shall I try?' Joss stepped forward. 'I have some power left.'

Jorrun wet his bottom lip with his tongue, then grabbed his wife's arm. 'Kesta. Healing is Chemmish magic, blood magic, but for some reason my father thought a sorcerer needed Fulmer blood, mixed blood. My sister, like he, thought it was to do with the purity of intent. I think Riddi was closer to the truth, though. Emotion flows with blood, flows strongly with *walkers*.'

'But you're not a *walker*,' Kesta pointed out.

'I know.' Jorrun's jaw muscles moved, and he clenched and unclenched his fists. 'I'm not explaining it very well. Kes, do you have enough strength to use your *knowing*?'

'I can for a while.'

'Good.' He knelt beside Cassien and Dysarta shuffled out of the way. 'I'm going to try his shoulder. Kesta, please try to understand how I'm doing it with your *knowing*. Then, transfer it to Alikan.' Joss protested, but Jorrun stopped him. 'Ali is almost pure Chemmish, and this is Chemmish magic, remember?'

Dia wrapped her arms carefully around herself as she watched. Perhaps it was the lack of doors, but the hall had grown oddly cold. She shivered. Jorrun closed his eyes, concentrating on letting his magic flow with tentative care into Cassien. Kesta placed a hand on his shoulder. After a moment, her face almost lit up.

'I feel it,' she whispered. 'I feel it, Jorrun. It's not emotion as such, but... but the magic flows from your heart! It moves through your blood, yes, but you're not drawing it from around you and controlling its purpose with your mind like other magic, it is literally made in your heart!'

Jorrun faltered as he almost lost concentration.

Catya gave a small cry of alarm.

'No, keep going.' Kesta urged. 'A moment longer so I can show Ali.'

Alikan knelt on the other side of Cassien, and Kesta took hold of his hand. Alikan gasped and tensed, then slowly relaxed.

'I have it.' He cleared his throat. 'I think I have it, it feels amazing.'

Kesta pulled his hand down towards the sword, and Catya ducked in to remove all the bandaging they'd wedged around it to stem the bleeding. Catya then grabbed for the sword hilt, closing her eyes.

Dia had to turn away. If it failed, it would be unbearable for all of them. She stepped towards Jderha's body, wanting a closer look at the creature who'd wrought so much destruction. She shrank back immediately. The head had not only been chopped off, but brutally hacked.

'I thought Cassien killed her by stabbing her through the heart?'

'He did.'

Heara's voice was muffled, and Dia turned to find her. The warrior sat slumped over a table, three empty flagons before her, one of which had fallen on its side. Heara looked up. Her eyes were red.

'Bitch killed my Vilnue, so I killed her again.'

'Oh, my honey.' Dia hurried around the table to put her arm around Heara and lay her head against her back, regardless of her own pain. Vilnue had only been meant as a distraction to Heara when they'd first met, some fun and comfort; but they'd developed a respectful and even loving relationship that had lasted over twenty years. Knowing how fond her husband was of Heara, it surprised her he'd left her to drink alone. She looked up at his chair.

The coldness blew through her again.

Her heart slowed.

'He isn't asleep.'

'What?' Heara slurred.

Dia shot to her feet. 'He isn't asleep.'

'Icante?' Milaiya looked up from where she was tending a wounded warrior, her mouth open.

Dia ran to the high table, all but those attempting to save Cassien stopping what they were doing to gawp. She slowed before she reached him. Merin stirred but didn't wake. Dia looked to the untouched beer, then at the sword propped against his leg that had slipped from his grip. She touched his icy hand, her eyes travelling over his still chest, his still face.

There was a peaceful smile on his lips.

The stubborn old warrior had held on until he knew the Islands were safe.

Dia dropped to her knees.

She tried to breathe, but it caught in her throat, strangled there by the pain.

The Icante of the Fulmers fell forward into her dead husband's lap and sobbed like a child.

***

Dia got up and paced the room again. It was too empty, the bed too big. The hole inside her too raw; fathomless. She crossed to the window, looking down at the sea, the moonlight dancing across the eternal ripples. She couldn't even bring herself to light a candle. There would be no Siveraell to keep her company through the long night.

Something prickled within her, and a soft voice started outside the door. It was a Fulmer ballad, a fisherman's song of the sea. She crept to the door and pressed her hands against the wood, then leaned her cheek against it. She sucked in a breath, tears pushing upward from the ache in her chest. When had Temerran arrived?

He was using magic to soothe her. Part of her didn't want comfort, part of her still needed to rage as Heara had, but she listened, not making a sound.

He changed to a harvest song, and she sank carefully to the floor. She closed her eyes, feeling the words but not hearing them. She drew in a deep breath, taking in the smell of the room, the scent of the man who had shared it with her for so many years. Like his life, the smell would fade, but like music and song, his memory would live on as long as it was shared by those who loved him.

As though reading her mind, The Bard moved onto a soaring ballad, the notes purer than starlight, striking the chords of her soul. Every note hurt, but she clung to it, letting her proud tears fall. Here in her room; she was not the Icante, not even a grandmother or mother; just a woman, a girl, with a bruised and battered heart.

As raw and vulnerable as she was, she dared not open the door, but her fingers pushed themselves into the imperfections of the wooden barrier. She let his love in; it compelled her heart to beat, stopped the ice of despair from consuming her soul. It was as wild as the sea, as pure as the stars, as warm as a hearth that heralded home; as deep as the ocean that lay between here, and Geladan.

Temerran sang to her through the long night, though it no longer felt so endless.

Chapter Forty-Nine

Arridia; Fulmer Island

'Riddi, would you drink something, please?'

She screwed her eyes up tight against the glare of fire, bringing up her arms.

'Azra, back off, just a little.'

Nip?

She groaned and opened her eyes, startled to find it was night. Leaves moved above her and somewhere a man and a woman spoke quietly together.

'Where are we, what's happening?' Her mouth was dry, her tongue clumsy.

Azrael darted in, but Nip shooed him. 'Let her have a drink, then you can tell her.'

Azrael huffed and buzzed to himself, but he waited.

Arridia sat up slowly, gazing around the forest clearing. Nip pressed the warm cup against her chest and she took it. 'Please tell me we aren't all that's left?'

'No, not just us.' Azrael couldn't wait any longer. He told her everything that had happened. Arridia held her cup against herself with one hand, placing the other firmly on the ground.

'Is there any news from the Hold?'

'There is.' Nip smiled. 'Eyraphin came to tell us, the hold is secure. Jderha is dead.'

For a moment everything seemed to swim away from Arridia. 'Dead? Was it Joss?'

Nip reached out to take her cup, and she realised she'd almost let it drop.

'It was Cassien.' Azrael turned a loop.

'Cass?' Arridia stared at the spirit. 'But what about the prophecy?'

'I don't know about that.' Nip frowned. 'But we need to get you safely home to your family.'

'Family.' She sat up straighter, memory tearing through her heart. Her hands flew to her mouth. 'Dierra!' Tears pushed against her eyes, hurting her throat.

Azrael gave a short wail, coming as close to her as he could. 'I can't give you a hug,' the little spirit said. 'But I can sing you a song.'

Arridia smiled and laughed despite the tears that dripped from her chin.

Nip reached out to wipe them away. 'Your mother is sending warriors out to us. They should get here by dawn, in just a couple of hours. If you can bring any of the ponies to us, it would really help with moving our injured.'

'Oh, I should try to heal them.'

Azrael crackled at her. 'You should not! You already knocked yourself out for two days using up too much power.'

'Azrael is right.' Nip handed her back the cup. 'Even reaching for the ponies might over-extend yourself. How do you feel?'

She flexed the muscle in her brain that controlled magic and tried to draw a little power. Immediately a mild, throbbing headache started, her nerves were raw, but power came. 'I can do it.'

Nip gave a nod.

Arridia reached out a shaking hand to touch his face. Nip was normally always very neat, but there was almost four day's growth of stubble on his chin and jaw. 'I quite like it' she said.

He turned his head to kiss her palm.

'Oh, for goodness' sake!' Azrael hissed. 'Your parents were bad enough. I am here, you know.'

'We know,' both Arridia and Nip said at once.

Nip stood, brushing down the back of his trousers. 'I need to get everyone ready.'

She nodded, watching as he walked away.

'Are you okay, my Riddi?' Azrael asked quietly.

She drew in a deep breath. 'I am, Azra, or I will be. This all seems so unreal. I was meant to be the one who saved everyone, yet I slept through Jderha's end.'

'Yeah, well.' Azrael blew a raspberry with his fiery tongue. 'Prophecy is nonsense.'

Arridia smiled, although it faded quickly. She still felt so uneasy. 'I'm going to try to reach the ponies. Keep an eye for me.'

She lay back on her blanket, reaching for the tiniest trickle of magic and dropping the barrier to her *knowing*. It was hard not to get snared on the emotions of the people and spirits in the surrounding forest. Their pain, grief, hope, exhaustion. Nip's quiet, sturdy love was everywhere, a web that ran between him and every hurt person he had tended.

She let herself drift outward into the forest, trying not to overexert herself by reaching. The world felt strange, dreamlike; like the sun shining on a wet landscape after a storm. There was an odd sense of unravelling that wasn't altogether unpleasant until she had the unsettling thought that it might be what dying was like.

She focused harder, searching for the feel of an equine. She found two, then one alone, then a little further out, a group of four. Some were content with their new life of wandering, some were anxious, twitchy, alert for the scent of predators. She offered them all home, food, and safety, and despite the darkness, all of them turned to make their way toward her.

She returned to herself too sharply, rolling onto her side and retching. Nip was there almost instantly, rubbing her back while Azrael fluttered helplessly.

'I shouldn't have asked you.'

She drew in several deep breaths. 'No, Nip, always ask me, and I'll do the same with you.'

'Agreed,' he smiled. 'As long as you are never afraid to say no if you need to. Speaking of which, fancy helping me make another litter?'

They worked together in companionable silence, Nip getting up to greet each pony that arrived and slip a harness made of woven plant fibres over the head of each. Mimeth woke and rummaged through their supplies to make an early breakfast, managing to get Beth to eat a little. Vorro and Sharne, who had been out in the forest keeping watch, returned, both looking animated.

'Our help is on its way,' Vorro announced, stopping short on seeing the ponies.

'Thank you,' Nip said. 'Your hand?'

Vorro glanced down at his bandages. 'Throbs a bit, but it's fine.'

'Shall we finish packing the camp for you?' Sharne offered, obviously keen to get back to the Hold.

'Please.'

They were all sat eagerly waiting, those unable to walk lying on litters, when the warriors from the Hold came to fetch them, led by Rece.

'Rece.' Arridia got quickly to her feet. 'It's good to see you. What news from the Hold?'

He regarded her, his smile fading. 'I don't know how much you're aware of.'

'Not much.' She frowned. Rece was scaring her. 'I know Jderha is dead, and that Cass slew her.'

'Ah.' Rece winced. 'I… This would have been better coming from your family. I must tell you first, that he somehow managed to go peacefully in his sleep, but your grandfather is dead.'

Pain burst inside her chest, and the world seemed to fall away around her. Arridia pivoted to search for Nip and Azrael. The little spirit darted straight to her side. Arridia drew in several breaths before she felt steady enough to reply. 'Thank you, Rece.'

The walk back to the hold was a blur of enduring pain to Arridia, trying to hold herself tightly together and shut out the emotions of those around her. She leaned against a pony, taking comfort from its warm presence, as Azrael buzzed along miserably beside her. Nip joined her often but had his patients to tend.

When the hold appeared before them, she was shocked, but heartened to see the *Undine* anchored out in the bay. The watchers on the walls saw their approach and several people, including Borrowmen, came hurrying out to meet them.

'We won't get the ponies across that causeway,' Nip told Rece worriedly. 'But I have promised them food and shelter.'

Rece placed a hand on his shoulder. 'I will ensure your promise is kept.'

Nip took a few steps back toward the trees. 'Gorchia, are you coming?'

Moments later, the small fox-like earth-spirit ran into Nip's waiting hand.

'Riddi!'

She drew in a sharp breath at her brother's voice, hurrying past the others to meet him, while Azrael and Doroquael flew circles around each other. Joss gave her a fierce hug, stepping back to rest his forehead against hers.

'Did you hear about grandfather?'

She nodded.

He took another step back to regard her. 'There is so much to tell you. Temerran arrived last night and brought news from Elden. King Bractius and Ayline are both dead.'

'No. How?'

'Come on, I'll tell you.' He placed his arm across her shoulders to lead her over the broken causeway. She looked behind for Nip, but the stable master was busy.

Joss chattered away, Arridia trying to take it all in. Her feet faltered when he told her of Eleanor's execution. A decision like that would kill Lucien inside. And now her friend was king.

'Rids?' He reached back to take her hand, thinking she'd halted for fear of the narrowed path. 'Anyway, with Elden secure, Temerran headed here to determine if we needed him. His men have been a welcome help in cleaning the place up. Oh, did you... you know about Cassien?'

'That he killed Jderha?'

'Yeah.' Joss turned to study her, his eyebrows raised. 'He gave his life in a gamble to kill her, only, well, Father taught Ali to heal, and now Cass is recovering.'

'Ali is a healer?' She stopped again, and Joss yanked at her arm to keep her following. 'Father thinks he has the key for lots of us to do it now.'

They passed under the wall, the two fire-spirits speeding over it; Arridia's eyes travelled over the broken gates and the scorched stone.

Everlyn's husband was busy trying to make some temporary doors for the great hall with help from two Borrowmen, a familiar figure looking on with his arms folded.

'Nolv!'

The *Undine's* first mate touched a fist to his chest and gave her a grin.

Dierra's absence tore at her again.

The great hall was busy, Milaiya instructing some warriors who were moving an injured man, presumably to one of the empty houses out in the ward. She scanned the room but couldn't find any of her family. She knew they were safe, but anxiety returned.

She spotted the red-headed northern sorceress. Dysarta was sitting cross-legged on one of the tables at the far end of the hall, gazing down at an empty spot on the floor. She was dressed in her black leather and white fur, her hair plaited but coming loose. Her eyes looked red and raw.

A brief spark of anger flared within Arridia, overriding her weariness. Dysarta looked up as she approached.

'The fire children,' Dysarta whispered.

Arridia clenched her fists. 'It wasn't me. It was never me. All those people dead because of some mad prophecy.'

Dysarta sighed, swinging her legs out to sit on the edge of the table. 'See it instead that it wasn't *just* you. Rarely does one person change the world, rather it is many people, small acts of bravery, moments of courage or inspiration, that come together to alter fate.'

'Did Edon see all that?'

She shook her head. 'He saw nothing, Arridia. And everything.'

'But that doesn't make any sense!'

Dysarta winced in sympathy. 'I'll tell you what Edon Ra told us. Jderha was a true prophet, just like Edon, but both of them learned there are loopholes, changing points. Jderha had years to study her dream, to look at all the possibilities. She knew a fire-priestess, as they called you, would cause her end, but what detail there was in the dream, we will never know. Whatever the case, Jderha would have planned to avoid that end, including running when you made her weak.' Dysarta shrugged. 'Perhaps she sought to weaken you in return by destroying your home and family. Whatever the case, Edon had a dream of his own.

'He perceived that at some point, Merin would face Jderha, and that Catya would try to save her son, and that Catya would fail. A minor detail in eternity, but a significant one. He and Catya manipulated things so that someone would be there who would not fail, someone faster than her. As it turned out, it was Cassien's nobility that saved us, not his speed.'

Azrael hummed. 'And long ago, Naderra gave her life to save two boys. One of those boys saved an unknown slave from the fighting pits, whose eyes stirred his guilt and his conscience.'

Arridia looked from Azrael back to Dysarta, her mouth open. 'So, Osun was the key?'

'No more, or less than you, or any other whose right or wrong stroke of a sword changed the path of time. We are all the threads that weave the final pattern, though a rare few are the foundations, the frame. Boggles the mind, doesn't it?'

Arridia shook herself. It was easier to believe the whole thing nonsense as Azrael did. She pivoted to look back up at the spirit.

Or did he?

'Come on,' her brother muttered, clearly as unsettled as her. 'Everyone is in Grandma's room.'

She couldn't help but pause as they passed her grandfather's chair. His mug of beer still stood there untouched. Taking in a ragged breath, she hurried after her brother and to their family.

Chapter Forty-Nine

Kesta; Fulmer Island

'Hey.'

Kesta glanced up at her husband, then back out to sea. His arm brushed hers as he joined her to lean against the stone wall.

'Hey,' she replied.

'We've news from the sea-spirits. They've confirmed none of the Geladanian fleet has survived.'

Kesta breathed out slowly, letting her shoulders sag. 'Why am I finding it hard to believe this is the end?'

'Perhaps because we have lived with this fear for too many years.'

She turned, leaning her back against the battlement. 'I keep going to look at Jderha's body to make sure she's still dead.'

'You're not the only one. We're just about to head down to the beach for the meeting.'

She straightened up. 'I'm ready.'

Over the last three days the Hold had slowly recovered and a few more survivors had been found or made their way back. The gateway remained broken, the causeway would forever be scarred, and some chairs would stand empty; but life was finding its way back to normality. The beach was busy, Catya's ship stood out in the bay alongside the *Undine*, and many of the grieving Rakinya had already made their way aboard. The Queen of Snowhold only awaited this meeting, before she would embark back to her adopted land.

The sky was overcast, and some shelters had been set up, though for the moment the rain held off. The Icante and Temerran were standing together, looking out to sea. Jagna, Rece, and Everlyn had taken seats; Worvig and Milaiya on their feet before them as they conversed. Heara sat alone on some wreckage washed up from a Geladanian ship, scratching at one of the planks with a knife, and Kesta's heart constricted.

'Who will speak for Elden with Vilnue gone?'

'I will myself, to an extent,' Jorrun replied as they took the path through the dunes. 'I am still a Thane of that land. But they have another spokesperson.'

Kesta followed his gaze. Arridia, Joss, and Alikan were with Catya, Dysarta, and Merin. The young boy was demonstrating to his father how much he had improved at controlling a small flame in his hand. Alikan wouldn't be leaving with them on the ship. He'd decided to stay a while and practice his healing skills under Jorrun's supervision, but later he would follow his son to Snowhold and spend some time there. Catya had spoken of a friend in the far north who had been tattooed by a Coven, and Ali wanted to be sure he could remove the inhibiting blood runes from her skin before he went.

'Joss is to be a prince consort in Elden,' Jorrun continued.

'But surely with Bractius dead, he will not need to hold to that?'

Jorrun looked down at the sand, a slight catch in his breath. The King of Elden's death had hit him hard. Despite Bractius's often harsh treatment of Jorrun, they had been boys together, and for many years he'd been Jorrun's only human friend. 'I guess that will be up to Joss and Scarlett. Lucien too, of course. I do not think our son will back out of a promise, even one he made under duress.'

Kesta didn't reply. She knew he was right. Part of her was proud of Joss, another part scared for him. She was fond of Scarlett, but the girl was very young and had a long way to go before she really knew who she was.

A noise behind her made her turn. Cassien was making slow progress over the dunes, Nip helping him, and Vivess hovering in case she was needed. Cassien's movements were stiff, and the pain showed on his face. Alikan had knitted together some of the broken flesh, but Jorrun had needed to complete the healing as his power returned. It hadn't been a neat process.

The small earth-spirit rode on Nip's shoulder. It was Gorchia who had been summoned to the meeting, rather than the stable master.

The whir of wings heralded the air-elementals, Aelthan and Eyraphin. Doroquael and Azrael immediately stopped playing with Merin to draw themselves up and look serious.

Hollow pain again ate at Kesta's soul. Siveraell should have been here to head such an important meeting, they would sorely miss his presence. It still seemed impossible he was gone.

There was only one representative missing. Temerran stepped up to the water, letting the small waves roll over his boots. He sang a short, simple song in the ancient language of the bards, and a wave rose, forming into the shape of a woman.

Dia turned, and Kesta held her breath. Her mother was broken, and yet she still found her grace and poise as she addressed them.

'Thank you all. Thank you all so many times over for what you have done for the Fulmers, and for each other. For the first time in many years, we face the possibility of a long and lasting peace. We will build the foundations together, here, on this sand.' She turned to Catya. 'Your Majesty, Queen Catya of Snowhold.'

Catya gave a nod. There was no pride in her posture. She held her wife's hand, her arm around her son who stood before her. This was Catya, the girl who Kesta had taken under her wing. A queen was *what* she was, but not *who* she was.

'Icante. My friends. Snowhold has stood separate for many years, mostly through my guilt and stubbornness, but also to protect the Rakinya and The People, the Northern Tribes. Much as I would love to declare us a Raven province, my duty to them must come first. However...' She looked from Rece to Cassien. 'Although we have traded for a while, it is long past time we signed official treaties. Rece, Cass, if you would sail with us back to Navere, we will draw one up. Most of the Raven laws we can adopt and set in stone, as they are compatible with the ways of the tribes. Snowhold is a Free Province of Chem, but it must always belong to the Rakinya, and The People.'

Rece glanced at silent Cassien and shrugged. 'I would be delighted to help draw up such a treaty.'

Cassien cleared his throat. 'As would I. But, no offence, I would like a Rakinya present also to witness such a treaty. An exchange of ambassadors would also be appropriate, and would be very welcome with me in Caergard, as well as Navere. Also...' He met Catya's eyes. 'My son, Raith, is a similar age to Merin, and I think they would get on well together. We might consider them both training under Alikan.'

Alikan looked up, his amber eyes wide, and Kesta smiled.

Catya tilted her head. 'I would happily agree to all those terms.'

Dia raised an elegant hand towards the two air-elementals. 'Aelthan, Eyraphin. You both came to us willingly to offer much needed help. Your people were brought here as prisoners of Geladan. What is it you wish? What do you need from us in return?'

It was Aelthan who replied, wings a whirr as it hovered. 'They took us from Geladan, but we do not wish to go back. However, free as we are, we have no home here. These islands are fire-islands.' Azrael gave a hiss. 'The Borrows, the province of the sea. We hear that Elden is a kingdom of earth, and that fire-spirits also lay claim to Chem. We have no animosity towards our fellow spirits, we wish only to live free, but we are without a home.'

Nip raised his hand. 'May Gorchia please speak? The earth-spirits face the same problem.'

'Of course,' Dia invited.

Gorchia stood up on Nip's shoulder, taking a handful of the young man's hair to keep his balance. Green foxfire briefly crackled across his eyes. 'There are a few earth-spirits who are native to the Fulmers and to Elden – like myself – but also many who were forced here from Geladan. For many years all spirits but those of the sea have hidden themselves away from people, for fear of capture and persecution. For years we have allowed ourselves to fade as our land is taken and destroyed.

'Nip has offered me some hope. Coming to this island and learning of the *walkers*, and the tribes of the far north over the sea, has given me hope. People will always be the bane of earth-spirits, as they live, they destroy, but...'

Gorchia faltered, but Nip took a step forward toward Dia, his hands pressed together. 'We could try a bit harder. Remember the old ways of *if you take, you give*. The spirits wouldn't need much. Just a small portion of the harvest. A bowl of milk left on the doorstep. If you cut wood for building, then plant a new tree. If you gather herbs, leave them some fruit, or some cake—'

'If they're getting cake, we should have biscuits,' Azrael muttered.

'They would...' Nip's jaw muscles moved as he contemplated his next words. 'They would ask though, that in return for the service they rendered you, and the lives they lost, that each land put aside a forest that is to remain just theirs, untouched by people. A sanctuary.'

Both Catya and Dysarta stiffened, and Kesta turned toward them with a puzzled frown.

Dia held up her hand. 'Thank you, Nip. And you, Gorchia and Aelthan. That is a lot to contemplate. Regarding a forest here, the Islands can promise you will have one. Your law of give if you take, I like very much and can certainly encourage. All spirits are welcome here, so long as they harm none, and remember that we are fire islands first and foremost.'

Azrael puffed himself up.

'I cannot, of course, speak for the other lands.'

Catya spoke up at once. 'Snowhold can abide by such an agreement in its northern territories without hesitation. The land that was owned by Chem will be trickier, though.'

'And Elden?' Dia asked Jorrun.

Jorrun didn't reply but held his hand out toward his son to speak. Joss gave a start, and Kesta bit at her lower lip.

'Oh.' Joss glanced at Alikan and Arridia either side of him. 'Well, of course I would have to consult with the king. But King Lucien is a... well, he is a gentle kind of soul, and I think he would agree, but, um... I'd have to ask.'

'Azra?' Dia prompted.

'We want biscuits!'

Doroquael flared at him and hissed, drifting toward the centre of the group. 'I assk only two things, Dia. First, that it be made unlawful in all the lands for a spirit to be trapped and used against its will. Such a thing should be severely punished.'

'I think we can agree to that?' Dia looked around and everyone there nodded. 'Your second request?'

Doroquael made himself small. 'I want to stay home now, with you, Dia. I love Joss very much, and I have guarded him for you, but you are my fire-priestess. I'm no Siveraell, but now Jderha is gone, I'd like to stay with you.'

Kesta put her hands to her mouth, her eyes watering. Her son's face had fallen, and Arridia took his hand, but he made no protest. Dia, however, turned away momentarily to hide her own tears.

'You are a free spirit, Doro.' Dia's voice was a little hoarse. 'And I would love to have you with me.'

Temerran took several sudden steps deeper into the water, and the sea-spirit drew herself up to tower over him.

'What of you, most magnificent and powerful spirits of the sea?' the bard asked. 'What think you of treaties?'

The spirit roared and crashed. 'We will never be bound. We are ruled by no one.' She subsided just a little. 'But should any who set sail wish to give us tribute, we would consider being… benevolent.'

Temerran bowed flamboyantly, while the Icante narrowed her eyes and gave a slight shake of her head. Kesta wondered if the sea-spirits felt any remorse at all at holding back in helping against Jderha.

'That leaves Elden, Chem, and the Borrows with whom we already have treaties,' Dia said. 'Are you all happy to retain them, with amendments to be considered regarding spirits?'

There were several 'Ayes,' but Jorrun rubbed at his beard. 'I have one idea, but it would again be for King Lucien to consider. North of Elden are two large islands known as The Towers, whose cliffs are so tall they are practically inaccessible. As such, no person lives there. They would make a suitable home for our air-spirit friends.'

Kesta sucked in a breath. 'That would be perfect!'

'But subject to agreement from the king.' He twisted to smile down at her.

'There is one more thing.' Temerran's voice rang out clearly; a shiver of foreboding ran through Kesta. Temerran turned again to address the sea-spirit. 'Years ago, I made a bargain to stay in these waters. I now ask to be released from that.'

The sea churned and darkened, but Temerran didn't move.

'Hear my reason.' He faced Dia. 'Jderha is gone, but we learned from Chem that removing a dictator can leave a land in chaos. I fear the repercussions in Geladan. I propose to sail there, or at least to the nearby islands of Hidarra and Mereck. I want to ensure this is really over.'

Kesta swallowed.

Her mother's hand was pressed against her chest, but she nodded slowly.

The sea-spirit grumbled, but subsided. 'It benefits us. It shall be so. But you must come back.'

Dia drew herself up. 'Thank you all for your time.'

Without another word, the Icante strode away, head down. Heara leapt from her perch to scurry after her. Temerran didn't move, the sea churning about his legs as he watched Dia leave.

Kesta went to follow, but Jorrun put his arm around her. 'We have some goodbyes to make.'

She looked up into his blue eyes and nodded.

Most of the Ravens were returning with Catya to Navere, only Jagna and Perta were waiting for their own ships to come for them, bringing back Fulmer refugees. Holin and Sharne were also staying to finish their term of training in Elden.

Kesta took a moment to say goodbye to them all as they clambered into the boats, saving the hardest goodbyes until last. She squeezed Rece's hands tightly.

'Take care, Captain.'

He nodded, stepping in to kiss her on the cheek. 'You too, *master.*'

She slapped him hard on the arm.

Beth, Jollen, and Rey were next, and she helped the Raven sisters into their boat, waving as Fulmer warriors and Borrow pushed them out into the water. She turned to regard Catya and Cassien, and a sob rose to choke her.

'Look after yourselves.' She sniffed as she held Catya tightly. 'Don't be a stranger.'

Catya nodded against her, then stepped back to wipe at her eyes. 'Come to Snowhold, when you have time.'

Kesta forced a smile as Jorrun took Catya's hand and hugged her. 'I'm so proud of you,' he said.

Catya's hands shook as she wiped at her face again, clambering into the small boat beside her wife and son. She lifted her chin. 'I love you both.'

Kesta's lip trembled, and she had to rub her eyes to clear her vision. Jorrun was carefully holding Cassien.

'Give our love to Kussim and the boys. We'll try to see you soon.'

Cassien clasped Jorrun's wrist, nodding as he stepped away.

'Cass.' Kesta placed her hand against his cheek, then put her arms around him. 'Thank you.'

They stood together for a long while until Kesta eventually let go.

'We'll see you soon.' She sniffed.

Kesta and Jorrun put their arms around each other, stepping back a little as the tide came in. They watched until they lost the ship beyond the northern horizon.

Chapter Fifty

Dia; Fulmer Island

Doroquael hummed to himself in the corner of the room, now and then using his magic to stir a subtle breeze to turn a page in the book. He cursed and muttered when he used a little too much force and several pages fluttered over.

'Is it the right thing for the boy?' Dia asked, studying Temerran's face as he gazed at the dancing candle flame.

'It will be his choice.'

'But you have been influencing his choice.'

He turned, his green eyes meeting hers. 'In all my years on the sea, he is the only one I have found who could take my place, though I invariably thought it impossible. I never offered him a home with me, but he has asked many times over the years. I gave him an opportunity to explore who he is, no more.'

'You were always freedom to his father's chains, affection instead of disapproval and discipline. Of course, he would turn to you.'

'Was I wrong?' Temerran's face creased in concern, his eyes vulnerable.

Dia had to look away. 'I guess we will see.'

Temerran sighed. 'I will not ask him. But this time, if he asks me, I shan't say no. And what of you? That frown you wear isn't just for me.'

Dia closed her eyes briefly. 'No. I am still puzzled, floored, by Edon Ra's sacrifice. He is as valuable to the north as I am to the Fulmers, and perhaps more valuable to the Land Beneath the Sky than I. What did he see that made him give his life for mine? He has left me with an enormous debt I can never repay.'

There was a soft knock at the door, and Dia went to open it. Vivess stood there, glancing from Dia to Temerran. She gave a bob of a bow. 'We are ready.'

Dia froze, her heart thrumming rapidly in her ears. 'Go on, I will follow.'

Vivess hurried away, but Dia remained in the doorway, unable to move.

'Dia?' Temerran stepped up behind her.

'I can't do this.' Her breath caught in her throat.

Temerran reached out and carefully tucked a stray strand of her greying hair back into place. 'Yes, you can.'

'I didn't think I'd have to.' She looked up to face him. 'I thought I would die before Arrus.'

Temerran caressed her cheek with the back of his fingers and bent to kiss her forehead. 'Edon Ra was a wise beast, and you are the strongest person I know. You can do this.'

'Do you know how exhausting it is to be strong?'

Temerran drew in a long, slow breath. 'You know I do. And I remember how you and Arrus were there for me when my heart was shattered, and I didn't think I could go on. Tonight, I will be here.'

'And me!' Doroquael chirped.

Temerran took her hand and squeezed it, then led her down the stairs to the great hall.

Traditionally, for important feasts, they decorated the hall with garlands of leaves and blossoms, but tonight colour and life were added by shrubs, flowers, and vines planted in pots and troughs. Dia smiled to herself. Nip and the earth-spirits had been busy.

A steady procession was making its way down to the beach and they joined it, Dia closing her eyes momentarily to draw in the flow of life.

They congregated on the shore where too many pyres stood in stark reminder of their loss. Kesta, Jorrun, and their children stood beside the one that held the body of her husband. To one side of it lay Dierra, on the other Merkis Vilnue. Kesta turned to look at her, but Dia couldn't meet her daughter's eyes.

Without a word, she picked up one of the torches and approached her husband's resting place. They had built his pyre from the shattered wood of the gates and doors of Fulmer Hold; the rest of the wood gathered from the destruction Jderha had wrought on their forests.

Worvig stepped up beside her, placing the mug of beer his brother hadn't had time to finish on top of the pyre.

Every nerve within Dia's chest hurt; her fractured ribs a relief in comparison. She held out the torch but couldn't bring herself to touch the pyre.

She jumped as Temerran broke into song behind her. Not a melancholy tune suitable for such an occasion, but a bawdy, humorous warriors' song, such as Arrus used to roar with laughter at. Several of the warriors joined in, including Heara.

Dia closed her eyes, drew in a deep breath, and held her torch against Arrus's pyre. To her right, Jorrun lit his niece's, and to her left, Heara flung her torch onto Vilnue's pyre. She let out a shaking sigh, her spine painfully rigid.

'Heara.' She turned to her friend. 'I noticed Jderha's body is missing.'

'Is it?' Heara poked out her lower lip and gave a shrug. Then the old warrior rolled her eyes and huffed. 'Okay. So, I chopped her up and threw her in the sea for the fish. It's no more than she deserved, and she was really starting to smell.'

Dia placed her hand over her face to hide her smile. She put her arm around her friend and Heara silently hugged her back.

Before them, the pyres slowly turned to ash.

***

Dia woke early, dawn only just pulling itself up from the horizon. Venturing out into the hall, she crept past those who snored and lay where they'd fallen after the funeral feast.

She found Everlyn and her husband, Calbri, out in the ward, sitting at a waulking table with parchment laid before them.

'Good morning.'

'Dia.' Everlyn sat up straighter and twisted around to face her friend. 'We've been looking at the causeway. Calbri says a stonemason would be better than he at repairing it.' She pulled the parchment closer. 'Calbri has suggested we take out more of the causeway and put in a lifting bridge such as they have over the river at Lake Taur.'

'I think that's a great idea.' Dia smiled at Everlyn's young husband. 'I will leave you to oversee it.'

'There's also Eagle Hold, we have some plans for its repair—'

Dia touched her arm. 'Later, my honey.'

She made her way down to the beach, her chest tightening at the sight of the piles of ash and charred wood. She walked slowly to the one that had consumed her husband, crouching to scoop up some ashes at its centre and place them in a small wooden box. The rest would be scattered over the fields and forest, given back to the island.

'Come with me.'

She gasped, standing up and pivoting to see Temerran a few feet away from her.

'Come with me, Dia. Sail on the *Undine*. Come and have an adventure with me.'

She squeezed the box tighter in her hand, smiled, and shook her head. 'My place is here. I have work to do.'

'There will always be work to do. Have some fun. Come with me.'

She regarded him; the handsome younger man with his charming smile, curly red hair, and sparkling green eyes. He was warmth, and freedom.

'I'm the Icante.'

He took a step forward. 'You are also Dia.'

She looked down at the box in her hand. She knew what Arrus would want for her, and yet she couldn't.

'I will stay here. I am still the Icante.'

Temerran's smile faded as he regarded her. 'I have been lucky enough to have had more than one great love in my life. The sea, the *Undine*...' He winced. 'Linea. And you, Dia Icante. You took my breath away the first day I saw you. When you need me, call me my friend, and I will come home.'

He turned and walked away along the edge of the water. Something tore in Dia's heart, but she held the box of ashes tighter and, drawing in a breath, headed back to the Hold.

Her farewells to her family were painful, but she knew they were only temporary, and she withdrew to her room rather than wave them off from the beach with Worvig and Milaiya.

It was hard not to go to the window and watch the *Undine* sail away. Even without her *knowing*, she felt its departure, because a little piece of her went with it.

'Hey, Dia.' Doroquael flew a little loop around the room. 'I've been learning stories. Do you want to hear one?'

Her painful heart tingled. 'Yes please, Doro.'

'Okay, then. Once upon a time...'

Dia sat slowly in her chair, her small wooden box cradled in her lap. The little spirit's words washed over her, and the Icante of the Fulmers smiled as she blinked away her tears.

Chapter Fifty-One

Scarlett; Kingdom of Elden

'They're coming!'

Riane slipped in the door and closed it behind her.

'Oh.' Scarlett flapped her hands and snatched up the dress on the bed. 'Can you help me?'

'Of course.' Riane held the elaborate dress while Scarlett stepped into it, then tied up the laces. 'Shall I do your hair?'

Scarlett reached up to touch it. As usual, it was hanging loose about her shoulders, a girl's style in Elden, not a woman's. As the aide and advisor to the king, that would need to change.

'Oh, but do we have time?' Scarlett turned to the skinny girl. Riane had decided to stay, and Scarlett was grateful. The girl knew little about court and hair, but she knew a lot about the real world and the real people of Elden, and had already given Scarlett a tremendous amount of insight. In return, Scarlett had arranged an appropriate allowance for the girl, and a generous amount to be paid to her family in compensation.

'They only just docked, so, um, I think so.'

'Maybe just a plait then.' Scarlett crossed to the dressing table and snatched up some silver pins inlaid with coloured stones. 'But dress it up a bit.'

Riane did a surprisingly good job, and the two young women hurried down to the throne room. Her brother, Tantony, and Rosa were already there, as were Dinari and Ylena. It still made her pause to see her brother seated on the throne. He looked different there. Older; less kind. Or perhaps that was just the memory of what he had done to Eleanor.

Their mother's throne had been removed; it was Jorrun's stark black chair that Scarlett used when she sat beside her brother. Merkis Tantony was standing at Lucien's side; Rosa seated on one of the benches at the edge of the room with the Ravens who had come from Chem to save them. Scorch marks still marred the flagstones, though the bloodstains had been scrubbed away. Scarlett tried not to look at them.

They'd received word from the Fulmers, but little detail. She hoped that, had there been any deaths that would affect them, they would have heard; but the fact Jorrun had asked for a private audience with only those now present made Scarlett fidget with unease.

When the steward opened the door, Scarlett sat up straight in her chair. Lucien didn't move. She scanned the group coming in. Jorrun, Kesta, Temerran, all looking well and unhurt. A fire-spirit flew with them, but she was certain it was Azrael, not Joss's Doroquael. She leaned forward. Arridia came next with the stable master from Northold; he had some kind of animal perched on his shoulder. A squirrel, perhaps?

Then Joss entered with Alikan and she let out the breath she'd been holding. Joss looked worried, tired, but unharmed. His eyes sought hers, lighting at once with a smile.

Dinari didn't smile. The powerful Chemmish woman shot to her feet as the Fulmer party bowed.

Jorrun took a step forward. 'Forgive me, your majesty. This is a little rude of me, but I have important family news to impart.'

'No, of course.' Lucien's demeanour altered at once, and he stood, jumping off the dais. 'I would much rather greet my friends first and be king later.'

No one else needed any prompting. Jorrun hurried to his sister, while Kesta almost ran to embrace Rosa. The King of Elden clasped wrists with Temerran, then hugged both him and Arridia. Scarlett used the steps to get down to the lower floor in a more dignified manner than her brother, flushing with pleasure when Joss came to meet her with a polite bow.

'Your Highness.'

'Joss.' She glanced around quickly, then stood on her toes to give him a quick kiss. 'Are you all right?'

He nodded, though the grin faded from his face. 'And you? I'm so sorry about your parents. And… and Eleanor. We were told she was executed.'

Scarlett looked away. 'It was Lucien. He didn't give her a trial, just took off her head.'

'She wasn't…'

Joss faltered, and Scarlett gazed up at his anxious blue eyes.

'I mean… was she carrying my child?'

Scarlett's hand flew to her mouth. She thought she'd be sick. It had never occurred to her; she wondered if Lucien had considered it at all.

Joss's jaw muscles moved, but he took her arm and gently steered her to a bench. She saw Kesta had her arm around Ylena, and Jorrun held his sister as she cried on his shoulder.

'What is it?' Scarlett demanded. 'What happened?'

'My cousin, Dierra.' Joss swallowed. 'She died defending Arridia.'

'Oh, no.' She squeezed his arm. 'I'm so sorry, Joss. She seemed really nice.'

He nodded. 'She was. My father is pretending to be all tough about it, but he's devastated, and blaming himself.'

She reached her hand out to touch Joss's face, but they both jumped as Lucien coughed, and sat down on the seat beside Joss.

'Your majesty.' Joss stood, but Lucien winced and grabbed his arm to stop him.

'It's just Lucien. Joss, I wanted to tell you I won't hold you to the vows you were forced to make under duress. You are free to be a Raven, or... or whatever you choose.'

'Oh, but...' Scarlett looked from her brother to Joss.

Joss straightened up, turning to face the young king. He regarded Lucien for so long, Scarlett feared for a moment they might actually come to blows. She knew Joss hadn't loved Eleanor, but he was an honourable man and would have no doubt died to defend any accidental child.

Joss's brows drew together, and he looked away, the pain in his eyes hidden. 'A vow is a vow. I intend to protect and serve the throne of Elden as my father did.' He slumped a little, turning back to study Scarlett's face in a way that made her flush. 'But, Scar, things with us happened very quickly.' Her heart plummeted. 'I would like to do this properly. Take things slowly, get to know each other. I guess... I guess I'm asking for permission to court you.'

Lucien gave a soft snort and pushed himself up off the table. 'I'll leave you to it.'

A smile grew rapidly on Scarlett's face. 'I would like that. Could you teach me Raven skills? Maybe get me some lessons with your mother? She scares me a bit, but I want her to like me.'

Joss grinned and took her hand. 'I'll see what I can do.'

***

King Bractius's funeral was an elaborate affair. In contrast, the queen and Princess Eleanor were buried without ceremony, only a plain stone with their names left to mark their graves. All the Jarls and Thanes had been summoned, and they stayed late through the night in the feasting hall, drinking and filling their stomachs. Scarlett wondered if any other than Jorrun genuinely mourned their king. He had not been a kind man, but he had worked hard, sacrificed everything, to keep them safe.

Jorrun and Kesta left early, Scarlett wished she could have too.

The following day was to be her brother's coronation. Arridia had joined Scarlett and Riane in her room as they got ready. Considering Arridia was more solitary than the new king, Scarlett guessed Arridia must be missing her cousin.

'So, will you no longer have a bodyguard now Jderha is dead?' Scarlett asked as she pinned up Arridia's hair. She had such lovely hair, soft and as dark as a crow's feather.

'No,' Arridia replied quietly. 'No, I shall be on my own for the first time in my life.'

Scarlett hesitated, not sure if her brother's friend was relieved or sad. 'I seem to have acquired one,' she said cheerfully. 'Meric.'

'Meric is a good man. But, if Riane is staying, you might want to get her trained up.'

'What, like the princess's assassin?' Riane asked excitedly.

They both turned to look at her.

'Careful.' Arridia gave a low chuckle. 'You might have a new Catya.'

'Who's Catya?' Riane demanded.

Scarlett shook her head. 'Come on. Let's get to the throne room.'

They had moved the benches that normally stood at the side of the room to stand in rows before the throne. It was already busy, and an excited buzz of conversation filled the long room. Jorrun's stark chair had been placed in the shadows in the corner, but the former king's sorcerer stood waiting in elegant black, the crown on a podium before him. Long ago, the king would have been chosen by the Jarls, but it had been many years now that the crown had been passed from father to son. By tradition, though, all the Jarls would attend to pledge their fealty.

Scarlett moved to take her seat at the front. The bench was empty. It hit her so hard she might just as well have walked into a wall. She and Lucien were all there were of their family. She pivoted to catch Arridia's attention. The older woman had moved past her toward her own seat but sensed something was wrong and halted.

'Highness?'

'Would you sit with me, please?'

Arridia gave a slight bow, aware of eyes on her. 'Of course.'

Jorrun broke his stern appearance to smile at them both. Moments later, a steward opened the door behind the throne and gave Jorrun a nod. The Dark Man held a hand out toward the waiting audience, and they all stood.

Lucien appeared in the doorway, not dressed in finery, but in simple green trousers and a hooded tunic. His sword was buckled about his hips, but a lute hung at his back. His long curling hair was loose and unruly.

There were gasps and mutterings from around the hall. Jorrun's eyes narrowed, but he said nothing as Lucien approached the throne. Butterflies danced in Scarlett's stomach. What was her brother doing?

Lucien stopped beside the throne, touching its arm with two fingers. He raised his chin a little to regard them all from under his curls. His voice was firm, his brown eyes showing more confidence than Scarlett had expected.

'I will not be your king.'

There were more gasps and cries of shock and even outrage. Jorrun held up his hand to shush them.

'There is someone much better suited to rule than I.' Lucien raised his voice and the room silenced. 'You all knew my father, he put his throne, this kingdom, above everything and everyone. But when we were attacked, there was someone he gave his life to save. In doing so, I believe he chose his heir. I abdicate in favour of my sister. You will accept Scarlett as your queen. I am leaving.'

Scarlett's eyes widened, and she clutched at the fabric of her dress. 'Luce? What are you doing?'

Jorrun rubbed at his forehead, his eyes closed and lips pursed as he shook his head, but he didn't stop Lucien.

'Luce?'

Scarlett stepped forward as Lucien jumped down off the dais. He took hold of Scarlett's upper arms gently and kissed her cheek. 'You will be fine, Scar. You were always the better choice, even Father knew that. I took Eleanor's death for you, so you wouldn't have to bear it. But now I have to go.'

'They'll never accept me!'

Lucien smiled, glancing past Scarlett to Arridia. He touched the cord around her neck that supported Rosa's hidden amulet. 'They have no choice. Take care, Scarlett. Be happy.'

He strode down the aisle, ignoring the muttering and angry shouts of his name. For the first time, Scarlett noticed Temerran the bard standing by the door, leaning casually against the wall with one long boot crossed over the other. The bard looked up at Jorrun, touched his chest in salute, then followed Lucien out the door.

'Go on,' Arridia urged softly behind her.

'Oh, but...' Scarlett looked around for something to focus on, something to tie down her fleeing thoughts. Jorrun came quickly down the steps, offering his hand.

'Your majesty.'

She tentatively placed her small hand on his larger one, and he led her up the steps to the throne. She sat, blinking up at him.

'All will be well,' Jorrun whispered. 'We will be with you until you are ready to stand alone. Now, show them your strength, show them their queen.'

Scarlett nodded, slowing her breathing and straightening her spine. As Jorrun stepped away to pick up the crown, she made herself meet the eyes of her audience. Kesta had an amused smile on her face; Arridia looked serious but gave her a nod. Joss was beaming, though his eyes reflected her own bewilderment.

Jorrun held up the crown. 'People of Elden. Before you sits Scarlett of Taurmaline, heir of Bractius.'

He turned to look at her and with a jolt, Scarlett realised she was meant to speak. She had nothing prepared, and for a moment her mind went blank.

Then she remembered her father's words, that a princess's duty was not to rule, but to serve.

She stood.

'People of Elden. I have only this to say. That I promise to faithfully serve this land and its people. I will do my best to keep you safe.' She looked down the hall to where Riane stood toward the back. 'And I promise to deal fairly with *all* our people.'

She sat back down, her hands shaking.

Joss stood, clapping loudly. There was a scraping of benches as others followed. Scarlett swallowed, feeling exposed, alone. She found Arridia's pretty eyes. Her betrothed's sister stopped clapping to place both her hands flat against her chest. Scarlett opened her mouth to gulp in a breath.

'Are there any objections to your new queen?' Jorrun raised an eyebrow.

Scarlett held her breath. How powerful had her brother's magic been? After all, he had failed before...

Without hesitation, Jorrun turned and placed the crown on her head.

Chapter Fifty-Two

Temerran; Kingdom of Elden

'Hmm. I may have to reconsider taking you on as an apprentice.'

Lucien looked up sharply, his brown eyes wide.

'We spoke before about you using magic to command, and when it's appropriate.' They hurried along the corridor. 'I can't have an apprentice who doesn't listen. What do you have to say for yourself?'

'I did listen,' Lucien protested. 'And... and I learned the painful way in that very throne room that words can't always save us. I thought very hard about whether to use what you taught me to secure my sister's place. Had I not done so, I would have left Elden in chaos. As it is, although they've been compelled to accept her, they won't like it, and they'll wonder why they did it. All I did is buy Scarlett time to prove herself.'

'And do you believe she will?' Temerran asked.

'Yes,' he replied at once.

Temerran smiled, and Lucien relaxed a little. 'You considered the consequences, that's a start. Do you have your things ready?'

'Yes, I just need to grab my bag.'

'And your goodbyes?'

Lucien hesitated. 'I won't make any.'

'You're sure?'

Lucien nodded.

'Hurry, then. Meet me out in the courtyard.'

While Lucien opened a door and hurried off, Temerran slowed and dawdled past the guards who lined the way to the castle doors. As yet these men didn't know a woman now ruled them. He couldn't help a quiet chuckle.

When he reached the courtyard, he crossed to the well, leaning back to wait. He turned his face up to the sun and closed his eyes.

'Temerran, a word.'

Temerran stood up straight, turning to see Jorrun striding toward him. 'Thane.' He held out his hand. Jorrun didn't take it. The Thane of Northold hid his temper well, but the slight flaring of his nostrils and the hardness of his eyes told Temerran he was angry.

'Bractius and I had a somewhat turbulent relationship, but he was my friend. You've denied his son his throne.'

'Luce never wanted the throne, you know that. He dreaded it.'

'I would have helped him. I believe he would have been a great king.'

Temerran drew in a deep breath. 'I gave him a choice. He deserved that much.'

Jorrun shook his head. 'You gave him an escape. Perhaps you should instead have given him courage and confidence. Is not the Bard of the Borrows meant to stay out of politics?'

'That's so.' Temerran was feeling uneasy. 'I only thought of Lucien's happiness. He has courage and confidence aplenty, away from the bullying of his father.'

Jorrun clenched his jaw and looked away. He sighed. 'Perhaps. In any case, it is done. Lucien left me with no option but to crown our queen. The burden is Scarlett's now. It will not be easy for her.'

'No.' Temerran's eyebrows drew together. 'It will not. But there is a great resilience in her.'

'I wish you had spoken to me about it.'

Temerran winced. 'I spoke with Dia, for what that's worth.'

'And she did not dissuade you?' Jorrun sounded surprised.

'She did a better job of opening my mind to all possibilities than a Bard of the Borrows.' The corner of his mouth quirked up in a fleeting smile. 'But she also felt the choice should be Lucien's.'

Jorrun wet his lower lip with the tip of his tongue and gazed over the wall at the fast-moving clouds. 'You are still heading for Geladan?'

'That is the *Undine's* destination. Yes.'

Jorrun turned his pale eyes on him. 'If Lucien comes to harm, I will hold you responsible.'

Temerran nodded. 'That's fair.' He held his hand out again.

After a moment Jorrun clasped his wrist, surprising the bard by yanking him forward into a brief hug and slapping him hard on the back. Jorrun took a step back. 'There are Jarls to soothe. Not my favourite job. Take care of yourself, bard. And take care of Lucien. He's family.'

'You also.'

Temerran watched the tall man walk away. He screwed his nose up a little and rubbed at his face. Jorrun had planted an element of doubt in his conscience.

'Tem!'

Lucien came hurrying around the side of the castle from the direction of the kitchens. Temerran pushed himself away from the well and directed the young man to the gate. Lucien's eyes were bright, the worry lines gone from his face.

Temerran breathed more freely.

They made their way down through the city, Lucien taking it all in with his eyes. Temerran wondered if the young man was memorising it to keep in his heart.

They walked the plank together onto the deck of the *Undine*, and Nolv came to meet them.

'We're all aboard, now, Captain,' the first mate reported.

'Very good. We'll set sail at once.'

'This the new boy, Captain?' Nolv looked Lucien up and down.

'It is. He can sail a bit, but we'll start him with the basics. What would you say, Nolv, the bilge, or scrubbing the deck?'

Lucien's mouth opened, and he stared at them both.

Nolv rubbed at his chin. 'Oh, I'd say bilges, Captain.'

'But...'

Temerran and Nolv both broke into laughter. Temerran placed a hand on Lucien's shoulder as Nolv strode off to get on with his work.

'The men will pull your leg,' Temerran warned Lucien. 'They mean no harm, it's their way. We'll spend a week or two sailing the Borrow Islands to give you a chance to find your feet. After that... After that we head south. Come.' Temerran gestured toward the prow. 'Say hello to your new lady.'

Chapter Fifty-Three

Jorrun; Northold, Elden

Jorrun shuffled through the reports, then put them down on the table and sighed. With Tantony busy in Taurmaline, there was a lot for him to get done in the three days they'd been granted at Northold. Joss had not surprisingly remained at the castle, but Rosa had come back with them to collect some of her and Tantony's belongings. Arridia would be staying here, and he couldn't help but envy her. His hopes of a quiet life to study and spend time with his family had once again been turned upside down.

He looked toward the fireplace and narrowed his eyes. Azrael had moved back into the Raven Tower with him but was suspiciously absent.

Instead of returning to his reports, he picked up some books he'd collected from the libraries downstairs. Looking among the clutter on the table, he found a ball of string to tie the books together.

Someone knocked firmly at the door. He frowned. People knew better than to disturb him in the Tower, and few had permission to be there. Kesta would be unlikely to knock. Rosa's knock was more tentative. Arridia, then?

'Come.'

The door opened, and Jorrun sat back in his large, comfortable, but battered old chair as Nip stepped in, closing the door behind him.

'Pardon the intrusion, Thane.' Nip met his eyes unwaveringly, not the slightest hint of nerves in his posture. *So much for the Dark Man.* 'Azrael told me you were free.'

'Did he, now?'

'I have an important matter to discuss with you.'

Jorrun had a very good idea what that matter was, especially if it involved Azrael.

'You had better sit down then.' He indicated the chair on the other side of the fireplace, watching as Nip carefully picked up the books from it and placed them on the table, his eyes scanning the spines as he did so.

Nip sat, leaning against the arm of the chair, before realising he was being too casual and straightening up. Jorrun had to work hard to stop his amusement showing.

'How can I help you, Nip?'

'I am of course here with Arridia's knowledge, but I wanted to do things properly. I... I have come to ask for your blessing. That is to say, Arridia and I wish to marry.'

Jorrun studied the young man's face. He couldn't help but be impressed that he didn't so much as flinch. 'What makes you believe you are good enough for Arridia?'

'It isn't for me to decide if I'm good enough, but for Arridia.' Nip swallowed and blinked, but still refused to be intimidated. 'You have known me almost all my life, Thane. I promise I will never give Arridia any reason to fear being anything but herself, completely, with me.'

Jorrun raised his eyebrows, quickly lowering them again to frown. He'd known this day was coming for a while. Arridia had been ten when she'd told him and Kesta she was going to marry Nip. They'd laughed it off as a sweet, childish crush; after all, Nip had been her protector on many occasions. A part of Jorrun had worried, though. But Arridia was sensible and patient – unlike her brother – and Nip a good man who would never take advantage of a woman, let alone a girl.

He leaned forward. 'How many times did you practice that?'

'I'm sorry?'

A grin broke out on Jorrun's face and he held out his hand. 'Of course, you have my blessing.'

A huge smile spread across Nip's face, and he took his hand. Jorrun wondered if Nip had practiced the handshake too.

'Tea?' Jorrun offered, getting to his feet. 'Or brandy?'

'Oh.' For the first time Nip looked startled. 'Tea, thank you.'

Jorrun removed the lid off a small pot, glanced inside, dumped in a handful of dry leaves, then swung the kettle over the fire. The wood wasn't lit; he called fire to his hand to boil the water. He sat back in his chair as the tea stewed.

'It was always my plan to give the Raven Tower to Arridia. As fond as I am of Scarlett, I don't want all this knowledge being controlled by Elden. I wish for it to remain in neutral hands. It doesn't seem likely Joss will be Thane after me, so I would like to bequeath my title to you, through Arridia.'

Nip's eyes widened, and his mouth opened. Jorrun could see the young man was struggling to find a polite way to say no.

Jorrun raised a hand. 'You need not be Thane nor run the Hold any more than I do, just get yourself a trustworthy and hardworking Merkis. But I would like the place that has become her home to go to Arridia.'

He poured the tea, giving Nip time to think about it.

The young man cleared his throat. 'The thing is, Arridia and I have plans.'

Jorrun handed him a cup, trying not to feel hurt. He and his daughter had always been close, or he'd thought they were. She'd mentioned nothing to him of plans.

'We want to set up a place for studying and teaching healing. Both magical and physical,' Nip said quickly. 'For helping animals as well as people. It would make sense to establish such a place in Taurmaline, but neither of us much like the city. We considered here, but, well, such a venture would disrupt the privacy of the Raven Tower. We were going to talk to you about building something on your land, along the lakeside, but away from the Hold, only it's a new idea and nothing is certain yet.'

'I think it's a wonderful idea.'

'You do?'

Jorrun smiled. 'I do. And we will discuss it fully when I next escape from Taurmaline. I also intend giving some of these woods to Gorchia. In the meantime.' He took Nip's cup from him. 'Why are you sitting there drinking tea? Don't you have news for my daughter?'

'Oh.' Nip pulled himself to the edge of his chair. 'Oh, yes.'

Jorrun stood, and Nip stood with him. 'And I suppose you had better call me Jorrun, not Thane.'

'Not Father?'

Jorrun glared at him and Nip grinned.

'Thank you,' the stable master said seriously.

'Just remember,' Jorrun warned. 'If you upset Arridia, it won't be me you have to deal with, it will be her mother.'

Nip gave him a nod, though he was smiling as he left.

Jorrun pretended to get back to work, and as he'd suspected, Azrael appeared out of the chimney.

'Hello, Jorrun.'

'Azra.' He continued reading his scroll.

'Was that Nip I saw leaving the tower?' The fire-spirit asked with feigned casualness.

'It was.' He carried on reading.

Azrael gave a little buzz of annoyance. 'What did he want?'

'Oh.' Jorrun waved a hand. 'He just asked if he could marry Arridia.'

Azrael gave an excited squeal. 'What did you say?'

'I said no, of course.'

Azrael froze, then he made himself huge, pulling terrible faces and shrieking while Jorrun ignored him. 'How could you? Jorrun! Jorrun! You'll break Riddi's heart!'

He couldn't keep a straight face any longer. He laughed out loud, his shoulders shaking.

Azrael shrieked at him again, shooting around the room and pulling more faces. 'That was mean, Jorrun. You're not funny.'

Jorrun tried to get his laughing under control. His stomach muscles hurt. He wiped at his eyes. 'That will teach you for being a plotting old busybody.'

Azrael muttered to himself. 'I'm not a busybody. Meanie.'

'Did you see if Rosa was still down in the library?'

'Yes, she was.'

'See.' Jorrun grinned. 'Busybody.'

Azrael squealed. 'Human!'

'Bug,' he retorted.

Jorrun picked up the stack of books he'd tied together and made his way down the tower steps. Rosa was sitting at the small table by the window, squinting over a page.

'Thane.' She looked up and smiled.

'I have some books for you.' He held them up. 'And a magnifier so you don't strain your eyes so much.'

'Thank you.' She brightened, although her smile quickly vanished. 'What books?'

'That's what I need to talk to you about.' He grabbed the back of a chair and pulled it around to sit on it. 'I intend to discuss the future of witchcraft and magic in Elden with Scarlett. Sadly, her mother and sister have tarnished people's view again of what could be a beneficial and benign craft. I would like you to help me continue to study and understand it. I also need to study you.'

'Me?' Her eyebrows shot up, then worry lines formed deeply around her brown eyes.

'Yes, Rosa. You have no magic in your blood. As far as I can tell, you can neither create magic like a sorcerer, nor channel, draw, and control like one. Yet the amulets you made worked. That is fascinating.'

Rosa flushed slightly. 'I just did what the book said and prayed.'

A sudden uneasiness swept away Jorrun's good humour, but he pushed it aside. 'Will you help me study it?'

'Of course.' Rosa pulled her shoulders back and beamed.

'Thank you, Rosa.' He put the books down on the table. 'Now I really must get on with my work.'

He made his way back up to his room, but instead of returning to his work, he went to the window that looked across to the Ivy Tower.

'Have you forgiven me yet?' he said to the seemingly empty room.

Azrael shot out of the chimney. 'I'll consider it. For a biscuit.'

Chapter Fifty-Four

Cassien; Free Province of Navere

Pain tore through him, and he sat bolt upright, gasping for breath and reaching for his lower ribs. There was no sword there, but he was soaked in sweat. He blinked several times, peering around the room to re-orientate himself. He breathed easier when he was certain that he wasn't back in the great hall of Fulmer Hold, but safe in a guest bed in Navere Palace.

With a sigh, he went over to the washstand to throw cold water over himself, then dried and got dressed. Cassien opened the shutters a little to look down at the gardens below. The sky was lightening, a pure clear blue without a cloud in sight. A thin film of mist rested above the grass. He drew in a deep breath of the dawn.

It was too early for breakfast so he took a slow wander about the halls of the palace, going first to the top floor. This part of the building had once been the prison of the women of blood purchased to strengthen the coven of Dryn Dunham. Now it was used by the visiting and training Ravens. One room along the corridor had belonged to Jorrun's mother, Naderra. Another to Osun's mother. He wondered if those women somehow knew how much they'd changed the world. He hoped so.

He left the quiet corridor, going back past the grand rooms now inhabited by the resident Ravens. His feet took him to the study where Osun and Jorrun had once plotted to liberate the women and slaves of Chem. Since Osun's death, the Ravens had continued to use the room to administrate the palace, the city, the province, and the country. Cassien tried the door and found it unlocked.

The partially drawn up treaty between the free provinces and Snowhold still sat upon the desk. He ran a finger over it, looking up at the portrait on the wall. Osun's image smiled down at him, a man whom some had hated, but most thought of as a hero.

'Did you know?' Cassien took a step toward the painting. 'What was it you saw, when you looked into the eyes of that boy in the market?'

He had been sure he would die in that market, just as he had been certain when he made his choice, when he saw the answer blossom before him, that he would die by Jderha's swords. Only luck, coincidence, had saved him. Dia's brooch turning a blade from his heart; Ali's conserved strength fixing the damage done by Jderha's blades. Osun had willingly given his life to save them all; he had done the same.

'Still trying to impress your master, Cass.'

He shook his head at himself, taking a moment more before he turned his eyes from the painting and quietly left the room.

The library was along the same corridor, and like many a sleepless soul, he wandered inside. Two pairs of eyes looked up at him, both amber, and he started.

'Merin. You found that scruffy old cat again.'

Merin stroked Trouble, who lay curled up in his lap. With his other hand, he wiped at his nose and sniffed.

'Hey, now.' Cassien sat in the chair beside him and reached out to smooth the boy's hair away from his face. 'What's wrong?'

Merin gave a small shrug. 'I miss Edon. And Grandpa Arrus.'

'Ah.' Cassien sagged a little. 'It's very hard missing someone. Having things you want to tell them, hugs you want to give them, and hugs you wish they could give you. When I miss my... When I miss people, sometimes I still talk to them in my head. Sometimes I even think they talk back.'

'Really?' Merin frowned, one eye partially closed in an unconvinced squint.

Cassien gave a firm nod. 'Try it. When people really touch your life, their wisdom, their words, often stay with you in your head and in your heart.'

Merin looked down and continued stroking Trouble. 'I'll try it. Thank you, Uncle.'

Cassien's heart swelled in a sudden surge, and he had to catch his breath. It was not unusual in Chem to call an older man Uncle, and yet Cassien clung to it like a drowning man.

'Shall we get some breakfast?' He held out his hand.

Merin scooped up Trouble. The cat groaned but didn't struggle as the boy held him against his chest with one arm. He gave his free hand to Cassien.

They were first to sit down at the long table in the formal dining room for breakfast, Merin hiding the cat on his lap. Calayna and Rece arrived next, soon after joined by her daughter, Sevi. It was almost an hour before Catya and Dysarta hurried in.

'There you are!' Catya put her hands on her hips, shaking her head. Although she smiled, Cassien could tell she had been worried. 'Merin, please don't go off without letting us know where.'

Merin flushed. 'I'm eight.'

'It's my fault.' Cassien stood up. 'I brought him here, I should have returned him to you.'

Catya narrowed her eyes and tilted her head. 'If he's eight, he is old enough to take responsibility for his mistakes. But, no matter.' She strode in, plonked herself in the seat beside her son, and kissed the top of his head.

Tyrin, Beth, and Rey also joined them later, and the conversation became lively. Now and then Merin snuck a little piece of meat under the table for the cat. When he saw Cassien catch him out, the boy froze, but Cassien winked and continued playing with the food on his plate.

'You are very quiet, Cassien,' Rece observed. 'You seem miles away.'

Cassien gave a snort and smiled. 'No, just wishing I was miles away.' He sat up straighter and turned to the former captain. 'I am going to leave for Caergard today. I need to be with my family.'

'Of course,' Rece replied at once. 'I will see to supplies for you and arrange you an escort, though we will be sorry to see you go.'

'You can't go yet,' Catya protested. 'We haven't finished the negotiations.'

Cassien looked into her wild, blue eyes. 'You don't need me for your negotiations, Cat. But I do need my family.'

She sagged a little. 'Okay. I guess I just I don't want you to go.'

Cassien stood. 'If you'll excuse me, I need to pack.'

As he headed up the stairs, he realised someone was following. Turning, he was surprised to see it was Dysarta.

'Will you forgive her?' The red-haired sorceress asked, her green eyes troubled.

He stopped, waiting for her to catch up. 'How many times have *you* forgiven her?'

Dysarta paused, her lips slightly parted. She smiled. 'Like you, probably too many.'

Cassien regarded the pretty north-woman, taking two steps back down toward her. 'Catya burns the people she loves. She doesn't mean to, but she does.'

She nodded. 'I know.'

'I bet she makes a formidable queen.'

Dysarta grinned. 'She does. You should come and see for yourself. You and your family. We would like that.'

Cassien drew in a deep breath. 'We would like that too. For what it's worth, I understand that she did what she thought was right, and I would gladly have given my life to save Merin. The rest of the world.' Cassien smiled. 'That was a bonus.'

Dysarta smiled back at him, blinking rapidly. She darted forward to kiss his cheek. 'Thank you, Cassien. Thank you from the rest of the world.'

Cassien's heart felt lighter as he gathered his few belongings. When he reached the stables, he found Rece and Calayna waiting for him with his horse and a baggage pony.

'There are a couple of gifts in there for Kussim and the children,' Calayna told him.

'You're kind.'

He hugged his friends, then signalled he was ready to the two scouts and four warriors who were to cross the provinces with him. He was about to swing up into his saddle when he hesitated. Cassien shook his head at himself.

'A moment. There's something I need to do.'

He strode back into the palace, taking the stairs two at a time, and banged loudly on the door. It was a Northman-warrior who answered. He looked Cassien up and down, moving out of the way to call back into the room. 'Your majesty. Cat.'

Cassien took a few steps into the room. Catya leapt up off her chair, her eyes wide.

'I couldn't leave without saying goodbye.'

Catya grinned and launched herself across the room. He picked her up off her feet, holding her tightly. It was sometimes easy to forget how small this ferocious woman was.

'Thank you, Cass,' she said into his shoulder.

He put her down. 'Look after yourself. Try to stay out of trouble.'

She looked up at him and nodded, unable to speak.

Dysarta and Merin were standing together, watching. Dysarta raised her hand.

'Bye, Cass,' Merin said.

Cassien smiled at them. 'Take care.'

* * *

It was three days into his journey home that Cassien found a Rakinya sitting in their camp. His companions all reached for their weapons, but Cassien told them to stand down.

Cassien sat beside the enormous creature. 'What's your name?'

'I'm Parvle. The Raven Queen has sent me to be Snowhold's ambassador to Caergard.'

Cassien nodded, then gave a soft snort. He smiled at the Rakinya. 'You will be very welcome.'

Their journey was without further incident and they reached the city of Caergard nine days after leaving Navere. The province's scouts had been busy, and Kussim was waiting for him on the palace steps, Enika in her arms. Raith came running to meet him, causing his horse to shy and toss its head. Cassien gently controlled the animal, soothing it before jumping down to hold his son. He breathed in deeply. Raith smelled of home.

'Dad.' Raith wriggled free. 'Is it true? Is it true you killed the monster?'

Cassien stood and regarded his wife. She looked well. She looked amazing. 'The messengers have been busy then.'

'They have,' she replied, jiggling Enika, a soft smile on her face. 'Who's your friend?'

He glanced over his shoulder. 'This is Ambassador Parvle of Snowhold. I'll introduce you properly and tell you everything, but first...' He crossed the remainder of the courtyard in four swift strides, kissing his wife, and caressing his youngest son's cheek. 'I want some time with my family.'

Chapter Fifty-Five

Joss; Kingdom of Elden

Joss looked up as the door opened and Alikan stepped out onto the battlement.

'You all ready?'

'I am.' Alikan placed a hand on his shoulder, then stood beside him to lean against the stone wall. Below them in the docks the Chemmish ship, *Whisper*, was being loaded for her home voyage. Dinari and the Ravens who had liberated Elden were returning to Farport; Alikan had decided to go with them and perfect his healing skills under Dinari's tutelage. From Farport he would visit Cassien and Rothfel, then travel on to Snowhold.

'How's it going?' Alikan broke the silence.

'Ah... well. It's going well.' He raised his eyebrows, forcing cheerfulness past the aching, hollow feeling in his chest. 'Scarlett signed The Towers over to the air-spirits as their protected home. Some Jarls tried to be awkward about it, even though the land's little use to anyone except as a watch-post, but she held her own. The earth-spirits are proving a bit trickier. No one wants to give up forest and timber except Father, it seems. Scar is thinking of confiscating her mother's family's land and using that.'

Alikan sucked air in through his teeth. 'Good idea, though a bit ruthless.'

'It was Rosa's idea.'

Alikan made a surprised sound in the back of his throat.

'The witchcraft thing.' Joss winced. 'It's still unresolved. I think Scar would just ban it outright, but father is convinced Elden needs its own magic back.'

'The evil is in the user,' Alikan said quietly.

'Yeah.' Joss's eyes were drawn to the ship.

'I have to go.'

Joss nodded, but he couldn't look at his friend. His brother. He wanted desperately to keep his pride. Other than a few months here and there for training, Ali had always been with him. He'd already lost Doro.

Alikan straightened up. 'Take care, little brother.'

Joss turned and hugged him, sniffing and blinking rapidly. 'And you. Don't go seducing any foreign queens.'

Alikan laughed, stepping back to regard him with his amber eyes. 'You mind your own queen! Seriously, though, Joss, stay out of trouble.'

Joss rolled his eyes and nodded.

With a last slap of his arm, his best friend walked away.

Joss turned back to the lake, wiping at his eyes with the back of his arm. He drew in a deep breath, cleared his throat, and made his way down to the training yard.

The two guards on duty gave him a nod, one of them greeting him with the title, 'Raven.' They moved out of his way but stayed near the doors to ensure the training ground's privacy.

Joss drew his sword, distracting himself from his melancholy thoughts by practicing his footwork, adding some swings and thrusts. Movement caught his eye, and he looked up to see the Queen of Elden hurrying into the courtyard. Her face was flushed, and she was a little breathless. She'd changed out of her fancy robes into plain trousers and tunic, with long boots and a sword buckled to her waist.

'Has Ali gone? Did I miss him?' she asked.

Joss relaxed out of his fighter's stance and nodded. 'Yeah. I feel kind of odd without him already. Especially with Doro gone too.'

Scarlett's face fell. 'I think I know what you mean. It's been so busy I've barely had time to think, but every corridor, every room, reminds me all my family are gone.'

He held out his hand. 'You still have me.'

She placed her smaller hand in his and smiled. 'Rosa wants me to select myself some ladies-in-waiting. If I'm honest, I'd be happy with just Riane and Rosa, but she says it's not so much about me, as protecting vulnerable ladies.'

'I'd never thought of it that way.'

'Neither had I.' Her hazel eyes were troubled. He wanted to hold her, but the guards were still loitering watchfully nearby. 'My mother chose her ladies for influence and power. But Rosa says the former queen, my grandmother, selected girls who needed protection, or those who were very good at different things. I'm going to ask Adrin's poor widow, Sonai. I'm not sure who else yet, but I want to surround myself with wise people, from all different lives and backgrounds, so I can learn. I never want to stop learning.'

He squeezed her hand.

'Oh, but I'm going on.' She gave a little toss of her head.

'Oh, no, I want to hear it. It's good to get things off your mind, then you can relax. Or, concentrate so I can't beat you so easily this time.' He grinned.

She opened her mouth in mock protest, withdrawing her hand. 'You did not beat me easily.'

'I'll guess we'll see.'

'I guess we will.' She unbuckled her sword belt and selected a wooden practice blade from the rack. Still grinning, Joss did the same.

'Ready?' he asked. He didn't wait for a reply but lunged at once, following with a slash upward from left to right. She parried and blocked quite well, if a little slowly, and he held back his own speed so as not to discourage her. As she gained confidence, he increased the power to his blows, then stepped in to disarm her.

'Ow.' She jumped back, blowing on her bruised fingers. 'How dare you strike your queen!' Her laughter belied her words. 'Do you want to spend a week in the dungeons?'

'I hear they're not very secure.' He tutted. 'Might be better to keep me close, where you can keep an eye on me.'

She glanced over her shoulder at the guards. 'Maybe I will. But first...' She grabbed up her sword. 'You'll teach me how to defend our kingdom.'

Chapter Fifty-Six

Kesta; Northold, Elden

Kesta took the old carpenter's hand as she jumped across from her husband's boat; she'd borrowed it to take her to the Fulmers. She looked around at the other light craft moored at the narrow wharf.

'Thanks, Kurgan. Is Jorrun home?'

'He is. He arrived but an hour ago.'

She gave him a nod, her feet taking her swiftly away from the small waterside settlement and along the tree-lined path to the main gates of the Hold. The warriors on watch called down in greeting and she waved a hand at them distractedly.

Only an hour.

She had no doubt where he'd be then.

She passed the keep, disturbing a gaggle of geese who'd wandered across the ward to graze. The tall Raven Tower loomed before her, several of its residents perched up on the steep roof. The warm glow of candlelight pressed against the leaded glass windows on the top floor. Kesta smiled.

The door stood slightly ajar, and she pushed it open, noting that none of the torches had been lit yet along the narrow, winding stairway. The doors to the libraries and the storeroom were closed, so she ascended to the top.

'Jorrun?'

She nudged the door open with her elbow; he almost dropped the large book he was balancing open in his hand.

'Kesta.' He put the book down, hurrying over to tangle his fingers in her hair and kiss her. He smelt wonderful; of wood-smoke and jasmine. 'I wasn't expecting you until later. Did you catch Ali and Dinari?'

'I did.' They still held each other, and she gazed up into his pale eyes. 'Just. I entered Taurmouth as they were leaving. The harbourmaster wasn't best pleased at the galleon blocking his harbour so we could say our goodbyes.' She grinned, and he shook his head and smiled.

'How was your mother?'

She did let go of him then, crossing the worn old rug and moving some books so she could sit down. He poured her a glass of wine and joined her.

'She was all right,' Kesta replied slowly. 'She's grieving deeply but getting on with things as the Icante. It was hard to see, harder knowing I could do nothing.'

He reached out and took her hand.

'She'll be okay.' She pursed her lips in a smile. 'I'm okay. Heara is missing, though.'

'Missing?' Jorrun tilted his head.

Kesta nodded. 'No one has seen her since the *Undine* left. Mother says she isn't worried, but she is. I think Heara is just dealing with things in her own way.'

Jorrun blinked, his eyebrows drawn together. 'Heara is very proud. I imagine she just needs some time alone.'

'Where's Arridia?'

Jorrun shifted a little in his chair. 'The stables.'

'Has she moved in there?' Kesta grinned.

'No,' he answered at once. 'She's just helping with the horses.'

Kesta's grin widened. 'Jorrun Raven, are you being a prudish Eldeman?'

He scowled at her and took a sip of his wine.

A voice whispered from within the chimney, 'He isss Kesta!'

'Come on out of there, you eavesdropping bug!' Jorrun shouted, though he winked at Kesta.

Azrael flew out, buzzing around Kesta's head and almost singing her name. 'How was Doroquael?' he asked.

'He is well, and sends his regards,' Kesta told the fire-spirit. 'And how are you? Have you made a truce with Gorchia yet?'

Azrael pulled a face. 'He knows this is *my* tower.'

Jorrun and Kesta exchanged a quick smile over their wineglasses.

Jorrun put his glass down, leaning forward. 'Was there news of the *Undine*?'

Kesta's smile faded. 'There was. It's gone south and Lucien was still aboard.' She shuffled closer to take his hand. 'Jorrun, Tem loves that boy like a son, he won't see any harm come to him.'

The muscles of Jorrun's jaw moved, but he said nothing.

'Hey, we have to let all our chicks fly some time.' She squeezed his hand. 'And Luce is doing what he loves, choosing his own destiny.'

'I'm still not sure—'

'Jorrun, you yourself could have taken any number of thrones, but turned away from them. Would you force Arridia to take a throne, knowing the woman she is, how unhappy it would make her?'

He sighed, his posture relaxing a little. 'No, no, I would not. Even though I would think her the best of queens.'

'And it is no different for Lucien. Talking of queens.' Kesta raised her eyebrows. 'How are Joss and Scarlett doing? We should see them soon.'

She didn't miss the face Jorrun pulled. The poor man had only just got away from Taurmaline.

'Actually.' He rubbed at his beard. 'Scarlett is doing very well. She isn't afraid to ask for advice when she isn't sure, but she'll make a decision quickly when she needs to. I think Scarlett will do very well. Rosa is blooming in her new position, and Tantony is... well, I'd best not leave the poor man at the castle without me too long, or he'll have no hair left!'

'And Joss?' Kesta prompted.

'Is being supportive, and patient.'

Kesta sat back in her chair. 'Who'd have thought it? All our children behaving.'

They held each other's eyes for a moment and laughed.

'What?' Azrael demanded.

'We were waiting for the sound of trouble,' Kesta smiled.

'This isn't quite what we planned,' Jorrun said quietly.

'Nothing has been.' She gave a shake of her head. 'But for those we have lost, I wouldn't alter anything though. We changed the world, Jorrun.'

He blinked twice as his eyes filled. 'We did.' He glanced up at Azrael. 'With help, of course.'

While Azrael turned loops around the room, Kesta pushed herself out of the chair to kneel beside her husband, taking both his hands to kiss him.

'I am here, you know!'

They both laughed.

Chapter Fifty-Seven

Arridia; Northold, Elden

Arridia left Nip sleeping, although she couldn't resist pausing at the top of the ladder to watch him for a while, before climbing carefully down. One or two of the horses moved restlessly, but mostly the stables were silent. She gathered her tack and opened Freckle's stall, stroking his nose and cheek before harnessing him and leading him out into the ward.

The hold was already stirring; Trella guiding her troupe of children to draw water from the well. Reetha was frail now, but still supervised the kitchens from her chair in the corner. Arridia looked up at the Ivy Tower. Its windows were dark. With her mother having been away, she doubted they'd see anything of her parents for several hours yet. She smiled. She hoped she and Nip were as close as they were after twenty years.

She pulled herself up into the saddle, giving the guards a wave as she rode through the first gate, increasing to a trot as they passed through the houses of the outer ward. Once beyond the fortified earthworks, they turned toward the lake. A low mist lay across it, the water eerily still. She drew in a deep breath and released the hold she had on her *knowing*. It felt better than undoing a tight corset, or letting down braided hair. Freckle was still a little sleepy, but happy to plod along the shore.

Arridia gazed southward. The city of Taurmaline was beyond her sight. She knew she ought to check on her brother sometime soon, but for now she still needed the healing quiet of Northold. She gave her head a slight shake. None of them should have been surprised at Joss ending up in a castle with a queen; he'd lived for Azrael's tales of heroes as a child.

They turned into the forest and towards the dawn. Freckle perked up a little and raised his head, and Arridia returned his energy, stretching forward to stroke his neck. Their house of healing was to be built along this stretch of lake, and already they had chosen the name Dierra Hall. The forest beyond it would be Gorchia's.

She took an apple from her saddlebag, reaching up to place it in the crook of a tree.

She rode a little longer, breathing in the peace, but eventually she felt the tug on her heart, and she turned Freckle. She glimpsed the Raven Tower through the trees and smiled. The day felt new. Her life stretched out before her with a multitude of paths to choose from.

She chose the one leading home.

***

Follow Temerran and Lucien as they sail south on the *Undine*, in 'Bard of the Borrows.'

Acknowledgements

I wrote this book during 2020, so like all of us, I was going through a very difficult time and adjusting to a new world. Whilst working as a key-worker throughout, I came to despair about human kind and their selfish, destructive nature, and I fell into a very dak place. Raven Fire kept me going; you see, I didn't want to let *you* down. I couldn't go without finishing the series, but by the time it was complete, I'd found some hope again. So when I said at the beginning of this book, *this is for you,* I really meant it. Every one of you who reached out to say how much you love Fire-Walker, you gave me a reason to keep going.

And my thanks as always to my Alpha readers, Maria and Kat, you are my little rays of sunshine whenever it gets too dark.

And my other wonderful Raven Apprentices, Kirsty C, Kirsty E, Val, and Linda. xxx

Thank you also to Jon, my kindred spirit, for your support and kindness. Jon has started writing and I can't wait for you to read it, he has such an amazing natural talent.

Wendy and the other amazing admins at the Fiction Café, who do so much to support authors. Thanks guys. Xx

And just a little nudge in case you haven't seen it, if you want to read Catya's full story of how she came to be Queen of Snowhold, you can read it in Queen of Ice.

Take care of yourselves xx

https://www.facebook.com/EmmaMilesShadow

https://mobile.twitter.com/EmmaMilesShadow

She'd killed a boy.
His face haunts her dreams.

With no notion of what she is seeking, Catya flees to the frozen and unknown province of Snowhold, leaving her friends and the Raven Scouts behind her. A glimpse of an intriguing face in a blizzard sets her on a path where her fate collides with that of ancient beasts, and a mysterious hidden people. Can she survive alone in a land where women are still slaves, and sorcerers rule?

Perhaps there is a chance for redemption. Perhaps she can lay the ghost of the boy to rest.

It's time to choose; to be a hero, or a monster.

Queen of Ice is a Land Beneath the Sky book, set in the world of the Fire-Walker series.
It can be read as a standalone, but fits chronologically between books three and four of Fire-Walker

UK **https://www.amazon.co.uk/Queen-Ice-Land-beneath-sky-ebook/dp/B08XP49MH2**
US **https://www.amazon.com/Queen-Ice-Land-beneath-sky-ebook/dp/B08XP49MH2**

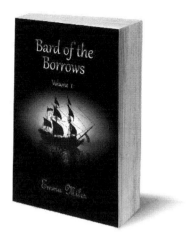

Bard of the Borrows: Volume One

Grieving for his lost friends, and battered by life and war, Temerran, the enigmatic Bard of the Borrows, sets sail on his graceful ship, the *Undine*. To protect those he loves, he must risk his crew and his beloved vessel, and guide them into enemy waters. Unknown lands beckon the audacious captain, and a new crew tests both his skill and patience as well as that of his loyal first mate. For not only has he taken aboard a feisty warrior-woman to help lead his crew, but also the absconded prince of Elden, who is more than a fish out of water.

Can he steer them through the perils of the sea, betrayal, loss, and scheming foreign lands, or will his quest be the end of the *Undine* and the Bard of the Borrows?

Bard of the Borrows is part of the Land Beneath the Sky collection, companion books to the Fire-Walker saga. Bard of the Borrows Volume one follows immediately after the last book of the Fire-Walker saga, *Raven Fire*.

UK **https://www.amazon.co.uk/gp/product/B09B3YG1V2**

US **https://www.amazon.com/gp/product/B09B3YG1V2**

Also by the same author.

Valley of the Fey books

Hall of Pillars

Hall of Night

Fire-Walker Saga/Land Beneath the Sky

The Raven Tower – Fire-Walker part 1

The Raven Coven -Fire-Walker part 2

Raven Storm – Fire-Walker part 3

Queen of Ice – Land beneath the Sky (Companion book to the Fire-Walker saga)

Raven Fire – Fire-Walker book 4

Bard of the Borrows volume I – Land Beneath the Sky

Bard of the Borrows Volume II – Land Beneath the Sky

The Witch of Elden – Land Beneath the Sky

The Wind's Children Trilogy

Shadows

Shadow Chase

The Shadow Rises

Printed by Amazon Italia Logistica S.r.l.
Torrazza Piemonte (TO), Italy

43289759R00277